FATED

BORNE
to
SALT
and
SIN

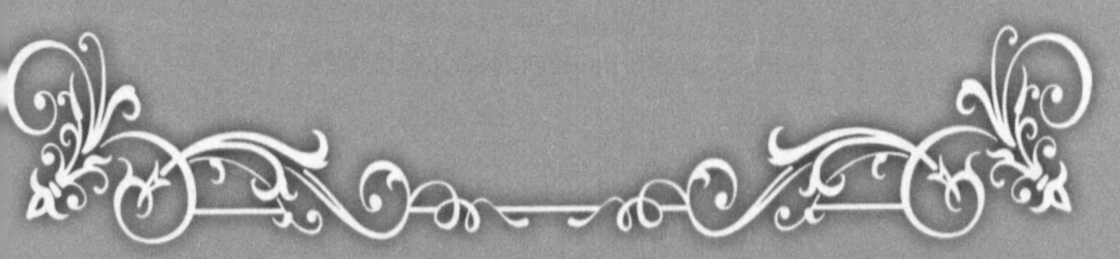

Content Expectations Including Triggers

1. Book III begins Zaria's journey as a New Adult. This is no longer a Young Adult story and it is not appropriate for teen readers. Mature sexual content is present throughout. **If explicit sexual material is not preferred, please do not read this book**.

2. Some potentially triggering scenes include (Spoilers): The witnessing of children captured for enslavement (brief) and the result of torture (confined to its aftermath). There is also the mercy killing of an animal and the death of a loved one.

3. Dark Romance (Spoilers):
This book contains Dark Romance. These encounters are gray and dubious. Unlike the potential triggers above, which are brief, this content is lengthy (spanning several chapters) and deeply explored. These scenes are not intended to be severely dark, but they are emotional and might be uncomfortable for some readers. Please do not read this book if you do not prefer this content.
Lengthy coercion, attempted force, manipulation, and physical aggression lead to sexual acts of very dubious consent.

If you have any questions about material not covered, please do not hesitate to email me at eloramorganauthor@gmail.com

Part I

Safe in Your Arms

CHAPTER 1

Safe within Kirwyn's embrace was my heaven.

I hoped it was worth risking, to save the next girl from hell.

"There's no way we'll all make it out alive," Kirwyn scoffed. The jerk of his trim hips jostled our favorite hammock in my aunt's garden. "I'm not leading us to our deaths."

His voice was deep and firm, but I could hear the grin in his refusal. He might not like my plan to find Mal-Yin and capture High Spire, but I had methods of persuasion. I worked my hand lower, teasing lazy circles on his abdomen, letting my fingers traipse beneath the waistband of his pants.

"You're the one quickly swayed by temptation," he chided, "not me."

I frowned. "Are you saying I'm easy to manipulate with your caresses? With promises of... something more?" Licking my lips, I teased, "It's only because I was touch-starved for most of my life and because you do it *so well.*"

Kirwyn made a sound of disbelief in the back of his

throat. "Are you trying to pressure me with both the attentions of your hands *and* flattery?"

"Is it working?" I asked, daring lower, close to what I wanted. I hoped Volmar's sentries weren't looking in our direction. The massive, ancient oak tree from which we swung afforded some privacy, but I never felt completely alone in the exile's heavily guarded estate.

"Nope," Kirwyn replied, though he hissed a breath between clenched teeth and his hips twitched again. He grabbed my hand, stilling its progress.

"Not so immune, are you?" I gloated.

"I was nearly as touch-starved as you my entire life, don't forget."

"And I do it *so well?*" I echoed, then pouted, "Or I would... if you'd let me."

Kirwyn refused me on two matters: one, leading us to Mal-Yin; and two, letting me explore his body as freely as he explored mine.

Astoundingly, it was the former on which he was more inclined to budge, knowing we'd likely have to trek north at some point because we had no better plan. But the idea that we could become accidental parents at our age, in our circumstances, would have been enough to deter Kirwyn even without the knowledge of how he'd lost his own mother and father. No matter how many times I assured him the birth control Jesi snuck me was working, Kirwyn didn't trust the efficacy of "hastily procured street drugs."

Not that I was complaining about the delicious things he did to me whenever we slipped into the woods. I just wanted to reciprocate... and progress.

"You didn't stop our night together on the beach," I reminded him for the thousandth time, propping myself up on his chest and rocking the hammock. With my fingertip, I traced the curve of his sinister mouth. It had new meaning to me now that I knew what it was capable of.

"I was young and foolish," he said, turning serious. As if it happened years and not months ago. But then, we'd both changed so much in a short time.

"Fine. Yet you still won't let me..." I dipped my other hand lower and Kirwyn seized it again.

"Not in your uncle's house," he whispered, grinning. "It's weird and the guards are always watching. One of us has to show restraint."

"Right," I tried to challenge him in my most commanding voice, "but you'll sneak off into the woods and wrap my legs around your shoulders until I'm satisfied?"

Kirwyn licked his teeth. "I said I'd show restraint. Didn't say I wasn't human." He paused, then added thoughtfully, "I like looking at you. I like your scent. The way you taste."

I choked on air, suddenly bright red and slapping my hand over my eyes. "You can't just say those things!"

"Why not?" he frowned.

"I – I don't know. Just admit that you're afraid you can't stop yourself," I challenged, changing the subject. "That it's easier to control how far we go when *you* do things to *me*, but you're afraid you'll lose control if you let *me* do things to *you*."

"Okay, I admit it," he shrugged.

I rolled my eyes and snuggled back onto his shoulder. I was blissfully happy, for the moment. We lazed beside a babbling fountain in one of Enith's gardens, drinking chilled elderflower cider. The sun kissed the earth, butterflies flitted about the flowers, and the light breeze set the leaves on the tree above to dancing. We lay together as we had so many afternoons, with me cocooned safely in Kirwyn's embrace and the both of us nestled tightly in our favorite hammock. Face-down, the book of poetry lay open on the grass beside us. I had listened, enthralled by the cadence of his voice dancing over such beautiful prose as Kirwyn read. He knew it calmed me, but I wasn't sure if he figured out it turned me on, too.

"Not a lot of boys I've met read poetry," I mused, glancing down at the book.

"Theodos required it." Kirwyn let out a breathy laugh. "My uncle didn't just choose the library for safety reasons. He was–*is*–what they used to call 'a renaissance man.' At night I watched him flip through everything from ancient mythology to quantum physics."

"I still can't imagine growing up inside a library," I said, shaking my head. "What was your favorite section?"

"The adventure books when I was younger. I wanted to be like the heroes in those stories. Until I realized that's the only place heroes can exist."

"You're not half as monstrous as you believe yourself to be," I argued, lightly slapping his chest.

He turned close to my ear. "You wouldn't say that if you knew half my thoughts."

I shivered at the rumble in his voice, *very* curious. Part of Kirwyn's head was a mystery to me and I wanted to know all of him, to be as close to him as possible. Besides, he had an irritating way of seeming to be in *my* head, knowing what *I* was thinking.

Kirwyn cleared his throat. "As I got older, I started to get interested in the mature section of the library," he chuckled. "When Theo found me there too often, he sat me down and slapped a stack of poetry books in front of me. Told me he'd make a fair trade. One *adult* book in exchange for every poetry book I read. He didn't want me to turn into too much of…"

"A sex pervert? An ass? The jury's still out on both accounts," I quipped, eager to use the knowledge I'd been acquiring. Juries were a thing of the past, but the expression lingered.

"Good," Kirwyn praised. Just as Theodos once instructed him, Kirwyn brought me to my aunt and uncle's library each day to teach me. It wasn't so different from my mornings in Rythas, but I enjoyed his tutelage much more.

I heard a rustle by the house and saw Damyre, one of Volmar's guards, darting into the rear gardens with alarming speed. At his urgency, the hair on my neck stood on end. Before I could even scramble off Kirwyn, he lifted me and placed me on my feet.

I braced for bad news, trying not to panic. Reaching us, Damyre whisper-shouted, "Braenese, come, you must hide!"

No matter how many times I insisted the guards use my name, they reverted to Volmar's rules – titles. But I was too concerned with my stomach-dropping to correct him.

Clasping my hand, Kirwyn quickly pulled us toward the back of the walled gardens.

"Who is it?" he asked, voice low.

A beat, during which Damyre's eyes shifted to me and then he said, "Rythas. Emissaries approach. Under the guise of a visit once more. But they'll poke around with colorful excuses."

I sucked in a breath while Kirwyn swore under his. "You said we'd be safe here," I reminded him, scurrying to keep up across the lawn while my knees threatened to buckle.

I won't go back. I won't.

"I thought we would. I'll talk to Volmar once they leave. We'll have to hide until then. I've done it before."

"But you said they can't connect you to my uncle."

"Doesn't mean they won't try. They're desperate."

Reaching a weather-worn garden shed at the rear of the property, Damyre threw the door wide and we slipped inside.

"Are we safe here?" I asked, looking around the wooden building, unconvinced.

Kirwyn shook his head as he knelt, fingers running along the floorboards. Some sixth sense in me knew what he sought even before I consciously comprehended it. *Of course.* Small, tight places seemed my constant torture.

Reading my face, Kirwyn said, "Don't worry, it's spacious. You won't feel too claustrophobic."

I exhaled, preparing to descend as he lifted the trap door.

"It's just..." he knit his brow. "We won't be alone down there."

What did that mean?

As light illuminated the dirt below in a patch of yellow, I watched the ground *move.*

Cockroaches, dozens perhaps, scurrying out of sight.

Oh god. A fish flopped in my gut and swam upward, making me feel as if I'd gag. Even on Elowa they were hated creatures; we never ate them. And I was barefoot. And as soon as the door closed, we'd be trapped in the dark, forced to remain silent. It was stupid, considering everything I'd faced, considering the danger we were suddenly in, but tears welled in my eyes because I did *not* want to go down there with them.

When I whimpered, Kirwyn said, "You have to be quiet, Zaria, okay? Until they leave."

"How long?" I whispered, looking pleadingly at Damyre.

He shrugged. "Shouldn't be more than fifteen minutes. Everyone knows this visit is a sham." Damyre thought a moment, then added, "Unless they stay for tea, which would take all afternoon."

I laughed with an edge of hysteria, throwing my head back and shaking it. *That would be my fate, wouldn't it?* Nobles or acclaimed guards from Rythas drinking tea in our house while I hid in the dark, crawling with cockroaches. Very queenly.

It's nothing compared to what would happen to me if I'm caught, I reasoned.

Lazlian's voice from the day I escaped, echoed in my mind.

"If you ever try to betray us, I will kill you. I will kill you so slowly you'll be begging to die for days – weeks."

Palms sweating, I wondered, *what if Juls or Laz is here, now?*

Kirwyn climbed into the dark roach hole and raised his arms up to assist my descent. "They can't hurt you," he reminded me.

They can't, I soothed myself in agreement. *But the Dorestes can.*

Whimpering, I lowered myself into the cool underground, pressing so hard against Kirwyn I was practically trying to crawl inside him. When the trap door closed above us and I heard Damyre retreat, I started to panic, digging my nails into Kirwyn's shoulders.

It wasn't long before I felt the first horrific tickle on my ankle. I jumped on top of Kirwyn's bare feet, sobbing as silently as possible, restraining myself from climbing up him like a tree only because I feared we'd be down there too long and he'd drop me.

"Shh…" he whispered against my ear.

As the minutes passed, more cockroaches came, crawling their disgusting bodies across my unprotected feet. Antennae ticked my skin, making me shiver and sob.

Please not my hair or my face, I begged, folding my lips between my teeth, imagining a roach falling from the ceiling into my mouth. I tried kicking and jumping, but sometimes I'd land on a bug, squashing it between the bottom of my foot and the top of Kirwyn's. I clapped my hand over my mouth to avoid puking and tried picturing what was happening in my uncle's house to distract myself. *Who had come? Any guards I remembered?*

I knew the horror of this roach hole was insignificant compared to the near threat of Rythas taking me back, but I also knew I'd have nightmares about it for years to come. Something tickled my arm, and I didn't even know if it was real or imagined, but I shook it out as I squeaked.

Above, I heard the door to the shed creak open and Kirwyn clamped his hand over my mouth, replacing my own. Fearing I'd hyperventilate, I tried focusing on the feel of his long fingers, his masculine and woodsy scent filling my nose… but the threat from above and the horror from below was too much to handle and tears pooled in my eyes.

Someone entered the shed. Slow, heavy footsteps pressed into the floorboards above us. I shook with the effort not to cry out as roaches caressed my feet.

Boots? A man? My heart hammered and sweat poured down my neck. The stranger stopped. Shuffled around a bit.

If he opens the door and grabs me, we can fight them off. Volmar has few men, but more advanced weaponry than Rythas. Guns capable of firing many rounds, quickly.

But could I kill guards from Rythas, just doing their job? Men and women I might even know?

If it came to that...

Slowly, the man retreated, the door banged shut, and I sighed in relief.

A few torturous minutes later and I heard the door to the shed squeak open again. This time, our trap door was thrown wide and I met Damyre's smiling face.

"They're gone," he said, reaching his muscular arms down to lift me.

A sob tore through me as I climbed out of the bug hole so fast that I scraped myself on the ascent. Barely hearing Kirwyn exit behind me, I ran onto the grass, swiping my skin and dancing around to shake off imaginary roaches still crawling on me.

By the shed, Kirwyn watched, strangely restrained.

"What?" I asked, heaving.

"Don't get mad but... it's kind of humorous."

My mouth dropped.

"I'm trying not to laugh," he protested, a smile ghosting his lips. "But I remember *you* did the day that tarantula crawled on me, back in your cave. I'm just saying, one day we'll look back on this and laugh about it."

Indignant, my mouth dropped further.

Kirwyn averted his eyes and mumbled, "At least I will."

With the all-clear, Aewna emerged from the house, coming across the lawn and looking a bit less serene than usual. She wore a white dress – not quite an Elowan tunic, but similar in length. Damyre gave a small, reverent bow of his head in her direction before departing. Even though she wasn't directly in line to any throne, Aewna's poise seemed to inspire an almost royal loyalty in the guards.

Kirwyn quickly joined my side, eager to hear news.

"I'm so sorry you had to endure that. They're gone now." Aewna smiled sweetly, but glancing at the garden shed, she wrinkled her nose. "I hate bugs. I know it's silly. My whole life I've been trained to face every imaginable mental hardship or emotional strife that accompanies political power… and while I've never faced such a real-life battle, I feel prepared, calm when it comes to those challenges. But I combat the cockroaches every day and I never get used to them." Aewna made a face of distaste. "To any insects."

"So Enith never cooks them?" I asked, surprised. "Not even grasshoppers?"

Aewna shook her head. "I'm afraid I have the same attitude toward eating bugs as Kirwyn does. I can't stomach it. Literally."

"Well, if we ever make it back to Elowa, I'll try to change your mind."

"Speaking of," Aewna said, turning serious, "my father wants to meet with you both."

Hand in hand, Kirwyn and I walked through the large, white manor, finding Volmar in his study. Most of the house was decorated in light, airy hues, but Volmar's private office was almost entirely brown and gray, wood and steel. It was a rare treat to be invited inside. I wondered if his wife was ever permitted. I wondered if she even permitted herself to ask.

Lording over the room's center, Volmar finished fixing himself a drink of some kind and turned to us.

"Have a seat."

Kirwyn and I sat together on a small sofa facing my uncle. He stood, one hand in his pocket, considering us.

"Well?" Kirwyn asked, impatiently. "What happened? Who was here?"

"A few men and women under the guise of a 'friendly' visit." Volmar's eyes flicked back and forth between Kirwyn and me.

"You said we were safe here," I repeated to Kirwyn.

He squeezed my hand. "They can't connect me to Volmar. We made sure of it. Unless your mother informed on us?" Kirwyn gazed into the distance, thinking. "But it's also not logical that you'd stay in the region. As far as the king knows, your only aim was to escape to me. By now, he's pieced together that I was the scout and that we've found each other. He'll assume we've fled and that his efforts should be concentrated on routes west. Maybe south, by boat. Not here."

"All the more reason we're safer fleeing north to Mal-Yin," I argued.

"Which takes us right through the thick of Spade sweeps," Kirwyn pointed out. "And now they're looking for you, too."

I frowned. "They knew of a freeborn hiding in Shreelos and maybe they wanted to capture her for her defiance. But I hardly think I'm important enough for them to expend any effort on a continued search now that they've lost the trail."

Kirwyn crooked a confused eyebrow at me. Volmar took a seat in his favored armchair.

"The Spades aren't stupid. They'll have figured out who you are," Volmar said. "And they've been increasingly interested in Elowans. Diplomatic relations on my part have kept them from causing trouble here in my home *for now*," he said ominously.

Volmar leaned forward, resting his elbows on his knees as he lectured. "Spade scientists have managed to re-create the technology for certain treatments in fertility assistance.

But they haven't been able to figure out how such advanced genetic engineering was done in the past. They haven't been able to replicate the science of the Optimal Election program. It's made them curious about us, the descendants. I suspect their soldiers won't make any *overt* moves, but if an Elowan girl—a Braeni, no less—is found running about the backlands," Volmar shrugged, "fair game."

"What are you saying?" I asked, chest constricting. "If they've realized who I am, wouldn't they deliver me back to Juls?"

Volmar spread his hands, "Depends on which of the Spades found you first. Those backing the politicians or those with allegiance to the scientists."

A memory slowly returned to me, like the tide washing in. Covering my mouth, I went back to High Spire in my mind, to the leering Spade Emissary I'd once met.

"There was a diplomat from Spade City before my wedding. For the Ceremony of Gifts. He kept *staring* at me like he was fascinated by me... I asked Juls about it and he brushed it off. I knew at the time he was hiding something, but I didn't know what." *Of course Juls was trying to be noble and protect me.*

"I thought you knew," Kirwyn said.

"The Dorestes liked to keep me in the dark, Juls especially."

"Do you think the king will send an army after you?" Volmar asked, swirling his glass of brown liquor I couldn't identify.

"No, I'm sure he'll want to keep this as quiet as possible," I insisted, remembering how much appearances mattered, how Lazlian never wanted the public to know about Kirwyn or my reluctance to marry. The Dorestes hated bad publicity. And even if they spun the story to make people believe I'd been kidnapped, didn't that make them look bad? Incompetent?

"Quiet? You don't understand," Volmar said condescendingly, spreading his hands once more. "Their queen is missing. How can they hide your disappearance? It's not a question of keeping it subdued, it's only a question of how many men are sent to track you down. The king is preparing to leave, to head the search for you. All of Rythas is frenzied in their attempts to rescue the kidnapped queen."

I blinked rapidly. "What?"

Juls sailing... here?

"The men who came today are preparing to meet him in a few weeks, toward Shreelos, where you were last seen. What I couldn't glean is if he'll bring small parties or an army," Volmar said. "Every day the shrine grows. Set upon the beach where it's believed you were whisked away. People leave coins, flowers, and seashells with prayers inscribed in the hollow. Torches have been lit that will not be put out until your safe return. Fundraisers to launch private rescue missions are underway; even in Mid-Spire everyone collects what they can."

From the corner of my eye, I noticed Kirwyn was equally surprised and displeased, to boot. Either Volmar wasn't freely sharing information with either of us or he'd only just learned more from this visit.

I groaned, dropping my face into my hands. The slick couch squeaked as I moved and I caught the scent of clean leather. Like Juls. Guilt gnawed at my chest as I imagined those in Mid-Spire with little to spare, taking what they couldn't afford to give, and handing it over for "rescue" missions with the best intentions.

I didn't want any of that. I just wanted to be free, with

Kirwyn. And for the next chosen braenese to be free. And for Elowa to be free as well.

"Because Rythas loves a good love story," I mumbled into my palms. "And reuniting the queen with her beloved king is an irresistible tale."

"They love you too, just you," Kirwyn said, rubbing his thumb in circles above my hipbone. "That was part of your plan, wasn't it?"

It was. But my escape had consequences that were backfiring.

"*Oh my god.* Son of a..." I snapped my head up, anger rioting through my gut. "He's *not* trying to keep it subdued and it's *not* Juls."

Snarling, I declared, "It's Prince Lazlian. I'd bet anything he's *encouraging* the underprivileged to empty their already-sparse pockets. Galvanizing the poor in Mid-Spire. He doesn't care if it bankrupts them. He knows it will upset me. That son of a *bitch.* Get it? The longer I stay away, the more they'll hurt. He's doing it to make me feel like goatshit."

"Then don't let it," Kirwyn protested, scowling.

"We have to go," I insisted, looking up at him pleadingly. "We can't stay here. You know it."

He ran a hand through his dark hair, sighing. "Alright, but we do it my way. Four of Volmar's guards come with us. Full body armor, full weaponry for all of us. Horseback through the long route. You need to learn to shoot and you need to learn to ride."

My heart picked up speed. *We were finally moving forward.*

Volmar leaned back in his armchair, sipping his brown liquor. "And Aewna goes with you," he added.

CHAPTER 2

Returning to our shared bedroom in the large, white house, I was first to wash the sweat and grime from my body in the mechanical tub. When it was Kirwyn's turn, I headed out to the rose gardens, intending to sun-dry my hair. But I hadn't even reached the patio when I realized I'd forgotten my comb and sprinted back to our room.

Something in the air felt different the moment I entered, though I couldn't put my finger on it.

Kirwyn hadn't heard me. The bathroom door was ajar, and he stood facing the other direction. My eyes widened as I approached. His shorts were bunched around his ankles as if he'd been too hasty to remove them.

I knew what he was doing, but I'd never seen a man do it before.

My mouth ran dry watching the muscles in the backs of his legs and rear tense as he rhythmically moved.

I wanted to assist him.

I wanted to give him privacy.

Did I cause that by teasing him in the hammock? Every night we slept together but we never *slept* together, and, in mutually frustrating attempts at keeping desire at bay, Kirwyn refused to let me go too far with his body. For a moment, I stood immobile, enraptured. I stared as Kirwyn's arm pumped. When he let out a low moan, I drew in a quick intake of breath --

-- and *landdammit,* with his superior senses, he heard it.

Kirwyn jumped, immediately ceasing. I couldn't help but laugh as he hastily covered himself shouting, "Get out, get out!"

"I'm sorry," I cried, quickly retreating into the bedroom. I felt terrible that I had watched and even worse that I *still* laughed.

I thought he'd either finish or... put it back down... but two seconds later, Kirwyn stormed out of the bathroom, wild eyes focused on me. I could see the erection tenting his short-pants and I burst out laughing again. Stalking across the room, Kirwyn picked me up and I squealed. He tossed me onto the bed, climbed on top of me, and practically slammed himself between my legs.

Finally.

I threw my head back and moaned. He hadn't removed his clothing, but I could *feel* the delicious hardness he'd denied me. Tilting my head back down, I met his deep green eyes as Kirwyn began to rock up and down, pressing himself against where I most needed it. Afraid he'd stop, I barely breathed. He threaded his fingers through mine and brought his head down to kiss me, thrusting all the while.

More... I needed more...

"I think about you, about this, all the time," I confessed, between kisses.

"Yeah? What do you think? Tell me."

"What?"

"I want to know what you think," Kirwyn instructed, planting kisses on my jawline. "Don't hold back. Be specific."

I swallowed. "Um... your hands." *God, I loved his hands.* "When they... pin me."

"Like this?" Kirwyn asked, fingers gripping my wrists.

I nodded and wrapped my legs around him, tilting my pelvis up to meet his movements.

"What else, Zaria?" His warm breath against my ear made me shiver. "What do you fantasize about?"

Panting, I replied, "You barely let me touch you. So sometimes I fantasize that you... let me, you know. Reciprocate."

He'd done delicious things to me between my legs. Wasn't it only fair to return the favor?

The first stirrings of that familiar frenzy built inside me. I arched into Kirwyn, rubbing my breasts against his hard chest. If we could keep going for a couple minutes...

"Be. Specific," Kirwyn ordered. "Or I'll stop."

Reddening, but too turned on to risk Kirwyn making good on his threat, I quickly confessed, "I want to make you lose control. I fantasize that you do. That you – you... lock your hands in my hair and guide me to my knees and... and... push yourself into my mouth because you just can't hold back any longer."

Despite the fact that I'd squeezed my eyes shut in embarrassment, my own words pulsed excitement through me – and Kirwyn as well. Breathing heavy, he rocked harder. When I opened my eyes, I was encouraged by the heat in his gaze and continued with a bit more confidence, "I- I want to take you in my mouth as you take me in yours. I don't care that I don't know what I'm doing. I want you to

just..." my face heated, "move inside me until I figure it out
--"

-- A knock sounded on our door and I squealed. Kirwyn
and I instantly froze.

"Zaria? Are you in there?" Aewna asked from behind the
locked door.

I called out as steadily as I could, "Yes, I'll be out in a
few minutes, okay?"

A pause and then I heard retreating footsteps. Kirwyn
hadn't resumed his grinding.

"Please," I whispered, feverish all over my body. "I'm so
close. I think I can, you know..."

To my disbelief, Kirwyn sat up, grinning sadistically
and entirely too pleased with himself.

"Now you know what it feels like to be interrupted."

My mouth fell. When I realized he wasn't going to
return, I countered smugly, "Fine. I don't need you." I slid
my hand down to where I ached --

-- but Kirwyn grabbed it. Our eyes locked. "Mine. And
we mustn't touch things that don't belong to us," he teased
with a grin I longed to smack from his face. "Don't you dare.
Not for the rest of the day."

He leaned down and rasped at my ear, "And I'll ask you
later and I'll know if you lie to me."

My face flamed again. *He would.* A sound between a
laugh and a groan tore from my throat as Kirwyn laid a
quick kiss on my forehead. I'd greatly improved in hiding
my thoughts from everyone else, but Kirwyn, unnervingly,
always saw right through me. I wasn't sure if I had a tell,
but I'd given up playing defense and focused on trying to
read *his* mind instead.

It wasn't going well. Yet.

As he backed up, I threw a pillow at his head, but he

easily avoided it by jumping off the bed. Leaving me alone and squirming.

"The jury is re-sitting the chair with a verdict," I declared, folding my arms. "Definitely an ass."

"Close, not quite right," Kirwyn said. I knew he meant my attempt at using the expression, but I amused myself with the possibility that he'd admitted to being somewhat of an ass. Before he disappeared into the bathroom, I called after him, "You're only torturing yourself, you know."

"Not this time," he called back. "And thanks for the… inspirational material," he added with a shameless wink, kicking the door shut behind him.

I slammed my fists into the bedding and clenched my thighs, but it didn't do anything to relieve the ache.

Ugh. I'd be frustrated for the rest of the night. Which, I suspected, Kirwyn would smugly enjoy every time he looked at me.

Just wait 'till we're in the backlands, I vowed. *I'll have my revenge.*

Not trusting myself not to peek at him again and needing a distraction from picturing what he was doing behind that door, I scurried out of the room to see what Aewna wanted. Ambling through the large house, I found her staring out the window in one of the sitting rooms on the second floor.

"My father wants me to accompany you," Aewna said pensively.

"I know."

"It's curious. Mal-Yin is the very sort of man my father preaches against. He's the sort of man I do not wish to associate with. Forgive me – I understand you know him and feel you have no better option. But this would not be my choice, were it my own."

I sat down beside her – near but not touching. Without me having to tell her, Aewna understood that I didn't want to be touched by others, and I was grateful for her insight. Despite the *sessions* my aunt insisted on having with me, I couldn't make sense of my feelings. Having gone from not being permitted to be touched by a male, to not being able to prevent it, left me confused. In too many ways I'd gone *from zero to one hundred,* to use one of Kirwyn's expressions. For now, the idea of anyone's hands on me—anyone but Kirwyn's—made me uncomfortable.

"Why is it not your own decision?" I asked Aewna, a little angry on her behalf.

She smiled. "I know what you're really asking. *Why don't I defy my father?* But the truth is, even if I thought this worth causing a row, it's what *you* are determined to do. And you are my sister, so I will go with you." Aewna flashed a teasing grin. "Besides, you'll need me to help you find your seat. I heard you fell off your horse yesterday before you even fully climbed into the saddle."

My face reddened. "Hey! I got spooked, okay? And I climbed right back up again," I added, lifting my chin stubbornly.

Aewna dipped her head in a slight bow, "You did," she agreed, smiling once more.

Still wanting to sun-dry my hair, I rose to leave. At the door, Aewna spoke so quietly I almost didn't hear her.

"Shoulders like a queen, hips like a whore."

I froze, disbelieving I'd heard Aewna, of all people, say something like that.

"What?" I blurted.

She bit her lip. "It's what instructors say when they teach you how to ride."

Shoulders like a queen, hips like a whore? Well, that's... Laughing, I replied, "I can handle that."

THE NEXT DAY, Kirwyn and I trekked to a nearby place in the forest he used for target practice, and he lined up weapons on a dilapidated table. I stared at the guns, gut twisting. I couldn't reconcile my revulsion for the object with the knowledge that it was a necessary protection.

In Elowa, we lived free of such killing devices, but our safety was wrapped up with so much other cruelty from our malicious rules and compromises. If I didn't want Elowa dependent on Rythas to defend us, how could I continue to depend on Kirwyn—or any other—to defend me?

"I don't think about it," Kirwyn said, sympathy crossing his face as he read mine. "I grew up here. I barely remember learning to shoot. I forget what it must be like for you sometimes."

I licked my lips, confused and buying time. "Am I a hypocrite? Swords and arrows... I don't like them -- does anyone, truly? But I guess I've become used to the sight. Guns and bombs though," I took a breath, "it's just a lot to process."

"Zaria, yes," Kirwyn said, and I didn't know what he meant until he continued. "Some people like swords and arrows a lot. Guns and bombs, too. We're going to come against those people in the backlands. And how else do you think Mal-Yin maintains his power?"

I groaned. "I see now why Rythas is such a special place. They keep," I shrugged, spreading my hands wide, "some of this at bay."

Kirwyn picked up the smallest gun and held it aloft. "This one has a safety. Some don't. The most important thing, for now, is to make sure you select a gun with a safety and keep it on until you're ready to use it. Let's just worry about the mechanics first."

"Shooting comes next?" I asked.

"Then proper stance and managing the recoil."

My instruction with Kirwyn began, not unlike when Lazlian ran down the basics of explosives. Slowly, we progressed to target practice. Kirwyn's closeness behind me, adjusting my hips or my arms, made it bearable.

For days we kept up a routine. Sometimes we practiced alone, sometimes with Aewna. Guns, daggers, and hand-to-hand combat. Though I never became truly skilled, I grew passable, which was better than nothing. Tracking and foraging in this territory were my best talents, and I liked learning about the new species.

By far, my biggest surprise about the mainland was the monstrous beasts. Tens of thousands of them in our region alone. Kirwyn showed me pictures in books from my aunt and uncle's library and drilled me in defense each afternoon.

"What do you do if you encounter a bear?" he quizzed one day, pacing our preferred clearing.

"Try to scare it off if it seems interested in you. If it attacks, fight back or lie on your stomach and protect your neck and head as a last resort," I responded, imagining the ginormous creature he'd shown me in books. It wasn't to be believed, yet the texts confirmed it.

"How about a black panther?"

I thought a moment. "Don't run. Make yourself look as large as possible and hope it decides not to attack. Fight back only if you have to."

"And an alligator or crocodile?"

"On land, run. If it's in the water, fight for your life, especially if it tries to roll with you. Attack its eyes or snout or... a flap-thing under its tongue?"

"Good," Kirwyn praised, resting his hands on his hips with satisfaction. But I didn't relax because this run-down didn't even cover the smaller, poisonous creatures. Or other clans.

I threw up my hands and asked with a groan, "Why are there so many things here designed to kill you?"

Kirwyn laughed. "To keep pretty princesses like you close by her protector's side."

I crossed to where he stood and urged him back until his legs knocked against the old, paint-chipped bench we used. I pushed him to sit and straddled his lap.

"Is that what you are?" I grinned.

"Mm-hm," he hummed, eyes dancing.

"Do I look like I need protection?"

"Here, yes." His hands found my hips.

"I seem to remember protecting you repeatedly in Elowa."

"Consider it repayment, then."

"I can find better ways for you to pay me back." The roll of my hips made my proposition clear.

Kirwyn's eyes darkened, but his grip on my waist tightened as he lifted me quickly into a standing position, frustrating me.

"You're a terrible student sometimes," he mock-scolded, but it struck a nerve.

"I know," I said, quietly. "I'm just scared. Aewna's not built for the backlands. She can ride better than me, but she's worse at self-defense. She freezes at the sight of a fly. I don't *like* killing anyone, but I know from experience that if it's my life or someone else's, I'll do what I have to. I can't imagine Aewna taking a life."

"It won't come to that," Kirwyn said. "Volmar is giving us four of his best guards."

"I don't understand why he wants her to come with us in the first place," I protested.

Kirwyn sighed, leaning back on the bench. He looked so damn sexy in that pose, and training with him always made me want to do dirty things with his hard body. "I think he doesn't trust us. He wants his own daughter keeping an eye out."

"But Aewna doesn't strike me as one to spy and report. I trust her, Kirwyn."

"So do I," he admitted.

"Then it doesn't make any sense. But there is one advantage." I chewed my lip, hesitating. "I've been thinking, she looks a lot like me. But she's... more even-tempered," I begrudgingly admitted. "For all his shortcomings, Volmar has trained her well in diplomacy." I let out a long breath. "She'd make a good match for Juls."

Kirwyn snapped his gaze to me, brow knit in displeasure.

I knew that was coming.

"She could replace me," I quickly suggested. "Kinda soften the blow, you know?"

Kirwyn's hands tensed on along the edges of the bench. I nervously shifted my weight.

"Are you suggesting we offer your sister up as queen? As some kind of negotiation point for the king? You, of all people, want to play family members as pawns?"

"No!" I protested, holding up my hands. "Not like that! I'm just saying, if they met, they might... naturally... be drawn to one another. It could be a solution and could make them both happy."

Kirwyn gazed into the distance, rubbing his thumb along his forefinger. I knew that look.

"You assume he'll be in a state capable of experiencing any kind of happiness," he said ominously.

"Kirwyn, whatever it is you're plotting, stop. Please. If Juls is coming here, don't try to kill him or hurt him. Don't set a trap. I know how your mind works. Didn't you mean it when you said it was my choice? You can't kill the king and we need more leverage than just his life -- he would sacrifice that. It has to be big, and it has to be in Rythas."

Green eyes locked on mine, but I didn't see the forest in them this time. I saw unyielding mountains beneath the foliage.

"*Don't.* It will all fall apart if there's another king. Juls is reasonable, honorable. He'll listen," I swore, then admitted, "if we force him to."

"What kind of honorable man forces his bride to marry him?"

I let out a long sigh. I knew that was coming, too. As time marched on, Kirwyn being assured I bore no love for Juls only made his anger burn brighter. Time was doing funny things to my emotions as well, and I didn't like it.

"You don't think I ask myself the same questions? You don't think I go 'round the whole thing in Enith's sessions every day? But it's complicated."

Enith fancied herself some kind of mind healer and every afternoon she encouraged me to talk through my experiences. My aunt insisted the onslaught of emotions nearly bringing me to my knees was *healthy.* She believed I'd been in some kind of survival mode until now, never allowing myself to *feel.*

Personally, I didn't feel I had the time or desire to deal with any of that, so I held it back, held it up as one would a collapsing building. When pieces fell, when bricks dropped, I dealt with them one at a time, as they came.

Your entire life is a lie. *Crack.*

You were forced into an arranged marriage. *Slam.*

A man with scorched-earth eyes tried to murder you. *Crash.*

Later, when this was all over, I'd let go, let it all fall around me. But I had more important things to do now.

"I'm just thinking ahead," I told Kirwyn, forcing a smile. "And saying that maybe, if they met, Juls and Aewna might naturally fall in love. It could be a solution where everyone wins."

Kirwyn's skeptical eyes told me he was unconvinced.

His scowl said he'd rather beat Juls senseless.

And my intuition whispered that we risked a confrontation turning deadly if I wasn't careful.

CHAPTER 3

I was never as sure on a horse as I was in the sea, but once I'd mastered my seat, the thrilling sense of freedom delighted me.

"Race to the stream?" I arched one challenging brow.

Watching Kirwyn ride made something heat, low in my gut. He moved effortlessly, like he was born to it. *What a struggle it must have been for Kirwyn to be horseless, weapon-less, and utterly dependent on me back in Elowa.*

"You must love losing," he mocked. "I'm going to beat you every time."

"Not every," I countered, tightening my grip on the reins and readying to run. "One day you'll let me ride Vesper and I'll win."

Kirwyn's mare provided an unfair advantage. No horse could outrun his dark, gray-brown filly. She even left the males in Volmar's stable in her dust.

My own horse wasn't as swift but *my god*, she was the most beautiful creature I'd ever seen. Szirena was a Cremello, Kirwyn said, not to be confused with an Albino. Her coat wasn't as white as the latter -- she bore more of a champagne coloring, as the name suggested. If the light on the beach hit her just right, she glistened with an almost rose-gold hue. But it was a Cremello's eyes that enchanted most people. Szirena's eyes were bluer than mine and uncannily soulful. I fell in love with her the first time she looked at me.

"You didn't believe in beasts for riding when I told you, back in Elowa," Kirwyn had reminded me. *"I wanted something special for your first horse."*

Who knew what he'd done to procure her, or his own mare? Barter, blackmail, steal? None would surprise me.

"Come on, girl," I whispered, leaning down to Szirena's pointed ears. "Help me wipe that smug look from his face."

The fluttery feeling rose, watching Kirwyn position Vesper next to me. He was so landdamn sexy as his hips moved in an act pantomiming something else.

It made it hard to hate him when he won. Again.

Riding, to him, was what swimming was to me -- second nature. Heck, maybe first.

"I'll tell you what," Kirwyn said, grinning sardonically when I reached the finish-line. "We can go for a swim later and I'll let you beat me in the water."

Cackling breathlessly, I scoffed, "As if you'd ever have any hope of beating me at sea."

"You're always so pleased when you win." Kirwyn nudged Vesper closer. He took my chin in his fingers and I grinned because I could tell by the gleam in his eye he was going to do something naughty. He leaned by my ear and said, "I like it when you're wet and happy."

I shivered and playfully smacked him, cheeks heating.

Would I ever get used to the way he spoke?

〜

We'd depart in a few weeks, causing the entire house to hum with tension. Fear and excitement warred in my gut like two swordfish slashing at one another.

"Are you *sure* we can't just threaten him with a missile or something Mal might have?" Kirwyn asked, one night in our bedroom. "It would be a lot easier and safer, too."

I shook my head. "After the Oxholde attacks, Juls will never abandon or surrender High Spire from any external threat. He'll dig in his heels and defend it; he said as much. There'll be no way to gain control without bloodshed in that case. The only way to win is to conquer the castle from within."

Every time I thought about a battle, I couldn't help but imagine an unlikely scenario – Jesi and I facing off, swords or guns raised at one another. I would sooner injure myself than harm her and I knew she felt the same. But if others bore witness?

She'd do what she had to. Capture me. And it would all fall apart.

If harm came to her through another soldier though... if, in the heat of battle, Erisio or Lida or Tomé were hurt or killed...

I had to do whatever was necessary to stop that from happening. Which put us at a major disadvantage. Kirwyn, finding the idea ludicrous, was sure *we* were going to die instead.

"Look at it this way -- it's sensible," I argued. "If we shoot up half the guard, the people of Rythas will turn on us and I'll lose support for any changes."

"Look at it this way -- if you take the throne yourself, it won't matter."

I gazed at my hands, sighing. We'd had this discussion many times and I didn't know what I wanted. Destiny was a funny thing; I felt like it called to me but from so far away I couldn't heed the direction.

"I- I don't know. It's not my throne to take and I don't want Juls to lose it. I don't think I see myself as Queen of Rythas."

Kirwyn clasped my hands in his. "That's because you don't see yourself clearly. Besides, you already are."

Was I? Technically, Juls and I never consummated our marriage. Technically, I'd never been crowned.

"Kirwyn, I've been thinking and if Aewna stays in Rythas I might... want to go back to Elowa," I confessed. "Maybe not forever, but, for a time. And I could rule there until Jona is ready. If she wants it."

Kirwyn's mouth scrunched in displeasure. "First of all, Aewna hasn't said for sure what she wants. Secondly, and no offense, but I don't want to live there. You're used to it, but I need more. More people, more modernization. Did you forget how backwards it is?"

"Of course not. But we can change it, just like we change Rythas. That's the point. Lida said Pentyr will preach new ways... If we oust my mother somehow..." I threaded my fingers through Kirwyn's, holding his eyes. "Think about it. I could rule. You could rule."

Kirwyn blinked. "I'm not royal."

"It means nothing. It's made up. I can't think of anyone more knowledgeable or more equipped to lead us into new ways for the future... no one more than you."

Kirwyn frowned. "I don't want to ride on your coattails, Zaria."

I'd never heard the expression, but I understood the gist of it. "You think I can do it alone? You're wrong. It would take me years to catch up with the reading you've already done, the learning you've had. Kirwyn, I need you. You wouldn't be riding my coat, I'd be riding yours. Well, we'd be riding each other's."

That made him laugh.

"Seriously, all I'd bring to the table is a title," I pointed out. "You'd bring the rest. You'd bring everything." I brought his hand to my lips and kissed his knuckles.

"What if you be my High Braenar? And I'll be your High Braenese?"

He shook his head, still grinning. But I could see by the gleam in his eyes I'd tempted him. He could deny it, but the idea of utilizing all the skills he'd acquired excited Kirwyn. I knew my own eyes glistened, imagining Kirwyn in a crown, completing that picture of sinister beauty.

"I don't know..." he hedged. "There's a lot we still have to do."

I nodded eagerly. "We can figure it all out later. If – *when* we succeed. First, we need leverage."

"First, we need Mal's agreement to help us," Kirwyn scoffed, but his eyes still gleamed. He knelt by our model fortress with little rocks and shells meant to represent the soldiers of High Spire and the men we hoped Mal-Yin would give us. "Let's play *capture the castle.*"

With a small smile curling my lips, I moved the stones according to what I'd planned and what I reasoned would be High Spire's necessary moves in response to ours.

It began with me.

All that time spent searching for a way *out* of the castle proved useful.

I knew best the way *in.*

CHAPTER 4

My anxiety rose as days passed and we continued training, but I cherished every moment of our time together. *People often don't know they're living in a golden age until it's gone,* my Aunt Alette once told me. But I knew. And I swore not to take any of it for granted.

Everything would change when we left Volmar and Enith's manor, anything could happen once we put our plans into motion.

It was a gift when Kirwyn came up behind me in the woods, sliding his hands over my shoulders and repositioning my stance to better hit a target. It was a gift when he selected another boring tome on a tedious subject from my aunt and uncle's library and insisted I read up on some long-gone clan or country.

Most of all, it was a gift when he held me in his arms, to sleep.

"It was *one* nightmare. That can happen to anyone," I argued one evening, mere days before departure. "I'm not traumatized."

Kirwyn shot me a chiding look.

"I'm a little traumatized."

"Your screams woke the house," he said, "Twice. Lie down."

My nightmares were usually about losing Kirwyn again, but the most recent had involved Lazlian suddenly appearing at the foot of my bed and scaring the sea out of me. In my dream, he'd held a dagger to my chest and pressed it straight through my heart while I screamed -- apparently in the real world as well.

Arms folded, Kirwyn and I engaged in a staring contest before I sighed and relented, climbing onto the bed with its strange, springy mattress.

"That's an exaggeration," I grumbled, half to myself. "I only woke you. And Aewna."

Not that he cared about technicalities like stretching the truth. Kirwyn didn't fight fair -- a habit he'd picked up to survive in the chaotic world where he grew up and now smugly applied to me to get his way.

But sometimes, in secret... I let him.

"I'm not about to go swimming in a Sea of Sorrows like Enith would have you believe." I huffed, adjusting the pillow. "I'm actually angry. Most of the time."

"I know," Kirwyn said, rolling up the sleeves of his crisp, white shirt. Each time he did so, I was riveted by the simple exposure of his forearms. They were beautifully toned and perfectly accentuated his confident, capable hands and long, nimble fingers.

I watched as Kirwyn worked methodically. While I didn't like being monitored, the ritual almost made it worth it. I'd feel the cool prep of alcohol he'd swab against my skin, then he'd attach a small, sticky patch meant to relay signals to the black device on the nightstand. It wasn't sexual, not really, yet having his attention so focused on me ignited a comforting warmth inside my chest.

"You're good at this," I whispered. "You could have been a healer, in another life."

"Doctor," he gently corrected, still centered on attaching the stickers. "I wouldn't have wanted to."

"Why not?"

"They had to take oaths in the old days," he explained, pushing aside my tank top to dab the wet cloth onto the flesh above my heart. He placed the accompanying sticky-tag on my skin. "Promises to heal anyone no matter who they were or how they came to you. If someone delivered a mass murderer to your doorstep you were bound to treat them, to save them."

"And you wouldn't? You'd let them die?"

"If they were truly horrible," Kirwyn nodded. His eyes flicked to mine. "If they were only somewhat evil, I might show mercy and help them depart this world faster."

Not the answer I was expecting. But it didn't surprise me.

"You're not as sinister as you think," I mock-scolded. "I know you couldn't hurt Gereth when you took him, and you never hurt me when you thought I was your enemy."

Kirwyn shrugged. "He's good and you're both innocents."

I narrowed my eyes, feeling as if I walked into a trap. "I'm innocent... but not good?"

"Oh no, you're bad. I think your mind is so filthy it's nearly a challenge for me to keep up." He smirked at me and teased, "But I'm good at challenges."

I rolled my eyes and snorted. "That's because you know you'll win because you cheat."

Well, it wasn't *outright* cheating, but he had a fishy way of bending the rules, stretching the truth.

Kirwyn leaned down slowly, giving time for gullbumps to rise on my skin before he even spoke. Too measured he came to my ear, sending my pulse racing.

"I think you like losing to me. I think it really feels like winning."

Nothing could stop my blushes this time. My mind returned to the game we played a few nights before, just outside my uncle's walled gardens. We'd wagered on the outcome and when I lost all my pieces on the board Kirwyn claimed the victory. But he was right. What he'd demanded as payment for the bet didn't feel at all like losing on my part.

I gulped at the memory. *It felt amazing.*

Kirwyn held my eyes, surely knowing where my mind traveled. I thought he might kiss me but disappointingly, he straightened instead.

"All done," he announced, flipping a switch on the black device. A red light glowed, letting us know it would record biofeedback data while I slept. Already picking up my rhythms, a set of numbers on the complicated screen began flashing and the device beeped in warning.

I looked below the numbers.

Heart rate.

Something worked behind Kirwyn's face, lighting it with devilish delight. Once more, he leaned down gradually. It seemed the slower he moved, the faster my heart thumped, making the device blare more frantically.

Against my ear he rasped, "What's making your heartbeat so erratic, Zaria? Tell me."

Before, it'd been the memories; now it was his tone. Kirwyn's husky, masculine command went straight to my head, making me dizzy.

"Your... voice," I admitted. My own voice came out hoarser than I expected.

"We could play another game," he offered, grinning with self-satisfaction.

I knew the truth would go right to his head.

"I already know you like to be teased, even though you pretend to hate it... What else? I could say or do various things and we could listen to the biofeedback. See which ones you like best."

I swallowed, thinking about all the secrets I wasn't ready to yet discuss. It made no sense, but half the time I longed for Kirwyn to speed up and the other half I relaxed into how slow he moved.

"No, thank you."

Kirwyn backed up, arched a brow and said, "Do you really think I need the monitor to tell?"

I definitely walked right into that one.

He laughed and licked his teeth. The only thing holding me back from smacking him was that I knew he'd catch my wrist, causing that stupid device to all but scream my galloping heart.

Kirwyn laid down beside me and blew out the flickering candle on our nightstand. Though my aunt and uncle's house glowed with modern lighting it hurt my eyes and unnerved me. I liked it best when my world contracted to this bed, to only Kirwyn and I. It felt safe, manageable, and sleeping in his arms soothed me like nothing else.

Knowing the monitor would beep if I upset myself too much, I took steadying breaths before confessing the frequent nightmare that haunted me in daylight, too.

"I'm terrified of how my life would have turned out if I hadn't met you," I whispered in the darkness. "I actually freeze, afraid to move. I'm afraid something will happen and you'll disappear again." I ran my hands over Kirwyn's biceps and squeezed, as if he might be cleaved from me that moment. "After all I've been through, in some ways I feel braver, more sure of myself. I know what I'm capable of and what I can withstand. But in other ways, somehow, it worked backwards. Maybe part of it is because I know I'm incapable of living without you and I'm scared of the risks we're taking."

"We'll have the best protection possible," Kirwyn insisted. "Your uncle's guards are well-trained."

I nuzzled into his chest and whispered, "It's you I trust. Keep me safe, Kirwyn. Don't let them take me back."

"Never," he swore, kissing my forehead. "Now go to sleep. I'll watch over you."

It felt like he said *I love you* every time he told me that.

"If you don't particularly like Volmar, why do you play cards with him so often?" I asked, eyes closed. As soon as I was asleep, Kirwyn was going downstairs for their game.

"*Because* I don't really like him," he replied. "I don't fully trust him. And he drinks too much when he plays. The man can't handle his liquor half as well as he thinks he can."

"So you beat him every time?" I asked, grinning.

Kirwyn turned serious. "No. About half. He's not an idiot. Just..." I felt him shake his head. "I don't know. Something is off, missing." Kirwyn kissed my temple again. "Now, shhh..." he said gently. "Go to sleep. I'll be back in an hour or two and I'll have the remote to hear if anything goes wrong."

I closed my mouth but in trying to find sleep so close to our departure, I couldn't stop my thoughts from turning to Rythas. If Juls vacated the throne to search for me, that left Lazlian to rule in his stead, and I still didn't know what had happened the last time the keylord was in charge. Before escaping, I'd told Lida I suspected Singen had betrayed the Dorestes to Oxholde, but what had come of it? Was I right?

Was that even a good thing?

Or did warning Lazlian and potentially saving his life—the life of the man who wanted to kill me—seal my own fate?

CHAPTER 5

ewna and I found Kirwyn in the sunroom the next morning. Already dressed, he'd slipped out of bed before I woke.

"There you are," I said. "Come on. We're ready for our ride."

Kirwyn's eyes flicked back and forth between Aewna and me, hesitating. He'd pulled his shoulders back, stiff, tense. As if he'd been caught unaware.

"Okay," he said, a bit reluctantly. "Let's go."

The hair on my arms stood on end. *What was wrong?*

I asked Kirwyn the question with my eyes, but his gaze darted over to Aewna and he shook his head, as if to say, *Wait. I'll explain later.*

The three of us headed to Volmar's stables to saddle our horses. Aewna, who'd been riding her whole life and was far better than me, always camouflaged herself when leaving her father's walled fortress. She'd tuck her long blonde hair into a hideous, green-and-brown mottled wig and don loose "camo" clothing that practically swam on her slim body, in order to blend with the forest.

However, in order to torture Kirwyn, I had knowingly dressed in a tight, white tank top and fitted pants, tucked into tall brown boots. The outfit clung to my body, and I couldn't help but smile every time his gaze lingered. For the first time in a long time, I had someone I wanted to look pretty for and it gave me a fluttery feeling in my heart. I'd also tied a pale blue ribbon in my shoulder-length hair, and one in Szirena's beautiful mane, to match. It was silly and a little flashy for the forest, but I always felt safe beside Kirwyn.

After a few minutes of riding, the path widened and I nudged Szirena to match Aewna's pace, needing to speak to her about something uncomfortable I'd been avoiding.

"Aewna, Kirwyn and I were wondering…" I bit my lip, wincing. "If you've taken the birth control shot? If anything were to happen in the backlands…"

"It's not productive to think that way," she dismissed, skirting the uncomfortable topic.

I pursed my lips. I didn't want to think about it at all, honestly. Considering the Spades, Rythas, the beasts in the backlands, and all other natural disasters that might bring danger, the horror of being attacked by men who forced themselves on women… that it could lead to unwanted pregnancy… was too much to handle. But I needed to know she was protected.

"Okay, well what about your cycles?" I asked, trying a different angle. "Do you want to deal with that while we're in the middle of the woods somewhere?"

Aewna looked to the trees, sighed, then turned back to me. "I suspect I won't have to. My moon cycles came upon me and quickly ceased. I don't have them any longer."

I stiffened, confused. *Was she saying something wasn't working correctly inside her?* Remembering how Jesi said it was difficult for many couples to conceive, I wondered if that meant Aewna might face issues.

She flashed a small, tight smile. "It's my eating habits, I think." I could tell she spoke as if to soothe *me* and it made me feel guilty that my face showed unwelcome concern. "Stress. I can't menstruate again until I put on more weight. So I most likely cannot get pregnant at this time and won't have to worry about cycles while we're journeying."

Something else to resent Volmar for, came the immediate, venomous thought. I blamed him for the unnecessary stress, sure his excessive grooming of her into the perfect braenese caused who-knew-how-much damage within.

Though I almost didn't blame him if it escaped his notice. Aewna seemed determined to put on a mask of silent strength no matter what she endured. Perhaps she'd inherited that from her mother.

"I wish we were going anywhere but to Mal-Yin," Aewna sighed. "You might know him as an ally, but I've heard terrible stories. I know what he's capable of. They say he murdered his father in cold blood to take control of the clan when he was only fifteen."

"I don't particularly like him either," I replied. "But sometimes you have to work with your enemies to get what you want."

Aewna nodded but seemed unconvinced. "True."

Kirwyn nudged Vesper beside me. In his hand he held a white frangipani flower, just like the ones dotting the trees outside my old cave. Holding my gaze, he leaned over and tucked it into my hair. The simple act made me blush, made my heart thump.

He's so different from other men, I marveled for the thousandth time.

Men like Lazlian, I thought, for just as many.

∾

By late morning, we'd rounded back toward the house. Kirwyn was in the lead, as usual.

"Stop!" he ordered, quick and low. The mainland was eerily flat in our region, but we'd crested what could be called a small hill when he pulled Vesper to a halt. My stomach instantly tightened as Aewna and I reined in our mares.

"What is it?" I whispered, nudging Szirena beside him. My eyes widened at the sight of maybe a dozen horse-riders surrounding my aunt and uncle's house.

"Spades," Kirwyn announced, brow furrowed as he surveyed the grounds. From our vantage point we could see their bustle of activity as they carried gear into the stately white manor, but they couldn't spot us if we remained hidden by the trees.

"Why are they here?" I gasped.

"I don't know," Kirwyn replied. "But we can't go back right now. We'll have to wait until they leave. This is... odd. Too coincidental."

We heard a rumble from the trees and Kirwyn drew his gun.

"Don't shoot! It's me!" Damyre exclaimed, emerging with his hands raised in surrender.

I sighed in relief. Kirwyn re-holstered his gun. "What's going on?" he asked, sliding from Vesper's back. Aewna and I nervously dismounted as well.

"The Spades have come to clear out the area of any free-borns. They're billeting at the house."

Billeting? I'd heard that word before but couldn't remember it.

"What does that mean?" I asked.

"It means they plan on staying. It means they didn't ask. *Fuck,*" Kirwyn swore.

My stomach knotted again. Kirwyn turned to face me.

"It means we can't go back. She can," he lifted his chin at Aewna. "But we have to stay away. We'll find a good spot to camp-"

"No," Damyre cut Kirwyn off, frowning with sympathy. "Volmar thinks it's too risky for her as well. The Spades are asking too many questions. He's not even sure if the mission is fully sanctioned or if they're rogue."

"What are you saying? Spit it out," Kirwyn demanded.

"I'm saying the Spades plan on staying several weeks." Damyre walked back to the trees and picked up something he'd dropped when he arrived. Eyes round with pity, he shuffled back, carrying one large, brown-and-green pack, and another bag I knew contained tenting supplies. He offered both to Kirwyn. "I was able to sneak out one of your bolt bags."

Bolt bag? Were we going somewhere? My eyes flicked nervously between the two men having a conversation I hadn't yet caught up to. Or rather, the conclusion I came to wasn't possible and I couldn't accept it.

"No," Kirwyn said firmly. "Not without armed guards and certainly not without more supplies than this."

"Kirwyn," I began, hoping he'd tell me I was mistaken before I voiced my fear. "What's going on?"

He turned to me. "He means for us to leave. To go to Mal-Yin. Now."

No. Not like this. I spared Aewna a quick glance. "Just the three of us?"

Kirwyn glared at Damyre. "You know it's suicide."

"Whatever's going on down there... something isn't right," Damyre muttered, eyes lingering on Aewna. "Your odds of surviving the backlands are better than if you return to the house."

"We stay here," Kirwyn insisted. "I know a place a few miles north where we can hide. We'll wait until you can sneak out more supplies and find a way for at least two guards to give the Spades the slip-"

"It's like they *know*," Damyre declared, shaking his head. "More Spades are arriving this evening and the sweeps start within the hour. You have to leave now and you have to get far away from here." Damyre's cheeks puffed with air he let out slowly. "So far you might as well head to Mal-Yin rather than linger in any disputed territories."

Oh god. My blood ran cold, finally accepting the truth. We were cut off from the house with little more than the clothes on our backs. *At least we're dressed for riding. At least we've had a few weeks to prepare. At least we have each other.*

Remembering my powder-blue ribbon, I reached up and yanked it from my hair. The frangipani Kirwyn gave me tumbled to the ground. I let it go, trying not to feel sentimental or a sense of foreboding as it lay in the dirt. There'd be no use for flowers on our journey. I slid the matching blue ribbon from Szirena's mane too, pocketing the impractical silk.

Aewna's resolute expression didn't betray her emotions, as usual, but I could guess what she was thinking. Physically, she was the least equipped of the three of us to survive in the backlands. She was likely resolving *not* to be a liability. I swallowed my own fears and crossed to where she stood so that I could comfort her with the right words -- hoping I found them. Hoping they worked on me, too.

"I have to go. My disappearance will be noted," Damyre said to Kirwyn, looking over his shoulder nervously.

I noticed that while I spoke to Aewna, Kirwyn bent his head close to Damyre, whispering to the guard. I could tell the conversation was dark, tense. I wondered if Kirwyn discussed our planned route.

Track us when the Spades leave, I imagined him saying. *In case we don't make it. Find out what happened, if you're able. Find our bodies. Bring them back for a proper burial.*

Oh god, how could this be happening? Not like this.

Kirwyn stepped back, holding the bolt bag and the camping bag. Damyre slowly looked at each of us, face grave. When he reached Kirwyn, he said with curious emphasis, "Send word when you reach Mal-Yin." His gaze slid over us once more before he gave a curt nod. "Godspeed," he added, before hurrying back down the slope and toward the house.

None of us spoke for several long seconds.

Kirwyn turned, forest-green eyes studying Aewna and me. From the quiet determination on his face, I guessed what he was calculating.

How to keep not one, but two Elowan princesses alive in the backlands. Without guards, our survival fell on his shoulders.

I lifted my chin, determined. I may not know the land the way he did, but I was capable of fishing and foraging. Growing up in Elowa, I had skills many did not possess. Maybe I wasn't the most talented rider or fighter, but I was quick, strong, clever. An asset. Far from helpless.

I brought my fingers to my face, absent-mindedly caressing my cheek. My gaze grew unfocused and I saw what Kirwyn saw.

Yet even the way I look makes me a particular kind of target, I thought with a shiver.

I suddenly felt foolishly exposed, especially compared to Aewna's olive-brown wig and her layers of loose, camouflaged clothing. I'd worn an outfit hugging my curves like a second skin because I wanted to look good for Kirwyn. Because we'd only gone out for a short ride, near the house. I hadn't even brought a gun.

Oh god, how had this happened?

At least our boots were sensible. Good for riding or hiking.

What lay ahead? There were worse things in this world than Juls finding me, bringing me back.

Even with Lazlian, my fate in High Spire was the devil I knew.

Out there in the backlands... was the devil I didn't.

PART II
LAND OF ETERNAL NIGHTMARES

CHAPTER 6

I gulped, dreading the first step toward...

Pain. Torture. Death.

No, I quieted the fearful voice in my head. *We'll survive.* All three of us. We had to.

"Should we wait?" I whispered. "See if Volmar can sneak us a message or more supplies come nightfall?"

"No. He won't... risk it. We need to ride. Far and fast," Kirwyn said. "Now."

Urgently, Kirwyn opened the bolt bag to assess its contents. Rummaging around he exclaimed, "What the hell? There's no guns, no extra ammo... no explosives! It's just... Spade bricks, water, a medical kit..." rifling through the pack, he continued with disbelief, "a compass, some cooking supplies, a few daggers, bear and bug repellant, tooth powder and soap shavings..." His hands fisted the straps until his knuckles whitened. "This isn't a full bag."

Cold water flooded my gut. "Did Damyre," I wondered aloud, "take out the weapons?"

Kirwyn swore under his breath and caught himself

before throwing the bag in anger. "I don't think so, no. He could have brought us nothing at all."

Kirwyn's gaze flicked to Aewna. She remained quiet but her eyes rounded slightly with alarm. Calming, Kirwyn said, "Someone probably just removed the weapons for cleaning or training. Bad timing is all."

I frowned. That didn't sound likely, and he didn't sound convincing. *He's trying to put Aewna at ease. Why?*

Reshuffling everything neatly back into the pack, he said, "Come on, we have to go."

Kirwyn stepped close to me, and, brows knit, he stroked my face.

"Don't do that," I said, jerking away.

"Do what?"

"Look at me like you're trying to memorize me. Like we're not going to make it to Mal-Yin."

"You don't like it when I lie to you..." Kirwyn murmured. I bat my lashes, once, impatient. *Of course I don't.* "I put our odds of survival at thirty percent."

I swallowed thickly, pulse picking up speed. *Not good.* But what were the chances I'd escape Rythas? That I'd make the swim from *The King's Light* without drowning? I'd faced worse odds with less resources.

"The odds are better if you don't take unnecessary risks, endangering yourselves to protect me," Aewna said bluntly.

"Out of the question," I dismissed her. "Don't even consider it."

But her comment did bring up a thought. In the past I had little help, but I also only had to worry about myself. Now there were three of us needing to make it through the backlands alive. Three times the risk.

Maybe Kirwyn's odds were overly generous.

But in all the world...

"There is no one I trust more in this entire universe," I said, grabbing Kirwyn's hand, "than the man who told me about the world in the first place. There's no one who makes me feel safer than you."

"Will you actually listen to me? Without questioning it if I tell you to do something?"

I nodded... but used the opportunity to negotiate. "I'll make you a deal. You know the territory. You're in command here. But once we reach Mal-Yin, once my plans are put into motion and *especially* on Rythas – I lead. You have to listen to *me,* no matter what I tell you. Fair?"

Kirwyn inhaled slowly.

"Stop it," I scolded, wagging my finger. "I can practically see you looking for loopholes. Swear it."

He sighed, "Fine. I swear it." Grumbling, he added, "I feel better about our odds of survival already."

"Why's that?" I narrowed my eyes.

"Because you're too stubborn to die before getting the chance to hold me to it."

I grinned but it didn't touch my eyes. He was trying to make me feel better but it only made me want to cry.

Kirwyn strapped the bolt bag to Vesper's saddle and the camping bag to Aewna's mare. He returned to me before mounting.

"I want you to stay close to me at all times, do you hear?" Kirwyn demanded, clutching my biceps. I nodded vigorously. "Unless I tell you to run, never leave my side. Swear it!"

"I swear it," I breathed, and he loosened his steel grip on my arms.

"Come on. Let's make it as far as we can before nightfall."

With one final glance at my family's white manor, we mounted our horses and took off northward at full speed.

∼

Kirwyn set a grueling pace, as if death nipped at our heels. Which might have been the case. The further we rode, the more my fear grew. I could feel the subtle change in Kirwyn too, as we passed beyond the most familiar territory and into the unknown. He'd traveled this region with his uncle, but he didn't remember it well. For direction we relied on the sun, the compass, and dusty trails – some well-worn, others barely traversable.

Inland, with no coastal breeze, the burning sun beat down relentlessly. The terrain was thick with dense, low bushes and trees. It was also eerily flat, which felt *wrong* to me. Beaches and coastal regions might be flat, but inland of Elowa and Rythas brought gently sloping hills or mountains of some height. I couldn't get over the creeping fear up my spine from the lack of change in elevation. It didn't feel safe somehow, as if it left a person exposed to attack.

The flatness unnerved me as much as the great ruins. No clans settled these areas, no one had reshaped or repurposed anything from the wastelands. Whenever we followed trails leftover from old roads, favoring speed over stealth, I couldn't fight a sense of chilling awe. Riding deeper into the backlands I witnessed a great, ancient war between a long-departed civilization and nature.

Nature was winning.

Slowly, steadily, she reclaimed swaths of black roads and sometimes narrow, felled towers alongside. Kirwyn had shown me pictures in books, but nothing compared to seeing it in person.

Giants once lived here, I thought. *Not physically, but mental giants, capable of building great things.*

Despite my amazement, I wasn't wooed and didn't wonder why Kirwyn had wanted to escape.

I don't know where my home is, I thought. *I don't know for certain if it's Elowa. But I know it's not* this.

We spoke little and stopped only to rest, drink water, and nibble on the dried, powdered Spade bricks. They were as tough and tasteless as Kirwyn once told me, but effectively stayed hunger pains. Using three mares eliminated the chance of trouble caused by ornery males, should our mares go into heat. Personally, I never wanted Szirena bred. Labor could be risky and she was too precious. By late afternoon, we left the Old World road again, heading into untamed forest. Our riding was slow, hindered by branches and prickly things.

As dusk fell, Kirwyn decided we'd put enough distance between ourselves and the Spades, and we dismounted to camp. Mindful of alligators and their nests, Kirwyn carefully harvested sawgrass from the edges of a pond and we cooked the edible, white core over a small fire. Even more than the coast, the inner mainland was riddled with snakes, alligators, and crocodiles. Cold-blooded and cruel, I saw Lazlian's eyes in theirs whenever I pictured them. For this reason, we checked the ground carefully before setting up our tent, just big enough for the three of us to sleep. Inside our camping bag we had three blankets as thin as sheets and no pillows at all.

"We'll use our clothing for pillows," Kirwyn instructed. "And keep your boots in the tent. You don't know what might crawl inside them in the night, and if they're wet with rain or morning dew it will take days to dry in this humidity."

Everything on the mainland is designed to kill, I thought wryly. *I shouldn't be surprised that even unguarded boots pose a threat.*

~

THAT NIGHT, Aewna retired to the tent first, but Kirwyn and I were too tense to sleep. I paced nervously, ears straining to listen for footsteps or hoofbeats coming from the endless darkness just outside our small campfire. Kirwyn felt reasonably safe in the location he'd chosen, so I didn't understand the hum of anxiety he emitted until after Aewna fell asleep. He watched me with his eyes until finally, rising, he grabbed my wrist, halting my pacing.

"Zaria," he said in a low, urgent voice. "I didn't get the chance to tell you before we left. I didn't want to say anything in front of Aewna."

My stomach tightened at his warning tone, and I held my breath.

"I snuck into Volmar's office this morning and I found the letter your mother sent him. *Letters.* It's not just the one I carried, they've been exchanging correspondence since you arrived."

My heart sank and I knew my face showed it because Kirwyn's eyes rounded with concern. Carefully, he said, "Your father is gone, Nasero is gone. There are no men left in Queen Pama's life. She wants Volmar to sail to Elowa to rule with her. I can tell from her letters she's always wanted him. But more importantly, your mother lost a lot of support with her scandal, and she believes that if Volmar reappears after having been gone all these years, after everyone thought he died... she can spin his return to make him look like a god himself."

My eyelids fluttered shut and I gritted my teeth. *The endless lies! Always using gods to make us believe whatever they wanted, to hold onto power.*

"It will solidify her rule and she'll get what she always wanted," Kirwyn said.

"No," I insisted, flinging my eyes open and fisting my hands. I might have been betrayed again, but I refused to be outplayed, in the end. "I won't let her."

Kirwyn took a deep breath. "That's not all. Zaria, I think you should sit down."

"Just tell me. Whatever it is, tell me now!"

"Sit," Kirwyn repeated, and, not giving me a choice, he scooped me up and sat me beside the fire. With my attention riveted, I didn't bother to fight him.

"This might be hard to hear," Kirwyn said, crouching in front of me. "I think Volmar arranged for the Spades to come. I think he was planning on having them take all of us out of the way. Maybe he made some kind of a deal with them. I'm not sure."

Kirwyn sat back on the dirt now, sighing. "We may have thwarted his plans by being out of the house when they arrived. But I think... he's hoping we don't make it. Maybe he's counting on it."

For a moment, I was speechless.

"Are you saying that he's trying to murder his own daughter?" A lump formed in my throat. "Murder us all?"

Kirwyn ran a hand through his hair. "Possibly. Or maybe he just wants the Spades to capture us... indefinitely. He might have sent them to track us. Which is why we needed to leave the area quickly."

"But he spent his whole life training Aewna!" I cried. "He seemed delighted by my rise to power in Rythas! It doesn't make any sense!"

"I think you and Aewna were his best horses in the race. But it quickly became clear that you had your own plans, and when your mother offered Volmar a place to rule beside her," Kirwyn shrugged, "he didn't pass it up this time."

I bit my nail as I considered the idea. As sad as it would have been for Volmar to marry my mother for a love of power when they were younger, it was infinitely more depressing that he might take the opportunity a second time around. Because he *must* have loved his wife once... so where did that love go?

Frowning, I mused aloud, "Volmar truly loved Enith when they were young, didn't he? Enough to marry her and risk everything. But somehow, along the way... Poor Enith."

"Familiarity breeds contempt," Kirwyn shrugged. "For some. I think over the years, Volmar began to regret his decision. When the shiny newness of Enith wore off and the quiet tedium of exile gave him the time to think about all he'd given up."

"Even so, my mother would never agree to this," I argued, gesturing wildly with my hands. "She might lie to me, but she wouldn't murder me!"

Although she'd tossed me into the sea as a baby.

I shook my head. "No. She truly believed she was giving me the best possible life with Juls. I think it was the life she wanted for herself."

Kirwyn clasped my hands to stop their flailing. Firelight danced shadows across his face. "I think you're right. And that's the only reason Volmar didn't dispose of us more quickly. I'm certain now that your mother knows we've been hiding at his estate. The only reason I can think that she wouldn't have reported it to Rythas is because Volmar convinced her not to. He knows if you return, you'll rock the boat, and that's a major threat to his power. He doesn't *want* you as queen. Not if you won't be his puppet," Kirwyn said. "I think he's been stalling, looking for a way to get rid of us quietly, without Queen Pama knowing it was his doing."

I waited for the devastation, but it didn't come. Kirwyn's theory didn't even shock me. Nothing about my dysfunctional relations shocked me anymore.

Ironic... I felt a prick of envy for the family I was a part of unwillingly and in name only. For all their faults, the Dorestes loved and protected one another, above all else.

"We have to make it to Mal-Yin," I said, mind racing. "Before they make any moves. We have to stop them both."

Kirwyn nodded. "We have an advantage, and it's a big one. Damyre is on our side and he thinks the other guards are loyal to Aewna over her father. They've watched her grow and she's very charismatic. But Damyre doesn't believe they will turn on Volmar without proof we have something to offer." Kirwyn lightly touched my face, drawing my gaze back to his. "I'm sorry, I wasn't lying, I just didn't get a chance to talk to you. It all happened this morning. I saw the opportunity to sneak into Volmar's office and I took it. I swear, Zaria, I was coming to tell you after I spoke with Damyre. But then..."

Then Aewna and I came for our ride and the Spades arrived.

Kirwyn continued, "If we can make it to Mal-Yin and persuade him to send soldiers to your uncle's estate, we can contain him there."

"So the guards will turn on Volmar for us," I said, thinking aloud, "if we give them a reason."

"But they can't until the Spades leave. And they won't,

not without word from us. Word that we're safe and that they have something, someone, to back. Who's also got their back."

I groaned, mind spinning again. "So we need to make it to Mal-Yin fast *and* persuade him to help us *and* send a small army right after the Spades depart."

"Exactly."

"And there's no way of knowing when they'll leave."

Kirwyn nodded again. "Damyre expects us to send word once we're safe. That's what we were talking about before we left. I didn't want to say any of this in front of Aewna. She's your sister. It's your decision how much you want to tell her, and when."

I didn't need to think about it. "I want her to know everything, even if it hurts. She's strong, she can handle it. And I never want to keep anyone in the dark the way I was."

Kirwyn nodded his agreement and wrapped his arm around me. We both fell silent, listening to the crackle of fire and watching the dancing flames for a few minutes before retiring to the tent.

"We need more weapons," Kirwyn whispered, as we readied for sleep. "We won't make it without them."

"How can get some?" I asked.

"With luck, maybe we'll pass travelers who will trade."

"We have nothing to offer," I pointed out.

"Our horses," Kirwyn said. "I could ride out on Aewna's mare and make the trade."

"What about Szirena and Vesper?"

Kirwyn's arms tightened around me. "You and Aewna will stay back," he said firmly. "You won't show yourselves."

I understood what he wasn't saying, and my stomach

knotted. *Travelers who saw us might want to trade something else.* Or worse. *They might not be interested in being friendly about it.*

It took me a long time to drift off and I spent a fitful first night's sleep with Kirwyn and Aewna in the backlands.

CHAPTER 7

We made it through the night without any attacks from bears or other people.

The next morning, I told Aewna everything as gently as I could while Kirwyn packed our supplies. My sister absorbed the information with a stoic grace I couldn't help but contrast to the way shocking news leveled me emotionally. At least, in the past. But I didn't think she was blindsided by it. Her crestfallen expression seemed to convey that her worst suspicions were confirmed.

"Are you okay?" I asked when she fell silent.

"It seems we have no choice but to go to Mal-Yin now," Aewna said, shaking her head with displeasure. "I agree that we need to contain both our parents. And we're going to need his help."

"He's not as evil as you've been told, I promise."

"And he's not as good as you've been shown," she countered with a frown.

We rode at a slightly slower pace than the day before, due in part from our shared soreness by the previous day's ride, coupled with our uncomfortable sleep. Every part of my body ached, but I supposed I'd grow used to it. I longed for a cool swim in the ocean, but we were miles from the sea.

Despite being a better rider, Aewna didn't have the stamina to go far that day and we stopped to camp in the early evening. Needing water and more nutrition than Spade bricks, Kirwyn and I made the decision to forage while Aewna stayed with our horses. I didn't want to leave her alone, but Kirwyn absolutely refused to leave *me* alone, and we found a nook deep in the woods he felt confident no one would stumble upon.

We got lucky when, on a few felled trees, we spied mushrooms growing which Kirwyn deemed edible. He'd left our dagger with Aewna for protection, so we used our hands to scrape the ruffled, orange fungi from the bark. I dusted off a section and was about to pop it in my mouth when Kirwyn's hand gripped my wrist.

I looked up, alarmed.

"Chicken of the Woods needs to be cooked first. Don't eat it raw." He gently took the mushroom from my hands and put it in our small bag.

Nearby, we also found a treasure trove of what Kirwyn called Hog Plum trees and I picked the tart, purple plums with delight. It was our second forage with stipulations as Kirwyn explained the fruit was safe to eat, but not in large doses.

"You know, this land is crawling with insects right at our fingertips," I said as we walked back to camp. "Everything we're doing would be easier if you ate bugs. I'd feel a lot better about our survival."

Kirwyn raised his eyebrows, looking down at me and countering, "Mal-Yin's compound is going to be overflowing with weapons. Everything we're doing would be easier if you weren't against bringing guns into the plan. I'd feel a lot better about our survival."

Unable to think of a comeback, I pouted. Kirwyn cocked a half-smirk. Playfully facing off against each other, we were caught off guard when a beast stalked out of the trees and prowled directly in front of our path.

My heart stopped and my knees buckled. Kirwyn threw himself in front of me and raised his arms high and wide. I blinked to be sure it wasn't a phantom, a nightmare.

The black panther crouched before us. Real. Terrifying.

"Zaria," Kirwyn said, low and steady. "Reach into my holster and withdraw the gun. Slowly."

Shaking and sweating, I removed the gun as silently as possible. I never took my eyes off the panther.

"There's no safety on this one. Just point it at him and if he moves... shoot. Just like we practiced."

I gulped and nodded, as if Kirwyn could see me from behind. He stood straight with his arms outstretched, making himself as big as possible. I was half-crouched, reaching around his midsection and aiming the gun at the panther.

"Shouldn't I-"

"No," Kirwyn cut me off, sharply. "Stay behind me."

How did he know what I was going to ask?

The panther bared its deadly teeth and rumbled a terrifying growl. I thought that if I hadn't taken care of it moments before, I would have lost control of my bladder at the sound. My wide eyes remained transfixed on the creature's long, sharp teeth. They could tear us to pieces in seconds. *And the claws.* I couldn't see them, but I knew they were sheathed beneath its paws, eager to slice our skin.

It felt like the rest of the forest quieted in horrified awe for our showdown.

Staring at the beast, Kirwyn growled in return. It was *inhuman*, from somewhere deep inside him, and utterly unlike any playful growling he'd done when we were intimate.

Something primal in me responded to it – a feeling of yearning and adoration shot through my chest. I didn't think Kirwyn even knew he was capable of such a sound; I didn't think he could repeat it under other circumstances.

The beast didn't move. His yellow eyes pinned us, weighing whether to attack, determining if we would make a good meal.

I swallowed again, finger tensing on the trigger, wishing my sweaty hands weren't so slippery.

Shoot straight, Zaria.

Slowly, the panther raised its head.

You might only get one shot.

It turned away from us...

...and casually resumed its walk across the path.

As if this hadn't been a moment of life-or-death.

I blinked rapidly and heard Kirwyn exhale. He lowered his arms and took the gun from my shaky hands. I moaned in relief but couldn't seem to make my limbs function. Thankfully, the creature had stalked off in the direction opposite of our camp.

"Hey, you okay?" Kirwyn asked. "Back away slowly. Don't run. Don't turn around yet."

Finally, I made my body move. "You just... fought off a panther for me," I panted.

Oh my god. We were almost killed. If Kirwyn hadn't been there, I probably would have been.

Kirwyn clasped my hand and pulled, leading us away

with a cautious gait. After a few moments we came to a silent, mutual decision and broke into a run, grinning like idiots and possessed by the surge of adrenaline.

Before we reached camp, Kirwyn halted and grabbed me. "Are you okay?" he asked again, breathlessly pulling back to search my face and my body as if I'd been harmed. His chest, though heaving, puffed with something like exaltation.

He looked sexier than ever. It was an odd thought to have but I couldn't stop it.

I was... turned on.

"You fought off a panther for me!" I cried, smiling and still disbelieving. Technically, he didn't wrestle the creature, but his posturing successfully scared it away and I knew Kirwyn would have physically fought it, if necessary.

"I'll always protect you," he swore. Kirwyn cupped my face and kissed me deeply. Adrenaline and arousal surged together, goading one another higher.

Please, I thought, feeling my nipples tighten against his chest. *I need you.*

The lust in his eyes told me Kirwyn felt the same. It was crazy at that moment, but I didn't care. His hands found my top and slid it from my body. My boots, pants, and undergarments quickly followed, stripping me naked. Kirwyn tore off his own clothing and I gaped at his toned body, naked and bold in the middle of the open wood.

Is this really happening? Finally?

Our panting only increased. Like a beast possessed, Kirwyn roughly swept me from my feet and onto the grass, pressing himself between my open legs.

"You're sure the birth control works?" he asked, confirming he wanted what I wanted.

"Yes!" I cried as his hard body collided with mine. "I haven't had my moon cycles, trust me."

He didn't need more convincing. Kirwyn's mouth locked on my throat and he nipped it a little too hard. I yelped, throwing my head back and running my hands over the strong planes of his chest. Kirwyn's fingers found my wet core and he groaned as he stroked it, as if it gave *him* more pleasure than *me*.

"Please," I begged. "I need you inside me."

"I can see that now," he teased, dipping two fingers within and curling them. "I can feel it," he said, pumping in and out. Kirwyn took my nipple in his hot mouth, licking and sucking, working me into a frenzy before pausing to line up with my entrance.

My eyes flicked down to his sizable erection and my mouth ran dry. I reached up to hold his back but lightning fast, Kirwyn gripped my wrists and pinned them over my head. The strength in his hands made me instantly moan and arch, seeking...

In one thrust, Kirwyn buried himself deep inside me. Hard.

I cried out as I jerked, fingernails digging into my palms.

He froze. "Is it too much?"

"No, it's just-"

The first time—the *only* time we'd had sex—it hurt a little, but he'd entered me slowly, gently, and I'd been quite inebriated. Not to mention, it'd been kind of... over too quickly. The soreness was minor and had passed by morning.

But experiencing the entire length of Kirwyn at once, without the time to accommodate myself, was a very different sensation. How did I explain that his full thrust teetered between pleasure and pain?

"Look at me, Zaria."

I looked.

"Is it too much?"

"No," I breathed.

"Liar."

I moaned, bucking and confessing, "Yes, but it's the good kind of pain. Don't stop."

Kirwyn let out a soft chuckle. "Relax," he whispered, kissing my jawline and letting go of my wrists. "You're tense. Everywhere."

I hadn't even realized I'd clenched my core -- tensed every muscle in my body.

"Relax," he repeated, kissing my lips, "and I'll make it feel good, I promise."

I nodded, forcing myself to uncurl my toes, loosen my shoulders, and unclench... below. He still filled me to the hilt, but he hadn't moved.

"Good," Kirwyn murmured, feeling the tension leave my body, "Just like that..."

Yet I couldn't stop from rolling my hips against him, desperate. I'd waited so long I thought I might scream if I couldn't finish like this, with the fullness I'd yearned for, connected to him as deeply as possible.

Kirwyn answered my plea by groaning and thrusting again, hard, making me cry out to the treetops.

This is what I'd wanted, what I'd longed for.

"Don't ever stop," I begged. "I need this. Always. Please don't stop."

"Never," he swore, angling his hips to rub the spot that gave me the most pleasure. I threw my head back and it felt like my eyes rolled back along with it.

Everything was so different from the first time it was like we weren't even the same people. Kirwyn drove into me far harder than I remembered. He repositioned my legs to hit something delicious deep inside me. He pressed the firm, flat area above his pubic bone against my clit as he moved, grinding to send waves of pleasure through my body.

Most importantly, this time, he kept going.

Until I was frantic, clinging to him, pleading. Words were Kirwyn's specialty but neither of us spoke much beyond base, animalistic moans and grunts. We were too needy, rushing on adrenaline and desire, tearing at one another. Kirwyn leaned down, sucking my throat greedily. He again nipped the tender region between my neck and shoulder with a possessive bite that made me yelp. He kissed a line back to my lips and plunged into my mouth on my next cry.

"Look at me, Zaria," he ordered, thrusting deep enough that I sometimes squealed with that pain-pleasure mixture. I could tell he was watching me, learning me. But I was too aroused to feel more than a pang of self-consciousness; I floated too far down the river of bliss to muster any playful refusal. My body felt like putty, obeying his commands, not my own. If Kirwyn said *look*, I snapped my eyes to him. If he guided my knee up and out in a move that stole my breath, I melted into the motion. I had the heady and slightly embarrassing thought that he led me as knowingly as he steered his horse, and I loved it. I felt guided in his confident hands, felt so desired by the powerful snap of his hips and his devouring mouth.

"Oh, god. I love you so much," I swore, running my fingers through his dark hair. "Please, please..."

He knew what I wanted and kept up the hard, shallow

thrusts, driving me toward that cliff's edge, poised to tumble into that heavenly sea.

"Kirwyn," I moaned as I climbed. His name was everything to me. My demon, my monster, my sinner, my savior. He responded by pinning my arms to the ground again, strong fingers encircling my wrists. The restraint of my body had the opposite effect on my desire, heightening it, strengthening its potency, until I could no more hold back my orgasm than I could hold back the stars.

I was too wrapped up in my own imminent climax to notice if he was close until I heard, *"Fuck, Zaria,"* and I snapped my eyes open, watching him watch *me.* It was *my* moans and the bliss flitting across *my* face making Kirwyn come undone. The intimacy made my heart feel as if it would burst. We came together like that, eyes locked, hands locked, hearts careening against our ribcages. It didn't matter that we were pressed against the dirt in the middle of nowhere, it was more than I'd dreamed.

Drenched in sweat as we came down, I had the sense to worry that our enthusiastic lovemaking re-caught the attention of the panther or something else in the forest. Some*one* else. We'd been loud, unrestrained and *fuck...* it was so good. I wrapped my arms around Kirwyn's body, loving the weight of his warm hardness over me. I'd never been so blissed-out in my life. Why was anyone unhappy, why did clans war -- when everyone could just be doing *this* all the time?

Part of me didn't want to return to Rythas or go anywhere near civilization again. I'd rather run forever with Kirwyn and couple in the woods, or the waves, or beneath the stars for the rest of our lives.

"That was... different than the first time," I said, cautiously.

Kirwyn let out a sound in the back of his throat. "I got better."

I bit my lip to keep from giggling. "That's an understatement. How?"

"What do you think I've been doing since I lost you? Thinking about what I'm going to do to you when I got you back," he answered his own question. "What do you think I've been doing since you returned? Figuring out what you like," he answered again, then mumbled under his breath, "And how to slow down."

Kirwyn laid on his back, pulling me onto his chest. Knitting my brows, I asked, "But do you like it too? What do you... like?"

"Everything when it's you. Especially when it's rough or I overpower you, you look up at me with such longing. This contrast plays out on your face. You blush but your eyes glaze with lust. Even when you're not fighting me, you're fighting yourself. I noticed it back in Elowa though I didn't fully understand it at the time. Eventually you're too aroused to continue the battle and you surrender to desire, to my hands or my tongue. That moment-"

"Okay, that's enough!" I cut him off, face growing hot from his easy manner of speaking and his way of seeing through me. "You could have just said *'I like it rough.'*"

Kirwyn laughed and pulled me tighter.

Quietly, I studied the last splashes of vibrant purple and orange twilight through the treetops. Birds or bats flit across the sky, too fast and dark for me to discern. I hadn't expected such an explanation from Kirwyn, the way he detailed changes in me like I was a play he watched unfold. Being unable to hide from him made me feel shockingly vulnerable. But he never used his ability to hurt me. Everyone else who had power over me had abused it. My mother and father neglected me, lied to me, traded me like an object. Grahar and Lazlian bullied me, terrified me. Even Juls, I had to admit, subtly controlled our dynamic to subdue me and to suit his desires.

No wonder it was a scary prospect, opening up to another person -- a man, especially. When I first met Kirwyn, I hadn't felt that way. I was too naïve to fully grasp the extent to which one person could emotionally destroy another.

But now... was I damaged?

I didn't believe Kirwyn would ever devastate or abuse me, but just the possibility existing irritated, like a grain of sand caught in an oyster. *Could we ever be as wild and carefree as we had been in Elowa, or was everything now tainted, spoiled?* I felt myself frowning. Funny that someone like Grahar would say I'd lost my innocence on the beach that night with Kirwyn, but I didn't feel that way at all. It seemed, to me, that what my parents had done ... what my marriage had done... the lies and battles and cruelty... that all of *that* chipped away at innocence. With my head on Kirwyn's chest, I could hear the beating heart of a man who loved me. What in the world could be better? Making love with Kirwyn made me feel closer to a state of grace, not further.

I winced. *Despite the fact that I'm technically married to someone else.* A soft groan escaped my mouth. *How did this get so landdamn complicated?*

Snapping Kirwyn's attention, a small animal of some kind scurried across the forest floor.

"We should go," he said, shifting me so that we could get dressed. "We need to get back before it gets dark."

"Aewna will be worried," I agreed. "And rightly so. We could have been killed."

Kirwyn gave me his hand to help me stand and we quickly re-dressed.

"You know, I just want to point out that we could have been doing *that*, long ago," I said, with a hint of waspishness.

"You were right."

I stilled, eyes wide with exaggerated surprise. "Can you repeat that?"

Kirwyn grinned. "You were right. We should have been doing that since I found you."

"Can I get it a third time?" Instructing primly, I said, "Nay, I'd like to hear you say it anytime you want to do it again. It'll be like a code, how you request to proceed. Say, 'Zaria, you were right,' and I'll consider your entreaty."

By the time I'd finished, Kirwyn had crossed his arms.

"Don't push your luck," he said, fixing me with *the look.*

"I'm not," I teased, "I'm pushing your buttons, and it's one of my favorite things to do."

"Keep going and I'll push yours right back," he threatened, pulling me into a one-armed hug. His other hand squeezed my backside and I squealed. "And we'll see who wins that game."

"Oh my god, you are, hands-down, the cockiest person I've ever met," I laughed.

"And you're the most stubborn I've ever met," Kirwyn countered. Kissing my forehead, he said, "And the bravest." Pressing his lips to my nose he continued, "And the most resilient." With a kiss on my mouth, he concluded, "And the sexiest."

Warmth spread through my chest. *A pearl,* I suddenly realized, feeling foolish that I'd missed the obvious. *Of course.*

If I had any trepidation about my vulnerability with

Kirwyn, if my thoughts worried like grains of sand caught in an oyster, I would simply work at them until I transformed them into something better, something beautiful to behold.

Hand in hand, Kirwyn and I returned to camp. After telling Aewna about the panther, we quickly fell asleep, readying to ride hard and fast again come morning.

The next day seemed longer than any I remembered. Kirwyn and I stole lingering glances at one another, minds wandering. When we stopped to water the horses, he came up behind me and I had gullflesh from the simple contact, even before he whispered in my ear, *"I'm going to make you come twice tonight."*

Butterflies took an excited wing in my stomach. I swayed, leaning against him. My entire body wanted to melt into his embrace right there, but we weren't alone.

Making excuses about needing to gather sawgrass, Kirwyn made good on his promise that night. *So* good.

It became our routine. Each evening, Kirwyn and I found a reason to sneak off for a few moments, alone together.

Aewna politely failed to notice the leaves in our hair upon returning.

CHAPTER 8

I wondered, at times, if we were insufferable to be around. Kirwyn and I moved as if we were invisibly tethered *before* we started having sex. Now our days of riding were filled with distracted daydreams, long stares, whispered promises, and blushes. At least, my cheeks heated whenever I thought over how I moaned or things I babbled at the height of pleasure. Shameless pleas and strings of nonsense fell from my lips whenever Kirwyn thrust inside me.

It was so powerful, if not magical. He entered my body and logic left. One look and I was in his thrall. One push to fill me and I was his. It was as if part of me moved aside to make room for him. His commands and desires. But I didn't feel less, I felt *more*. Perhaps that was the reason reason departed. To allow space for the greater thing we became together when we merged.

But each morning bumping along on Szirena's back, I bit my lip and flushed. Did other women say such things? Did they feel the same as they neared their climax? I wanted to ask someone, most especially Jesi or Lida, in whom I longed to confide. I didn't feel comfortable talking to Aewna about sex -- not yet.

Kirwyn never had anyone his age to talk to, but at least he'd been surrounded by books. How fantastical it must have been, growing up, to have a question and to simply find the answer at your fingertips.

I remembered all the naughty stories he perused in his youth. *To find answers you didn't even know you were looking for,* I thought.

I wanted those stories too, to see if other women felt as I felt. Besides the book Jesi gave me, containing mostly pictures, I'd never opened that kind of tome. Rythas had such material, but I was in no state of mind to read it then.

Nor would I have wanted to risk Lazlian catching me. God only knew what he'd say.

Reading for whores, most likely, stealing the book from my hands and reporting me to his brother.

Kirwyn led us northwest in a circuitous route, trying to steer clear of coastal clans. Blessedly, we hadn't encountered anyone up close, and if we heard a noise in the distance or spied what might be a campsite, we changed course to avoid it.

My legs, back, sides, even my arms were never *not* sore. We didn't make good time; the inland forest was dense and swampy. Often, we had to backtrack and circle areas too mucky to cross. Mosquitoes swarmed, even in midday, and the area was thick with black bears. Afternoon rains were a frequent and welcome respite from the heat.

On horseback we were safer than in our beds at night. Kirwyn slept with the gun and I held a modern device especially designed to deter bears. It flashed colorful lights and made such a cacophony of noise it repelled *me* the one time I'd practiced with it. We'd run out of water on the second day, and collecting it presented the problem of never knowing which stream or lake concealed alligators just below the surface. Kirwyn skirted the edges, scanning, then quickly filled a pot and ran. We boiled it for purification over the campfire before refilling our containers for travel.

We'd only been able to wash off the worst of our grime and sweat with the minimal supplies in the bolt bag, so before long I felt too achy and dirty for any intimate activities with Kirwyn at night.

"There's a cold spring we'll reach soon. We can safely bathe there," he promised. "No crocodiles or alligators to worry about. Usually. We should reach it tomorrow."

That night, Kirwyn climbed into our tent early, so that I could speak with Aewna about our plans. We had no intention of ever working against her, but we didn't know what *her* intentions were, especially after what her father had done.

I sat beside her, watching the fire, and when I broached the subject she surprised me by declaring, "I always knew my father was being dishonest. It's my gift and my curse, you see," she said, absent-mindedly adjusting her camouflage wig.

"What is?"

"My Elowan talent. I'm very good at telling when people are lying."

"What do you mean?"

Aewna looked at me with her big, blue eyes. They were darker than mine but shaped the same.

"You know we were created with more than beauty in mind, don't you? In the Optimal Election program they selected the finest DNA for every trait possible."

I shrugged. "I know a bit. Aunt Alette said our ancestors

chose the best gene sequencing they could, to make sure we were intelligent, athletic..."

Aewna nodded. "It's something we don't talk about because it makes us even more desirable to others. We can't hide the way we look, but we can hide our abilities," she explained.

A fearful, queasy feeling roiled in my gut, but at the same time I bristled at the idea of having to hide so much.

"I'm skilled at homing in on body changes when a person isn't telling the truth," Aewna said. "The change in their tone of voice, direction of their gaze or pupil dilation, body movements and so on. Anyone can do it, but I'm exceptionally good." She spoke pensively, not boastful. "It's not supernatural, it's science. Even though there are times I can't identify *how* I know, that doesn't mean it's anything mystical. I just can't always distinguish the tell on a conscious level. But it's there, and I'll subconsciously pick up on it. It's not just with truths or lies, it helps give me direction to figure out what a person is thinking. I'm not a mind reader," Aewna insisted, "I just read body language exceedingly well."

I listened, mesmerized by Aewna's confession. In truth, it sounded mystical to me.

"I don't know if it's by chance or if somewhere in my ancestorial line these abilities were a specific focus for election. Perhaps I had ancestors in public safety or government," she shrugged. "Deep down, I always knew my father wasn't being completely honest. But I'd always hoped he'd make... better choices."

Aewna forced an encouraging smile. "Have you discovered your abilities?"

I thought a moment, then shrugged, "I can swim better than most."

"I've noticed you're double-jointed," she remarked. "You probably have a better lung capacity too, and other internal advantages you're not even aware of. Anything else you've observed that's different from other people?"

Chewing my lip, an odd one hit me. "*Yes*, smell. I swear I'm more sensitive than others because I never hear people talk about it the way I do. To me, everyone has a distinctive scent. Jesi smelled like coconuts or orange blossoms, depending on the soap she used, and Kirwyn smells like the forest..."

And Juls smelled like sandalwood and clean leather... and Lazlian smelled like blood... and fire.

Aewna gave a soft laugh. "Another gift and a curse maybe. You probably have more than one enhanced sense, most of us do. My father's vision was like a falcon's. But what about more cerebral talents?"

"I don't know." I shrugged again. I didn't have a mind like Lida or Tomé, who could learn anything once and commit it to memory. "I'm a good schemer I guess."

"I'm sure you have many Elowan skills you don't even know yet," Aewna replied.

We both gazed into the small fire for a while, silent. I wasn't sure how I felt about enhanced abilities. I was already different enough on the outside. Perhaps I would feel less trepidation in a world where it didn't make me a target.

It's why Elowa is the safest place for me to be.

"I know what your father wanted, but what do you want, Aewna?" I asked. "Do you want to return and rule Elowa? Do you want to be the High Braenese?"

"It's not that I want to be a queen," she said carefully, "but I want be in a position where I can make the most difference."

I didn't want to get my hopes up at her answer, but I did anyway.

"Hear me out. Kirwyn and I have been talking and this is going to sound a little crazy because I know he's technically my husband, but would you ever consider sailing to Rythas for... Juls?"

Aewna blinked, surprised.

"I don't want to push you into something the way I was – that's not what this is. I'm just... I know Juls. I know who he is and what he likes. And I know you too, or I'm starting to. And I think your temperaments align. I think you would make an *ideal* Queen of Rythas. I think if you and Juls met you might..." I pushed myself to finish, "fall in love."

In her silence, I added, "He's a good man. Very handsome. He cares about his people. You're both so similar."

"I know enough about him to know he's good," Aewna said. "Or he tries to be," she added, taking into account Juls from my conflicted point of view.

"Would you at least consider meeting him?" I asked.

"I would consider it," she said slowly. "Then do you mean to return to Elowa?"

It was my turn to hesitate. "I think so. I think it might be best if Kirwyn and I go back. Something must be done about my mother. Someone has to watch over Jona as she grows into her role. Someone has to usher in a new era. Together, Kirwyn and I can blend the old and the new, we can help move things forward in a way that, most of all, safeguards our people."

Aewna studied me and I didn't know what to make of it.

"But I wouldn't take it from you, if that's what you want," I quickly amended. "I know your father has been preparing you for claiming some sort of power your whole life. I would step aside, or help you, if you want to be the High Braenese until Jona matures."

"I want what's best for everyone," Aewna said, diplomatic but firm. "It sounds like you have a plan and the will to execute it. If it's the wisest course, I would be happy to help it come to fruition."

I smiled, relieved. Aewna was selfless, well-spoken, and intelligent, with an abundance of inner strength. She might be just what Juls and Rythas needed.

Could it work? A plan where everyone was happy, in the end?

Most girls coerced into a union like I was would simply slit their husband's throat in his bed at night, or they would return with an army and take his crown. Certainly, most forced brides didn't introduce their husbands to a beloved sister and wish the couple every happiness.

We only needed to survive the backlands... and persuade Mal-Yin... and thwart our parents... and capture High Spire... and negotiate a truce...

Ugh. It was a lot.

But still, this could be the beginning of a new era, I thought. *We are two filthy Elowan princesses on the run in the backlands, watching a dying fire while mosquitos swarm, making plans that might determine the fate of two kingdoms.*

Stranger things had happened... right?

THE NEXT DAY we reached the spring and it was heaven.

I never wanted to leave that cool water, that oasis in the punishing inland heat. Why anyone would choose to live far from the sea was beyond me, and selecting an area rife with monstrous beasts was sheer madness.

Though, I had to admit it was probably a wise location for freeborns to stay free. Spades avoided the thick, muddy woods.

We took turns scrubbing with the last of the soap from Kirwyn's bolt bag. In Elowa we didn't have water spouting from mechanical devices like Volmar did, nor an abundance of soap bars, but everyone smelled like the sea anyway. Fresh and beachy and *good*. Unless, of course, they'd recently toiled in the woods and I could smell the verdant earth and leafy trees on their skin, the way Kirwyn often smelled.

But everything the past few days reeked of swampy muck and unwashed flesh.

"How far to the next spring?" I asked, wrapping my legs around Kirwyn's waist and my arms around his shoulders. He kicked the water, spinning us together.

"I don't know," he said. "I can't remember. My uncle committed maps to memory, but I'm drawing a blank past this one."

"I don't want to leave," I whispered in his ear, grinding against one of my favorite parts of his body.

"Stop it," he hissed through clenched teeth. "You'll get me hard and your sister will see."

I grinned and kept going. We'd all stripped down to our underwear and used the opportunity to wash our clothing, which now hung to dry on nearby tree branches.

"Zaria... last warning," Kirwyn cautioned.

"Or what?" I teased, wiggling in his lap with renewed vigor.

Kirwyn stilled, giving me a hard look. "If you're going to test me like that, keep your hands around my neck," he said, enigmatically. "If you move them, I swear to god I will carry you out of this water and spank you right in front of your sister."

My eyes bulged and my core clenched. *What did he just threaten?* I gulped. *Why did it turn me on?*

Kirwyn slid his fingers beneath the waistband of my underwear and without hesitation, rubbed my clit.

"Remember, keep your hands around my neck," he warned as he stroked.

Softly, mindful of Aewna swimming on the other side of the spring, I moaned, rocking my body in time with Kirwyn's ministrations. I couldn't imagine this wasn't making him hard anyway, but that was his fault.

"God," I whimpered by his wet ear, closing my eyes, "you are so good with your hands."

It wasn't long before my legs tightened and my hips gave their first hard jerk --

-- and Kirwyn instantly removed his fingers.

What the fuck? Forgetting Aewna, I squeaked. *I was just about to come.*

"Shh..." Kirwyn hushed condescendingly, stroking my sides while I squirmed, as if were an animal he soothed. I heard the grin in his voice as he chided, "I did warn you."

Lost in frantic desire, it took longer than it should have to realize he wasn't going to let me come, that he'd done to me what I'd started to do to him... but ten times worse.

Collapsing my head against his shoulder I let out a painful groan and he laughed. He laughed! *I was in pain and he laughed.*

Yet, mind-bogglingly, I was more turned on than ever.

"I knew you were trouble from the moment we met," I sulked.

Kirwyn took my chin in his thumb and forefinger, bringing my gaze to his.

"I thought the exact same thing." He leaned over and kissed me. "But even I couldn't have conceived of how much. Trust me, when it comes to trouble, you take the prize."

"Good," I lobbed. "You deserve it."

"And you deserved that."

"I hate you right now."

"Stop grinding against me and maybe I'll believe you," he whispered in my ear.

I stilled hips I hadn't even realized I'd been canting.

"Cocky demon."

"Stubborn princess."

We were both distracted with laughter when we were interrupted by Aewna's shout from the spring's bank. I hadn't even noticed she'd exited the water and I wondered if she'd suspected what we were up to.

In a flash, Kirwyn and I broke apart and raced toward her.

"Ow," Aewna cried, having collapsed on the ground. She threw her head back, rocking in pain as Kirwyn and I crouched beside her.

"My ankle..." she moaned. "I... it's twisted maybe."

Kirwyn's entire demeanor instantly changed. He gently held Aewna's leg, examining it. "You might have sprained it. You can't ride. Not well. It should heal in a few days but," he surveyed the area, calculating, "we can't linger here, it's not safe."

Kirwyn grasped Aewna beneath her arms and lifted her to a standing position. "Can you put weight on it?"

One tentative step and she hissed, "No."

"You can't ride," he repeated.

"I can," she said. "Just not well."

He looked around again thoughtfully and relented,

"Only until we find a safe place. You need to rest. Elevate your leg. *Shit.* I wish we had ice."

With no choice but to move, I helped Aewna re-dress and Kirwyn carried her to her horse. She wasn't in terrible pain, but she couldn't walk and Kirwyn was right, she couldn't properly ride.

With Aewna struggling to maintain her balance, we made slow progress northward. The boost we'd all received from our break in the spring faded fast. My cracked lips constantly longed for more water. My aching back needed lengthier rests. My hot skin screamed for a dip in the faraway ocean. It could turn quite cool in these regions, Kirwyn insisted, but now was not the season.

Midday, we came upon a slight bend in the trail where the road dipped and turned. Trees blocked the view, but I saw the curve of something unnatural, man-made.

"What is that?" I asked, eyeing the metal bars of...

"The Crossroads Cages," Kirwyn replied as we rode closer.

"Cages?" I repeated, coquina clams creeping up my spine.

"For those whose fate hangs in the balance. They're used to imprison people and to let," Kirwyn shrugged, "god decide whether or not they deserve to be saved."

I scowled. "How does that work?"

Kirwyn stopped and studied the metal bars poking through the trees. Following his lead, Aewna and I brought our horses to a halt.

"Men and women locked in one of those cages can't get out themselves. The keys are kept out of reach. But they're there." Kirwyn looked at me. "Anyone passing by can retrieve a key and release the prisoner."

I blinked. *Oh. Us. We determined someone's fate.*

He pointed. "See that one on the right? It's swinging. I think someone's in there."

CHAPTER 9

"Y ou've *got* to be kidding me," Kirwyn scoffed.

My mouth fell. Inside the last cage squatted the scoundrel who'd taken Kirwyn and I prisoner after Kirwyn had rescued me, the day we first rode to my aunt and uncle's house. I scowled at the man who threatened to turn us over to the Spades.

Farip Fabroni.

Even from five feet away, I could smell him. He must have been in that cage for weeks without access to appropriately relieve himself or to bathe. Grease spread through his blonde hair and dirt encrusted his face. Those sharp, dark eyes hadn't dimmed, however.

Fabroni threw back his head as he barked a laugh.

"My luck never runs out." With his face still tilted skyward, he spoke to the clouds, "You had me going there for a while, I'll admit it."

Who was he talking to?

Fabroni fixed his gaze back on me.

"I've heard rumors that the king himself left the throne

to search for his missing queen." Fabroni grinned. "And I've found her, *twice.*"

My stomach tightened at the mention of Juls. *So it was true. He'd left Rythas to hunt me down.*

Oh god, that left Lazlian on the throne. What a thought.

Fabroni's head volleyed back and forth in his strange manner, as if debating. "I was hoping to use my favor for something... shinier. But now I've got a prize in mind that's just as sparkly." He grinned, revealing teeth in need of brushing. "Justice."

"You want us to let you go because you let us go," Kirwyn remarked, dryly.

Fabroni looked at me. "I want you to let me go because you promised me a favor."

True, I thought. *And this is an easy one. I'd thought he'd find me in Rythas or Elowa someday and demand something grand.*

"And then I want you to retrieve my bag from the men who put me in here." Flashing his teeth, Fabroni added, "Traitors. The men I traveled with turned on me. Stole what was mine and left me here." He grinned. "But I know where they've gone."

Speaking directly to Kirwyn he said, "I've seen you in action. They're holing up in the safehouse, I'm sure of it. Guarded, but nothing you can't handle. You can sneak in there and get my bag back for me."

"That's two favors," Kirwyn said.

"You want to play word games?" Farip asked. "Then my favor is that I want to be able to use the contents of my bag. In order for me to do so, you need to get *it* out of the safehouse and get *me* out of this cage. Not my concern that it's a two-step problem."

"You tried to sell me," I reminded Fabroni, crossing my

arms. "You threatened us with torture. We're not inclined to bend the rules in your favor. Violence is a rather unappealing quality, after all."

Fabroni leaned forward, clasping the metal bars with his dirt-encrusted hands. "So is grudge-holding." Looking up at the sky again, he yelled, "Isn't that right?"

I blinked. *Wonderful.* He was talking to a god. How long had he been in his cage? Had he gone mad? I scrutinized his face. *But his eyes are as sharp as ever.*

Fabroni smiled at me. "Besides, you gave your word of honor."

And certainly not mad enough to forget.

"How long have you been in here?" Aewna asked. "Who's to say the men who betrayed you have lingered in this area? They could be anywhere."

"They won't have moved on." Fabroni cocked his head. "Probably."

Kirwyn scoffed, his chest vibrating with the sound. "No can do. We'll release you, but we won't be hunting dogs to retrieve this bag of yours."

An unpleasant feeling pressed down on me. I didn't want to help Fabroni, but the thought of not having honored my word didn't make me feel good either.

"Kirwyn," I said. "I think we might... have to try."

He turned scolding eyes on me. "What's one of the first things I ever told you? Back in your cave?"

I shrugged.

"Kindness gets you killed," he reminded me of his long-ago declaration. "You have to trust me."

"I gave my word, Kirwyn," I said softly.

"You gave it when you got married, too," he bit out, jealously. "Did it matter then?"

Pouting, I protested, "That's not the same thing. I was forced."

"And you were forced when you made a promise to this jerk."

"No. I came up with the deal myself. I made it in good faith."

"Is this little task of his worth the risk to our lives, compared to what we're doing?" Kirwyn challenged. "What if we die? Your life is too important. It matters too much to too many people."

My shoulders slumped. He made a good point. Could I weigh honoring my word to a dishonorable man, against the importance of what I was about to do for so many?

But what did it say about me if I didn't keep my promises?

I'd be less than Lazlian, I thought. *Even he keeps his vows, however horrible they are.*

Fabroni watched us with keen interest.

"I don't know..." I hedged. "If I don't honor my word, then haven't I've already lost so much of myself that I'm not worth saving? You want me to be a queen? Then how can I fail to keep the first promise I made as a queen?"

"You won't *be* anything, won't be able to help *anyone* if you cease to exist," Kirwyn pointed out.

As I stared at the grass in defeat, Fabroni piped up. "I've got firepower in my bag," he baited. "You look to be in short supply of... everything."

Without moving his head, Kirwyn looked up and narrowed his eyes. "What kind of weaponry? Be specific."

Fabroni cocked his head side-to-side in his strange manner. "I can't know what they've used or traded. But there should be enough to bolster you. Some guns. Ammo. Explosives."

We needed guns, and not having to ration bullets so carefully would also be a boon.

"And you can take half the Spade tokens you find," Fabroni added.

Kirwyn made a sound in the back of his throat. "You mean we can take back the tokens you stole from me in the first place."

Fabroni grinned, first up at the heavens, then back at us. He spread his hands widely. "It's like it was meant to be."

Kirwyn ran a hand down his face and swore under his breath.

"He has a point," I sighed. "If not to honor my agreement, then to get more firepower."

Kirwyn groaned. "Your sister can't ride and we can't leave her alone."

"She won't be," Fabroni said. "I'll stay with the girl."

"You mean you'll sell her to the Spades the moment we turn our backs. I'm not leaving her out here, unprotected," Kirwyn insisted. "You're in no position to look after her, even if I trusted your intentions."

In truth, neither Aewna nor Fabroni were in good enough health to travel, let alone fight. Aewna's ankle wouldn't let her get very far and Fabroni looked like he needed several days of sleep to even function.

"There's a bunker, not far from here," Fabroni said, quickly. "If you can give me a ride, we can make it in under an hour. It's not large but I've got food, water, and a dry place to sleep. Even books to read to pass the time until you return."

"You've got places all over this territory?" Kirwyn asked, disbelieving.

"It's how we're able to travel and trade," Fabroni replied.

"I will stay."

We turned our heads in Aewna's direction, startled.

"He won't hurt me." Looking at me pointedly, Aewna said, "I can tell."

Perplexed, Kirwyn started to argue, but I grabbed his sleeve and said in a low voice, "I'll explain later. But if Aewna says someone is telling the truth, they are. She's safe with him."

Kirwyn scrutinized my face, brows knit.

"Please believe me. I swear I'll explain later."

"We can't afford to be emotional out here," Aewna said. "The most logical course of action is to retrieve the bag."

Cautiously, Kirwyn asked Fabroni, "How far is this safehouse?"

"Less than two days ride. You'll be there and back in three days."

Please, I pled with my eyes. *We'll all feel better with weapons and Aewna needs a rest anyway.*

"Dammit," Kirwyn sighed. "Fine."

He crossed to the rather unremarkable box atop a waist-height stand by the trees. He opened it and retrieved what I assumed to be the cage keys, though they didn't resemble any keys I'd ever seen. Kirwyn held a flat, circular object of some kind.

"Spade technology," he explained. "It's a release disk."

Since she could barely hold herself astride, I took Aewna on Szirena with me and Fabroni rode Sun Bolt, her horse. I almost didn't believe Farip until we arrived and, true to his word, he uncovered a hatch built into the ground. The bunker was just a small, camouflaged hide-away, consisting of three low-roofed, tiny rooms built underground. It wasn't anywhere a person would want to stay for long, but it wouldn't be too bad for a few days.

Easing his dirty body onto a chair with torn upholstery, Fabroni said, "I won't hurt her. If you don't trust that promise, trust that what you're retrieving is more valuable to me than she'll ever be."

Aewna flashed us a small, encouraging smile, but Kirwyn didn't unclench his jaw.

"I wish we had ice," he mused once more, examining Aewna's ankle before we departed. "Keep it elevated as much as you can. The swelling should heal by the time we return." To Fabroni, he ordered, "Make sure she stays hydrated."

Before leaving, we had no choice but to tie Sun Bolt, Aewna's horse, to a tree. Kirwyn took our only gun, as usual, and I strapped the dagger to my waist. He didn't know the territory well, so we carefully followed Fabroni's instructions southwest, trying to make as much time as we could before nightfall.

I didn't like continually heading away from the ocean.

"I only agreed to this because we need more guns," Kirwyn insisted that night, setting up our tent.

"I don't want to die this far from the sea," I whispered, drawing my knees to my chin. "This is the farthest I've ever been and it feels very wrong. Why would anyone want to live so far from the ocean?" It was a rhetorical question. "If something happens, promise me you'll carry me to the sea, Kirwyn?"

"Stop it," he scowled. "I won't have you talking like that, do you hear me?"

I tried, but no light shone in that black forest to banish the onslaught of dark, intrusive thoughts.

"How many people have you killed?" I asked, spiraling.

Kirwyn stilled. "I don't know."

"So many?"

"No. Not countless. But when I was younger, I tried not to think about it and now I just... don't. Everyone who lives in the backlands has killed someone at some point. Otherwise, they wouldn't be alive."

I stared at Kirwyn's skilled hands and his muscled torso as he finished setting up the tent. His strength, his speed, his clever mind... everything about him that made him dangerous kept me safe.

"It feels like a black mark upon my soul," I confessed. "I'd do it again, if I had to. But I feel like it changed me. Like something in me is different and I can never go back to the way I was." My lip trembled as I said, "It makes me feel unworthy. Of ruling, of... love."

"Hey, stop that. No." Kirwyn said, lifting my chin. "You can't think that way. Those choices you made that you believe changed you into something unworthy? Those are the very choices that made you *worthy*. Do you think not having to face difficult decisions means anything? Keeps you pure or something? You've got it backwards."

In the dimness I saw Kirwyn knit his brow. "It's like... imagine a sword, forged by fire. The molten heat sharpens it, burns away all the impurities. What remains is what was meant to be. You're who you're meant to be because of those hard decisions you made."

"You're saying I was always fated to tragedy," I said sadly, "to make me into what I am today?"

"No," Kirwyn insisted. "I'm just saying those decisions you made in response shaped and continue to shape you. You're not set like stone." He flashed a grin. "You're like water, remember? You can take any shape you want."

"Which is it? Am I a sword or water?" I asked.

"Which one makes you feel better?" he teased, cocking one eyebrow.

I smiled, cupping his face. "You. You always make me feel better. Do you know how smart you are? You always know the right thing to say."

"I grew up in a library, remember? Plus my uncle was, *is,* a damn good teacher."

I raised one challenging brow. "You may have had access to more knowledge, but how you've used it is all *you.* Look at what you're doing right now. The way you lift me up, the way you make hard decisions, even cold ones? I know you're hesitant about going to Elowa and being king, but you're a leader whether you like it or not."

"Look at what *you've* done, what *you've* survived," Kirwyn countered. "Anyone else would have broken under those conditions. You're a leader too, whether you believe it or not. You lead by example."

And you just lifted me up again, I thought, laughing softly.

"I didn't believe in other land when we met, but you didn't believe in kings and queens. You need to start having faith because that's your fate," I decreed in my most regal voice. "We'll return to Elowa. You'll be my king. I'll be your queen."

Kirwyn rubbed his stubble, sighing and smiling. He leaned down and kissed my forehead.

"You already are."

CHAPTER 10

According to Farip's directions, we'd reach the safehouse by nightfall and we had no idea what to expect as we journeyed westlands less familiar to Kirwyn.

Traveling a wide, dirt path, the sun beamed high in the sky when Kirwyn suddenly halted. He brought a finger to his mouth in a *shh...* motion. Immediately, I heard it too – and would have heard it sooner if I hadn't been lost in my own thoughts.

Daydreaming can be deadly in this world, I thought, panicked.

A party was coming up the trail behind us. They weren't bothering to be quiet, which meant they were well-armed.

"Spades," Kirwyn whispered. I gulped. He scanned the forest. "This way."

We steered our horses into the foliage, but Kirwyn almost immediately stopped. I tilted my head in the direction we headed, asking the question with my eyes. *Should we continue?* He shook his head and I understood – we'd risk making too much noise and alerting the party to our presence.

We dismounted in tense silence and Kirwyn tapped repeatedly on Vesper's legs. I didn't know what he was doing until she finally laid down beneath the tall brush. Thankfully, Szirena followed her lead because I didn't know that trick. Kirwyn and I hunched beside our mares, praying we were effectively hidden by the bushes and leaves. My heart pounded as he wrapped a protective arm around me.

By the time the travelers came into view a sheen of nervous sweat covered my body. I recognized the Spade clothing and weaponry as about ten soldiers traversed the path. They didn't drive modern machine vehicles, as Kirwyn once described, but walked and rode horses alongside a wheeled, wooden cart, pulled by four of the strongest-looking stallions I'd ever seen. Built onto the cart was an ominous wooden cage.

My stomach sank when I saw what it held.

Children. Three boys and two girls, though they were so filthy it was hard to tell. Immediate tears sprang to my eyes. One girl, with especially tangled hair, crouched sadly, alone at the rear. Her hands clasped the bars and she stared outward with longing.

My heart stopped when the little girl rolled past and her searching eyes met mine beneath the leaves. I froze.

She sees me. She's going to point and expose us.

Wide, wet eyes stared into my soul. "Help me," she mouthed.

I couldn't breathe. Time stopped. But it couldn't have stopped because the wagon kept rolling.

My fingers tightened around the dagger strapped to my waist. *When had I reached for it?* I swung my head up to

Kirwyn. I didn't like the look on his face but couldn't figure out what it meant.

The Spades rolled forward enough that I could chance to whisper, "We have to help them."

Eyes bright with warning, he shook his head.

My shoulders slumped. I searched the ground wildly as if there might be something in the grass to help me.

Help them. Panic rose as the party continued to pass by. I had to do something.

Help them. The wagon is getting further away. My breathing grew rapid, heavy. Not a good idea because I'd need to remain calm to attack. My fingers tensed around the dagger's hilt again.

I looked back at Kirwyn and his expression was even stranger. I couldn't figure it out.

He doesn't want to help. Of that, I was sure.

But we can't let children be taken.

A wild thought appeared – there and gone. *What if I scream? If they hear me scream, Kirwyn won't have a choice and he'll have to help me.* My mind raced ahead to the future awaiting those children.

What fate will befall them? They're innocents. Oh god, what kind of world allowed this to happen?

Lightning-fast, Kirwyn's hand reached out and grabbed my neck, seeking, pressing hard enough to hurt.

I gasped, wild eyes searching his for understanding. I could have easily raised my dagger, but this wasn't an enemy, it was Kirwyn -- and he'd probably deflect it anyway. Instead, I instinctively clawed at the fingers painfully choking off my airway.

His expression didn't bear the slightest trace of pity; it was the demon-face of the boy I'd met in my cave. I hadn't seen that cold look in his eyes since Elowa.

Within seconds it was happening again. Blackness edged my vision. My knees grew weak.

I might have imagined it, but I think I felt myself slump into Kirwyn's arms.

~

I AWOKE to the loamy smell of the forest floor and the familiarity of Kirwyn's own woodsy scent from his shirt, bunched under my head as a makeshift pillow. Blinking, I noted he sat a good ten feet across from me. My dagger lay in his lap.

In a flash, the memory of the children returned.

"Why did you do that?" I cried, pushing myself into a sitting position. Dizziness washed over me from moving too quickly but I didn't care. "You just let them-" breaking off in a choked sob, I covered my face. After a breath, I looked back at Kirwyn, "How dare you? How dare you do that to me... whatever that move was!"

"How dare I stop you from getting us both captured? Easily."

"You're not even sorry!"

"No, I'm not. I'd do it again. I'm sorry it has to be this way. I'm sorry you were about to do something foolish. But I'm not sorry I stopped you. If anyone should be apologizing, it's you." He pointed at me for emphasis.

"Kirwyn, she looked me dead in the eyes and begged me to help her. How could you just let them be taken away?" My heart twisted at the memory of her pleading gaze.

"Because the only alternative was for us to get caught or killed along with them. We couldn't take down ten Spades alone, even if we had ten guns. I could tell you were going to do something... make a run for it or scream."

My cheeks pinked at how easily he read me. I shot to my feet, full of anger.

"I- I wasn't going to. Maybe the thought *did* cross my mind, but I wasn't going to do it. You have to trust me not to endanger us. And I have to trust you to do the right thing!"

Kirwyn folded his arms. "I *did* do the right thing. What was one of the first things ever I told you?"

I stared at him, fighting frustrated tears. If I blinked, they'd fall. If I blinked, I'd see that little girl's future.

"In this world, kindness gets you killed," Kirwyn repeated.

I snarled to combat sobbing. "I hate it here! Why is it like this?" My lip quivered as I fisted my hands in anger.

Kirwyn's face softened. "Zaria, I understand and I don't blame you. You've spent your entire life sheltered away. But this is exactly why I asked you to let me lead. You don't understand what it's like here."

"I'm not a child, Kirwyn, stop talking to me like I've never seen violence or been a part of it." My hands flailed as I spoke. "Just because it is this way doesn't mean it's right. Just because I don't like it doesn't mean I'm naïve."

I took a deep breath to calm myself. "This is not the way the world used to be. Should be." *Was it possible to feel a longing for something I'd never known? Did others?*

"I didn't say you're a child," Kirwyn argued. "I agree with you. Why do you think I don't want to work with Mal-Yin? He's evil. And I don't think you're foolish." Kirwyn's mouth twitched into a small, sad smile. "Sometimes you remind me of my uncle. Sometimes I think you're what I wish I could be. But you were about to *do* something foolish."

Funny. Sometimes Kirwyn was what I wished I could

be. How many times did I think that, back in Rythas? So clever and confident. And more than a little calculating, when necessary.

"I told you, I wasn't going to do it," I sighed. "I just thought it. Please believe that I'm trusting you here. As I ask that you trust me once we get to Rythas."

Kirwyn studied my face. "I couldn't be sure."

I groaned, rubbing my eyes. Was I mad at Kirwyn for knocking me unconscious or was I mad at myself for putting him in a position where he had to do it? Because the thought *did* cross my mind and he knew I *could* be impulsive. But we'd watched children carted off to their doom... what was the normal reaction?

Covering my eyes with the balls of my hands, I shouted, "I can't think about it. Can't picture what's to become of them. That girl..." I began hyperventilating. "I'm going to go mad!"

Kirwyn was instantly before me, gripping my wrists in his hands.

"Hey, hey, look at me," he said, gently tugging down my arms. "Look at me, okay? That wagon is headed northwest, not northeast. I'd bet ten thousand tokens they're going to Kanstead. The worst of your imagination won't happen there. I'm not saying she'll live as a queen. But it's a small, outlying territory where she'll be treated better than she would in Spade City. She'll have some freedoms. In time she might even gain clan status."

Mind racing, I searched Kirwyn's face as I pictured what would happen, the unfairness always being forced upon girls. "Status through what?" I challenged. "Hard work... or marriage?"

His sigh told me I'd hit it correctly.

"What's marriage but another kind of prison in that scenario?" *I knew that better than anyone.*

Kirwyn inhaled deeply. "I won't lie to you. It's possible some of those children might one day be set free by other means, but yes, that's her likeliest option. She might marry a clansman. Especially if she's capable of having children."

"That's not a happiness, that's a horror!" I shouted, letting my head fall onto Kirwyn's chest. "I hate this world. Dreams cannot exist here. Love cannot exist here."

"It can it's just... harder to find," he sighed, stroking my hair. "I found you. You found me."

I looked up, trying not to whimper, "Then we'll leave this world together?" I asked. "Return to Elowa and rule? We'll let everyone love whoever they want and protect our people from all this? Say we'll do it, Kirwyn. Promise me."

Kirwyn kissed my temple. "Okay. I promise we'll try."

My face fell. "What do you mean?"

"I mean that it's going to take more than the two of us to protect everyone from *all this.*"

CHAPTER 11

"I'm still mad at you," I reminded Kirwyn as we rode.

"I know."

I half-rolled my eyes at his flippant tone. "Thank god Vesper knew how to lay down at your command. I could never have gotten Szirena to do that without her lead."

Kirwyn affectionately pat his mare's mane and used a voice he only ever used with me. "You're the best horse in the world, aren't you?" he praised.

We didn't reach Fabroni's safehouse until well after nightfall and quickly saw we had little hope of breaching it at any time of the day. We tied our horses a good distance back and crouched under the trees, eyeing the low building nestled into the dark forest.

"Fuck," Kirwyn swore, rubbing his stubble and studying the log cabin. A few dim lights glowed inside, illuminating the windows enough that we glimpsed what looked to be ten or so men sleeping within. I guessed many of them would have been the same we'd encountered a few months ago, when Fabroni captured Kirwyn and me. Unfortunately, all the windows had been barred, making sneaking in impossible.

Only one man stood alert, guarding the front door. Kirwyn could take him out, but not with the guarantee of silence, which would immediately rouse the men inside the cabin. There was also the problem of not knowing where the bag was kept. Even if we soundlessly disposed of the guard, Kirwyn risked causing a disturbance when searching the cabin for Fabroni's bag.

"So there's no way in?" I whispered, balancing on the balls of my feet beside him. "Not without getting captured."

Kirwyn stilled. A slow smile spread across his face. "Have I told you today that you're brilliant?" he asked, suddenly clasping my cheeks and kissing me. "That's exactly what we're going to do."

ANXIOUS, I tightened my grip on the gun. *Maybe it would have been better if I'd been the captive.*

I watched the blur of Kirwyn through the trees, sneaking around the house with an intentional lack of stealth -- not enough to be noticed as clumsy, but certainly less than Kirwyn was capable of. Even I could hear the crunch of dirt underfoot from where I hid.

Between the trees, our eyes locked.

As planned, the guard by the cabin's front door turned his head in Kirwyn's direction. My heart skipped a beat as Kirwyn's noise lured him away from the safehouse. The sentry was short, but to my dismay I noticed he was very muscular and quick on his feet.

Seemingly unaware of his attacker's presence, Kirwyn crept through the forest toward me, and, believing himself to be unnoticed, the guard stalked toward Kirwyn.

I tensed on the trigger, ready.

Pouncing and pointing his gun at Kirwyn's head, the guard demanded, "Don't make a move."

Kirwyn froze, then sprang into action, maneuvering too fast for me to see in the dark. He tried to push the barrel of the gun from his face and to wrest control of the weapon, but the guard was equally skilled. In a flash, Kirwyn wound up on the ground beneath the man, struggling to keep the barrel from his head.

With my heart in my throat I raced forward, trying not to make noise.

As they struggled, Kirwyn managed to press the gun into the dirt, but he wouldn't be able to hold it long from his disadvantaged angle.

Exhilaration shot through my chest as I reached the guard, pointed my gun at his temple, and clicked it in warning.

"Don't move, don't make a sound. Drop the gun or I'll blow your head off."

The harshness of my own words startled me, as well as my unfamiliar tone of voice. Cold. Threatening.

The guard didn't doubt me. He paused for the span of one breath, considering alternative options, then relented and released his weapon. Kirwyn quickly scooped it up as the guard raised his hands in surrender.

We did it.

Turning to face me, the man's eyes widened and he stilled.

"I'd ask if you're an angel, were you not pointing a gun at my head."

"Don't look at her, look at me," Kirwyn said, sliding to

block me. "And keep your voice down. Fabroni sent us. Where's the bag?"

The guard snapped his attention to Kirwyn. "I can't tell you! They'll kill me for the betrayal. They're probably going to kill me when they find out I've failed my watch."

"What's your name?" Kirwyn asked.

"Arle," the guard said, after a moment's hesitation.

"Well, Arle, then you've got nothing to lose," Kirwyn pointed out. "And I can make you a far better offer. You help us and I'll give you a portion of the spoils. Tokens, weapons. Whatever you've got in there, we'll share. Take it, take your horse, and run. Start a new life somewhere else."

Arle gritted his teeth, fisted his hands, and considered the two guns pointed at his head.

"Shit," he finally hissed. "Alright. It's beneath Madolix's bed."

"Who's Madolix?" Kirwyn demanded with impatience.

"Redheaded guy, asleep in one of the middle cots. Can't miss him."

"If I find out you're lying to me, if anything goes wrong and it's your fault, her face will be the last thing you see before she puts a bullet in it."

The guard gave me an appreciative once-over lingering on more than my face. "It's not like a man could hope to see better before death," he said, tongue tapping his lips.

Kirwyn angrily pushed the barrel of his gun against Arle's head, shoving it to the right. "Watch your fucking mouth."

"Sorry, but it's the truth," he grumbled. Staring at me adoringly, he said, "You're the most beautiful girl I've ever seen."

I blinked, unsure if there was a trick in his words. "I'll

still shoot you if you make one wrong move." *For Kirwyn, I will. Without hesitation.*

The guard's eyes flashed. "I believe you and it only makes you more alluring," he replied with a crooked grin. Something about the way he uncomfortably shifted his weight caught my attention. I fought not to let my mouth drop when I realized *he had an erection.*

Oh my god. Me, pointing a gun at his head, made him hard. Oh no. *If I'd noticed it...*

Kirwyn grabbed Arle by the scruff of his neck and shoved him to his knees.

Don't! I wanted to protest. *I think it will only excite him more.*

"If you don't stop looking at her that way, *I'm* going to shoot you. Or carve your eyes out."

Arle looked down. But his eyes quickly flicked back up again. This time, to include Kirwyn. He was visibly aroused... by us both?

Oh, good lord.

For the first time, I realized what Kirwyn and I must look like, together. His sinister, chiseled face and beautiful bone structure paired with my *optimally elected* genes... was it vain if I admitted we made an attractive couple? Appearing out of the dark forest in the middle of the night, emanating danger... to this man, we probably both seemed like demons or dark Fae.

"Just go," I urged Kirwyn, almost wanting to laugh. Our threats only excited the guard. *At least he isn't much of a threat himself.*

Kirwyn gave me a kiss, holding my head possessively, and tucked Arle's gun into the waistband of his pants. He crept toward the front door of the cabin while I stayed behind, my gun aimed at the sentry's head and my stomach doing acrobatic feats.

We all cringed at the *creak* as Kirwyn opened the front door and he tensed to bolt in the opposite direction if needed. Luckily, no one woke and he slipped inside.

Through the window, I could see Kirwyn stealthily moving toward the middle row of cots. Hands raised, he crept toward the redhead, centrally sleeping.

My heart stopped when a man toward the door stirred in his bed. Catching the motion, Kirwyn froze.

No, please.

The man lifted his head and I nearly screamed in fear, but I folded my lips between my teeth, whimpering.

Why had I done this? Why had I jeopardized our lives? It was the wrong decision.

Tears pooled in my eyes as the man sleepily beat his pillow, reshaping it. In the darkness, he hadn't yet noticed Kirwyn.

Suddenly, the man shot upright into a sitting position and my stomach dropped to my feet.

God, no, no... Please. This was the wrong decision and I'll never make it again. My honor isn't worth the risk to our lives and certainly not Kirwyn's. Never.

Twisting, the man gave his pillow one angry punch, then flopped his head back onto it, facing away from Kirwyn.

I audibly exhaled. *Oh, thank god.*

Kirwyn, panting, met my eyes. For several painfully long moments he didn't move, waiting for the man to fall back asleep. Finally, he crept toward Madolix's bed and crouched. Unable to now see him from my angle, I held my breath as I waited.

One, two, three... I counted, bargaining, *he'll make it up by the time I reach ten.*

He didn't.

By twenty, I renegotiated, sweating.

Sixteen, seventeen, eighteen...

Kirwyn's dark head popped into view and I exhaled.

Now he just has to make it out...

At that thought, I remembered when I was in Lazlian's bedroom, having nearly escaped without getting caught. It was a very inopportune time to have the memory, but I couldn't stop it. There were too many similarities.

Please don't let it end the same, I begged to the sky.

Kirwyn disappeared from view again as he approached the door. Once more I held my breath...

...and the door swung open.

Kirwyn slipped from the house and crept across the grass as I exhaled in relief. As soon as he reached us, the three of us sprinted in the direction of our horses. I didn't even bother training my gun on the guard, he was invested and I had Kirwyn with me.

"We split the spoils and go our separate ways," Kirwyn said, tossing the bag onto the ground as we reached our mares.

We crouched to examine the contents.

"Jackpot," Kirwyn grinned.

Inside the bag were several guns, bombs, daggers, handcuffs, Spade tokens... and a box containing a necklace with a small silver medallion hanging from the chain.

"That must be what Fabroni wants," Kirwyn mused.

"It has sentimental value to him," Arle confirmed.

Shrugging, Kirwyn pushed it aside, "Not our business."

We gave Arle two guns, the handcuffs, and several tokens to begin a new life somewhere else. Before departing to his own horse, Arle lingered, eyeing Kirwyn and me. With a start, I realized he wanted to come with us.

"You really are the most beautiful creature I've ever seen," he told me, shaking his head. "Ethereal... it's almost... inhuman."

Kirwyn narrowed his eyes. I held back a snort. If I thought about it, Arle wasn't far off. All the features of an Elowan were very human, but they were unnaturally chosen and clustered to reach perfection. It almost was inhuman.

There are thousands just like me, I thought. *You're only enchanted because I'm the first you've seen.*

By the time Kirwyn and I rode far enough for him to feel we could safely camp, dawn was only two or three hours away. Adrenaline still coursed through my veins and I bounced a little, riding the high from our achievement.

"We make a good team," I said, smiling.

"I know that." Kirwyn thumbed my chin, lifting my gaze to his. "I've always known that."

"Are you reminding me again that I took longer than you, back in Elowa?" I asked, brows raised. "It was a big decision. Don't forget you were asking me to give up a god for you."

"I can be your god now," he smirked.

"Pfft." I rolled my eyes. "Don't push it."

He leaned closer, stroking my neck. "You say it enough when I'm between your legs. *"Oh god,"* he teased. *"Oh god Kirwyn, oh god Kirwyn."*

My face heated. Combined like *that,* he made a point. "Is that really what I say? Like... how I say it?"

"Yeah," he smirked. "I love it." His hand slid down my shirt and thumbed my nipple. I guessed he still rode a high, as well. "Let me show you right now."

"No," I protested, despite closing my eyes and arching into his touch. "Maybe later."

"You're only torturing yourself, you know," he taunted, rolling my hard peak between his fingers and referencing the time when I said the same thing to him, back in Volmar's house.

"We'll see," I said, slapping his hand away.

I hadn't forgotten his little trick to make me faint… and I had plans to make sure he knew it.

CHAPTER 12

We awoke late the next morning but if we hurried, we'd make it back to Fabroni's bunker by nightfall. We'd only needed three days, just as he said.

As Kirwyn and I packed up our supplies, I couldn't help but compare the three men in my life. If Juls and I had journeyed together, he might have rushed in to save those children alongside me. We'd both have died, or worse. If Lazlian had been my companion, he would have stood back with a smirk and let me charge in alone to die, just like he had at the Battle of the Glass Gardens. Only Kirwyn did what he had to do... even knowing I wouldn't like it.

And if someone threatened me? Juls would die for me, but it wouldn't really be *me*, it would be his sense of honor. Lazlian would kill for me, but it wouldn't really be *me*, it would again be for himself, his own twisted version of family honor.

Kirwyn would kill for me and die for me and it was because he loved me.

And I would unquestioningly do both, for him.

But as we packed up, it still irked me a little that he'd made me faint by the mere press of his fingers. That he had that power over me and could wield it whenever he wished. I wanted power too.

"You look so sexy when you're fighting someone, you know that?" I said, studying him with a seductive smirk.

I nearly laughed as he *immediately* stopped fussing with the saddle and returned the look. "Is that so?"

I ambled over, swaying my hips. "It is. *So* seductive, *so* dangerous, *so*... arousing."

I pushed him backwards and down onto the grass and he allowed it. The heat in his eyes told me I had him right where I wanted him.

Did all men require just a sexy smile and a few words, or was this only so easy because of what Kirwyn and I shared?

"I'm still not pleased about what you did with your fingers," I cooed. "Making me faint."

I slid slowly onto his lap, letting my breasts first hover near his face. Kirwyn eyed them with hunger and his hands cupped my backside, pulling me closer.

"But I understand," I said, settling right on top of the hardness forming in his pants.

My god, were all men this easy to arouse or was it just us?

"I forgive you," I hummed into his neck. Straddling Kirwyn's lap, I rocked against his sizable erection. When his breathing deepened, I smiled to myself and snaked a hand beneath his waistband until I found what I sought. Gripping him tightly, I stroked, satisfied by his answering groan. I kept going until I knew he was in a state of irreversible passion.

"Kirwyn..." I moaned in his ear, breathless. "I need... need..." With a whimper I trailed off.

"What do you need, Zaria?" he asked hoarsely, squeezing my breast.

Stilling my ministrations, I pulled my head back and decreed, "I need you to know I think you're an ass for knocking me unconscious." I stood, abruptly. "How's it feel to be misled?"

Kirwyn's eyes blazed and *damn* if he didn't look sexy. But I would hold onto my vengeance. I would.

"Zaria. Get back here. Now."

I shrugged, trying to look bored but biting my lip to hold back the grin. "No." To emphasize my refusal, I stepped back.

"I'm going to give you three seconds to return," he growled in frustration. "If I have to get up and drag you back, you'll be sorry." His eyes glistened with an enthralling kind of danger, making it hard to keep a straight face. "You're determined to make me your monster... I can be your monster, Zaria."

I stepped back again. "Try to drag me anywhere and we'll see who's sorry."

"You," Kirwyn declared, grinning his threat and revealing those sharp canines.

"One."

I scowled. "Stay where you are."

"I suggest you use your time to come back over here right now. Or run," he shrugged, adding, "Two."

"Kirwyn, I swear to god!" I yelled, but I was laughing nervously so it didn't sound menacing. I backed away further. "Don't you dare."

Kirwyn rose slowly. *God, was he always so tall?* He made a show of rolling his broad shoulders.

"Zaria?"

"Yeah?"

"Consider this your last chance," he warned darkly, head bent, eyes up, readying to attack. His voice was low and oh-so-satisfied as he declared, "Three."

I ran.

Trouncing ferns and shrieking my position, I sprinted through the woods as fast as my legs could pump. There was no point in hiding my direction, Kirwyn wasn't far behind – him and his damn long legs. A strange thrill shot through my chest as he chased me. It reminded me of the day we met, when I'd attacked him and fled my cave -- though our relationship was entirely different now.

As well as his intentions. Whatever they were.

Two strong hands gripped my waist, my legs were swept from the ground, and together we landed in the grass.

"Caught you," he gloated.

Kirwyn folded himself on top of me and I could scarcely catch my breath through my laughter and shouts. I flailed but he was always too strong, too fast, and he had me pinned face-down in seconds. Though Kirwyn successfully tugged my pants and undergarments past my knees, the move cost him control and I slipped from his grasp. I couldn't immediately stand, tangled in my own clothing. Crawling away, I made it farther than I would have thought... because I hadn't realized Kirwyn was busy shoving down his own pants. I was still laughing and shrieking when his hands gripped my waist again, tugging me backwards on my hands and knees --

-- and to my astonishment, he lined up with my core and in one determined stroke, buried himself inside me from behind.

Oh my god. In one whoosh of air, all my laughter suddenly dissipated. I gasped, back arching at the new sensation. Kirwyn stilled, giving me time to adjust, I think; or at least to gauge my reaction.

He'd never... entered me like that before. So deep. I felt so full. Of *him*. Whimpering, I clenched around his hardness. In response, Kirwyn slowly pulled out --

-- and drove deep in another thrust of exquisite pleasure. At the same time, his fingers tightened on my hips, guiding me back to meet his push.

Oh my god, it felt incredible.

More... yes... don't stop, I wanted to beg. But, enraptured, I only moaned, hoping that communicated everything.

Wait, no. I forgot I was supposed to be mad at him.

Attempting to escape, I wiggled forward. Possessive hands immediately grabbed my hips once more and pulled me back, firmly holding me in place.

I couldn't help but smile.

"Stay," Kirwyn growled the order with a deep, lust-filled voice. I hoped he didn't feel the responding clench of my core around his shaft, but he might have, because he added, "Or I'll be forced to tie you down until I finish."

"*Mmm...*" I let out a soft, whimpering moan, almost unconsciously adjusting as my body melted into his.

"That's it," Kirwyn instructed. "Spread your legs wider, bend down lower, arch your back."

I meant to playfully resist his commands, but my body had other plans and submissively did as it was told. I spread for him. Bent as ordered. Arched to please.

I was rewarded by Kirwyn fucking me with vigor. His quick, strong rhythm from this new angle had me making noises I'd never made before. I rocked my hips to meet his thrusts, pushing against the springy underbrush and hard-packed dirt for leverage. Our movements stirred the forest floor, filling the air with the loamy scent of earth. Coupling in such an animalistic manner right out in the open wood, a wild and wicked dizziness surged through me, leaving room for nothing beyond base desire.

The primal need for Kirwyn to *take me*. Like that, just like that...

If he felt half as blissed-out as I did, he wasn't going to last very long. But it was an exquisite torture because I was hovering at the pinnacle and couldn't fall over without...

Like a magician reading my mind, Kirwyn's hand snaked beneath me and his fingers found the spot I needed, rubbing in frantic circles. I knew he was near the throes of ecstasy, knew he hurried to catch me up by his less-than-steady ministrations. It didn't matter -- between his hard-ness filling me within and his fingers stroking me without, I'd never experienced anything so amazing in my life. I felt completely held by him, from behind and in front.

Shamelessly the words tumbled out now. *Kirwyn. Oh god. Yes, like that. Please. Please don't stop.* Euphoria rose as he stroked... His fingers, *god,* his fingers.

The last thing I heard when rapture seized my body was Kirwyn swearing *fuck* under his breath, and then my mind blanked, the ocean roared in my ears, and powerful waves of pleasure swept through my body, tumbling me spent upon the sand.

Grass.

We were laying together in the grass. As we finished, I'd barely felt Kirwyn roll me onto his torso, resting my head upon his chest. *Oh my god.* For several minutes neither of us spoke. I listened to his ragged breathing until it slowed, to the quickened beating of his heart until it calmed.

"We've never... done that before," I whispered, awed.

"I'm aware," he deadpanned.

"What made you do it?"

I could feel his half-shrug beneath me. "I don't know. Just wanted to."

"When girls say they want to be swept off their feet," I teased, "that's not what it means."

Kirwyn breathed a soft chuckle. "It does for you."

I buried my burning face against his chest. Biting my lip, I confessed, "It kinda hurt. But I want to do it again."

Kirwyn barked a laugh. "Give me a couple minutes."

Was it like this for everyone? I wondered, enchanted by the woods around me, by Kirwyn's embrace, by the afterglow. *Or were we special?*

"This is rare, isn't it? It's real. I didn't know before. I didn't have a basis for comparison. But the more I see, the more I'm sure. What we feel for each other, it's not common, is it?" I whispered.

Kirwyn's hand stroked my cheek. "I don't think so."

I wanted to hold onto this moment forever, with the sun beaming down on his beautiful face and the birds chirping in the trees around us.

"Kirwyn," I began softly.

"Yeah?" he asked.

"I know you're torn inside," I whispered. "I know you wonder if you did the right thing, holding back when I was in High Spire. I know you think you failed to save me."

Beneath me, he stiffened. I propped myself up on my elbows to look at him; I wanted him to know how seriously I meant what I said. "But please listen to me. If I hadn't met you, I would have had nothing to escape to. No reason to try. In time, I probably would have accepted my fate with Juls. And slowly, it would have diminished me. I would have become like those creatures you told me about... the ones that look like humans but are empty inside... robots. I'd have smiled when I was meant to smile and laid with

Juls when he bid me lay with him. But I would have been an empty husk."

I cupped Kirwyn's face and our eyes locked. Infusing my words with my whole heart, I swore, "You saved me because you gave me the courage and the will to save myself."

Pensive, Kirwyn brushed the hair from my cheek, tucking it securely behind my ear.

I swallowed back a lump before concluding, "The idea of what would have happened to me if I never met you, terrifies me."

"We did meet," Kirwyn said, cocking that dazzling smile just for me. "And I'll never let that fate happen to you. I swear it."

I traced his lips with my fingers. Everything Kirwyn did was inherently erotic, to me. The expansion of his chest as he breathed. The deep base of his voice as he spoke. The flash in his eyes as he lined up a shot for target practice. And of course, the movement of his confident, capable hands.

And that was just the physical.

"Lida said you look like a god, but she's wrong. There's something sinister about your smile, a diabolical gleam in your face. You're a demon, I'm sure of it."

With a tempting bat of my lashes, I said, "It has a nice ring to it... King Kirwyn. King Kirwyn Holt. The Holt dynasty."

"You want my name?" he asked, surprised.

I shrugged. "I don't have one anyway. Why not take yours?"

An uncomfortable silence descended as we both realized, technically, I did have one. I was Zaria Doreste.

Lazlian's long-ago words echoed in my mind.

You are not our equal. You will never be our equal.

Maybe, I supposed, annoyed the insult still hurt. But looking at Kirwyn's gorgeous face, I thought, *but you will never be* his.

"When this is all over, Juls will grant me a divorce," I said, fidgeting with my shirt as I quickly stood.

"Will he?" Kirwyn raised disbelieving eyebrows, standing and dusting his pants.

"We'll make it part of the terms."

"I don't think it will be so easy," Kirwyn said, as we walked back to our campsite. "Besides his reputation, divorce is a stigma there for regular people; the royals haven't had one in their history, ever."

I looked at Kirwyn in surprise.

"I read up, asked around," he shrugged. "Volmar knew a lot."

"I won't stay married to him," I insisted as we reached our horses.

"He might try to negotiate it. He might offer for you to keep me, quietly, on the side."

"How hypocritical," I scowled, mounting Szirena. "Though it doesn't surprise me. Jesi once implied there had been clandestine arrangements to maintain power in the past."

Kirwyn slung into Vesper's saddle with ease and we headed onto the trail.

"Come on," he grinned. "If we ride fast, we'll make it back to Aewna well before the sun sets." Kirwyn leaned down on Vesper, patting her mane and giving the top of her head a quick kiss. "Ready to leave her in the dust again?"

I tightened my grip on Szirena's reins and bent my head, accepting the challenge.

Of course Vesper took the lead as we raced. Kirwyn was

just ahead on my right when I narrowed my eyes with determination and braced to go faster. I hoped to at least keep pace since I couldn't overtake him.

Low in the brush, someone appeared from the overgrowth, mere feet in front of us.

My stomach dropped as a sword flashed, slicing Vesper's legs.

With a neigh, she went down, taking Kirwyn with her.

CHAPTER 13

"Kirwyn!" I shouted, yanking Szirena to a halt. Thankfully, Vesper hadn't crushed him with her body. He'd already rolled to stand and was grappling with a scruffy, dark-haired man on the ground. Bent on beating the stranger with his fists, Kirwyn didn't even draw his gun. Even I could see the man had no hope of besting Kirwyn in hand-to-hand combat. They were matched in size, but Kirwyn was a lot more skilled.

I jumped off Szirena, but before I could run to help, a second man grabbed me. Holding me flush to his chest, he reached around and pressed a blade against my throat.

Kirwyn, now wielding his dagger, straddled the dark-haired man screaming and thrashing beneath him.

"Call to him."

My assailant's hot breath hit my ear as he panted, digging the tip of his knife into the delicate flesh on my neck. I folded my lips between my teeth and he pressed harder, nearly breaking skin.

"Call to him or I will."

I refused but, strangely, the man seemed reluctant to do it himself. Perhaps he was too frightened by what he saw unfold. Vesper, lying on ground, partially blocked my view. I could see Kirwyn sliced his dagger somewhere along the lower abdomen of the man who'd attacked her, and an agonized scream cut the air. I couldn't tell exactly what Kirwyn had done, but he pulled something *out* of the man that should have been *in*. I fought waves of dizziness from both the blade at my neck and the horror unfolding in front of me, even though I didn't fully understand what I was seeing.

"Kill me!" the man pled between blood-curdling screams. "Kill me now!"

Kirwyn wasn't even looking at him, his full attention had snapped to me. As he stood, the man on the ground fainted.

My assailant's knife pressed tightly against the veins in my neck and his shaking terrified me more than if he'd remained deadly calm. He trembled like he might make hasty decisions in any direction. One cut and I'd die.

Tears pooled in my eyes but I was too scared to really let loose the sobs I wanted. Blinding, red rage boiled in me too. That this man, this *no one* was going to end me, end *us*, end hope for Elowa with one slice... A strange determination surged through me to stay centered on Kirwyn. If this was the last time he saw me alive, I didn't want to be blubbering.

Kirwyn was *terrifyingly* focused.

"He hurt my horse," Kirwyn grit out. "Look what I did to your friend, and he hurt my *horse*. What do you think I'll do to you if you harm one hair on her head?" His words were too furious to be called calm, yet nothing like the torrent of emotions I felt reflected on his steady face.

The man behind me didn't answer but I hoped his imagination ran wild.

"I'll cut you a deal," Kirwyn said, slow and measured. "Put down your fucking dagger and run. Turn around and run away, right now. Unless you want to meet a fate worse than evisceration. I can make your friend's death look like mercy."

Evisceration?

On cue, the man awoke and his horrific sobs erupted once more. I kept my eyes focused on Kirwyn, trying not to think of entrails spilling out or whatever was happening mere feet away on the blood-stained forest floor.

"I have your word?" the man behind me bargained in a shaky voice, fingers digging into my rib cage. His sweat dripped onto my neck and ran down between my breasts, making me want to gag. The tortured cries of his dying friend didn't help.

"You have my word. I swear it on her life," Kirwyn replied steadily. His eyes blazed. "The deal expires in five seconds."

The man behind me panted rapidly through his nose, bursts of air hitting my neck. Suddenly, the pressure around my torso disappeared. I was given a hard shove and I fell onto my hands and knees. The man turned and bolted.

Kirwyn didn't immediately look at me. My eyes grew wide as he raised the hand holding the dagger, carefully took aim, and threw it across the trail.

It embedded deeply into the man's back with a thud I'd never forget. One cry and he fell to the grass. I blinked at his lifeless form.

"You just... killed him... in the back," I gasped, as I stood on wobbly legs. The field was quiet; the other man must have passed out again. "You swore you'd let him go and you killed him."

"I swore I wouldn't kill him as slowly as I killed his friend," Kirwyn corrected. "I never swore I'd let him go." He quickly crossed the field and grasped my chin, turning my head, inspecting. "Are you hurt?"

"No!" I blurted, but I contradicted it by letting loose the sob I'd been restraining, feeling like I was breaking apart. "I should be used to men trying to kill me by now. But I don't know, I just... can't take anymore Kirwyn. I just want to be safe! Why is that so hard?"

I didn't expect an answer -- certainly nothing other than generalizations. *Life is hard. It's unfair.*

Kirwyn pulled me into his arms. "Because you want things that require risks. Big ones."

I moaned, fantasizing about turning back *right now*. We could escape to the blank port, live a quiet life somewhere, unknown. Tend a vegetable garden or whatever the hell we wanted. God, it was so tempting. I didn't want to do this anymore.

The expression *'whatever doesn't kill you makes you stronger'* was total goatshit. Each trauma was another cut, weakening me further. Maybe it was because I'd never had time to properly heal. Even holed up at my aunt and uncle's house, we'd been training for the next battle, risking even more. I felt battered and tired. I longed to just *be* for a while. Not plotting an escape. Not readying to fight. Not even performing as royal. To simply... exist. With Kirwyn. To find out who we were without the world telling us or forcing us into roles we didn't want to play.

But you did choose this, came an annoying voice in my head. *It is how you wanted to play.*

I was pulled from my reverie as Kirwyn released me and

slowly walked over to Vesper. Kneeling, he wrapped his arms around her neck and pressed his forehead to hers. I thought he'd soon break the hug... but he didn't.

Cold water filled my gut as belated understanding washed over me. I hadn't been around horses as long as Kirwyn and was too caught up in the imminent threat to our lives to think ahead, as he had.

As he understood from the moment they cut her legs.

Oh god. She couldn't walk. We couldn't carry her.

Kirwyn was going to have to...

Oh god. No wonder he... did *that*... to the man who cut her.

I covered my mouth to quiet my sobs. I didn't want to interrupt his goodbye.

Kirwyn sprang to his feet and *roared*. It was so anguished that I jumped. Face to the sky, back arched, hands fisted. The cry echoed through the forest. For a few seconds, he panted, alone in his thoughts. Tears streamed down my face. For Vesper and for him.

Kirwyn raised his gun and, struggling not to wince so much he'd miss, he shot Vesper, once, directly in the head.

The few birds remaining after his cry took flight at the boom -- and then there was nothing. I'd never been in a forest so eerily quiet.

Half-turned from me, I could see Kirwyn wipe his tears with the back of his hand. He didn't move.

He's ashamed, I realized, with a thump of my heart. He did what he had to but didn't want me to see how it made him weep. Stunned, it hit me that I was looking at the last vestiges of a cuspate boy, almost a man. *But men didn't cry* he'd surely been told, somewhere along the way. Probably in one those books of his.

Don't you know how I feel? I wanted to cry in return. My

heart swelled with a mixture of sympathy and love. What he'd just done, seeing him now... made him more of a man to me than any other I'd met. Made the rest of them look like children pretending to be men.

But I didn't know what to do, either. My instinct was to comfort Kirwyn, yet I didn't want to overstep or intrude. Tentatively, I crossed to where he stood and wrapped my arms around him from behind, letting my own tears fall quietly. He didn't turn, but his hand squeezed mine, telling me to stay. Resting my head against his back, I could feel his soft cries – or the struggle to suppress them – by the uneven breathing shaking his back.

After a while, Kirwyn muttered, "She was... my friend. She was..." he shook his head, "the best."

"She was special," I agreed, softly, reverently.

Kirwyn knelt beside Vesper, stroking her head for a few moments. Finally, he withdrew his dagger, cut off a length of her mane, and pocketed the hair.

Wiping my nose, I resolved to plait it for him later. I still carried the powder blue ribbons from the day we left. I'd tie up the ends of a braid to make Kirwyn a sturdy keepsake.

Kirwyn detached our bag from Vesper's saddle. A cold determination glared in his eyes when he finally turned to face me. Anger? Had he moved on to the second stage of grief? Or was it the third? I could never remember what Enith prattled on about.

Angry at me? I wondered guiltily. *For bringing us on this journey, for causing Vesper to die?*

"Let's go," Kirwyn said, striding toward Szirena and grabbing her bridle. "I want to walk a bit. Are you okay to ride?"

I shook my head. "I'll walk with you."

A groan caught our attention, followed by horrifying

moans and sobbing. The man who'd cut Vesper's legs had regained consciousness again. He would die a slow, painful death alone in the woods.

He must have known it when he pled, "Kill me. For the love of god, kill me."

"Let's go," Kirwyn repeated, leading Szirena down the trail.

I froze, unable to bear the man's agonized cries. "Kirwyn, wait. Please. You can't leave him like this. You have to... show mercy."

"Mercy?" Kirwyn blinked.

The chill in his tone raised gullbumps on my skin.

"Kill me!" the man sobbed. I covered my ears, ready to weep anew. For this man, for Vesper, for Kirwyn and for myself. It was too much to handle.

Without breaking eye contact with me, Kirwyn raised his right hand and *boom!*

I jumped as he fired, hitting the moaning man in the head. There were no birds left to fly this time.

Kirwyn hadn't even spared the dying man a glance. *How did he aim so perfectly?* Dark green eyes held mine the entire time.

"There's your mercy," Kirwyn said, quiet but firm. "When the time comes, don't ask me to show any to the king. Or his brother."

CHAPTER 14

We walked solemnly, silently, alongside Szirena until our feet ached. At least, mine did, but I didn't want to disturb Kirwyn's quietude with any complaints. He'd searched the bodies for anything useful but found only their daggers to be worth taking.

Vesper wouldn't have died if it weren't for you, accused a horrible voice inside my head. *This is your fault.*

When the sun dipped low in the sky and it became clear we wouldn't reach the bunker before dark, Kirwyn relented and we mounted Szirena with me sitting behind him.

I didn't want to admit it but a gnawing fear ate away at my heart. Finding out my whole life was a lie and having things that seemed impossible come true, made it difficult to ignore intrusive thoughts. My mind often conjured up horrors and why wouldn't they be real? They had been in the past. I'd been exposed to such prolonged *gaslighting* and *brainwashing,* as Enith called it, that how could I tell what was real any longer?

Because of this, a part of me wondered if Aewna was mistaken in trusting Fabroni and we'd find her hacked to pieces upon our return. But when we reached the bunker, Sun Bolt was tied up where we'd left her and to my surprise, we found Aewna and Farip both fully healed and...

...*laughing* together.

I blinked. They played some kind of card game on the floor. Fabroni sprung to his feet when we entered.

"I kept her safe," he swore anxiously. "You have my bag?"

With a thud, Kirwyn dropped the black bag onto the floor. As predicted, Fabroni dug straight for the silver necklace. He lovingly stroked the circle, then slipped it over his head.

"Are my men still alive?" he asked.

Kirwyn nodded. Farip shrugged.

While I checked on Aewna, Kirwyn and Fabroni divvied up the spoils. We kept most of the guns, bombs, and daggers, while Farip took two thirds of the tokens.

"I'm fully healed," Aewna announced, twirling her ankle.

"Can you ride?" I asked, still cautious.

"Better than you both," she teased, yet coming from her even the jab managed to sound endearing.

We all agreed to sleep in the bunker overnight and go our separate ways in the morning. Aewna and Fabroni chatted late into the night. He seemed to be telling his life story and she eagerly absorbed the details.

"Luckily, Volmar's guards took to her the same way," Kirwyn whispered, as we settled ourselves into one of the tiny chambers for sleep.

"She always knows the right thing to say to charm people. Like you," I pointed out, a little envious. "I'm not like that."

Kirwyn chuckled. "What did I tell you? You might feel at

a loss for what to say, but you always know the right thing to *do*. Why do you think everyone in Rythas calls you the Queen of our Hearts?"

"If we survive," I mused, deflecting, "she'll make an enchanting new queen for everyone, that's for sure."

IN THE MORNING, we said goodbye to Fabroni. I had a feeling it wouldn't be the last time I saw him, but I imagined our next encounter couldn't be any more unusual than finding him locked away.

Aewna and I re-acquainted ourselves with the weight of a weapon and strapped them to our waists. The three of us headed northeast to regain our previous trail and it wasn't long before we passed the Crossroads Cages once more.

We pushed on through new forests.

Without three horses our progress was slow, but steady. At midday, we stopped beside a stream and shared a lunch from Fabroni's private stock including canned beans, peaches, and a tough, salted jerky of some meat I didn't know and didn't want to.

Despite losing Vesper we'd been so fortunate in our journey that, as we ate, I silently thanked whatever inland gods listened to prayers.

Ironic.

Mere hours later, Kirwyn, riding in front of me, brought Szirena to a halt and cocked his head.

"What is it?" I whispered.

"Stay here," Kirwyn ordered, jumping to the ground.

I didn't follow as he disappeared up a nearby hill, but I slid from Szirena's back to anxiously await his return. Tense, Aewna did the same.

Less than a minute later, Kirwyn's head poked back into view.

"They're coming," he called, sprinting toward us. "It's as they said, the king is here, hunting you."

Here? A fish flopped in my gut. *Juls is here?*

"How many?" I asked. "How far?"

"I don't know," Kirwyn said, hastily tugging the bag strapped to Szirena's saddle to ensure its security. "Only half a dozen or so. It's a small royal party, designed to move fast. They're tracking us. Maybe they've got some of your old clothing, dogs, I don't know."

"Can we outride them?" I asked, panic rising. My heart thumped with fear, waiting the eternity for Kirwyn's reply.

He paused, briefly closing his eyes. "No."

Working his jaw, he said, "They'll likely catch up as soon as we break to rest or camp. Our best bet would be hiding, but they're on our trail."

For a few heavy seconds no one spoke as we looked at one another in silent panic. My heart broke the moment I knew what I had to do.

"Then you ride!" I cried, reaching up to touch Kirwyn's face. "You both ride. It's me he wants. I'll go. If you two get away, there's hope you can save me. But if we're all captured, I'll have no hope. You have to save yourself to save me."

He might kill you if he catches you, I thought, but refused to say aloud. *Even if Juls didn't want to, he might need to in order save face in front of his men.*

"No," Kirwyn protested, slicing his hand through the air for emphasis.

"Yes," I insisted. "Juls won't hurt me."

Be strong, I scolded myself. *Don't cry.* But I felt tears leak.

"I'll say I escaped my kidnappers so the soldiers have a

story to tell. They'll take me back. If I return to Rythas quietly and play my part-"

"No," Kirwyn snarled, squeezing my biceps to hold me in place. "We stay together."

"We are *not* sacrificing you," Aewna declared, standing beside Kirwyn.

"No, Kirwyn," I pled, tears streaming down my face. Rising fear choked me, making it hard to breathe. "I can't lose you! If you die, then I have no reason to go on."

Kirwyn's clenched jaw told me he wasn't persuaded.

"Or if you won't let me go then we take a stand here, together." Desperate, I swore, "I'd rather die with you than live with him."

"You don't mean that." Kirwyn scowled, furious fingers digging into my arms.

"Yes, I do. I won't live without you."

Kirwyn gazed into the distance over my shoulder. He was pensive for long, tense seconds we didn't have. I held my breath waiting for him to speak.

"I know another way," he sighed. "There's a bridge we can take. It crosses the ravine about thirty minutes ride from here?" he asked the question to himself, shaking his head. "I can't remember exactly. But if we can make before they catch up, we can blow it up behind us so they can't follow."

I blinked, confused. *Why didn't he suggest that way before?*

"Let's go. Hurry!" Kirwyn ordered.

He doesn't want to go this way. Something dangerous lurks beyond the bridge. But what?

In a matter of seconds, Aewna sat astride Sun Bolt, ready to run. Kirwyn mounted Szirena and gave me his hand to help swing me up behind him. I threw my arms around his waist and held on as tightly as I could. My heart stopped when I heard the distant clamor of the hunting party just as we kicked our horses into action. Even though Szirena struggled with our combined weight, we took off at a stomach-dropping pace to the west. My hope was that Juls and his men hadn't expected us to spy them -- we needed every advantage we could get. But I doubted we were so lucky and since stealth wasn't an option, we blazed an obvious trail and made too much noise.

Faster, faster, I thought. My imagination ran wild, as it did whenever I was chased. I knew it did no good, and probably caused harm by distracting me. But clinging to Kirwyn's waist, I had no task but to ensure I didn't fall off. I pictured soldiers of Rythas coming up right behind me, ready to grab me any second. How could I face Juls again? Would he look at me with hurt in his eyes or anger? Both?

The trail became rockier and less pronounced after about ten minutes of riding. Another ten and the trees thinned, revealing a wonder before us.

My mouth dropped eyeing the deep but narrow ravine cut into the earth, stretching far beyond what I could see as it rounded a bend. It had to be artificially created. I didn't know enough of the world to be sure, but it didn't seem organic. It looked purposeful, built for defense. Perhaps long ago the divide had been dug out or blasted into existence. Perhaps something once naturally existed that had been subsequently expanded upon by man.

To defend what? What exactly lay on the other side?

Even as I sweated, a cold chill ran up my neck. Because if this was a shortcut, why didn't Kirwyn want to take it until we were forced?

It had to be preferable to Juls... right?

I pushed the thought away. I had no time to ask questions and no choice but to trust Kirwyn. Racing northwest for another ten minutes or so, we hugged the intimidating ravine until Kirwyn brought us to an abrupt halt and we dismounted.

I spied one long bridge slung between the two sides of the narrow canyon. Rope-and-wood, the bridge looked as sturdy as could be hoped, considering the material. I gulped. Heights were better than tight spaces, but not much.

It dawned on me that our horses couldn't make the crossing and my heart sank. It was my turn to say goodbye. I looked at Kirwyn and, reading my mind, he nodded.

I quickly unbuckled the bolt bag from Szirena's saddle and gave it to him. At least Szirena would live. Free. Wild. I wouldn't be with her, but she'd be alive. My hands fumbled, wanting to release her from the bridle, if not the saddle entirely. I sliced to free her from the bit and the noseband. It would have to be enough.

"Zaria, we don't have time!" Kirwyn shouted, sliding the bag onto his back.

I brought my face to hers, nuzzling the short, soft hair on her head. "I love you. I'll miss you. Thank you."

Did she feel I was abandoning her? I wondered, with a pang.

"It's stuck!" Aewna cried, behind me.

I turned to see her struggling with our tenting supplies, attached to Sun Bolt's saddle.

"Forget it!" Kirwyn shouted, grabbing my hand. "We don't have time!"

Horseless, the three of us stepped onto the bridge. Aewna took the lead, I was in the middle, and Kirwyn followed close enough behind me to steady me if I needed assistance. Despite the bridge feeling securely built, my stomach dropped as soon as I made it three steps. I'd never loved heights, perhaps because I hadn't experienced many until High Spire. But the castle was solid rock beneath my feet and this was wooden planks and hempen rope, jiggling with our combined weight.

I moved as fast as I dared and it wasn't just for my own life that I hurried. If Juls and his men caught up, if they set foot upon the bridge... then there was no way I could let Kirwyn explode it.

I couldn't let it come to that.

But Kirwyn would fight me on the decision and I'd have to make the horrible choice between letting Juls capture us or killing him and his men.

And if I let them take us, what would they do to Kirwyn? Drag us back to High Spire together or kill him on the spot?

God, please don't make me have to make that choice. Please.

"Faster!" I cried to Aewna, reaching her heels.

We had to outpace Juls enough to both clear the bridge entirely *and* set up the bomb. *Please god, we have to.*

Impossibly steep but narrow, at least the width of the ravine was on our side.

My heart beat faster as we reached the last few planks.

Just a bit farther...

Behind me, I heard dogs barking when I set my foot on solid ground.

CHAPTER 15

"Zaria, the bomb! Hurry!"

I fell to my knees and fumbled through our bag for the device. When my fingers hit the hard-metal explosive, I quickly grabbed and tossed it to Kirwyn. He caught it with ease and sprinted a few feet onto the bridge.

"Stand back!" he cried. Aewna and I stumbled ten or fifteen paces away, skirting the cliff's ledge, while Kirwyn crouched, arming the device. After he initiated the sequence to trigger it, he ran toward us and shoved me behind his broad frame.

Time stood still and my heart pounded out the questions as we waited, eyes glued to the bridge.

What if it didn't explode?

What if it did and Juls already set foot on the planks?

What if it didn't explode and they caught us?

What if it didn't explode and...

Boom!

Instinctively, we ducked our heads then quickly looked back in time to see the bridge shatter; wood and rope shooting up into the sky and falling into the ravine. As support vanished, the rest of the rope bridge floated downward, smacking the walls of the gorge.

We did it!

Each side was still anchored where it had been mounted to rock, but the rest hung limp and useless down the cliff walls. Any hope of using the bridge as a crossway was destroyed for the near future. Maybe forever.

My heart leapt as Kirwyn and I exchanged a look of joy, but I was too anxious to be completely elated. Adrenaline surged through my veins as the smoke began to dissipate, clearing our view to the other side of the narrow canyon. Tense, we eyed the treeline, waiting for Juls and his men to come into view.

My heart pounded like an Elowan drum. Blood rushed in my ears as the figures emerged -- six or seven men stuck without passage.

As the final plumes of gray smoke dissolved before my eyes, they spread and thinned to reveal one tall figure perched on the edge.

My heart stopped. *The rumors were wrong.*

It wasn't Juls hunting us down.

It was Laz.

CHAPTER 16

My eyes widened. Prince Lazlian. The keylord. Brother of my husband. The man who tried to kill me, more than once. The man who still wanted me dead. *Here. Now.* Separated only by the narrow ravine keeping me safe.

How did he cross the ocean?

Where was Juls?

The rumors were wrong.

He couldn't have crossed the sea. He couldn't.

We were separated only by the gorge...

"If you ever try to betray us, I will kill you. I will kill you so slowly you'll be begging to die for days – weeks."

The distance was too great for me to make out facial features but unmistakably, Lazlian stood on the other side of the rocky ravine in front of half a dozen soldiers and four dogs barking excitedly. Taller than most, Lazlian's arms arched slightly behind him and his hands fisted, as if ready to take a swing. It was the first time I'd seen him dressed in something other than the clothing of Rythas, though I couldn't make it out clearly. Riding leathers and boots of some kind. Unmoving, he gazed across the narrow canyon. Staring at us, I presumed.

How is he here on the mainland? The ocean roared in my ears. I had a funny feeling in my stomach. *Right there, across the gorge?*

Entranced, it wasn't until I felt Kirwyn's firm grip on my bicep that I realized I'd unconsciously moved forward like a sleep-walker and now hovered dangerously close to the steep drop. I blinked in horror, jarred back to reality, to the fatal fall a mere step away.

How very like an encounter with Lazlian. We were separated by an impassable canyon and still he endangered my life, simply by appearing.

I swung my gaze up to see Kirwyn looking down at me with concern and... something else. Searching my face, he brought his hand to my chin and held it while he leaned down...

...and kissed me.

I was too stunned to do anything other than kiss him back. *Maybe I'd frightened him by walking perilously close to the edge.* One of his hands wove beneath my hair to hold my head steady while his tongue swept slowly in my mouth. The move felt deliberate. *A show?* Was he taunting or claiming or... could anyone on the other side see clearly what we were doing?

Bewildered, when our kiss ended, I quickly looked across the ravine to gauge how much could be discerned, to figure out if Kirwyn might have done it... to mess with Lazlian?

I turned just in time to catch one of the Rythasian soldiers raising a gun in our direction.

"No!"

Laz's shout echoed across the canyon as he leapt, pushing the man's arm -- but not before the shot fired.

Instinctively, Kirwyn, Aewna and I ducked to avoid the bullet without knowing in which direction it flew. I crouched low to the ground, Kirwyn folded himself above me, sheltering me, and slightly higher up on the slope, Aewna slipped. As she tumbled, Aewna's full body weight slammed into Kirwyn. Imbalanced in his squat, it knocked him forward and sent me screaming and flying --

-- right over the edge of the cliff.

My stomach dropped and instant tears sprang to my eyes as my legs dangled over air.

"Kirwyn!" I shouted, though it was needless. He had me by the arms already – had never let go. Yet I couldn't stop screaming his name as my legs kicked wildly, seeking purchase in the air where none could be found.

Would I die instantly? How badly would it hurt?

Plummeting to my death with Kirwyn having to watch was a bad way to go. Not that our chances of survival had ever been great, but I always hoped we'd at least make it to Mal-Yin.

"I've got you," Kirwyn swore. "Listen to me, I've got you. Zaria, *look at me.*"

I looked.

"You're twisting too much. Stop kicking. I've got you, calm down. I just don't want to scrape you as I pull, okay?"

By this time, Aewna had joined him, clasping my forearms. I nodded, and, understanding all my flailing was making it harder for Kirwyn, forced myself to relax.

"Hang on," he said, as both he and Aewna tugged me over the ledge and back onto solid ground. Legs sprawled before him, Kirwyn pulled me into his lap and held me against his chest. Shaking too badly to be shamed, I curled into a ball and clung to him until my heart rate slowed.

After a moment, Kirwyn tried to stand us together, but my knees buckled. In one swoop, he lifted and cradled me. I wrapped my arms around his neck and he took off into the forest.

Over his shoulder, I couldn't stop staring at Lazlian and his men, poised on the cliff's edge, powerless... and pissed off.

It was enough to tie my stomach in knots even with the safety of the canyon separating us. As we disappeared into the trees, I stared at the keylord, still disbelieving, until I made out only a hint of black attire and then... nothing at all.

For a few seconds we scurried through the forest, wanting to put distance between ourselves and our pursuers. Kirwyn soon set me on my feet to move faster.

"How far are the other bridges?" I asked as we hurried. "Will they be able to track us?"

He scrubbed a hand down his face. "Possibly. But I don't think they will. If I recall, the other means of passage are pretty far and we're in Biohazard territory now. Too noxious to risk chasing us. If the toxins don't deter them, the women will."

"But Kirwyn, what about us? What about you?" I asked, remembering what he'd said about the clan, long ago, back in Elowa.

He didn't reply. He'd stopped walking and stared at something behind me. I turned to follow his gaze.

A sign stuck out of the grass. Its eerie, dripping letters looked as if they'd been written in a mixture of paint and blood.

No mercy will be given to men who enter Biohazard land.

You've been warned.

Turn back if you value your life.

The three of us looked at one another in silent horror.

If ever *I wished for our horses, it's now.*

Journeying by foot through poisonous terrain was the least ideal means of travel. How contaminated was the land? Would it infect the soles of my shoes? What if I touched something toxic and then touched my face and it melted the skin clear off my bones while I screamed?

Our agonizingly slow progress was terrifying. The longer we lingered, the greater the risk for Kirwyn getting caught and...

I didn't want to finish the thought. Coquina clams climbed up my spine with every sound coming from the trees. I imagined Biohazards attacking us from the front and Lazlian catching up from our rear. I pictured mutated beasts, more fearsome than normal, charging out of the grass. Of all the land we'd covered, this scared me the most.

We moved quickly and spoke little. After a few hours, dusk settled and we found an acceptable location to camp. The terrain was rougher here and the site we chose protected us on one side by a steep, rocky hill. With no pressing need to cook, we didn't risk a fire.

"We'll leave at first light," Kirwyn said. "I don't know how toxic the air is. The water isn't safe for drinking and anything we'd collect or kill would have fed from the same polluted earth, so we'll have to eat what we've already harvested until we're clear of the area."

"We need to get you out of here," Aewna said gravely, looking at Kirwyn.

"I know."

We'd passed no less than three more foreboding signs with very specific warnings.

Men will be slaughtered on sight.

Turn back. You've been warned.

"They will kill you," Aewna said, voice tight with worry.

Kirwyn squeezed my hand, as if I were the one whose life was on the line. "It won't come to that. We'll leave at dawn. I don't know this territory, but I know it's not large and this way, Mal-Yin's is just past their borders... somewhere. I think we can make it out in a few days. We just have to be careful not to touch more than we have to."

When it came to sleep, however, we had no choice but to lay against the ground. Worrying about toxins from merely touching the dirt was probably unnecessary paranoia, but no one truly knew the extent of the venomous territory. More concerning were snakes or other small, poisonous creatures we hoped didn't attack in the night. At least we were comforted by a strong wind, keeping the mosquitos at bay.

Aewna succumbed to exhaustion, but my nerves pricked at me, forcing me awake. I was terrified for Kirwyn, and I couldn't stop thinking about seeing Lazlian across the gorge. *Where was Juls?*

Kirwyn was distracted as well, though I couldn't figure out why he seemed more pensive than anxious. Sitting up, he scrutinized me with his ever-perceptive gaze until we heard Aewna's even breathing, indicating she'd fallen asleep.

Silently, Kirwyn stood, nodding for me to follow him as he walked away from our camp.

"What is it?" I asked, quickly catching up.

He turned to face me, hands on his hips. After a pause,

he said, "It makes sense that King Juls wouldn't, *couldn't*, abandon the throne -- especially after recently thwarting plots to overthrow him, as you mentioned. But that's the second time I've witnessed the king's brother doing the dirty work for him where you're concerned." Kirwyn crossed his toned arms. "What exactly does the keylord want with you, Zaria?"

"He wants to kill me!" I whisper-cried. *What was Kirwyn implying?* "Trust me. He not only told me as much, he tried to do it. More than once."

Kirwyn tilted his head, eyebrows raised.

"Then why did he try to stop his man from shooting at us?"

I squirmed. Why did this feel like an inquisition?

"Because he doesn't want me to die quickly," I explained. "It's too merciful. Prince Lazlian told me that if I ever betrayed him or his brother, he'd kill me slowly. Make me beg for death." I shuddered, remembering how close I'd come to getting caught by Laz before I escaped High Spire. *He must have been shamed and enraged when he learned I'd slipped right through his fingers that night.*

I chewed my lip nervously. I didn't always understand the keylord, but I understood this. His vengeance.

"Before I die, Lazlian wants to do to me what he thinks I did to him," I whispered. "Humiliate me. Hurt me."

Rubbing his thumb over his forefinger, Kirwyn's deep forest stare pinned me, watching carefully as he spoke. Nervous with his tense, elongated pause, I twisted my hands.

"Then why was he on his knees when you fell?" Kirwyn asked.

"What?" A school of minnows darted around my stomach. "What do you mean?"

"When you went over the cliff's edge," Kirwyn spoke carefully, eyes never leaving my face, "why did he drop to his knees like a man gripped by terror? Like a man who begged God not to let you fall?"

The minnows in my gut frenzied.

"That's not..." Kirwyn must have mistaken what he saw. Lazlian didn't kneel. He didn't even kneel to pledge loyalty to his brother when Juls became king. "...possible."

Kirwyn laughed, once, licking his teeth. There was nothing joyful about it.

"When we get to Rythas," he said, turning to walk away, "I'm going to kill him first."

CHAPTER 17

"**K**irwyn, stop. You can't kill the king *or* his brother. It will all fall apart if you do."

Kirwyn continued walking until I was forced to tug his shirt. "If Lazlian truly wants me alive and unharmed it's because Juls requires it. The only person in the world Laz loves more than Laz is his brother."

"Men don't fall to their knees for their brothers' wives." Kirwyn's hands rested impatiently on his hips. His eyes were forceful, determined. "He wants you alive. For his own reasons. *Personal ones.*"

Personally, I wasn't going to entertain Kirwyn's ridiculous implication. But it did confirm my suspicions of one thing, and I narrowed my own eyes with ferocity.

"Is that why you kissed me so pointedly back there? Marking your territory, like a dog?" I ran my hands down my body with a flourish. "Why don't you just pee all over me?"

Kirwyn shrugged. "I will if I have to."

I stomped my foot in my old manner, teeth grinding. My fear of confinement... it wasn't just physical, I realized.

Whatever games Kirwyn and I played in private, intimately, I didn't want them spilling over into our real life, real matters.

"Don't. Don't make me feel like a possession. I hate it." Knowing he'd know who I meant, I pled, "Don't be like them."

Kirwyn's gaze softened as he ran a hand through his hair. His eyes darted to Aewna, making sure she remained asleep before speaking. "You can't blame me for wanting to show him you belong to me." Before I could argue, he continued, "It's not the same thing. Because it was *your* choice." Softly, he said, "Because I belong to you too."

I inhaled a shaky breath. Why was that so hard to trust, to relax into? Was I too damaged by lies? Or was it because... I was scared of losing him again?

Studying the chiseled beauty of his face and recalling all my nightmares, I blinked.

I am absolutely terrified and it's messing with my head.

A lump formed in my throat as I thought about it. I couldn't endure the pain of being separated from Kirwyn a second time. And if something happened...

"Do you want to know what I said that night on the beach, back in Elowa? The first time we slept together?" Kirwyn asked suddenly. "The words in Gaelic?"

I stared at Kirwyn, rapt.

"I said that I read all the books and I fantasized for years. About a girl like you. Except when I met you, you shattered those fantasies to nothing, blew them away to dust. Because you were better than anything I'd ever read, more astounding than anything I could have imagined. I said you were *more* than my fantasy. You were the fantasy I never even knew I had."

Gullflesh rose on my skin. I swallowed several times

before I could find my voice and knew it would be shaky anyway.

"I feel the same and it terrifies me." I looked down, chewing my lip hard to keep from crying. "Because I lost you and I could lose you again. Nothing is certain in this world. And whenever I get too scared, I – I don't know. I convince myself it wasn't real or I distract myself or I fight or shut down because *Kirwyn-*" the tears fell anyway, streaking my cheeks. "I can't lose you again. I won't survive it."

I buried my face against his chest and spoke half into his shirt as I mumbled, "Sometimes... no, a million times a day... I want to turn back. I'm scared, in a totally different way than I was afraid in Rythas. Then I had nothing to lose, now I have so much. Why are we doing this, why are we risking it? We're not heroes. You said it yourself, many times. Heroism only gets you killed. Maybe we should forget Rythas. Forget Elowa. Forget the world," I rambled. "We could be happy and safe. Picture it. Just you and me on a beach somewhere, away from all this."

If I closed my eyes, it was so real I almost felt like I could touch it. A beach in the south continent or beyond the Cold Mountains, where less people warred. Kirwyn and I had survival skills, we could live on our own. But staying here... Even now, strange shadows in this rocky terrain might hide monsters impossible to imagine. They could jump out at any minute, tear us apart.

Kirwyn stroked my hair. "I already told you I would leave with you if that's what you wanted. But that's not who you are. If you abandon your people, if you don't save the next chosen braenese, I don't think you'll ever forgive yourself. It will eat away at you for the rest of your life. I know what it's like to be tortured by a regret that haunts you."

Kirwyn tucked my hair behind my ear and wiped my tears. "Every day I sat on that goddamn beach and thought about how I wanted to storm that castle and take you back. But even if I *physically* could, I couldn't. For you."

"Is that why you're doing this?" I asked, pleading with my eyes as I pulled back to look at him. "For me? Because what you did back at the gorge wasn't about me."

Kirwyn scratched his stubble, debating before he answered. He flicked his eyes over to Aewna again, making sure she remained asleep.

"You don't understand. *They took you from me, Zaria.* It will eat away at me for the rest of my life if I don't kill them. Or at the very least, destroy their reign and watch them live a lifetime of suffering."

I groaned, shoulders slumping. "Kirwyn, no…"

I couldn't blame him because if the situation were reversed, I'd slaughter any woman who touched Kirwyn. But the more he spoke like this, the less likely I felt that we'd all make it out alive. If Kirwyn and I were captured, Juls might spare Kirwyn's life, but Lazlian wouldn't… and Lazlian had a way of getting what he wanted. On the other hand, if Kirwyn and I succeeded and he had the opportunity, he'd kill the Dorestes. Unless I could persuade him otherwise.

"Why didn't you shoot Lazlian from across the ravine?" I asked. "Didn't you have a clear shot?" A foolish part of me held out hope that reason stilled his hand.

"Unlikely. It would take more than one shot and they'd have started firing back, with more guns. There's no way I could have risked it with you and Aewna standing there beside me."

I sighed. Hence the taunting kiss in place of a bullet.

"So you took a different kind of shot instead."

"Yeah." He cocked a smirk. "One that I think will piss him off more. And the angrier he grows, the sloppier he'll get."

I half-rolled my eyes and groaned, "Listen to me, Lazlian isn't interested in me in that way. Trust me. He has tried to *murder* me."

"Think about it, Zaria, it doesn't make much sense," Kirwyn said, switching into his instructor-mode voice, rubbing his hands up and down my biceps. "The first time the keylord tries to kill you, he uses a shark? What are the odds that it would attack? It's sloppy, it's public, it's trace-able back to him. It's as if he didn't want to succeed or maybe even wanted to get caught." Kirwyn clucked his tongue. "He's clever, but he tries to murder you in the sloppiest and least covert manner possible? If he truly wanted you dead, he could have sent someone to assassi-nate you."

Kirwyn had a point. Could it have been half-hearted? Did Lazlian want to fail or get caught? I fell onto the grass, head in my hands.

I'd once wondered if there was something masochistic about the way Laz came at me. As if he wanted me to come back harder to justify a feeling of self-loathing. *But why in the world would Lazlian feel less than utterly pleased with himself?* That didn't add up, it wasn't who he was at his core.

"I don't know, maybe there's more to it," I admitted, studying the grass. "But the second time he meant it. I was there. Laz let me run into the crossfire alone, hoping I'd die. It was awful."

Kirwyn let out a long breath, squatting in front of me

and taking my hands in his. "I don't know. He's as erratic as Volmar. His actions don't follow reason."

They don't, I thought. *It's frustrating... and frightening.*

❦

THAT NIGHT, Kirwyn and I slept together on the forest floor without a tent, sleep sack, or even a pillow. He shouldered the brunt of the discomfort by pulling me to lay on his chest, but it was fitful for us both.

I awoke to Aewna's blood-curdling scream.

The only thing more shocking than the sound was the way she clammed up immediately after. As if she vacated her body and left a shell in her absence. Kirwyn was beside her in a flash.

"Shit," he cursed, lifting her arms to examine her. "It's ticks. Dozens or hundreds embedded in her skin, *fuck!* She must have slept near a nest that hatched in the night, I don't know."

Aewna's skin turned from ash to a ghostly colorlessness. I'd never seen a human look so pale before.

"Oh god, Kirwyn, do that neck thing! Make her faint!" I cried. "I think she's going into shock or something."

I didn't think Aewna was cognizant, but she shook her head rapidly.

"Aewna, hey, look at me," Kirwyn ordered, gesturing to catch her attention. "We're going to get these out. One at a time. It will take a while, but we'll do it. Can you take a deep breath for me?"

Aewna didn't respond.

"Listen," Kirwyn said, sharply. "I've got it under control. Look at me. Breathe."

Aewna looked. To my great relief, she took a visible breath but continued to stare, wide-eyed and possessed.

"There's tweezers in the medical bag and a small bottle of rubbing alcohol to sterilize them," Kirwyn said in his calm, instructor-mode voice. I jumped to get what he needed.

"Another deep breath, okay Aewna? Just keep focused on me, keep breathing. I'm going to remove these, one at a time, but it might hurt a little. I need you to stop shaking because I don't want to accidentally squish one while it's inside you. That can make the tick regurgitate the contents of its stomach, which increases the risk for infection. Nod if you understand me."

Aewna frantically nodded, struggling to keep her body still. Her lips were thin, white.

"Get them out," she begged.

"After I remove each one, I'm going to wipe the area with alcohol. Zaria, grab the cotton pads too."

"Get them out," Aewna repeated, eyes glazed as if in a trance.

Kirwyn turned to me, pointing to a flat, broad rock next to him. "I'm going to put each one here. Crush it with a rock. Don't use your fingers."

I helped Aewna strip to her undergarments, but it was difficult because her limbs didn't cooperate. Thank Keroe she wore the wig – it saved her scalp from a worse infestation. Some ticks had burrowed beneath, but most attacked her chest, neck, arms and legs. Her face was so pale it was almost inhuman, and I hated to think it, but she looked rather grotesque with the sheer number of ticks raising black bumps on her everywhere.

I found a small rock to use and positioned myself beside

Kirwyn. Eyebrows arched, he looked at me as if to ask, *you ready?*

I nodded and he dug out the first tick.

⌁

ABOUT AN HOUR LATER, we'd removed each insect from Aewna's skin. There wasn't much we could do after that, but Kirwyn gave her a dose of antibiotics and some kind of vitamin-concentrate pill to help combat infection, making me thankful we at least had his bolt bag. We traveled northward on foot, slow without horses, but determined to make it out of Biohazard territory by nightfall, if possible.

"You're good at everything," I marveled as we walked. "Seriously, what can't you do?"

Kirwyn made a sound of disbelief in the back of his throat. "Cook. Make anything grow. Especially the way my uncle did. You should have seen his gardening skills. Flowers, vegetables, whatever he got his hands on. Without a weapon, I'm not likely to beat a man in hand-to-hand combat if he's bigger than me. But I've seen my uncle do that too, once. He's the one who can do anything." Kirwyn continued determinedly, "And Enith would say I'm not good at managing my anger or listening to others when I should heed their advice or experience."

"You're improving in those areas," I grinned.

Kirwyn didn't smile in return. His face hardened and he halted.

"We're being followed," he whispered, making my stomach drop. His jaw clenched and his hand tightened on the gun at his hip. "And we're outnumbered."

CHAPTER 18

I reached for my gun, but Kirwyn gave a quick shake of his head. Withdrawing my hand, I gritted my teeth in frustration.

"You can come out, we know you're here," he called into the forest. He moved his hands away from his weapon and spread them low, halfway between a *stop* and a surrender position. "We don't mean any harm we just want to pass through your territory."

A beat and then --

"*We can come out?*" mocked a voice from the trees. "Did you hear that, hazards?"

A woman with dark skin, dark hair, and unnatural, red eyes sauntered onto the path. She was dressed in black and had a very large sword strapped to her side.

I gawked. *It's true. Their eyes have been altered from the toxins.*

"Why am I not at all surprised that the first words out of a man's mouth would be trying to tell us what to do?" She grinned, fingers drumming threateningly against the hilt of her sword. "I bet his last words will be *begging* us what *not* to do."

A giggle came from the left and another woman appeared. She was pale skinned, with flaming red hair and white eyes – including her ghost-like pupils. Completing the image, she wore a billowy, white blouse and a cream-colored pants, tucked into faded, tan boots. The pale woman joined her clanmate, casually leaning her arm on the shoulder of the first woman. I couldn't decide whose eyes frightened me more – the red or the white.

"Don't kill me, please, don't kill me!" the white-eyed woman taunted in a fake voice. "Am I right?"

The first woman sighed. "It's always the same."

"Always," the second woman agreed.

"You can't kill us!" I shouted. "We've done you no harm."

"Not you," the dark-skinned woman said, pointing with one long finger. "Just him."

I stepped in front of Kirwyn. "No. He's helping us. He's our guide. He hasn't done anything wrong."

"Hasn't he?" the pale redhead asked, flipping her fiery hair. "How many signs did you ignore on your way here? How many warnings? Arrogance. Every time." She fixed us with her creepy, white stare. "And the outcome is the same, every time. Men who enter Biohazard Territory are put to death. You two may continue on without your friend."

"No!" I shouted again, heart pounding, sweat dripping down my neck. "Why? He isn't going to hurt anyone, he's helping us. We'd be lost without him. Alone, you'd condemn us to death."

The dark-skinned woman shrugged. Her blood-eyes held no mercy. "Not our problem."

Behind me, Kirwyn started speaking carefully. "My

name is Kirwyn," he said. "This is Zaria and Aewna," he introduced us, surprising me by giving our real names. "What's your name?"

The dark-skinned woman frowned. But she shrugged and said, "I'm Nalice. This is Frayde."

Kirwyn held out his arms cautiously and spoke slowly. "It's nice to meet you, Nalice. Frayde. We were hunted by men at the borders of your region. Men who would hurt Zaria. I apologize that I entered your territory, but I had no other choice to keep her safe."

"We understand," Frayde said, and for a moment my heart leapt. But she added, "And we apologize that we have no choice but to kill you."

At her words, the other hazards Kirwyn referenced as hiding in the forest stepped into view. Eight, nine... eleven in total. My stomach twisted. More than we could beat. Adrenaline shot through my veins, preparing for a fight. A fight we'd lose.

Two women raised arrows and pointed them at our heads. The others twirled a variety of weapons – swords, daggers... Five of them held guns.

"Step forward," Nalice ordered, unsheathing her sword. "And accept your execution like a man."

"*No!*" I cried.

Kirwyn immediately lunged between me and the sword, giving Nalice what she wanted. He held his arms wide, shoulders tensed as he searched for an escape.

"Hold the women," Nalice commanded.

"Stop!" I screamed, tears pooling as I leapt away from the closest.

Kirwyn's muscles coiled. He wouldn't go down without a fight, but I could see his mind working furiously to figure out another way. Because it wasn't a fight we could win.

Nalice, noting the tension in his body, slid her eyes to Frayde, "If he doesn't kneel for execution, kill the..." she considered Aewna and I, debating, "blonde one."

A short-haired clan member stepped forward and pressed a sword to my neck as two other women grabbed me from behind.

"Don't hurt her!" Kirwyn shouted, dropping to his knees.

"Please, he's on your side!" I cried.

Two of the hazards pointed arrows at Aewna's head. Hysterical tears soaked my face.

"I was forced into a marriage I did not want and he's helping me escape it!" I sobbed. "Me and other girls! Please, if you care about us, let him live. Saving his life saves the lives of others. Please!"

For a moment, Nalice cocked her head, listening to my plea. She exchanged a look with Frayde, but the pause didn't last. Nalice firmed her grip on her sword, readying to cut off Kirwyn's head.

"No!" I screamed. Tears filled my eyes so heavily they blotted out the spinning world and I felt hands firmly restraining me when the threat of the sword at my throat wasn't enough.

This was it. If Kirwyn died, I'd ask them to kill me too. I couldn't, *wouldn't* go one step without him.

Nalice stood beside Kirwyn, readying to swing her sword.

"No! Stop!" My heart screamed in time with my mouth. I thrashed so wildly that more hands clutched my body, restraining me.

"Your clan leader must have some kind of appeal rule," Kirwyn spoke quickly, looking up only with his eyes as his head bowed in submission. "Where we can request an audience to be heard. Where we can tell her our story and she can decide whether to grant us passage herself."

Frayde cackled. "Really? That's your move? *Take me to your leader?*"

Kirwyn stared hard at Nalice, who had paused.

"But I'm right, aren't I?" he bit out, panting.

There was a pause and Aewna piped up. "You're governed by rules of fairness, are you not? You believe in justice. It's why you placed all the warning signs. You *tried* to give us a chance. You *must* have a process of some kind – a method for individuals to request a leader's appeal for a pardon."

Did they? My galloping heart needed to slow down or it would explode. I held my breath though another long pause.

Frayde laughed. Her milky white eyes seemed to dance and glow. "Right you are. We can take you to Lysette to plead your case. But it comes with a price."

"Anything!" I shouted, ignoring the warning coming from her malicious grin.

"If Lysette doesn't grant your appeal -- and I must warn you, it's never been granted in the past-"

"Well, it has *once*," a small voice murmured. It came from one of the women holding a bow and arrow. Frayde shot her a cold look, quickly silencing her.

"As I was saying, when your request is denied, *no one* will be allowed to pass any longer," she informed us, creepy white eyes settling on Aewna and I. "You'll have been privy to our stronghold and that means all *three* of you must be put to death. That is, unless Lysette believes you two can provide value." Frayde jerked her chin at Aewna and me. "Then you may be granted permission to join us. But otherwise, you'll all be executed and you'll lose your chance at passage," she declared, with relish. "Do you accept these terms?"

I didn't need time to consider. "We accept!" I agreed, dizzy with hope.

Pushing the women off me, I ran to Kirwyn and threw my arms around him as he regained his feet. Inhaling deeply, I took solace in the piney, comforting scent of his skin. I clutched him for a long time, trying to calm my racing heart.

"I love you, I love you," I murmured, pressing my tear-soaked face against his sweaty neck.

No one has a way with words like Kirwyn does, I assured myself. From the first day we met, I knew he was a gifted storyteller.

And thank Keroe.

Because our lives depended on that talent now.

CHAPTER 19

So much growth covered the Biohazard's concrete building it was almost entirely hidden by the forest. With our guns confiscated, Kirwyn, Aewna, and I were led as prisoners into a great chamber made of metal and even more concrete. Behind us, a door scraped the floor and slammed shut with ominous finality. I picked up the scent of dust amongst the strange smells, but that was the only one I could identify. There was something synthetic, a chemical in the air. Luckily, it was mostly covered by the scent of earth permeating through whatever cracks existed in the windows or walls.

Lysette, the clan leader, waited for us on an unusually high dais, obviously having been informed of our arrival. Her skin and hair were a human shade of light brown, but her eyes, like that of the other hazards, were inhuman.

Yellow. Sickly. Terrifying.

Those eyes alone squashed my hope.

We approached humbly but I already panicked, knowing that no matter how well Kirwyn spoke, this clan leader wouldn't be persuaded.

Our journey ends here, I thought with a sinking heart. This concrete hall would be my tomb.

Would Juls mourn my death? Would Lazlian mourn the fact that he didn't get to kill me himself?

I'd never know.

Kirwyn stepped forward, bowed his head, and opened his mouth –

"Denied," Lysette pronounced, bored.

"But we haven't even-"

"Denied," she repeated.

"Please," Kirwyn insisted, humbly bowed. "Hear me out. I confess that I disrespectfully entered your lands. But I only did it for love. To keep the woman I love and her sister alive. Men who would hurt her were chasing us. I had to bring them to the safety of your territory."

"Your actions were noble. They were just," Lysette agreed, staring down at Kirwyn. "And they will cost you your life."

No! Why? Was this all a sham? Had she mounted her throne just to gleefully sentence Kirwyn to death?

"But rejoice in knowing you die with honor. Take him," she commanded.

"Stop!" I shouted, shaking and sweating. I jumped forward and clung to Kirwyn. They'd have to kill me before they could pry my hands away.

Aewna approached with her head bowed and I prayed she had something clever to say, but her face already held defeat. If Aewna could read people, I feared she already knew nothing would persuade Lysette.

Please god, let her be wrong. Please help.

Aewna drew a breath, but before she could speak, everyone paused at the sound of voices coming from an adjacent hall.

From the other side of the room a party of women entered, looking as if they'd just returned from some mission in the woods – hunting or tracking or... killing. Jubilation rose from the cacophony, but that didn't mean they hadn't recently slaughtered someone. *They could have easily murdered a man and now celebrated the dead,* I thought with horror.

One girl, taller than the others, waltzed backwards into the hall with a springy step. For a moment, I was reminded of Lida and my irrational heart gave a hopeful leap, despite knowing it was impossible to see her there. I had glimpsed the same shade of olive skin and brown hair. She'd also swept her thick mane into a high goat's tail, as Lida often did, which jostled as she bounced backwards.

But as she turned to face me, the similarity ended there. For starters, her features were not Elowan and her body was more muscular than Lida's. But what really struck me was her movement. Lida – bookish, watchful, pensive – was unmistakably a cerebral creature. The proud way this girl bounded into a room, the booming laugh, and even the manner in which she stood with a wide stance conveyed a confidence in her body that signaled her to be a very *physical* creature. *Sporty,* came the thought.

Beside me, Kirwyn gaped.

"Mack?" he asked, disbelief coloring his tone.

I froze, eyes darting back and forth between Kirwyn and the girl. *Mack?* The girl also froze, mouth and eyes wide as she gazed at Kirwyn -- before running and throwing herself into his arms.

I gaped, too stunned – and I'd like to believe too level-headed – to feel anything like jealousy... until her hands came up to Kirwyn's hair, running her fingers through it with familiarity. Face pressed intimately against his, she laughed. Her eyes were blue, but it was a strange cobalt not found in nature.

"I can't believe it!" she cried. "Is it really you?"

I was frowning – or trying not to – by the time she threw her arms around Kirwyn's neck in another tight hug. *Who was she? Who was she to him?*

"Oh my god, you're alive, you're alive! Teddy!" Mack yelled. "Teddy, hurry up! Kirwyn is *here!*"

What is going on? Who's Teddy?

A distinguished-looking man quickly entered the room. From his graying hair and slightly creased face, he seemed to be in his forties. I watched his stunned expression turn to teary-eyed joy as he looked at us. Kirwyn stood frozen, mouth slack.

"Theo?" he breathed, disbelieving. A slow smile lit his whole face. "Theo!" he laughed, before running up to the man and wrapping him in a bear hug.

Oh... my... god. I blinked as my brain slowly pieced it together.

Teddy... Theodos... Kirwyn's uncle. I was staring at Kirwyn's long-lost uncle.

"Kirwyn, my boy!" his uncle bellowed with delight, clapping his nephew's back.

"You're alive!"

"What are you doing – how did you get here?"

"Where have you been?"

They both spoke over one another, trying to get it all out. Amazed, I stared at the man's features and saw the similarity: sharp jawline, beautifully sculpted mouth, straight nose. Theo's eyes looked more blue than green, but it was hard to tell from a distance.

Before I had time to speak, Mack knelt before Lysette, bowing her head. "I will vouch for Kirwyn. He saved my life. By the laws of our land, he should be granted passage."

Lysette, who'd been watching the scene with mild interest, said calmly, "You've already vouched for his uncle under the same exception and by the book, it's only for those who haven't seen our compound and can be escorted beyond our territory."

"They *both* saved me. I wouldn't be alive without their help. Kirwyn's veins flow with the same honorable blood as his uncle. He will not bring any harm to our clan."

"This is exactly why we do not make exceptions," Lysette snapped. "One leads to another. Two is too many."

Theo quickly knelt before the clan leader. Nothing diminished his aura, even as he humbled himself on his knees. If anything, the act made him somehow look *more* admirable.

"I exchange my pardon for his," Theo said, gravely. "Take my life and let him live."

"No!" Kirwyn shouted.

"Silence!" Lysette ordered, yellow eyes searing into us all. The room fell quiet as Lysette studied Kirwyn, Aewna and me. I dug my fingernails into my palms, praying fiercely.

If Kirwyn dies, I will die with him, I swore. *We will go down fighting, together.*

When the clan leader spoke, her words were merciful, but the glare in her eyes was not.

"You may stay on probation," she decreed with ill-concealed malice. "But it comes with a price. I will henceforth not be hearing any clemency pleas for a period lasting no less than one year." Raising her yellow eyes to the gathered crowd, she said, "None of you are to seek leniency for *any* reason. That means that even if a man saves your life, he will not be granted passage. He will be given your sword, not my ear."

Lysette turned hard eyes to Mack, "This is my decree. Allowing Teddy's nephew to stay may cost the lives of others -- others you wish to save. Do you accept these terms? Do you all?" she asked, looking around.

Kirwyn looked hesitant, but Mack cried, "I accept!"

To my astonishment, an eager chorus of *"we accept"* echoed around the room. It wasn't on behalf of Kirwyn, I was sure. No one even knew him. But the clanswomen in the room all seemed protective of Theo.

Lysette looked sternly at Kirwyn. "It is not because of what you have done for these two," she said, pointing at Aewna and me. "It is only because you have saved Mack's life and only because of your blood ties to your uncle, who has proven his worth amongst us. You have been granted a probatory stay *only.*"

Head bowed, Kirwyn said, "I haven't the words to express my gratitude. But I'll start with *thank you.*"

"Go," she dismissed us. "You are responsible for them," Lysette told Mack, her eyebrows arched threateningly high. "And you are accountable for his behavior," Lysette warned Theo, indicating Kirwyn.

"We understand," Mack said, bowing and backing up. She grabbed and pulled Aewna and me out of the cavernous room. I yanked my arm back but tried to flash a grateful smile, not wanting to be touched but not wanting to offend her. I'd had enough unwanted contact as we were dragged into their stronghold.

Mack didn't even notice as she whispered excitedly, "With me. I'll get you settled."

"You're alive!" Theo marveled, cupping and lightly clapping Kirwyn's face. I noticed he was missing three fingers on his left hand, as Kirwyn once told me, long ago. With his arm still around Kirwyn's shoulders, both men had tears in their eyes. They chatted rapidly between themselves as we hurried away from Lysette, and I swallowed a lump in my own throat, overjoyed for Kirwyn. I heard bits of his story, catching Theodos up on everything that had happened since they'd lost each other.

"Oh, I should introduce myself," Mack said, stopping so quickly I nearly slammed into her. "My name is Mackenzie, but everyone calls me Mack. I met Teddy and Kirwyn on the road years ago."

"Wait," I protested, holding up my hands. "We can't stay here. What about the toxins?"

Mack roared her laugh. "There are no toxins. Sure, there were before, but it's long since been mitigated. We maintain the myth to keep out the other clans."

"But what about your eyes?" I asked, disbelieving.

"These?" Mack asked, pointing and shrugging. "They're just contacts. Deters those who'd threaten our safety and frightens anyone who sees us. Well, those not smart enough to heed our warning signs," she teased Kirwyn, punching his arm.

I frowned at how freely she touched him but he barely noticed, focused on his uncle.

"I still can't believe I found you *here*, of all places," Kirwyn marveled, then added, "though if one man in all their history was ever going to be granted a stay in Biohazard territory, it would be you."

"And if one boy were ever to fall off into the ocean and bring back a radiant sea queen," Theo said, turning to me with a warm smile and a twinkle in his eye, "it would be you."

Before Theo approached, Kirwyn's eyes – wide with

alert – found mine. I nodded to answer his unvoiced question and my heart swelled with adoration to know that, even with a beloved family member, Kirwyn made sure I was okay with being touched.

Theo gently took my hand and gave it a small, gallant kiss. It didn't unnerve me. Like Kirwyn, something felt *safe* about his charming uncle. I was sure that comforting aura he radiated contributed to both his being granted pardon and the way the Biohazards seemed to buzz around him. Theodos was tall and dashing, like Kirwyn. I think I even blushed a little when he kissed my hand. Teddy probably had that effect on everyone.

"Let Mack get you settled," Theo said, eyes shining with unshed tears as he looked over his nephew. His hand moved back to rest against Kirwyn's cheek, as if he couldn't believe he was real. "Clean up, have a rest. We'll meet for dinner."

Theodos sighed, happily, shaking his head.

"I'd given up hope. What a rookie mistake to make at my age."

KIRWYN and I were given a tiny concrete chamber to use as our bedroom. There was no private bath attached, but the quarters were clean and safe – a welcome respite after all we'd suffered. *Well,* I amended, *the room is safe as can be expected in a stronghold where we'd almost been put to death.*

I couldn't stop licking my teeth with pleasure. We'd been given a chemical paste to brush them, and it was the first time in a long time my mouth felt fully clean.

"So how do you know Mack?" I asked Kirwyn, brushing the knots from my hair to make the question seem casual. I didn't know why I bothered hiding my emotions, Kirwyn always saw through me.

He worked his jaw. "Remember when I told you I'd done some things before? Back in Elowa, when we picked mushrooms and you were angry that I had a past?"

I stopped brushing. "It was her."

Kirwyn gave a curt nod.

"How?" I dropped the brush and threw up my hands. "How in all the wide world is it possible to run into her again?"

"We're not really covering much ground, compared to the wide world," Kirwyn pointed out.

Chewing my lip, I paused before asking questions. I had been young and sheltered when we'd first met. *I was past such childish jealousy now, right?*

"How much did you do with her?"

Kirwyn rubbed his newly-shaved face with the backs of his knuckles. "If you're asking if we had sex, we didn't. Not fully, I mean."

Not fully?

"You were my first. But she-"

"Went down on you," I finished. I didn't know how I knew, but I knew. Odd that when I found out Juls had two women at once I wasn't bothered at all, but possessiveness flared in my chest at the idea of Kirwyn sharing intimate moments with someone else.

How had he borne it, knowing I was *married* in Rythas?

Kirwyn nodded. "We fooled around a couple of days after we rescued her and she put her mouth on me. I'd never done anything with a woman before. Mack can be assertive. She knows what she wants."

Unlike me? I wondered. My face must have fallen.

"I didn't mean it as a comparison," Kirwyn said quickly.

"I just meant... we drank one night. She made a move." He lifted one shoulder in a shrug. "I found her attractive but I wouldn't have initiated anything with a girl we picked up on the road. I didn't know much about her. Mack doesn't like to talk about anything deep or serious, she likes to keep it light."

I frowned again. *And I keep it dark? Heavy?*

Kirwyn rubbed his forehead, frustrated. He pulled up a chair and sat beside me. "I mean, the way we talked, it was never the kind of conversation that nurtured any real intimacy. We were just kids on the road, drunk and curious one night."

"Did you enjoy it?"

Kirwyn ran a hand down his face and leaned back in the chair, long legs sprawling forward. "If you're asking if I came, then yes. If you're asking if I'd have done it a second time if we had the opportunity..." He shrugged. "I don't know. Being young, exploring, that was all good but when I looked back on it later, I wondered if Mack had other motivations. I wondered if somewhere in her mind, even subconsciously, she felt..." Kirwyn grimaced, "obligated or something. For me saving her life." He winced. "Or as persuasion to let her stick around."

I pressed a hand to my stomach. *This world is disgusting. No wonder Mack wanted to stay with the Biohazards. I would too. It's better than the alternatives.*

But I shook the thought from my head and flashed Kirwyn a look of disbelief. "For all your cockiness you can't seriously believe that. Half the girls in that hall couldn't take their eyes off you. You're gorgeous, you know it. I wouldn't have been surprised if they wanted to spare you just because you're so good-looking. *Or worse,*" I shivered. "Shared you before they slaughtered you. What makes you think Mack didn't desire you? She has eyes, however falsely they've been enhanced. Did you part on bad terms?"

"No. But I got the sense before we split ways that she had a crush on my uncle."

I blinked several times. Kirwyn and his uncle did look alike, but... "O...kay," I stuttered, skeptical. "I find that hard to believe, given he's almost twice her age. But that only proves my point. If she was attracted to him, she was likely attracted to you too."

Odd that I was defending her desire for him -- or anything that happened between the two of them. But I couldn't let Kirwyn believe she'd been intimate out of any sense of obligation. Even if he didn't possess that sinister beauty, Kirwyn had a magnetism that drew people to him. His confidence, his humor, and the way he told a story as if holding court, entranced others.

Kirwyn cocked a half-smile, but it didn't touch his eyes. "Theo's not as old as he looks. Losing his family and having to raise me at a young age, aged him." Kirwyn's smile widened into something genuine. "I wasn't an easy kid. I was a bit of a rebel. Maybe a nightmare. Theo's only thirty-eight, he just looks older."

"And Mack's almost twenty years younger!" I countered, throwing up my hands. "Whatever. Weird. You're probably mistaken." I fisted Kirwyn's shirt and pulled him close. "But I do want to hear some stories about what a not-so-easy kid you were."

Kirwyn grinned. "Actually, do you mind if I-"

"Go," I said, grinning, knowing what he'd ask.

"Thanks," he replied, eager to reconnect with his uncle. Kirwyn gave me a quick kiss. "I'll see you at dinner."

As he reached the door, Kirwyn paused, palming the handle. "If I hadn't met you, if we hadn't decided to trek north, I would have never found him again." He stroked the doorknob, lost in thought. "You've brought so much into my life I don't think I'll ever be able to thank you enough."

Oh, Kirwyn, I thought as he departed. *You've got it backwards. It's me who can never thank you enough.*

❧

We sat together that evening in the Biohazard's dining hall. The room was up three flights of stairs, but the building was covered in so much foliage that the windows were blocked by vines and leafy trees. I had to admit I enjoyed the treehouse style. Evening light shone through the glass, but only in patches. The hall burst with carefree chatter and laughter, helping me relax into a feeling of safety. Somewhat.

Theo held court when he told a story, just like Kirwyn. I watched the two men beaming at one another and my heart warmed. Like Kirwyn, Theo was remarkably handsome. He had straight, white teeth and was blessed with a full head of dark hair. Like his nephew, Theo's ears stuck out just a little too far.

I cocked my head, frowning.

Now that I'd been around more people outside of Elowa, I realized it wasn't as severe as I'd once thought. Coquina clams crept up my spine and my gut tightened with something like distaste or even disgust. The way our Elowan ancestors modified their genes to a certain standard was... unsettling. We were designed to be physically pleasing, but, to whom? Why with the same specifications?

"Tell me another story," I asked Theo, smiling with encouragement. I loved getting this rare peek into Kirwyn's past. My demon boy could tell a good tale, but I had a feeling he only shared the ones that made him look favorable.

"When Kirwyn was about, oh, seven, we grew watermelons," Theo began, "and you know what he did one morning? He took his knife and cut into each one, trying to pick which was the ripest, the juiciest. Cut himself a nice little square from each melon, ruining the entire batch. It took months to grow the crop and he spoiled the whole thing in minutes."

Everyone laughed. Kirwyn ducked his head, sheepish.

"We had to eat watermelon for days," Theo said, eyes glistening with the memory.

"You made me juice and can the leftovers," Kirwyn added. "Ugh, I never wanted to see another melon after that. I remember we'd stored so much we even drank watermelon juice on Christmas morning that year."

"What's Christmas?" I asked.

Everyone's head turned in my direction.

Theo beamed at Kirwyn, bringing a fist to his mouth to hold back a cry. "We'll have so many Christmases," he said, eyes crinkling with his smile. "As a family."

DINNER LASTED for hours that evening. The Biohazards were all curious about Teddy's handsome nephew and they continually stopped by to ask questions. I kept my tale brief and vague, bringing the focus back to Kirwyn whenever possible, whose story intrigued them more than my own, being related to Teddy. Throughout the entirety of Biohazard history, only Kirwyn's uncle had ever been granted stay. Seeing his charm in action I wasn't surprised, but I hoped to get the full story later.

At the overabundance of vegetables served, I couldn't help but wonder aloud, "How do you grow so much food?"

"The land is ours. Everyone believes it's toxic and that we're mutated as a result of persisting on such polluted earth. Sometimes," Mack laughed, "we dress up half-zombified around the old Hollow's Eve and scare anyone foolish enough to settle too close."

"I know you don't allow men in your territory, but what about the boys?" Kirwyn asked. "I saw a few very young ones at that far table. How is it that you repopulate? Is there a storage of uh, fluid you utilize? You don't seem to have the technology to separate the samples based on gender."

I didn't understand all the science, but I caught the gist of what Kirwyn asked.

"Nothing that sophisticated," Mack dismissed, propping her foot on her chair and resting her arm on her knee. She fished an almond from a bowl of nuts and popped it in her mouth. "We do it the old-fashioned way. When a woman decides she wants a child, she seeks a partner outside our borders and returns when she's done."

"But... if a child is conceived naturally, it might be male, like those children." Kirwyn pointed out, brow furrowed. "What happens when they grow up?"

"We have a deal with the Spades," Mack shrugged. "It's why they don't attack us. Male children are conscripted into their army when they reach eleven years of age."

"You hand your children over to the Spades?" I asked, wide-eyed.

Mack scowled. "Just the boys. And only after they've had a good decade with their mothers."

My head spun. "But to the Spades? To be used in their army?"

Mack folded her arms, defensive. "It's not like that.

They're well-trained here and even more so there. They're given positions of honor within Spade ranks, they're not just foot soldiers. It's a good life. Maybe a better one than they'd have with us."

Mack offered me the bowl of almonds, but I shook my head. She popped another in her mouth, shrugging again.

"The Spades can't be conquered. You can fight them, feed them, or fuck them," she declared. "In our case, we found another way. By fighting *with* them."

I sat back in my chair, letting her information sink in. *Fight them,* as in the warring clans of the mainland. *Fuck them,* as in the way Rythas served in part as a Spade playground. *Feed them,* the way men and women of Shreelos farmed for their overlords.

I looked at Kirwyn and his uncle, who didn't fall into any of those categories. Freeborns found another way too, protecting their liberty by clustering in small numbers, living in hiding or on the run.

My whole life I'd been ignorant to the way the world worked. The idea of tearing a child away from his mother, even at eleven, made my stomach roil. It was preferable to being carted off in a wagon for slavery, but it still wasn't a future I'd envision, given the choice. I wondered if any of the fathers knew they'd had sons or daughters. Did they want to? Did they care? Did hazards ever fall in love, change their minds, and run away with someone?

What a fucking mess the world is. Every time I thought it showed me all its terrors, new ones were revealed. When the world could be anything we wanted it to be, why was it shaped this way?

A tiny ball of dread nudged at my stomach. Would it be possible to change things in Elowa and Rythas without dragging them into... all this?

"Before we leave, I want to soak up as much knowledge as I can about your way of life here," I told Mackenzie.

"Leave?" We all jumped a little in our seats, not realizing Lysette strolled nearby. Her yellow eyes bore down on us.

"You were never given permission to leave our territory."

CHAPTER 20

I saw my own shock reflected in the faces of Kirwyn and Aewna. For a moment, no one said anything.

"I don't think I understand your meaning," Aewna spoke up, offering a friendly smile. "We couldn't intrude upon your hospitality indefinitely. We'd never wish to impose upon you and forever burden or strain any limited resources."

"You understand precisely what I mean," Lysette snapped. "Are you so ungrateful? In all our history, Teddy and his nephew are the only men ever granted permission to stay. And now you seek to leave, to spread word of our secrets?"

"No," I quickly protested, straightening in my seat. "We wouldn't do that. But we have to move on. We have important things we must do, a life to lead."

Under the table, Theodos grabbed my knee and a second later Kirwyn's foot found mine, so I guessed his uncle had signaled him as well. I met Kirwyn's eyes and stopped talking, relieved that Theo seemed to have a plan.

"They're new," Theodos announced, tossing his napkin on the table as he stood. His voice was soothing as he continued, "And young. Restless. Naïve. Give them some time to grow and learn our ways here. They each have their own unique strengths. Each will prove an asset far surpassing any risk."

Lysette's sickly yellow eyes bore into mine. "See that you make yourselves valuable," she said. "Nalice will meet with you in the morning to discuss these assets and acclimate you to our ways."

A tense silence descended upon our table in which I worried my panicked thoughts were visible all over my face. I tried my best to school my expression into one of deference, as I'd grown used to pretending in High Spire. We all followed Lysette with our eyes as she strolled out of the hall.

Alone, Theo's handsome face lit with urgency as he whispered, "We'll leave the table separately, slowly. Meet in my room."

A FEW MINUTES LATER, Kirwyn, Aewna, and I scurried down the concrete corridors to Theo's room. Kirwyn knew the way, already having visited. We found his uncle waiting with Mackenzie in chambers much bigger than our own, stuffed with books from floor to ceiling and gadgets I couldn't name. Despite the quantity of objects, everything was tidy, orderly, just like Theo himself. The only thing disrupting the space was the tension we brought with us, charging the air.

Kirwyn broke the silence. "What do we do? She knows we won't stay, I can tell."

"We have to leave tonight," Theo instructed. "Before Lysette assumes we'll make a move. She's going to think we'll take our time to form a solid plan."

Things were unraveling so rapidly my head spun. We'd just found safe – somewhat safe – quarters, and now we were jettisoning into the backlands again? I opened my mouth, but before I could speak, Mackenzie's face fell into shock.

"If you leave, I'm coming with you," she declared.

Theo gently grasped her bicep with one hand and said calmly, "No. It's too dangerous."

Mackenzie broke free of his grasp, only to frantically grasp *him* in return. "No! Remember when I knocked and you didn't open the door? You *knew*. We both knew why I'd come. And I walked away because I could try again. Because in time you'd see things differently. But if you leave, I'll never have a chance to knock again. I'm coming with you."

I sucked in quick breath. *Kirwyn was right. Mack is in love with his uncle.*

As they argued, Kirwyn, Aewna and I all found the pores in the concrete very interesting in an attempt to politely avert our stares and give them some modicum of privacy. But we couldn't close our ears.

"You have your whole life ahead-" Theo protested.

"With you. My life is with *you*. We'll get away from where we're not allowed to be and go where no one cares."

Did she mean no one would care about them being together as in it was against the Biohazard rules or because of their difference in age? Both?

"It's too dangerous out there," Theo shook his head.

"Then you'll need all the help you can get. Don't argue with me because I'm not changing my mind."

Theo scrubbed a hand down his face in a manner that

reminded me of Kirwyn in frustrated defeat. Sighing, he turned to us and ordered, "We'll need to gather supplies. Mal-Yin's compound isn't far from here, but disputed territories are dangerous. Mack, take what you can from the armory. I'll sneak extra rations from the kitchens. And you three," Theo said to Kirwyn, Aewna, and me, "bring whatever supplies you have from your rooms. There's a back tunnel leading a good distance out of here. It's unguarded – the doors don't allow access in, only out. We'll use it to leave tonight. If we delay, we give her time to prepare."

My heart gave quick, fearful thumps and adrenaline coursed through my veins.

Kirwyn clasped my shoulders and spoke in his instructor-voice. "We'll return to our room and do as my uncle says. Act natural."

I wasn't surprised he addressed only me; Aewna was skilled at hiding her emotions while I struggled. I nodded, getting my breathing under control, but I must not have looked convincing.

"Zaria, having Theo guide us in the backlands is as safe as we can get. And I've got you," Kirwyn swore, cupping my face. "I won't ever let anyone hurt you."

Knowing what I'd probably say, he added, "Which includes keeping myself safe too."

LESS THAN AN HOUR LATER, we all reconvened in Theo's room. Mackenzie's anxious gaze kept sliding to Teddy as if he'd slip away, and I could feel Kirwyn watching me as if I might have a breakdown before we broke out.

Mackenzie approached Aewna and me, unfurled her

hand, and revealed a small, encapsulated medication of some kind.

"What is this?" I asked.

"It's a way out." Mack's eyes were hard as she stared. "A suicide pill. You secure it under your tooth, here-" she said, showing me on her own mouth, "and bite down if things ever get too bad. If you're captured or separated from Kirwyn. Taken and-"

"No," I protested.

"You don't know how bad it is out there."

"And you don't know how much I love Kirwyn. If we're ever parted and there's a chance he's alive, no torment could be too terrible for me to endure."

I would know. I've done it before.

"You say that now," Mack countered. "But what if you're passed around? Beaten bloody? What if Kirwyn is killed in front of your eyes before it happens?"

"Then I'll stay alive long enough to kill everyone who hurt him," I bit out, "and find another way to join him in the afterlife."

Whatever she saw in my face made Mackenzie shrug and pocket the pill. She offered the other one to Aewna.

I watched carefully, unsure what Aewna would do. She was tougher than she looked, but more familiar with the horrors that could befall a person on the mainland. She was also terribly worn down from our journey -- her strengths weren't physical and she'd already been pushed past her limits. Most importantly, I knew the betrayal of her father hit her harder than my own parents had hit me. Thinking about Volmar, rage rose in my breast.

Who knew if we were already too late? If we didn't reach Mal in time and my mother presented Volmar as some kind of god having returned from another realm, we'd never get the Elowans to listen to the truth.

We could also reach Mal and have him refuse to help us.

"Thank you," Aewna said, clasping the pill. She didn't put it in her mouth, but she slid it into her pocket. I couldn't tell if it was a diplomatic move on her part or sincerity when she said, "I'll consider it."

We waited anxiously in Theo's room for the clan to fall asleep. Kirwyn and Theo talked privately on one side of his large chambers, by the many books, catching each other up on what had transpired since they parted. I knew we didn't have a better choice, but it was all happening so fast. I'd imagined we'd spend a few days with the Biohazards, resting and getting to know Theo, before journeying as a family together.

Sometime in the middle of the night, Kirwyn and his uncle divvied up the guns and explosives Mack smuggled from the armory, renewing our depleted supply. We each strapped a bag on our backs containing weapons, rations of food, and the sleeping packs Theo had collected.

I found Aewna's hand and gave it a reassuring squeeze, my own fear reflected in her eyes. *This is bad,* I thought. *But there's no good choice.*

I gulped as we faced the doorway.

"I won't let them hurt you," Kirwyn reminded, pulling me close.

You can't stop them, I thought, but didn't say. *There's too many of them.*

The five of us lined up, waiting for Theo's command.

"I'll take the lead," he said. "We'll reach the back exit in a few minutes and once we've made it to the tunnel, we'll know we're not being followed. We'll emerge well past the stables and must journey on foot. We push as far as we can before dawn."

Everyone nodded. Theo peeked his head out his bedroom door and signaled us to follow. Artificial lights illuminated the Biohazard's concrete corridors, dimmed to keep their stronghold secreted within the forest, I supposed. I was grateful for the advantage as we slipped down one shadowy hallway and the next.

The floor gently sloped as we neared Theo's tunnel. The farther we made it, the more I panicked, until we finally reached a set of double doors and I exhaled.

"This way," Theo whispered, ushering us into a long corridor. At the other end sat a similar pair of metal doors. "That's the tunnel. It will lead us about eight hundred feet beyond the stronghold," he whispered, waving his hand back-and-forth to indicate it was a rough estimate.

Quietly, we shuffled down the hall toward the second set of double doors and threw them wide, cringing as they screamed in protest.

It was as if the landdamn doors were cognizant, because their cry was answered by a screech at the other end of the hall. My stomach dropped to my feet and I could feel the color drain from my face.

We turned in horror as shots whizzed past our ears.

The Biohazards had found us.

Aewna cried out and I cradled my head in my arms as the five of us ran beyond the doorway. Kirwyn slammed the metal doors shut and looked around frantically. He found what he wanted and smashed a modern panel on the wall with the butt of his gun. Sparks flew and the panel darkened – disabled, I assumed.

We quickly sprinted a few feet down the corridor, but Mack's scream brought us to an abrupt halt.

Shrieking, her hands flew to either side of her face.

Theo fell to his knees. Bright, heavy blood plumed from a wound on his stomach.

"He's been shot, he's been shot!" Mack cried as Theo slumped the floor.

CHAPTER 21

Please God, no.

"Theo!" Kirwyn shouted, falling to his knees beside his uncle.

My heart stopped, then twisted in agony.

Reaching us, pounding came from the other side of the doors as the Biohazards tried to break them down. The doors weren't thick; they wouldn't hold up very long.

"Run, go!" Theo choked out.

Kirwyn's head whipped back and forth with anguished indecision.

"Go," Theo insisted.

A wretched cry left my mouth. From the pooling blood, it was clear Kirwyn's uncle was going to die.

No, please. This can't be happening.

Mack sobbed, throwing herself on top of Theo. "You stupid, stupid man! You should have opened the door, see? What was it all for? You should have let me in!" Her forehead pressed against his, tears streaking her cheeks.

Boom, boom.

More pounding came from the other side of the door.

Fear roiled in my gut and my heart bled for Kirwyn, kneeling on the other side of his uncle. I covered my mouth to stifle the sobs. Everyone cried. Everyone but Theo.

"Son," Theo panted urgently, blue eyes on Kirwyn. "I'm so proud of what you've become."

"*Stop it! You hold on,*" Kirwyn demanded, clutching his uncle's shoulders. His face twisted in wretched pain. "If anyone can, it's you!"

Kirwyn attempted to lift his uncle under Theo's shoulders, but Theo protested and groaned in such terrible pain that Kirwyn was forced to lay him back down.

Bam, bam. The doors shook with the thump from a buttress beating the other side.

"Get out of here," Theo croaked the order between stunted breaths. "Don't mourn my death, do you hear me? Giving my life to help you is the best I could have asked for. I have no regrets." He looked at Mackenzie and sputtered a sad laugh. "Except not opening the door for you."

Mack let out a strangled cry and leaned down, kissing Theo all over his face.

Bang, bang. We jumped as someone shot at the door locks, but they held. For now.

Kirwyn roared an animalistic cry of pain. Holding his uncle, he cried urgently, "I couldn't have asked for a better father, a better life in this world than the one you gave me. I'm sorry for all the trouble I gave you when I was young, all the times I didn't listen and put our lives in jeopardy."

"Then listen to me now. Get your queen somewhere safe. Go make little princes and princesses. Name one for me," Theo said, scrunching his face in what I think was an attempt to wink.

Mack's sobs reached new heights. Aewna covered her mouth to stifle her own.

Crunch, crunch. Something new was being used on the doors to push or pry them open. Amidst the outpouring of grief, Aewna said quietly, sadly, "We have to go."

Theo turned to Mack, who was sobbing and clinging Theo's torso.

"Go."

She shook her head. Teeth gritted, she withdrew her guns and looked up at us. "Go! I'm staying. You'll never make it unless someone holds them off." Looking at Theo with tears streaming down her face she said, "Don't argue with me. I was right the last time and I'm right this time." Face set with a mixture of grief and rage, she commanded, "Go! Don't waste your time fighting me, I'm not fucking leaving. Go!"

I hated that she was right. If we didn't flee now, the Biohazards would capture us, kill us, and Theo's sacrifice would be for nothing.

Kirwyn wiped his tears with the back of his hand. "I always wanted to be like you," he swore.

Bang, crunch -- the doors creaked and this time something popped and snapped.

I summoned my courage because I knew what Kirwyn would do for me if the situation were reversed.

"We have to go!" I cried, grabbing Kirwyn's arm and pulling.

With one last, tear-filled look at his uncle, he pressed his forehead against his and cried, "I love you, Dad."

My heart shattered into a million pieces. The lump in my throat burned like fire.

But I couldn't lose myself to hysterical crying because we'd lose everything if I didn't pull it together.

Kirwyn knew it too. Summoning *his* courage, Kirwyn grabbed my hand and the three of us sprinted down the hallway. The last thing we heard was Mack's anguished scream, followed by her rapid gunfire.

Feet beating the floor, we ran our hardest and made it to the exit about a minute later. I was too distraught to feel relief when we emerged into the balmy night air. Aewna and I took off running again, but Kirwyn stopped us.

"Wait!" he shouted.

I turned to see him fumbling in his bag, withdrawing *all* our explosives.

"It will buy us some time!" he yelled.

Aewna and I watched as he ran back inside the tunnel, knelt, then ran back out again. "Let's go!" he cried.

We ran, turning back seconds later as the bombs exploded, lighting up the night. I slapped my hands over my ears as the tunnel collapsed on itself, effectively sealing it off. The hazards would need to spend precious time digging out or circling back to another exit.

"Kirwyn, I'm so sorry!" I shouted.

Face tight, he gritted out, "There's no time. We only have a few minutes lead. Come on."

Kirwyn grabbed my hand and the three of us ran into the dark forest. It wasn't long before my nose caught the musky scent of wet soil.

"There's a stream!" I cried, leading us in its direction. We reached a body of water ten or fifteen feet wide, disappearing around a dark bend.

"Let's go," Kirwyn said. "We'll swim downstream. Far. Don't give them any tracks to follow."

All three of us waded into the cool water, praying nothing slithered underfoot that wanted to kill us. The stream's center was deep enough that we couldn't touch the bottom and unfortunately, our bags weren't entirely waterproof. The current wasn't swift, but it helped us move along. Trying to keep our splashes quiet, we swam for a few minutes before passing a rocky bank that would work well to hide footprints.

"Should we get out here?" I asked.

"No," Kirwyn said, paddling next to me. "We have to keep going. As far as we can."

We waded downstream for another twenty minutes before Aewna reluctantly protested, "Wait. Slow down. Or stop, please. I can't swim anymore."

"You have to," I told her. "Please, just a little further."

Don't let Teddy's death be in vain, I thought, sniffling.

Aewna continued to struggle, not just with the swim, but our packs. After another few minutes, I was going to tell her to let hers go, to sink it, when Kirwyn spied something and grabbed my arm.

"Here, let's exit."

I began treading to the far side of the creek when he pulled me back.

"No, let's leave on the same side. They're going to be looking over there," he said nodding his head across the stream. "And we'll buy time with their fruitless search."

Dragging our tired and soaked bodies onto the bank, we stumbled back into the dark woods. Kirwyn led us northeast on a path he thought would be the most difficult to track. Utterly devastated and terrified, we spoke little.

Just a bit further, I bargained. *We'll be safe if we go just a bit further.*

I guessed we hiked about five miles through exceedingly thick forest before we decided to camp, dragging our soiled mats from our packs and laying them onto the hard ground.

"I'm so sorry, Kirwyn," I whispered, hugging him tightly.

His only reply was a brief fluttering of his eyes, as if shutting out the pain, and a curt nod of acknowledgement.

"Do you think he could have-"

"No," Kirwyn cut me off. "The wound was fatal."

What about Mackenzie? I wondered, but didn't want to ask. Did she survive? *If so, what would be her fate?*

"They might still be chasing us," Aewna whispered, drawing her knees to her chest. "We should make a plan."

Kirwyn's nostrils flared in anger. "Whatever happens, I won't let them take us. I won't let his sacrifice be in vain. Which means we all need to get some sleep, now, so that we can move quickly in the morning."

Laying on my side, I curled into Kirwyn's arms on the damp bedding, too exhausted and heartbroken to care about the mosquitos attacking me or the discomfort of the hard ground.

As we lay in the strange, dark wood, I felt Kirwyn's body shudder behind me and I knew he was swallowing back his grief for our survival.

CHAPTER 22

No hazards slit our throats while we slept and we made it through the night. But the agony of losing Theo felt raw and even more exposed in the morning sun, as if the unforgiving light shone cruelly upon its sharp, serrated edge. What right did the sun have to shine down, illuminating our pain? The skies should have clouded and storms should have raged, matching our grief. Instead, the world carried on. Butterflies flitted happily about the bushes and birds sang merrily in the trees.

I would have done anything to take that pain away from Kirwyn. I hated it and I hated myself too. If I hadn't insisted we travel to Mal-Yin, he'd have never lost Vesper and never lost Theo. I wouldn't have blamed Kirwyn if he hated me, screamed at me, abandoned me right there. When he was forced to shoot Vesper, my heart ached. Now, it was utterly broken. I badly wished I could somehow siphon pain from his body and inject it into my own to share the burden.

"Kirwyn," I tentatively whispered, wrapping my arms around his back as he knelt to roll his mat. "I'm so sorry."

He stiffened. I heard him take a steadying breath before speaking. But his voice flowed with anguish as he said, "We don't have time... I'll... mourn later." From an angle, I could see Kirwyn close his eyes. When he re-opened them, a hard shell coated his face. I knew he wasn't closing himself off *to* me, but *for* me. Steeling himself to get us through to a place where he could safely grieve.

With aching hearts and aching feet, we made poor time over the next two days, traveling in a less-direct route. The mainland forest carried a different scent. It wasn't unpleasant but it wasn't citrus or floral or briny, like home. I often closed my eyes and imaged the frangipani outside my old cave or the paw-paw orchards behind our Elowan palace... I even thought of High Spire, locked between the sea and the lush royal gardens. Sometimes, I remembered the smell of those mango trees in Jesi's favorite courtyard or recalled the whiff of the rushing fountain from the stunning Water Stairs flowing down the King's Gate.

Here, the stagnant, humid air of the mainland felt so thick it was as if we traveled through soup. Our clothing clung to our sweaty bodies. The straps of our bags chaffed and reddened our flesh. Painful blisters formed on our heels and toes.

Nightfall brought minimal relief. The sun no longer burned our scalps, but each day it seared the earth so hotly it was as if the forest still baked, even in the darkness. Kirwyn didn't swim in a Sea of Sorrows, but he spoke little, mostly when needing to assist as we climbed a few rocky hills and Aewna and I slipped, suffering bruises along the way. Kirwyn, a creature of the land, climbed as naturally as he rode.

Looking for a good place to camp on the second night

we pushed on after dark, but we came to an abrupt halt when the forest ahead suddenly disappeared.

Blinking to ensure I saw correctly, we stood before a large, wide circle in the middle of the wood. Unnaturally huge, it couldn't have been created by anything other than man. The eerie clearing made my skin prickle.

"Did a bomb make this?" I asked.

Kirwyn shook his head. "No. Look over there," he said, pointing.

I squinted in the darkness to see decaying, tiered stands of some kind on one side of the circle. Directly across from us, there also looked to be one smooth road leading into the clearing, but it was difficult to tell.

"It's a Reaper's Ring," Kirwyn explained, giving me chills. "Long ago they gathered people and murdered them here. Or made them murder each other. Spectators watched; it was a killing arena for sport. Tens of thousands, if not hundreds of thousands, lost their lives on this ground."

I shivered. Why was the mainland such a world of nightmares? No wonder so many fled to any island they could.

"If it was so long ago, why hasn't nature reclaimed this horror? There's hardly any new growth," I pointed out. "They must have salted the earth, but what kind of salt does this?"

"No salt. Nor any chemical I know," Kirwyn mused. "Maybe someone's maintaining it."

Surveying the ground with a shuddering breath, I imagined the land was cursed, poisoned by the deaths of so many innocents.

"Come on," Kirwyn said, grabbing my hand. "The forest

is too thick here. We'll make better time if we cross directly and take the road."

"Kirwyn, I don't like this. What if it's still in use?" I gulped. The night seemed unnaturally still and the lack of a breeze already had me sweating. "What if someone is waiting for people like us to pass by, to make us fight each other to the death?"

"It's not out of the question," he admitted, frowning, "but not likely here. We're barely beyond Biohazard lands, if not still in them. No one wants to mess with this territory."

Exhaling, I squeezed his hand and the three of us entered the enormous clearing. We'd made it maybe a third of the way into the ghastly circle when modern lights from the far side suddenly snapped on, making me jump. Aewna squealed and Kirwyn instinctively raised his arms in front of us both.

Squinting, I saw the lights were attached to modern vehicles of some kind, previously camouflaged in the shadows. From our distance they were muted, but up close those lights would be blinding. At least, to me. Kirwyn and Aewna never seemed sensitive to modern bulbs.

I fumbled for my gun, though we were no match for the advanced weaponry surely behind the vehicles. *Go down fighting* I resolved, as I gripped the handle of my weapon, stomach knotting. But I also pressed into Kirwyn as I had the terrible thought, *hold him close in case it's your last moment together.*

"Is it Spades?" I asked, voice quaking.

"I don't know," Kirwyn murmured, eyes glued to the vehicles. "I don't think so, but I'm not sure. Spades would have attacked already. Those look like APATs – alternatively powered armored tanks," he said slowly. "They were designed to run on a variety of fuel sources. They're small and compact for personal use and armored for protection. I haven't seen any this well-maintained in... ever." He took a deep breath. "I'll see who they are, what they want. Stay back."

"No!" I protested, gripping his sleeve.

"Yes. We can't outrun them and we can't outgun them. They might not be hostile but... if anything should happen to me, run."

Kirwyn looked at Aewna. "Get her out," he said, and she nodded.

My eyes flicked back and forth between the two of them. *Was he serious? Me?* Aewna was the one needing protection, not me.

"Kirwyn-"

He gave me his hard stare. "You're the one in the most danger."

I silently fumed at what seemed like a secret understanding between he and Aewna to put my life before hers.

We'll see about that.

Kirwyn leaned down and kissed me, eliciting a nervous whimper from my mouth.

"If you hear the smallest noise, if anything seems even the slightest bit off... run for the trees. You promised to listen to my decisions here. Swear it."

I licked my lips. They tasted salty from my sheen of sweat, already present due to the heat and now worse from fear. "I swear it."

I meant it, but only because temporarily saving myself might make it easier to save Kirwyn, should something go wrong.

Kirwyn turned his back to us and walked toward the lights. Aewna and I waited with pounding hearts as he crossed the huge, unnatural field. From his silhouette I could see he didn't hold his gun—obviously a wasted effort and trying not to begin with violence—but his hand tensed, hovering near the holster. Cautiously, he moved forward to meet the strangers, but no one exited the vehicles... as if they baited him to come closer. I didn't like it and couldn't understand why Kirwyn was so willing. The further he walked, the faster my pulse raced.

Oh god, please, I begged, as he was halfway across the clearing. I strained my ears, dreading what I might hear. The spirits of this haunted land seemed to gather in the darkness, rising -- ghastly cries from the dead, moans and wails for the loss of loved ones... even faint, cruel cheers from the audience.

Gunshots. What if they shot Kirwyn?

My stomach dropped when the first sure noise I heard came from *behind,* not in front. I cocked my head, a new fear gripping my heart as I slowly turned.

From the darkness at our backs, riders emerged, breaking the treeline and barreling into the clearing.

No...

My mouth fell as I recognized the same hunting party from the gorge.

Lazlian.

"Kirwyn!" I screamed, turning and breaking into a run with Aewna close behind me.

CHAPTER 23

Kirwyn whipped around, saw the riders, and sprinted toward me.

No!

He was too far across the field; he'd never make it. I nearly burst into tears as I ran. Wild, sloppy gunshots whizzed overhead as Kirwyn tried to shoot and run at the same time. The vehicles behind him suddenly roared to life and sped forward.

What was happening?

Aewna, struggling beside me, was losing ground as the riders gained it. In a desperate attempt at saving her, I bolted sideways, hoping they'd follow me.

"Kirwyn!" I cried into the night. From the corner of my eye, I saw the lights of an APAT head in his direction. *Why had they gone to him?* I heard the clattering of many hoofbeats close behind me and didn't know whether to be relieved that my ploy at diverting the riders worked, or terrified that I had absolutely no hope of outrunning them. Stumbling in darkness over uneven ground didn't help, nor did the sweeping beams of bright light, dizzying me. One horse sped in front of the rest, beating the earth closer and closer. Without turn-ing, I knew in my pounding heart it was Lazlian.

All around me, lights scattered the field as the tanks moved quickly in one direction, then another, attempting to avoid some of the riders who'd turned to push them back. For some reason, the vehicles didn't simply barrel down the horses, though Laz's men shot at their armored hulls. I wondered if any APATs were coming for me and I turned my head to check --

-- when a horse jumped in front of me, blocking my path. At such a speed in the darkness, I slammed into it.

No, no, no... how did he get ahead *of me?*

I looked up to see Lazlian with mad triumph in his eyes as he leaned into one stirrup. My knees turned to jelly at the same time he reached down and grabbed me around my waist.

Oh god, oh god.

"Kirwyn!" I screamed, punching Laz while he struggled to haul my flailing body up and over his horse with consid-erable effort. The harshness of his grip and scrape of my body against the saddle made me cry out in agony. I couldn't stop thrashing and screaming, though it did no good. Thrust face-down over the beast's back, blood rushed to my head and roared in my ears. The saddle's edge jut painfully into my hipbone and my arms and legs kicked at air.

"No!" I shouted, feeling Lazlian fumbling to remove the gun at my waist while I was helpless to reach around and stop him. Hysteria blinded me, making it hard to know how I maneuvered from being slung over the horse, to an upright position. Lazlian's rough yanking helped, only, I think, because the alternative of having me bent precariously over his horse made it too difficult for him to break into a faster run. I fought to hit him throughout, so when Lazlian pushed my leg astride, I was backwards, facing the keylord -- who crushed me to his chest.

"Lazlian."

I was only able to breathe a plea before it became too difficult to speak. He rode intentionally fast to evade the APATs and to make it impossible for me to escape. Straddling Lazlian's lap and jostling in the saddle, I was forced to cling to my abductor. Everything was a blur; both our speed and our frenzied struggles made it difficult to say much beyond his grunts and my cries. Lazlian's strong arm caged my waist like steel; furious fingers embedded painfully into my flesh. Pressed so hard against his chest, I couldn't meet his eyes. He faced forward while I faced our rear; my cheek against the side of his head. Ineffectually, my fists pummeled his back. Both of us sweated from the sweltering night and our exertions; I felt his hot skin against my own in the places where it met.

Where was Kirwyn? Where was Aewna? My heart pounded out the questions. *Were they safe or had they been captured?*

My mind warred -- half of me was terrified to the point of swooning, the other half disbelieved that it was all happening. Being on Lazlian's horse – *in Lazlian's lap --* was almost too surreal for my mind to grasp.

Fear won out and I felt the pull to give in, to go under. My head sank into Laz's shoulder. I hadn't realized my body slackened too, until I noticed Laz adjust his hold to keep me from falling. He released the punishing grip on my waist and his arm crossed higher on my back now, almost to my shoulder... part cage, part embrace. I knew from my weakening body that I was seconds away from slumping into unconsciousness.

You must not swoon, I warned myself, limp and dizzy as I jostled in his lap. *If you faint, you will lose any hope of escape. The last time you were unconscious, Lazlian mixed your blood... this time, who knows what he plans to do to you?*

One of the strange, tank-like vehicles looped around and chased us, gaining ground. The blinding lights jarred me to wakefulness and I focused on the beams to stay conscious. Straining to maintain speed with our combined, unbalanced weight, Laz's horse stumbled and the heart-stopping jolt helped wake me as well. Unfortunately, when my muscles re-tensed so did Lazlian's arm.

Fight back. But how? Should I yank Lazlian's hair, gouge his eyes? I needed to free my body of his iron grip without killing him or myself in the process. It was a long way to the ground. There were so many things I wanted to scream but I knew he'd ignore my cries... nor did I want to expend the energy when escape was the priority. Concentrating on the opposing goal, neither did Lazlian. The tense, furious silence made me feel like he saved his rage to explode later, and that frightened me more than if he was already shouting at me.

Lights bobbed as the vehicle behind us bounced over the rocky field, easily gaining ground against Lazlian's horse. But my heart skipped a beat as I realized the keylord headed back toward the thick forest... where it would be difficult for anyone to follow on wheels. Lazlian's guards flanked us at various distances, shooting fruitlessly at the tanks. Bullets bounced off their armored sides, the sounds echoing across the clearing.

I didn't know whether to be more or less frightened when an APAT paced alongside us. It was a hulking, metal machine, not like the smaller, nimble racers Kirwyn once explained resembled Old World motorcycles.

Once level, a hatch door on the vehicle's side opened, revealing...

...Kirwyn!

Lazlian yanked his horse so abruptly into another direction, I was again forced to clutch him. *Or would it be better to fall?* I glanced down, but it was like he knew my thoughts. Lazlian tightened the arm caging my waist, making it unlikely to pull free, even if I did want to chance a jump.

Which, I did not.

"Zaria!" Kirwyn shouted as the tank again caught up to us, faster than Lazlian could outmaneuver. This time, I reached out my hand and Kirwyn caught it. Gripping my left arm, he helped me gain leverage against Lazlian's hold while the vehicle continued speeding alongside our horse. I reached for Kirwyn with my other hand and he gave a firm pull, half-freeing my torso from Lazlian.

But a heart-stopping tug-of-war began.

Lazlian yanked back on my waist while Kirwyn clasped my arms and, depending on the bump we hit, my shoulders. Having hooked his leg within the tank for stability, he had the advantage of using both hands, while Lazlian was forced to use one to steer his horse. But Lazlian had the advantage of the bulk of my weight resting on his side. For Kirwyn to pull me across the divide and to shoulder my weight without the benefit of Lazlian loosening his grip meant Kirwyn would risk dropping me.

Splayed precariously between the horse and the vehicle, the ground moved at scary speeds beneath my helpless body. I heard Lazlian curse and realized that he was forced to ride straight and maintain speed. If he changed direction with half of my body now unbalanced in the air, I might fall. And if I hit the ground in that position, either his horse would trample me or the tank would run me over.

It was a terrible stalemate with my life in the balance. Sweating and crying, my heart beat furiously fast. We couldn't ride like this forever, one of the men would have to let me go to let me live... but whoever released me lost for good. If Kirwyn pulled me to safety and the APAT sped onto the wide trail, the horses wouldn't be able to keep up. But if Lazlian managed to detach me, he'd race off into the thickest part of the woods where the tanks couldn't follow.

And if someone didn't relent soon, we'd hit a bump, one of the men would lose their grip, and I'd fall to my doom. Or at least, to serious injury. Both men tugged and I involuntarily screamed again, watching the ground speed beneath my tear-soaked face.

Let me go, I thought, terrified. *Please, one of you has to let me go.*

With a sinking heart I realized it would be Kirwyn. He'd release me before he endangered my life. Lazlian wouldn't make that choice.

No... we'd come so far!

Something moved in the vehicle's interior and I glimpsed a dark-haired woman. Holding onto the edge of the open door like Kirwyn, she raised a gun and pointed it at the keylord's head.

"Let her go. Make a move toward your weapon and I'll shoot you," she yelled above the noisy engine.

For some reason, the keylord didn't seem to care.

"I'll shoot your leg or the horse out from under you," she augmented the threat.

That must have worked because I heard Lazlian curse. I met Kirwyn's eyes with rising hope and elation.

Ready? We both seemed to ask and *ready,* we both seemed to answer.

Lazlian's grip on me tightened in fury --

-- before he hissed and loosened his hold.

Feeling the slack, Kirwyn immediately bolstered my weight and his strong arms lifted me on a stomach-sinking pull across the open air and into the safety of the vehicle's hull. We fell onto the floor, clutching one another.

"I've got you, I've got you," Kirwyn promised, kissing my head, arms clamped around me as he tried to soothe my shaking.

The dark-haired woman clung to the door, keeping her gun trained on Lazlian, who roared.

Still keeping pace, Lazlian shouted with the rage of defeat, "She belongs to the Dorestes! Harbor her and we'll declare you our enemy!"

I scrambled to my knees to look at him, finally taking in his appearance. The keylord was clothed as I'd last seen him across the gorge, in black boots and riding leathers of some kind. But his hair was more disheveled and longer than it had been in Rythas and he'd grown a very short beard. Even safely inside the tank, my heart pounded in fright at the sight of him.

Losing ground as the APAT picked up speed, he swore, "I'm going to fucking kill you!"

I assumed he meant Kirwyn... but I wasn't sure if he meant me too. His eyes never left mine, chest heaving as he rode. Trembling on my knees, I stared back, ignoring the wind whipping my hair about my face as our vehicle raced away.

Oh god, how close I'd come to capture. I was literally in his hands. *What would Lazlian have done to me?* I wondered, cold water filling my gut. *Hurt me until he broke me? Until I returned to his brother meek and willing, an empty shell to fill with whatever they chose?*

The distance between us widened and Lazlian eventually reined his horse to a halt, howling and cursing. I didn't see my sister anywhere.

"Aewna!" I screamed. "Where's Aewna?"

"She's in the other APAT, safe," Kirwyn said. "They got her too."

"*Who?* Who has her? Who has *us?*"

"Mal-Yin has been looking for you," the dark-haired woman announced, holstering her weapon and closing the vehicle's door with a slam.

Mal? I was suddenly alert with hope once more. *Were these Mal's people?*

"It took you long enough to find your gun," Kirwyn said pointedly. "Funny how you didn't help until the last second. She could have fallen to her death."

"But she didn't," the woman replied.

"And why didn't you show yourselves sooner? Why make us cross the clearing like some sort of game?" Kirwyn demanded.

"You look as if you'd hit me, were I a man," the woman drawled, a smile playing at her lips.

Kirwyn refused to confirm or deny her comment. "Was this all a game to you?" he repeated.

The woman paused, debating whether to reply. "Assessments," she corrected. "Mal likes to call them assessments."

"I'm assuming we passed, since you rescued us," I said through gritted teeth, breathless but annoyed.

"It's not pass or fail," she answered vaguely. "It's more about seeing what's inside you."

Of course. I remember Mal-Yin's strange manner of conversing with me at the Fae Fête. As if he toyed with me.

"You would have had a *literal* peek inside her if she'd fallen and been trampled," Kirwyn yelled, pointing at me. "And if that had happened, I promise I'd have gotten the same peek inside *you* in return," he declared. "Slowly."

The woman sat on a low bench and lazily propped up her feet. She cocked a half-smirk at Kirwyn.

"Oh, Mal's gonna like you, I can tell."

Part III
The Devil Will See You Now

CHAPTER 24

Bumping along as we sat a bench inside the vehicle, Kirwyn confessed, "I considered the possibility that the APATs belonged to Mal, but I didn't want to get your hopes up. His territory edges the Biohazards, but I wasn't sure how close."

I folded my arms and shot him a look, but I lacked the energy to scold him. He wasn't outright *lying,* but he was bending the rules again in his typical manner to shield me from something as simple as getting my hopes dashed. I was equal parts annoyed and soothed because I had to admit, his actions always did make me feel safe, especially with Lazlian and the Biohazards behind us and the unknown of Mal's compound before us.

As we rode, nervous little fish darted around my stomach and I leaned against Kirwyn, his arm protectively slung over my shoulders. Would Mal's compound be crowded? Would his clanspeople get too close, eager to meet me?

"Don't let anyone touch me," I whispered.

He kissed my temple. "Never without your permission."

We couldn't have driven for more than thirty minutes before we arrived at our destination. The vehicle came to an abrupt stop, nearly throwing us forward. A moment later, the hatch door opened.

We made it, my mind screamed. *Thank Keroe, we are safe.*

Kirwyn helped me jump from the vehicle's hull and we quickly found Aewna, exiting the other APAT. None of us had seen Mal's compound before, not even in books. It seemed to stretch as wide as High Spire, but it wasn't nearly as tall. Also, where firelight illuminated the towers of High Spire, here modern lights glowed. Like Volmar's estate, men and women patrolled both the rooftops and the grounds below with large, intimidating guns.

Seeing our stare, the dark-haired woman explained, "For safety, we've built more under the ground, than above. But you'll find the compound expansive and there are plenty of inner courtyards for fresh air. We've even got vegetable farms and orchards within."

I didn't know how I felt about rooms underground, but it sounded large enough not to make me too uneasy.

"You'll enter there," the woman said, pointing to a large, central doorway.

"You're not coming with?" Kirwyn asked, suspicious.

Her only reply was to smile and turn on her heel.

"Games," Kirwyn muttered as she departed.

"Assessments," I corrected.

"I don't see a difference," he scoffed.

Turning to Aewna, I asked, "Are you alright?"

"If I'm honest," she said, smoothing her wig, "I'd rather be taken by Rythas than willingly walk into Mal-Yin's stronghold. If it were just me in question."

"He's not that bad, I promise," I told her. "A lot of what he does seems a game to confuse us. Underneath it all, he's-"

"Evil," Aewna cut me off, frowning.

I sighed. "I don't think so. But there's only one way to find out."

She nodded and the three of us walked into Mal's entry hall cautiously, without any guard or guide. Before the door slammed shut behind us, I gasped at a horror I could never have conceived without seeing. Beneath us, the floor was made of some kind of plastic. It was like a clear, solid sea.

And floating within this encasement were dead bodies.

Several dozens, if not hundreds. Some clothed, some naked. Spared the ravages of rot by whatever encased them.

"I told you he's the devil," Kirwyn bit out.

"Why?" I breathed, covering my mouth, unable to comprehend.

"My guess is it's a deterrent and an intimidation," he whispered. *"Don't cross me or see what happens."*

"You don't think... they were alive when he did this, do you?"

Kirwyn shrugged.

Instantly, I began to doubt all my plans. Jesi had alluded to Mal doing bad things... but I couldn't reconcile the horrors I saw before me with the playful man I'd met in Rythas. Which version was real? How many other sides did he have? *Could he do this to us?*

As we crossed the macabre entryway, my gut riled like slippery eels twisted within. By design likely, stepping over the dead was unavoidable, though I respectfully tried.

Were we wrong to come here?

Even if there'd been mercy in their deaths, being eternally encased like this was unimaginable to me – a fate *worse* than a land-burial. At least the earth held water far underground. At least a body would decompose, and parts might someday be absorbed into the soil and swept away. But *this*. Such a horror had a different meaning to an Elowan. A spirit would never find rest in this plastic hell.

Dizziness swept over me as we crossed the massive room. The ceiling rose tall, but the floor pressed too close. I longed to grow wings and fly over the bodies.

"It's just another test, Zaria," Kirwyn whispered as I wobbled, grabbing my elbow to steady me. "I bet he's watching us to see how we react."

I gritted my teeth and narrowed my eyes at the opposite door, not too far now. *I'm always being tested and I hate it.* Glancing beside me, I was relieved to see that Aewna looked pale but carried on with relaxed, steady breathing.

Wait, no... Aewna's breathing wasn't steady so much as... measured. She was struggling to remain calm, just as she'd done with the ticks. Her shoulders were back and her back was straight, but her chin dipped.

"Aewna? Are you okay?"

She could only blink her confirmation, so it didn't carry much weight. Her nostrils flared with a sudden, deep breath, as if she struggled to find air.

Nearing the exit, Mal-Yin appeared, standing beneath the arched doorway. He was just as I remembered him, although he wore all-black mainland clothing now – a shirt with buttons and slim trousers. We were only a few feet apart when everyone paused, tense. Mal's gaze swept over Kirwyn and I before lingering on Aewna. He gave a slight cock of his head before rushing forward.

Mal had just enough time to catch Aewna as she collapsed into a faint.

"Aewna!" I gasped, hurrying over.

Crouching with Aewna's limp torso draped over his knees, Mal-Yin looked up. One side of his mouth curled into a grin.

"That's a first," he said dryly. "I've made girls swoon in the past, but never with our clothes still *on*."

CHAPTER 25

"Ugh," I scowled, crouching beside Mal and ignoring him to press my hand against Aewna's forehead. "Is she alright?"

It was a rhetorical, knee-jerk question. I didn't mean for Mal to answer it.

"If anything is wrong with her, she's in the best place possible for care."

Considering the horror to my back, I shot Mal a look of disgust.

"I'll take her," I said. The last thing I wanted was for Aewna to wake up in Mal-Yin's arms. Luckily, Kirwyn was already beside me, lifting my sister. I could tell he'd meant to carry her, but she blinked her eyes open in the transfer.

"Oh," she gasped. "I'm sorry."

"Are you okay to stand?" Kirwyn asked.

She nodded vigorously, seemingly coherent and eager to re-establish her usual state of self-possession. I guessed we had fainting in common, but when I woke, I was annoyed and only wanted to be brought up to speed, *immediately.*

On her feet, Aewna looked at Mal with slightly wide eyes while he regarded her curiously. Then Aewna's face became a mask of haughtiness I recognized as one of my own.

"I ask that you forgive my discourtesy," she said, speaking even more carefully and formally than usual. Tilting her head to indicate the macabre scene at our backs, she added, "However, we cannot forgive yours."

Mal-Yin's lips did not smile, but somehow, his eyes did.

"Fair enough," he said, extending his hand to escort Aewna out of the chamber of horrors. Back rigid, she did not accept it.

"Queen Zaria," Mal drawled as we walked. "I've been expecting you."

"Yes, they said you were looking for us. It's a shame you didn't find us sooner." My voice was laced with subtle accusation. The continued testing hadn't put me in a friendly mood, though I was mindful of how badly we needed his help.

"I didn't know you had... company," Mal-Yin replied, as we walked through downward-sloping corridors. "But you couldn't expect me to pluck you out of a territory where the Dorestes would receive word that I'd done it. I had to wait until you were closer to my region."

You mean you wanted to see if we made it. Another test.

"So you knew we were coming all along?" I gritted my teeth, remembering all the danger we faced in the backlands. "But you never sent help to find us? Escort us?"

Mal-Yin shrugged. "If word got out that I assisted you and we didn't come to an agreement, how would it look?" He sighed, "Now, we've lost that advantage."

"What do you mean?" I asked.

"Prince Lazlian is well aware who stole you from his grasp tonight. He'll know you've been brought here."

Kirwyn threw back his head, cursing under his breath. "That's why he knew your soldier wouldn't shoot him," he said. "She had to threaten to shoot his horse out from under him. *Shit.* He knows we're here."

Oh no. I'd thought his declaration about making an enemy of Rythas was just a vague threat to an unknown adversary. My heart sank. Whatever we did going forward, we'd lost the element of surprise. But whose side was Mal on?

"Will you give us asylum?" I asked. "Or will you send me back? Will you protect us if Rythas attacks-"

Mal held up his hands. "Let's take it one step at a time. You all look like you need some rest, and you certainly could use a bath." He looked toward the end of the hall. "But first..."

Two dogs moved forward. Their slow stalking made them more intimidating than if they'd rushed to attack. I was sure they were part Dobermann, but I didn't know what they'd been mixed with -- Great Dane and maybe a little German Shepherd.

Sensing our nervousness, Mal said, "They just want to smell you. They're here to protect me."

"What are they looking for?" Kirwyn asked as the canines approached. We stood still while each dog ran his wet nose up and down our legs. I thought Aewna might be frightened but when I glanced at her face, she looked annoyed or insulted. I couldn't figure out what she was thinking.

"Bruel can sniff explosives and other chemical compounds," Mal explained. "Terisine can sniff... intent."

"What's that supposed to mean?" Kirwyn asked. Both

dogs sat on their haunches, cocking their heads at Mal in a silent communication I couldn't discern.

"He can scent if you're hostile. I like to say he can catch a whiff of any dislike for me."

More assessments.

"And?" I asked, slightly exasperated. "Do we dislike you?"

"Yes," Mal smiled. "But I hold that decision in your favor. It's wise, after all."

I fought not to roll my eyes. "You think very highly of yourself, don't you?"

"The Beloved Queen of Rythas is begging for help at my door," Mal replied, grinning. "Should I affect false humility?"

"Do you even know how?" I asked rhetorically, then pressed again, "Please, just answer the question. Will you give us sanctuary or not?"

Mal's eyes flicked to Aewna. "For now."

Kirwyn and I were shown to one room and Aewna, another. The sleek style was nothing like I'd seen in Rythas or my aunt and uncle's estate. Even Volmar's office wasn't this glossy. The furnishings and accents were dark or metallic and the walls were a deep gray with onyx trim. Yet a glittering chandelier and lush bedding gave it a luxurious feel. A carafe of water with matching glasses waited on a bedside table.

Attached to the bedroom was a modern bathing chamber. Interestingly, the floor was made of polished stones and muted light shone behind wall panels, giving it the feel of being outdoors, even though we had no window access.

The tub, ready for guests, was stocked with an array of washing products.

Catching Lazlian's scent on my clothes brought a wave of unwelcome memories -- his hot skin pressed to mine, his controlling fingers digging into my waist. I began stripping too quickly and winced when I felt immediate pain.

"Let me help," Kirwyn said. Slowly, he peeled off my shirt and pants, running his eyes up and down my bare skin. "You're bruised," he said. "Quite a bit."

"I know," I whispered. And we both knew that most of it came from Lazlian hauling me onto his horse and struggling to keep me there. Kirwyn reached for my bra with a question in his eyes and I nodded for him to proceed. When he'd removed my underwear as well, he circled me and kneeled to survey my waist.

"Is it bad?" I asked, too afraid to look.

"Miraculously, after everything, you're not cut or bleeding anywhere. But these bruises are going to take a while to heal," he said gently.

"Ouch!" I jumped when his fingers merely ghosted the area above my hip.

"I'll run a cool bath," he announced, standing. His jaw clenched and I knew what he was thinking. *Revenge.* But Kirwyn surprised me when he returned.

"I'm sorry," he whispered, resuming his examination with a frown. I noticed he'd indicated the skin on my arm where he'd gripped me, back in the APAT. It was ringed with purple bruises in the shape of his fingers.

I shook my head and stroked his face. "Don't ever apologize for saving me."

He placed a soft kiss on my sore arm, guilt still clouding his eyes.

"Better already," I whispered, forcing a small smile.

I wish I could kiss you somewhere inside, I thought. *To help heal the pain of losing Theo. The pain I know you're holding back.*

As water filled the tub, I summoned the courage to look into the modern gazing glass -- and sucked in a breath.

It wasn't just Lazlian, though I suspected his marks would grow to be some of the worst. Mottled black, purple, and yellow bruises—acquired at various stages over the last two days—dotted my hips, waist, and neck. My sides and arms where Kirwyn grabbed me were starting to color too. I stared with macabre fascination at my bruise-covered skin. Everywhere hurt -- and it looked like it.

"You're hurt, too," I said, lightly running my fingers over the back of Kirwyn's neck where I could see the top of a bruise. "Come in the bath with me."

"I'll shower later," he said, shaking his head. He always liked the pounding sensation of water against his skin. I'd found it delightful at first – like a waterfall. But after the novelty wore off, I preferred going back to languid, luxurious baths over utilitarian showers.

I took Kirwyn's hand and stepped into the tepid water, wincing as I lowered myself. When I reached for the soap, he swatted my hands away and proceeded to wash my hair himself.

"You always take care of me," I whispered, though he'd never actually bathed me before. Something about the moment felt reverent, making me use hushed tones. With my skin so sensitive, Kirwyn used his hands instead of a washcloth or a sea sponge. Not that Mal's compound likely had any sponges. Closing my eyes, I sighed into the safety of Kirwyn's gentle hands.

By the time we finished, the tub water was so dirty I wondered if I should re-fill it and bathe again, but I couldn't muster the energy. In a chest of drawers, Kirwyn and I found basic black sleepwear – loose tops and bottoms – in a variety of sizes. I put on one set and climbed into bed to wait for him to finish showering.

Despite my exhaustion, thoughts of Theo kept me awake. I refused to cry, refused to have Kirwyn comfort *me*. But the guilt was unbearable.

When he joined me in bed it was as if a dam broke and I whimpered, "I'm sorry, Kirwyn. This is all my fault. You lost everything because of me. You're not saying anything, so I don't know how you feel. If you hate me, if you want to end this mad journey and leave me, I'll understand."

The change in Kirwyn was sudden and fierce. "It is *not* your fault Theo died, get that out of your head right now, do you hear me? And I am never leaving you. Do you understand?"

I bit my lip as hard as I could stand to hold back tears. "You have no family now. I took that from you."

"*You* are my family," Kirwyn insisted, cupping my face. "And I am yours."

With a terribly aching heart, I searched Kirwyn's face for clues about what he needed. Saying anything more made it about me and I didn't want to do that. I just wanted him to know how sorry I was.

"This is going to sound..." he began, "I don't know, conceited or something. But my uncle wanted nothing more than to protect me. I know he did everything he could when they died, but he always felt like he failed my parents, in the end. He dedicated his life to *me*, to trying to fix that. But it was never enough. When he thought he'd failed me too, unsure whether I was lost at sea... I can't imagine what that did to him."

"I know this sounds strange but giving his life to save

me is what my uncle would have wanted, if he had any choice in how to die." Kirwyn stroked my hair, locking his deep green eyes on mine. "I know because he raised me, he is my blood, and it's how I feel about you. I'm *never* leaving you. I will have a life with you, or I will die for you. Those are the only options."

I felt like his words reached through my ribcage and gently stroked my heart. I couldn't stop the tears from falling as I nuzzled my face into his hand.

"I've never had family that loyal, devotion that fierce," I whispered. Inside, I felt as if I'd been built to *give* such unwavering love, but I had never received it. Until Kirwyn.

"But there is only one option," I vowed, shaking my head. "Have a life with me forever. Because if you died for me, I would die too."

CHAPTER 26

The next day, a strange mixture of tension and sorrow permeated the air as the three of us held a memorial service for Theo in one of Mal's gardens, while also preparing to dine with Mal to discuss our plans.

"We can make a land grave for him in Elowa, if you like," I promised Kirwyn, clasping his hand in the sunny courtyard. "Near our home. So that you have somewhere to visit. Unless you prefer a ritual at sea?"

Kirwyn shook his head. "The mainland was his home. Here is where he'll rest, where I'd like to keep him in my mind." Struggling to find the right words, he shrugged, "Or... somewhere... with my parents."

I returned to our room in the sleek, sprawling compound, but Kirwyn stayed alone in the gardens for the rest of the day, saying his goodbye to his uncle... the only father he'd ever known. A part of me felt relieved to be safe and clean after all our time in the backlands, but it warred with guilt at allowing space for anything but grief. Whenever these two emotions exhausted themselves in battle, nerves took over and I rehearsed what to say to Mal.

A knock on our door that evening brought fresh, formal attire from our host. Kirwyn was given a dark gray shirt and even darker pants, and I was provided an airy, light-gray dress, skirting my knees. We met Aewna, whose room was just down the hall from our own, to find she'd been given a similar dress in blush pink. I'd left my hair loose, though it only grazed just past my shoulders. Aewna still wore her mottled, olive-and-brown wig. Out of habit, I supposed.

"Are you okay?" I asked Kirwyn.

He gave a curt nod and squeezed my hand. I was sure his thoughts swarmed, but his clenched jaw told me he was resolved to focus on our task ahead.

Mal's dining hall was as dark and luxuriously appointed as the rest of his stronghold. A huge fireplace lined one wall, and three crystal chandeliers hung above a long table. Mal stood, formally awaiting us. He presented a more reserved version of himself in his own home than the mischievous man I'd met at the Fae Fête, but sometimes that playfulness came through too. I still didn't know what was real behind his chameleon-like persona.

When we arrived, he took the head of the table and Aewna and I sat on either side, with Kirwyn to my left. Dishes were served as they were ready, without set courses, and Mal wasted no time in asking questions.

"Queen Zaria," he drawled, "what is your plan and what role do you see me having in it?"

I swallowed and straightened my spine. Replacing my wine on the table, I tried to meet his directness with my own. "We want to capture High Spire and pressure King Juls to change the laws. Our demands will be that he throw away the custom of taking the Daughter of Elowa for a bride and for Rythas to free Elowa from ignorance by opening her up to the world beyond."

A beat and then, "You want my soldiers to take the castle for you?"

"Yes—but no. I don't want violence. I don't want anyone to die."

Mal's eyebrows rose. "You want to take the castle without bloodshed?" he asked, disbelieving. "It can't be done. You're wasting my time. It's madness."

Kirwyn made a sound in the back of his throat, grinning at Mal. "That's what I've been telling her. But she won't listen."

"Make her," Mal declared.

Kirwyn barked a laugh, leaning on the table and spreading his hand in offering. "You try."

"I'm not the one who has her in his sway," Mal said, pointedly.

I held back a groan and cleared my throat to interrupt. *As if Kirwyn needs his ego further stroked.*

"I believe High Spire can fall under our control another way. And I would know, I'm the one who's lived there."

"Go on," Mal bade.

I paused, taking a stalling breath. *Here goes nothing.* Once I revealed my plan, we were screwed if Mal didn't agree to help us. His eyes gleamed just like Kirwyn's did when Kirwyn knew he was about to win a game in the next few moves. In fact, I noticed that while Mal and Kirwyn did not have similar faces in general, something about their high cheekbones and keen eyes echoed one another. I chewed my lip a moment longer. With the information I was about to give, Mal could betray us to the Dorestes. But without it, we had no hope of proceeding.

"There are three gates into the castle," I began, recapping information he already knew. "The Garden Gate, the Bone Gate, and the King's Gate. The Garden Gate is the most commonly used. The King's Gate sits high upon the Water Stairs, and the Bone Gate abuts the rocky shore."

In my mind I went back to the day Jesi showed me the inner workings of the gates in an attempt to find escape from High Spire.

It never came in much use for getting out. Ironic that I'd now apply it to get *in*.

Mal listened patiently as I continued. "Your men could easily storm these gates if they were constructed according to the Treaty of Red Ridge, but they've been illegally reinforced with stolen technology. Guards would pick off your soldiers before you broke in and you'd be forced to blast through... lives would be lost."

"But there is a fourth way into the castle." I paused, holding Mal's eyes. He probably knew this as well, but not how I planned on using it. "The Black Passage. It was how my escorts wanted to bring me the night I was taken from Elowa." I suppressed a shudder at the memory and took a sip of water before continuing.

"Unfortunately, the passage floods at high tide. Fortunately, it's not heavily guarded at that time. There are but two palace sentries who pay very little mind when it's seemingly impassable. At least, by boat."

I noted I had Mal's rapt attention and couldn't help but smile. I glanced at Kirwyn who looked back at me with a pride in his eyes, giving a reassuring squeeze to my leg under the table.

"Now, your ship wouldn't be able to get near the passage without causing suspicion within the castle. *But,* if a boat stayed back far enough-" I grinned wider, "-if a person could swim that distance... she could make it across the sea and through the Black Passage at high tide. She could sneak into High Spire." My chest swelled with hope. "The only problem is she'd just need scuba equipment to do it. You know, those air tanks where a person can breathe underwater."

Mal moved very little throughout my speech, except to stroke his chin.

"Which I can obtain," he said. "It's not too difficult, you could have as well. What else?"

"That would be part one of our plan," Kirwyn said.

"And what's part two?"

"Zaria and I," Kirwyn began, and I immediately shot him a look.

I'm not letting you risk your life. The Dorestes are too dangerous.

He sighed. "Whoever swims through the passage will need to neutralize both guards and move on quickly. There's an elevated section behind each gate, housing the equipment responsible for reinforcing them. According to Zaria's information, they're connected through a series of halls or rafters," Kirwyn tried to explain, without the benefit of having seen it himself. "We can take out the modern consoles strengthening the gates by exploding them. The only issue with this part is that we need a more silent type of grenade to do it."

Mal thought a moment. "Not a grenade. An e-bomb."

My heart leapt. "What's that?"

"A small device that wipes out the electronic power of anything in its vicinity. You would simply attach it to the console and activate it. The pulse would disable the technology bolstering the gates. But if we're storming the Garden Gate, they already know we're there. So why does it need to be silent?"

"That's where stealth and the rest of your army comes in," I said, my heart beating faster just discussing it. "Which is what we need most. Our plan is to position soldiers at the Garden Gate waiting for us to disable it. But we need it to look like a fluke or as if it's been battered down naturally," I explained. "We want to make a show of it, of not hiding the attack there. It would be part diversion. Even if Rythas had any suspicions that the gate fell from someone inside sabotaging the modern locking system, once it's open, Juls and Navere will send all their men to defend it. They'll have no choice in the ensuing chaos."

I took a deep breath and felt a surge of nerves and excitement. "Meanwhile, I will run through the halls to the console above the Bone Gate and repeat the process. Below, we'll have hidden a second party of soldiers. Once the Bone Gate's been disarmed as well, your men will flood the castle." Holding Mal's dark brown eyes, I continued, "We don't want to kill any Rythasian soldiers. With only one gate open, the army of High Spire will do their best to overwhelm an attack funneling through the doors and our fight will need to turn bloody to succeed. Breeched from both sides, however, Juls will be engulfed and will have no choice but to surrender."

Mal remained quiet for many long, tense seconds. "And how do my men remain unharmed in this chaos?"

"Protective gear. Bulletproof vests, helmets, shields," Kirwyn said. "You've got the equipment to withstand the weaponry of Rythas."

"You want me to play defense?" Mal asked. "To bring my army to the gates and then take a beating?"

"Only until Zaria explodes the Bone Gate," Kirwyn pointed out.

"Have any of you ever been through a battle?" Mal asked, eyeing us haughtily.

"I have," I said. "I fought with Rythas."

"Then you know there's no way to control the turmoil once it's unleashed. There will be injuries."

"The way I hear it," Kirwyn said, "no one keeps a tighter leash on his clansmen than you." Mal said nothing but his eyes gleamed. "So *control* them," Kirwyn concluded.

"My army is disciplined," Mal boasted. "But even if they obey orders not to kill, parties on both sides *will* sustain injuries in the struggle. It's unavoidable."

"All we're asking is that you don't run in, guns blazing. That your aim is to disarm and capture. Some might get hurt, yes, we understand. We just want to eliminate casualties. It behooves us. We believe that if we keep the fight contained to High Spire, to who controls the castle and tweaks the laws, that the people of Rythas won't be too affected by or overly invested in the outcome. The nobles won't be happy, and the Dorestes will..." *despise me,* I thought, "the Dorestes will be angry. But if the people of Rythas don't lose loved ones in the fighting or see their daily lives change very much as a result of our demands with Elowa, peace will be maintained."

Everyone fell silent and my heart pounded. Servants appeared to remove our plates. Pensive, Mal-Yin leaned back in his chair and lit an herbal-smelling cigarette of some kind. More servants entered carrying dessert – pink, rectangular cakes sprinkled with coconut, like pictures I'd seen of falling snow. I didn't know what they were, but they looked delicious.

Aewna had quietly observed our conversation, but unlike most occasions, she was neither as reserved nor as charming as I knew she could be. Displeasure turned down the corners of her mouth. I chalked it up to not wanting Mal's involvement in our plans.

When the servants departed, Mal slowly rose from his chair and, surprising us all, walked over to Aewna. He invaded her personal space and flouted mealtime manners by boldly leaning back on the table, just to the left of her plate. I wondered if he was intentionally provoking her, as he'd done with me at the Fae Fête, but something was different that I couldn't put my finger on.

"I don't like the smell of Verdnal smoke," Aewna stated, clearly perturbed and referencing some kind of herb or tobacco I'd never heard of.

"I don't like people who make indirect remarks instead of stating exactly what they want," Mal replied smoothly.

"Oh? Mirrors can be uncomfortable, no?"

A palpable tension permeated the air. *What was happening?*

"Not at all. I simply think, between you and I, we don't need to hide our true desires behind the games of society."

I nearly choked on my wine at the oddly provocative-sounding remark. *Was this another quip to assess, like those he made to me at the Fae Fête? Since when did Mal have any information about Aewna to make that kind of remark?*

"You don't know anything about me," she dismissed, echoing my thoughts.

"Let's start with this." We watched in bewildered silence as Mal made a gesture toward Aewna's wig. I wasn't sure what he meant when he asked, "May I?"

"You may not," Aewna replied, tightly.

Did he want her to take it off? Kirwyn and I exchanged a look of confusion and I caught the side of Mal's smile.

"Indulge me, please. As you're here asking that I indulge you," he said pointedly.

Aewna and I both narrowed our eyes at Mal's thinly veiled threat to halt our negotiations. Aewna's eyes practically burned with the hottest blue flame of hate as she gave one tight nod, jaw clenched.

What the fuck was happening? This was the smooth, taunting man I remembered from Rythas. I felt like I witnessed something illicit as Mal reached up and unburdened Aewna of her wig. He took the liberty of removing her pins and running his fingers through her unbound hair, an intimacy she suffered with wide-eyed, pink-faced displeasure.

"Stunning," Mal smirked, studying her flowing locks.

"I'm not feeling well," Aewna announced, placing her napkin on the table. "I'm going to lay down. Please excuse me. It came upon me with *stunning* suddenness."

She pushed her chair back and left the table from the side Mal wasn't blocking. He didn't move his head but watched her with his eyes as she left the hall.

What the fuck just happened?

I had no time to ponder because Mal shifted direction. Once again with *stunning suddenness.* He retook his chair, placed his napkin back on his lap, and turned to Kirwyn and me to immediately launch back into business.

"Let me recap," Mal began, while my head spun. "You want me to go to war against Rythas, a country my clan has been trading with peacefully since before I was born, to save one girl every generation?"

I shifted in my chair. "And to free Elowa."

"You know what I'm going to ask," he stated, dangerous eyes on me. "What are you planning to offer in return for my help?"

I pushed back my shoulders. *This is stupid. But it's all I've got.*

"Rythas is in possession of a data cube. I've seen it. They don't have the means to read it, but I know you do. It contains information on Spade defenses." *Might contain,* I didn't amend. "If we capture the castle, you can take it."

"I have dozens of silver cubes," Mal dismissed.

I blinked, cocking my head. "This one is a yellowish gold. Do you have gold ones?"

Mal became very still and he couldn't hide the flash in his eyes. My heart fluttered with hope. "No. I do not."

"It's yours, if we win," I vowed, even as I wondered, *what's on it?*

"It's not enough."

Kirwyn and I exchanged a look. "If Elowa is free you can trade with her directly, instead of filtering her goods through Rythas," Kirwyn said, an idea he'd come up with on one of our discussions about Elowa's future. "We can arrange that. It will be profitable enough to mitigate some of your losses from Rythas, should business relations sour."

"Good, not enough," Mal replied. The amused tilt to his mouth returned and I didn't like feeling that he was playing with us.

"Look," I said, growing impatient. "I know you want something. So why don't you just tell me what it is and I'll give it to you?" I licked my lips. "And if it's not something I have now, I'll get it." I jut my chin.

Kirwyn drummed his fingers on the tabletop. "I wouldn't underestimate what she's capable of," he advised, with a hint of a teasing tone.

Mal gave Kirwyn a smile. "No," he said. "I won't make that mistake twice."

Was that an actual compliment?

"What happens if you succeed? What role will you play?" Mal asked.

"Zaria and I will return to Elowa," Kirwyn explained. "We'll rule there until Jona comes of age and we'll help usher in a new era for the people."

"Braenese Aewna does not want to make a claim on the throne?" Mal asked, not hiding his curiosity. "She has royal lineage."

"She was never directly in line for it," I replied, brows knit. "And we think she might prefer to live in Rythas." I toyed with the stem of my wineglass. "We think she might like... the king."

Mal cocked his head and I explained, "Juls and Aewna are very much alike, inside. But outside, she and I share similar looks. She's an excellent replacement for me and she'd make a good queen. It could be a solution where everyone is happy."

"Let me think over what you've told me," Mal announced, now drumming his fingertips on the tabletop, much like Kirwyn. "We'll dine again tomorrow night." Mal stood, preoccupied as he eyed the door. Kirwyn and I started to rise, but Mal waved us to sit. "Stay, enjoy dessert. I've got business... the compound is yours, roam anywhere you like. You'll have my counteroffer tomorrow."

I inhaled, chest swelling with hope. He'd said *counteroffer*, not *decision*. Kirwyn and I shared a smile this time.

"Wait," Kirwyn said, standing to block Mal. "There's the matter of Aewna's father. We need to neutralize him, as well as Zaria's mother, before we make any moves." He ran a frustrated hand down his face. "It's... another matter entirely. We can discuss it tomorrow. But we need to move fast, and we'll need your help."

Mal nodded, leaving Kirwyn and me to what turned out to be raspberry cakes. It felt odd to sit alone and eat, but ruder to leave it unfinished. Mostly because of Mal's command, but also, Kirwyn and I weren't accustomed to leaving food uneaten if we could avoid it.

"What was *that?*" I whispered between bites, nodding my head toward Aewna's empty chair.

Kirwyn shrugged. "Maybe he thinks she's our weak link. He seems to want to rankle her, but... my money's on him having taken a liking to her."

I dropped my fork, wide-eyed. "Good thing she hasn't taken one to him."

At Kirwyn's sheepish look, I demanded, *"What?"*

He shrugged. "Well, I might have... developed a better opinion of Mal."

Eyebrows raised, I asked, "Are you serious? All this time I've been telling you he's not that bad and all this time you've been fighting me. I only needed to let you have one conversation with him and you'd change your mind?" My voice was louder than before and I realized the wine had warmed my blood, making me a little giddy. Mal did have the good stuff.

Kirwyn raised his hands in surrender. "He knows what he's talking about. And I don't believe half the image he presents is real. I think he likes playing the devil."

At my look of impatience, Kirwyn laughed and added, "You were right. I'm sorry."

"Prove it," I challenged.

"Oh, I'll prove it," Kirwyn teased, tilting his head with a predatory threat. Maybe the wine had hit him, too. Maybe we were both relieved to be over the tough part. I jumped from my chair and backed away, grinning.

"What are you doing?" I laughed.

"I'll prove it..." he repeated, stalking toward me.

"What are you doing?" I shrieked, but it was too late. I tried to wrestle him to the ground, but within seconds

Kirwyn picked me up and thew me over his shoulder. Making me blush, clansmen returned to clear the table as he carried me out of the hall and back to our room.

I couldn't say Kirwyn proved anything about being sorry, but he certainly proved he knew how to make me forget about... everything. Everything but the feel of his confident mouth exploring the most sensitive places on my body and the delicious surrender of coming apart in his arms.

CHAPTER 27

Kirwyn, Aewna, and I anxiously awaited our dinner the next evening, barely able to eat or concentrate on much beyond walking aimlessly through Mal's inner-farms. I worried that Lazlian would attack at any moment, but Kirwyn spoke to Mal who promised us the keylord would not make a move he was sure to lose. Mal speculated that the prince had sailed back to Rythas to plot with Juls.

I hoped it was true, because I felt a lot safer not worrying that Lazlian paced outside the walls, waiting to grab me. On the other hand, a Lazlian with time to scheme alongside Juls and Navere was an alarming thought.

When dusk fell, we once again dressed in new clothing and met Mal in his luxurious dining hall. The evening prior Mal seemed curious, but now a sense of anticipation hummed beneath his surface. As soon as the servants departed, Mal replaced his wine on the table and announced bluntly, "I have two demands if I'm to help you."

My heart leapt and I stilled, waiting.

"The first is a long-term goal, but I want to work toward a transfer of power after we succeed."

No. My heart sank.

In the stunned silence, I gasped, "You... want to be king?"

"No," Aewna declared in a clipped voice before anyone could speak. I whipped my head in her direction, surprised she'd spoken up. "If he wanted to be king, he would have done it already."

Facing Aewna, Mal's eyes flashed. "Kings come and go," he said.

"Then what? Emperor?" Kirwyn guessed.

"Again, forgotten," Mal dismissed.

Aewna cocked her head. Her hands, which she usually kept at her sides or in her lap, rested flat upon the table as she studied Mal. "You seek immortality."

He gave her a rare smile.

"What's that supposed to mean?" Kirwyn asked, eyes narrowed. "Elaborate."

"He wants to be something new," Aewna answered. "Something that will make history. Something they'll write about in books or emulate... or maybe something old?" she mused, thinking aloud. "Like a president or a prime minister?"

Aewna had an extensive education in politics, but I didn't know what those roles were.

"The title couldn't be less important," Mal replied. "All that matters is that the leader is chosen by the free will of the people and that a peaceful transfer of power occurs after completion of the term served."

"You want to reintroduce or recreate some kind of democracy on a large scale," Aewna scoffed, speculative brow furrowed. "Not because you're a good person or you care about people, but for your own ego. Because you want to be *remembered.*" She threw her head back and laughed with scorn. "*That's* your immortality."

I sucked in a breath. Mal-Yin's price was too high if he was asking to oust Juls. It also didn't make any sense.

"How do you expect to obtain this position?" I asked. "If you're not seizing power, if it's by the will of the people-"

Mal's eyes gleamed. "You."

"I don't understand. You can do whatever you want. If you want fuck with Rythas, what do you need me for?"

Mal-Yin smirked. "Call it lubrication."

Kirwyn tried to suppress a chuckle. I scowled and waited for Mal to continue.

"The people love you," Mal said. "You are impossibly beautiful and you are queen. They either seek to emulate you or they want a woman in their bed who does. That alone would be enough. But you showed you'd sacrifice for them when you threw your ring into the sea. You followed through on that promise when you swam out and saved everyone from the Oxholde warships. And despite having no aptitude for combat, you fought bravely at the Battle of the Glass Gardens. I don't think you truly grasp how much they adore you. You're untouchable. And your words are powerful."

The wheels in my head spun. "You want me to sing your praises for you... Sway people to support you as some kind of new leader of a new system?"

I won't, I silently swore. *This price is too high.*

"I think she wants the same," Mal mused, swinging his gaze to Aewna. "A new, fairer system of governing to spread."

"Yes, but not for myself," Aewna insisted, impassioned, breathless. "Not in any manner that will dupe the people into making them believe I am a good person if I am not. Not by covering up my past evil deeds and presenting a new public image I expect Zaria to bolster on my behalf!"

"I will not overthrow the Dorestes," I swore. "No. Juls remains king. I won't support you taking his crown and it can't be done anyway. You can have something else. A compromise."

Mal arched a brow. "You'd give up the freedom of the girls to come after you, the freedom for all of Elowa, just to allow the man who forced you into marriage to sit his outdated throne?"

"I don't have to," I countered, smugly, tapping the table with one finger. "Because I know if you've waited this long, I'm the only shot you've got. And I know you won't give up your only real chance. We'll come to a compromise or we'll both lose." My chin automatically gave a stubborn jut.

"Let me ask you this," Mal said. "If Juls had been cruel or if, say, his brother Lazlian had been the one you were forced to marry and escape... would you then be amenable to tossing him from the throne and dismantling his rule?"

My face and neck suddenly heated. "I – I..." I tried shaking the image of Lazlian from my mind. He complicated things and I knew what Mal-Yin was really asking me. *If I'd been forced to marry someone horrible, would I vow vengeance in the form of destroying them?*

I was saved from having to reply by Mal continuing, "Because the next king or the next might not be as benevolent."

Before I could speak, I felt Kirwyn grab my hand beneath the table.

"You'll compromise," he announced. "Because it's been done in the past. Countless times. There's a historical precedent for it. Power can be shared between the crown and," he waved a hand, "whatever new leadership you're envisioning. A system of checks and balances can be put into action. It will be reasonable, and it will be easier for Zaria to sing this song to everyone. You can play at being George bloody Washington or whoever you want, but with compromise."

Who? I struggled to follow as everyone waded into waters beyond my depth. Not for the first time, resentment at my lack of a proper education, at the willful infliction of ignorance upon me and other Elowans, flared inside my chest. I might forever strive to keep up with what others had leisurely years to acquire. I possessed a clever mind, *landdammit,* I'd proved that by bringing into fruition this very conversation at this very table. But I wondered with regret -- what could I have achieved if I hadn't been kept in the dark all my life?

Before anyone could interrupt, Kirwyn announced to Mal and Aewna, "There's too much inherited power in this world. I agree with you that a fairer process of electing leadership needs to take root and spread throughout the larger clans, if possible."

Since when were they in agreement? Since when was every-one? This was happening very quickly and I didn't know how I felt about it.

"You can work with Zaria and me to enact those changes in Elowa. In some ways, Elowa is a blank slate. It will be easier there. Once we open her up and a new system is born, it'll spread. Rythasians and other clans will take a look at what's being done and they'll want it for themselves. If you're seeking a legacy, you can shape the new government. Be known as the father of it and *maybe* the first elected, but that will take a number of years."

"You're not even Rythasian," I scoffed.

"Neither are you," Mal replied. "Clans conquer other clans every day and leadership changes."

"But you don't want to actually conquer," Kirwyn said. "You can't do this alone or with force, you need a separate being – a powerful one like Zaria - to talk up your ideas on your behalf. I'm assuming you'll want clan status for some of your people and time to integrate yourself and establish a reputation. So you're looking at a long game of enacting change."

"I *might* be amenable to a dual system," Mal hedged, after expelling a long breath. "And I'm very patient. But it cannot be done the way you say."

"Why not?" Kirwyn asked.

"Because Elowa is too small. And because I have a second condition," he reminded.

Kirwyn, Aewna, and I looked at one another. I braced.

"Zaria must return to Rythas to speak out in support of a more egalitarian system with an elected leader, per her *enlightening* discussions with me and according to the ways I'll advise."

"You mean sing your praises," I corrected, frowning. "So that you can be the one who goes down in history as accomplishing it." *What a shady bastard,* I thought. *Making it look like free will when he'd be pulling all the strings behind the scenes.*

"The world is ready for change again, can't you feel it?" Mal asked, passionately. "And this way will do the most good for the greatest number of people."

I crossed my arms, frown deepening. When he put it that way, I couldn't deny it.

Shrugging, Mal said, "Someone has to be recorded as leading it; it might as well be me."

Mal shifted his eyes to Kirwyn and titled him loftily,

"The Man Who Stole a Queen. I'll assume you'll stay together wherever you go..." His gaze moved to Aewna and he declared, "And Aewna will not yet set foot in Rythas."

What? No, that's not our plan, I thought, panicking. *Why?*

"These are my terms if you want my army," Mal concluded.

Aewna threw her napkin on the table and once again stormed out of the room. Shocked, I was at a loss to understand what was happening as Mal quickly followed at her heels. Kirwyn and I stared at one another, ears straining to hear what sounded like a whispered, heated argument in the hall outside.

What the hell was going on? Mal and Aewna had never been alone together and it seemed, wordlessly, each one knew what the other was thinking.

I jumped a little in my seat when I heard what I thought was a slap. I started to rise, but Kirwyn laid a hand on my arm, holding me back with a meaningful glare. His furrowed brow told me he was working something out. I re-sat, frowning.

Mal returned to the dining hall, slightly disheveled.

"What is going on?" I demanded. "Did you upset my sister?"

"She's gone to her room, to rest," he said, a bit breathlessly.

Goatshit, I thought. *I'll pry the truth from her later.*

Retaking his seat at the head of the table, Mal stated candidly, "I don't want Aewna in Rythas. My second condition is that she returns to Elowa." He nearly knocked me over when he said, "To rule."

"Why?" I gasped.

"She will make the best interim leader there, until such time as new governance can be put into place. You know she's been well-prepared for it. Not by her father of course, but by the books she sought out herself. She too wants a better future."

His reasoning sounded plausible but didn't explain what the hell just happened in the hall. It also didn't explain how he knew that about her. I was beginning to suspect Mal sought out Aewna to converse over the past two days.

"What am I missing?" I demanded.

"He doesn't want her to meet King Juls," Kirwyn chuckled beside me, leaning back in his chair. "He doesn't like the idea of her falling for him. He doesn't want her to marry him."

Was Kirwyn serious?

While I gaped, Mal and Kirwyn shared a look I could only describe as a kind of delight or conspiratorial glee. I frowned. In two days, had Mal become so interested in Aewna he was trying to claim her before Juls did?

"You can't be on board with this," I said to Kirwyn. "You want to be king, don't you?"

Kirwyn shrugged and gave me an apologetic look. "Elowa is small and not very modern." His eyes flicked to Mal. "There are other ways to succeed."

I knew he'd been hesitant about Elowa at first but... "In Rythas?"

"If the right means are in place," Kirwyn hedged.

I didn't know what those means were. I didn't know what *succeed* meant. But I caught on to what he alluded to. *With Mal's help.*

"It is my second condition and I will not compromise," Mal said. "If we're going to craft some system of shared power between kings and elected rulers, you've already received enough concessions on the first stipulation. Zaria needs to physically reside in Rythas to support the changes. She can liaise between myself and the crown. These are my terms."

In the following silence, I collapsed my head into my hands.

So this was it? This is what Mal wanted? A chance to go down in history as some kind of hero ushering in a new era of dismantling thrones and... my sister to remain in Elowa? For him to... what? Court her?

I couldn't see a way around his demands. My mind scrambled to catch up with this new scenario, to picture a world where Kirwyn and I somehow existed in Rythas and Aewna returned to Elowa. I'd need Juls to divorce and pardon me. I'd need Lazlian not to kill me. *No big deal, certainly not after staging an invasion.*

Once again, everything in my life shifted, turned upside-down. The hall was quiet but for the crackling in the large fireplace before us, when suddenly, there at Mal-Yin's table, words from long ago sounded in my head as if they crossed oceans and years between.

You've come to the right place, but you're the wrong person.

I sucked in a lengthy breath, stunned.

It's what the Arch Priestess had said to me when Kirwyn and I climbed Mount Flame to speak with her. Had she known of Aewna and believed her best suited to usher change in Elowa?

Of course she knew about her, I realized. The Arch Priestess had directed Kirwyn on how to find Volmar in the first place.

"Oh my god, it's Aewna," I whispered, half to myself. "The Fire Maidens couldn't tell me at the time; didn't want me to know."

I met Kirwyn's deep green eyes. "Do you remember the

night we met the Arch Priestess and she'd spoken in riddles? She said I was the wrong person, and I didn't understand who the right one was. They want *her*." I covered my mouth, shocked, then slowly removed my hand. "They've been waiting for *her*."

All this time.

I was the wrong person. Never meant to rule Elowa.

Maybe never meant to rule anywhere.

Did I truly even want to? I asked myself.

"I - I have to speak this over with my sister," I stammered. "We'll all decide together."

I tried picturing the complex future Mal envisioned and his place in it. My mind raced, wondering what he'd done to work toward these goals in the past, and I remembered we never learned who supplied Oxholde with modern weapons to attack Rythas at the Battle of the Glass Gardens.

"It was you, wasn't it?" I mused aloud. Cocking my head at Mal, I accused, "You've wanted to take down Rythas all along. You're the one who gave Oxholde weapons before they struck that night. You did it behind Rythas's back, didn't you? I wasn't sure before coming here, but-"

"No," Mal protested, cutting me off. "That was the Spades."

What? I sat up straighter. That didn't make sense.

"You're lying. It was you."

Mal shook his head. "They discovered it was a special interest group in Spade City, funded by the scientists who've been eying Elowa."

"Who's they? What are you talking about?"

"I think it's time to caution you on two points before we proceed," Mal advised. "Out of fairness."

Mal sipped his wine before continuing. I narrowed my eyes, disbelieving he'd do anything out of a sense of *fairness*.

"Some of the Spades are getting restless, and that restlessness is spreading," Mal began. "They can accomplish many things, but they cannot give their offspring what Elowans naturally possess. They cannot replicate the science of the past."

Kirwyn and I exchanged a look as Mal echoed what Volmar once told us.

"Whether or not there existed some manner to scientifically alter the genes of future generations, or whether your enhanced abilities are simply the result of your exclusive breeding pool, remains unknown. But it's increasingly looking like the best way to find out all the necessary answers is by studying you."

My palms sweated hearing talk of my people as objects to study; imagining us being carted off like those poor children I'd seen.

"There's only one thing standing between the Spades and Elowa..." Mal drifted off.

"*Rythas,*" I gasped.

"The TORR pertains to more than just technology," Mal nodded. "If you start changing the way things are done, if there's unrest that upsets the treaty..."

"The Spades will use it as an excuse to invade Elowa," Kirwyn guessed, resting his elbows on the table and rubbing his chin. "To take her people and study them in labs or enslave them."

"Rythas isn't just your prison-keeper," Mal said. "She's your protector."

What a fucking mess. I chewed my lip, feeling like I was always in over my head. It was as if I kept kicking frantically to the surface and taking desperate gulps of air, only to be pushed back down again.

"So what do you suggest?"

Mal shrugged. "It's a problem that's likely going to come to a head one way or another. I'm just warning you that this could expedite things. Somewhere down the road, we are going to have to deal with the Spades. And it will take the unity of Elowa, Rythas, my clan and more. And even that might not be enough." Mal raised a cautionary hand. "But we have time before that happens."

I nodded, though nervous little minnows darted about my stomach.

"What's the second thing you wanted to mention?" Kirwyn asked, suspicious.

"I want you to think about if you *really* want to go to battle against the Dorestes and make an enemy of Prince Lazlian?"

I flicked my hair from my shoulders and lifted my chin. "Lazlian is already my enemy."

"If that were true, you wouldn't be sitting here right now," Mal said sagely.

"Perhaps he wasn't before," I admitted. "But in escaping High Spire, I made him genuinely hate me. There is no affection lost between us."

"But there may still be mercy. For you…" Mal-Yin's dark eyes flicked toward Kirwyn, "and for him." At my confused frown, he continued, "Perhaps you might be persuaded to use more caution around the keylord if you saw his handiwork."

Mal raised his right hand and snapped. The move's casual arrogance was tempered by the pitying look in his eyes. I heard a door swing open and two figures shuffled forward through the shadows and into the candlelit dining room. One was a thin, male guard of Mal-Yin's --

-- and the other was Singen.

What was left of him.

Oh god.

I shot to my feet, sucking in one loud, shaky breath. Instant tears sprang to my eyes. Instinctively, I shook my head, as if refusing what I saw could make it not true.

No, please.

Holes existed where Singen's eyes used to be. Arms ended in stubs where his hands had been sliced from his body. The word *traitor* had been burned into his forehead. He swayed so badly on his feet I knew they'd been lacerated or broken beyond repair somehow.

Tears spilled down my cheeks.

"You recognize him," Mal-Yin confirmed softly. "Good. Because he can't tell you his name any longer. He has no tongue. Or teeth."

Singen gave no sign of understanding his surroundings and the guard had to hold him steady.

"This is what happens when you betray the Dorestes," Mal-Yin said, gravely. "Prince Lazlian doesn't show mercy."

I tried to get my whimpering under control but couldn't. Kirwyn reached for me, but I stepped away. I didn't want comfort; didn't deserve it.

Lazlian did this? I did this too. I'd suspected Singen and handed him right over to the keylord.

I cradled my head, rocking on my feet. Everything I touched, I destroyed. Worse – I created a long list of casualties simply by existing. The first death in my name I'd caused when I was only a child myself, when the Mystics thought a boy touched me. I left a trail of bodies in my wake.

Now Singen. Not even merciful death but horrific mutilation.

"I'm sorry, I'm so sorry," I whispered, tasting the salty tears as they fell into my open mouth.

"He can't hear you unless you shout," Mal said. "His eardrums have been damaged as well."

Kirwyn reached for me again and this time I slumped into his strong arms, crying for Singen, crying for myself, crying for this landdamn world that seemed bent on destroying itself.

"He planned on killing the king and his brother. It's almost certain he would have murdered you as well," Mal-Yin said, nodding toward Singen.

"I- I know," I whimpered. "I was the one who reported him. I'm not sure what happened when I left, but I suspected Singen and I asked my friend keep an eye on him. I-" I broke off in a choked sob. "I asked her to tell Lazlian if my suspicions were correct. I never though Laz would torture him!"

"That's what the keylord does, don't you know?"

"He's a liar!" I cried, half-slapping my own face as I wiped my tears, but new ones quickly took their place. "He told me prisoners of war aren't tortured! When we captured men and women of Oxholde from the Bloody Shoals..." I trailed off, shaking my head at my own stupidity. *God, I was an idiot.* "I knew it. The night I asked him about it, he brushed me off. Said we didn't need any more information out of the prisoners and I knew it didn't make sense. But I believed him," I added bitterly.

Lazlian lied right to my face. God, he probably tortured

many prisoners that night. No wonder I found him alone, drinking on the balcony... And I'd delivered them all right into his hands! Just like Singen.

Wiping my running nose, I asked, "I don't understand. H – how is he here now?"

Mal-Yin lifted his chin toward the door and the guard guided Singen from the room, but the image of his mutilated body wouldn't depart my head. I doubted it ever would.

"Death was too kind a fate for him. Prince Lazlian intended him to live a long life, but it had to be out of the notice of others. He doesn't want the public aware of what goes on behind the dungeon walls."

"People know," I spat, remembering the times Jesi mentioned it. "They're not stupid." *Like me,* I thought, bitterly. *Like I was.* So stupid to believe the keylord.

"Some whisper. Suspect. They cannot confirm," Mal said, smoothing his shiny, black hair behind his ear. "The prisoner was being transferred to a secluded location when sympathetic friends mounted a rescue."

"But why is he *here?*" I asked.

"They brought him here because they believed I might take care of him in exchange for inside information about the Dorestes. Provided he was able to communicate in some fashion."

I swallowed the lump in my throat. "And have you? Cared for him?"

Mal took a sip of wine before answering. "There is no information he can tell me that I don't already know. Besides, his state of being already communicates what I need."

I blinked. *Communicates to whom? Me?*

"Did you hold him here just to show me?"

"I thought you might benefit from an enlightening," Mal replied.

I didn't want to hear any more. I fled the hall in tears.

CHAPTER 29

I was livid at Mal for callously springing such horror upon me, furious at Lazlian for lying, and angry at myself for believing him.

I was so fucking stupid.

It wasn't long before Mal-Yin knocked on our bedroom door, and he and Kirwyn spoke in hushed tones about me while I sat on the bed reeling. I was a little perturbed with Kirwyn too. He may have come around to liking Mal more, but I liked him less. Pride kept me from demanding to know what they were saying to one another, but I gathered Mal eventually asked if he could speak to me alone, because Kirwyn kissed my head and told me he was going for a walk and would return soon.

Before departing, Kirwyn gave Mal a friendly clap on the back and I wondered how extensively the two of them had spoken earlier that day. The ease with which Kirwyn willingly left me with Mal told me he at least trusted him. Begrudgingly, I admitted they were alike in some ways... both cunning, both charming.

Both romantically involved with Elowan sisters?

"You don't like me, do you?" Mal broke the silence.

"Less than I did when we first met," I flashed a small, tight smile. "I'd think someone like you would appreciate the bluntness."

Mal-Yin closed the door and sauntered deeper into my room, uninvited.

"I appreciate the honesty. I value honesty."

"Ha," I threw my head back. "Coming from someone as duplicitous as you, that's rich."

Mal-Yin shrugged and drew back a chair. I frowned. *By all means, have a seat.*

"My father dealt in true duplicity. When I was a boy, he wanted me to befriend the young Dorestes. On the surface. He arranged for us to play together," Mal said, cocking a smirk. "Juls and Lazlian were eleven, I was fifteen. It wasn't really going to work out."

"Were you plotting to kill your father then or did that come later?"

"He was a monster," Mal-Yin said automatically, as if he'd said it so many times before. "Do you know why we have the wine and control many of the vital routes west? Because everywhere my father went, he set off the wildfires razing forests and destroying towns for miles. Killing him saved many others."

"And seizing power held no allure? Would you have done it even if he wasn't a monster?"

Mal-Yin didn't bat an eye as he asked, "If I say yes that makes me a monster, doesn't it?"

I shivered. He could be so cold. Far beyond Kirwyn and even Lazlian. Come to think of it, their tempers ran rather hot and Mal never lost his.

"I've seen enough evidence to call you a monster, regardless," I replied, remembering his macabre entryway and how casually he'd presented Singen, "and I'll do whatever it takes to keep my sister from your clutches."

"Clutches," Mal smiled, amused. He stood and lazily sauntered around my room once more. "I like that." Confirming his intentions he said, "You don't have the power to stop me from engaging with her."

"Then why are you here?" I countered, following him with my eyes.

"You have the power to make things... difficult."

"It makes you uncomfortable, doesn't it, wanting something with a mind of its own? Someone who can choose not to want you in return? Needing from not one but *two* Elowan women."

Mal dragged a chair closer to me, sat, and folded his hands in his lap. "I'm only asking that you let us get to know one another."

"Aewna is even more repulsed by your methods than I am. You'd have a better chance at seducing me," I mocked, recalling the night we first met and Mal toyed with me, implying I might try to seduce him.

Or a better chance with Kirwyn, I thought, nearly rolling my eyes. *You seem to have impressed him.*

"I underestimated you," Mal repeated, and I knew he remembered that night as well. "The Dorestes intended to keep you like a caged pearl, to display and lock away. I thought the people would enjoy you as such – a pretty bauble to briefly admire and cast you aside once they tired of you. I never anticipated you'd genuinely win their hearts. And I never thought you'd escape Rythas." Mal cocked his head, entertained. "I still don't know all the details of how you did it."

"That almost sounds like an apology," I said.

"Almost."

I rolled my eyes. "If you want me not to intervene while you try to woo my sister or whatever evil plan you've concocted, you're not off to a great start."

"I'm getting there," Mal replied. "I have something for you. Information. About Prince Lazlian."

I froze, curious despite wanting to tell him where to shove his information. Mal paused for dramatic effect.

"They might have been too young for me to bond with the Dorestes as my father originally hoped. But I was old enough to entrust with certain knowledge and observations. When we visited, I learned what had happened only weeks before our arrival."

Why is he telling me this? I wondered. *Is it a bribe?*

"When the twins turned eleven, Grahar brought Juls up to the throne room and sat him on that oaken chair while the king stood beside him, passing judgement on petitioners. But he took Lazlian down to the prisons and stuck a dagger in his hand."

For some reason, my hands anxiously gripped the bedsheet.

"The king told Lazlian that it was his job to protect his brother. The keylord had no qualms about that duty; he'd already taken on the role on his own."

I didn't know whether to believe Mal, but that part sounded true.

"Grahar explained to Lazlian this meant not only protecting Juls's reign, but the crown and all of Rythas with it. He pointed his son to a prisoner and instructed him to torture the man. Young Laz balked, so his father threatened that if he did not do it, he'd release the prisoner, hand the dagger to other man, and let the captive do as he pleased to

Lazlian instead. He promised to intervene before the prisoner killed him, but that Lazlian would forever bear whatever wounds and scars the man inflicted."

I could hear my heavy breathing as I hung on Mal's words.

"Grahar couldn't sully his golden son, you see, the one he'd prop up to the people as everything honorable and noble. And since Lazlian already showed an aptitude for severity his brother did not, the late king took the young keylord under his darker wing, training him in how to torture."

I didn't want to admit that my heart pounded and hot tears welled in my eyes.

"I don't know exactly what Grahar made his son do," Mal admitted. "I only know the story as my father later told it to me. Throughout it all, the man screamed and the young prince cried."

I almost couldn't picture it: Lazlian, crying. Shaking my head, I mouthed, *no,* as if it undid anything.

"It was the first instance, but it wasn't the last," Mal-Yin continued. "The castle whispered of horrors, but most preferred to look the other way, no one had solid proof, and many secretly thought the torture was effective, after all. The king kept such ill-doings tight to the chest. Family business. He tasked Lazlian with carrying out all torture from the time he was eleven."

Horrified, I covered my face. *Poor Lazlian. He was just a little boy.* "Why are you telling me this?" I whispered through my palms.

"I thought you should better understand past events if you seek to change future ones."

My heart broke for young Laz having his innocence so cruelly ripped away. I squeezed my eyes shut, but I could only more clearly picture the terrors, so I flung them back open.

But why was he still doing it? Why didn't he refuse his father once he'd grown up? Why had he inflicted those horrors upon Singen?

"It's not my job to save him," I whispered, though I wasn't sure why I suggested it. Mal hadn't. "Even if I pity him, Lazlian is a man now. He knows better. And he's still doing it."

A whimper tore through my lips and Mal gave me a moment to collect myself. When I got my tears under control, Mal declared, "I think Grahar underestimated one son and overestimated the other."

"You think Laz could have done more?" I asked, surprised. "What, been king? You think Grahar underestimated his abilities?"

"No, the other way around," Mal corrected. "I think the late king underestimated what Jullik could handle and overestimated what Lazlian could. He's been carrying that dark burden since he was a child with no hope of ever sharing it."

Something about the way Mal-Yin spoke of *sharing* sparked a memory, illuminated it in my mind like the candle's light on the tabletop the night Lazlian and I drank wine together... the night on the veranda, after I'd bombed the ships. We'd been speaking of Juls making tough decisions.

"He's not willing to kill for it, like you are," I'd said to Lazlian.

"Like we are," Lazlian had corrected.

And I'd immediately refuted his assertion, refused that we were alike in any way.

Could it be... was Lazlian... hoping he'd found a kindred

spirit? Was he looking for someone – me – to share his dark burden?

And, *oh my god,* when I next spoke, I insisted I'd help *Juls* make those tough decisions, help his brother rule... and for some reason my declaration upset Lazlian. At the time, I instantly knew it was the wrong thing to say, but I couldn't figure out why. Laz verbally attacked me directly after and I'd forgotten about it, caught up in our constant battling.

Was it possible Lazlian was upset because he'd been condemned to the darkness for so long and subconsciously wanted me to... be some kind of companion beside him?

Maybe. With Lazlian it was hard to tell. He seemed to admit so little even to himself.

"I don't understand how the Dorestes get away with it," I said. "Don't the people see the evidence? I mean, Lazlian can't do to anyone what he did to Singen and still have the person publicly hanged. Everyone would know."

"Prisoners sentenced to hanging aren't tortured, of course," Mal replied. "Only those who meet other fates."

The Isle of Walking Corpses, I remembered.

King Grahar created this mess. Just one man. Maybe Mal was right and something should be done. Not every king would be as good as Juls. And Juls was looking the other way to what his brother did, wasn't he? I blamed his father for that, too.

"Grahar was a terrible man," I declared. "Who made terrible decisions."

Mal cocked his head back and forth and shrugged. "I see a hard man who made hard ones."

"You would."

"But you see now why it might not be so bad to have a more equitable distribution of power?" Mal asked, as expected.

"It's not your right to take it," I countered.

"And it's not anyone's right to inherit it. All I'm asking is to let the people decide for themselves."

I glowered at Mal. "All you're asking is that I help foster such a decision in your favor. If not for you personally, for the ways you'll preach."

His eyes danced with unapologetic amusement. "Think it over," Mal said, rising to leave. "We've got some time. You can stay here as my guests until we come to an agreement."

"My sister won't be charmed by you," I warned, knowing what Mal really planned to do with our time. "She despises evil and violence of all kinds."

Mal gave me a strange look before departing. "Then maybe the right man can shield her from it."

A few minutes later, Kirwyn still hadn't returned and I was alone, carrying a glass of water across the bedroom. A thought so wild hit me, I lost my grip and the glass fell to the floor, shattering.

I froze. Not only because I'd step in the shards if I moved but because I was rooted to the spot by my spinning thoughts.

If prisoners were to be hanged, they weren't tortured.

Oh my god. *Oh my god.*

After we'd captured the prisoners from the Bloody Shoals, could Lazlian have manipulated me to push for a hanging for Milicena, the clan leader's daughter I'd often visited in prison... because it spared her such a fate?

Was it possible?

I'd argued against sentencing her to the Isle of Walking Corpses because I found it barbaric, but Juls wouldn't be persuaded. Lazlian was supposed to be the one to oversee her execution there. With his fear of the sea, I was certain he didn't want to sail to the isle in a small boat. I didn't doubt his selfishness. He had no desire to bother with her eventual execution whether it would have been watching from the ocean or standing upon the King's Stair for a long and boring ceremonial hanging, as he'd once said. He wasn't sorry when she'd hanged herself instead.

But could there have been anything else? Was there a part of Lazlian that didn't want to torture Milicena, either for her benefit or for mine?

Oh my god.

If so, by using me to do his bidding... he manipulated everyone and got his way in one simple maneuver. My head spun with the implication. He played me. He washed his hands of the prisoner. He outwitted his father, whom he obviously couldn't tell the truth. Maybe Laz even circumvented having to directly discuss it with his brother, who likely pled Grahar to change Milicena's sentence because of my wishes. I remembered Juls and the late king were in a room together when I sent my plea. Maybe there were political reasons they teetered on her fate, but somehow, having me send that letter at that time was the necessary push to tip the scales.

Oh my god. Laz sat back in that chair—literally, leaned back—and watched me scurry around according to plan. He watched us all play our parts, just as he'd known we would. He didn't even lift a finger.

But after... if Lazlian did it because he didn't want to torture Milicena... why had he tried to strike me? Was he mad that I didn't know and couldn't express the gratitude he felt he was owed? Did he watch it happen according to his plan, but regret the decision? Why did he come at me so hard, almost to the point of backhanding me?

The keylord, as usual, was impossible to figure out.

I looked down at the glass all around me, trying to guess where to step, barefoot.

Just like Lazlian. He isn't even here and I am in danger, simply by thinking of him.

CHAPTER 30

While Kirwyn was showering the next morning, I found Aewna in her room, holding a tattered, leather-bound book in her hands.

"An edition that was rare even in its time," she said, stroking the raised lines along the spine. "It's from Mal."

I sat on the bed beside her. "Is he upsetting you? I swear I heard you slap him at dinner last night."

Aewna visibly swallowed. "I did," she admitted. "And then he... kissed me." Not meeting my eyes, she mumbled, "And then I fled to my room."

"You slapped him?" I repeated, suspiciously. "And he kissed you and you fled to your room? In between, did you... kiss him back?"

Aewna still didn't meet my eyes. "It all happened so fast. Actually, his kiss was rather slow. But still so passionate. And deep..." She rambled softly, speaking more to herself than to me.

"But you hate him," I reminded her, rubbing my temples. "You've always hated him."

"I- I still do," she said. "Mostly. I'm not sure."

"It doesn't sound like you hate the way he kisses," I pointed out, dryly.

"He tastes like red wine, you see," Aewna confessed, blushing and covering her face. "Velvety and intoxicating. And I... I was drunk on it. On his wine-kisses."

I swear to *god,* I nearly burst out laughing, hearing Aewna speak that way. I didn't think I could be more shocked if Mal's compound collapsed around us.

But this was serious.

"So there *has* been something going on between you two?"

"No!" she quickly swore. "But yes. In a way. That's what's so odd about it. We've barely spoken. He asked me a few questions when we passed in the hall once, about my upbringing. It's all been," she struggled to find words, "with our eyes. It's like the only way I can stop it is to close them. That's why I keep fleeing. If I look at him, it's like he's already doing things to my body just with his eyes! And not only physically; it's like he knows me in here," she said, touching her temple.

Fuck. My own eyelids fluttered shut, understanding. My sister wasn't so different from me after all. She hated Mal but didn't really. She'd slapped his face but felt drawn to him anyway. I knew what she was talking about because the same thing happened when I met Kirwyn.

And you tried to slap Lazlian, came the unwanted thought.

That was different, I argued. *Lazlian almost hit back. Twice as hard.*

"But what about Juls?" I pled. "Don't you still want to meet him? He's noble and honorable and Mal is the devil, you said so yourself. You could be Queen of Rythas."

Aewna pursed her lips. "It's a lot to consider and I'm considering everything."

"I know you are," I sighed. *I just never thought* he'd *be any sort of consideration.*

Head spinning, I left Aewna to return to my room and finish getting dressed.

Kᴉʀᴡʏɴ ᴡᴀs busy talking to Mal's generals the next time I saw Aewna, later that morning. I'd ambled into the orchard to pick paw-paws and immediately spied her wandering through the leafy trees. Before I could catch up, I glimpsed Mal, not far behind.

He was like a cat catching sight of a bird and pouncing. When he approached, Aewna subtly backed away, but she never tore her wide-eyed gaze from Mal's face. Once again, I felt like I witnessed something intimate. Mal may have been eye-fucking Aewna this entire time, but now I saw she engaged in return, despite moving away. Mal was slow but persistent in moving forward with Aewna's every step backward. I knew he knew *exactly* what he was doing; I could practically feel the sexual energy rolling off him from across the orchard. It was as if he shepherded Aewna. She could have run, could have told him to stop, but she didn't.

It had been going on from the moment they first locked eyes, I realized.

I wasn't sure if I believed in love at first sight and Mal had to be the *least* likely of all people to get swept away -- yet I'd watched the improbable event unfold.

My sister backed up until she hit the garden wall. Mal purposefully placed his hands on either side of it, keeping

Aewna within. Mesmerized, she never looked anywhere but his dark, dangerous eyes.

I wasn't at all surprised when, right there under his ripe fruit trees, Mal leaned down and kissed her. Wanting to give them privacy, I left, nearly groaning aloud because I had the feeling that kiss sealed our fates.

It's done.

Juls was out. Aewna was falling for the devil.

My head spun and our destinies spun out in new directions along with it.

Damn Mal-Yin and his kiss that cracked kingdoms.

"IT'S ALL FALLING APART," I moaned to Kirwyn, back in our bedroom. "This isn't right. Aewna should be with Juls, she's perfect for Juls!"

Kirwyn leaned against the bathroom doorframe in nothing but a towel, wet and sexy. He'd showered again after some impromptu training with Mal's men. Even distracted, my stomach tightened watching the water sluice down his lean muscles and toned abs. He crossed one ankle over the other, arms folded. "Give me one good reason. Besides your guilt."

"I can give you two," I snapped. "One, if Juls is to be a good king he needs to not be miserable. Having someone to love will help make him happy. And two, if you want some kind of future in Rythas, I need him to grant me a divorce."

"Zaria, you were forced into that marriage *and* it's unconsummated. It's not real."

"It is to Juls." I threw up my hands. "It is to the people."

"So you'd offer your sister as a sacrificial lamb?"

"That's not what I was doing," I insisted. "I was just

playing matchmaker. I truly believe they'd both find happiness in each other and be good rulers and, yes, if you think about it, she's the perfect substitution for me. She and Juls are so similar. They'd bring together Elowa and Rythas. It was perfect." Frowning, I spat, "Then Mal-Yin has to saunter in with his dick in his hand and ruin everything!"

Kirwyn tried and failed to suppress a laugh. I scowled.

"Look, I don't think he's just thinking with his equipment below, okay? I think he's fascinated by her. And whether she likes it or not, he intrigues her too."

I crossed my arms and stared daggers at Kirwyn, in no mood for persuasion.

"I'm sure it helps that she's a good political card for him play," Kirwyn said, holding up his hands in defense. "But in my opinion, Mal isn't maneuvering this for the advantage. In fact, I think it's a bit of a disadvantage to him. If he doesn't view it as a weakness, he at least sees it... her... as a vulnerability. I think that makes him nervous."

"Fuck me," I muttered, flopping back on the bed.

"Later," Kirwyn quipped, raising his brows suggestively. I shot him another look, but he shrugged, "You know you're sexy when you're angry. You pout. It makes me want to do things with that pouty mouth."

"Is she even safe with him?" I asked, refusing to be distracted by sex. Which, in Kirwyn's defense, was probably a first. Not to mention a feat because *god, I love him wet.* His slick muscles were terribly distracting.

"She's probably safer with him than any other man in a thousand-mile radius. That might, subconsciously, be some of his appeal."

I threw my arms above my head, and groaned again, "It's all falling apart. How did this happen?"

"It's not. Alright, look at it this way," Kirwyn said,

sitting down next to me and sinking the mattress a bit with his weight, "going with your delightful visual – and thank you for that by the way – even if Mal came in with his dick in his hand, you've got him by the balls now."

I knew Mal wouldn't go to war for the promise of a data cube. I'd always known he wanted more. But I never guessed he wanted *everything*. Maybe in Kirwyn's eyes he wasn't so much the devil any longer, but I couldn't think of a more devilish prize to claim than power *and* my sister. I snorted. Not just power. Going down in history as the founder of... whatever the hell title he came up with to *usher in a new era*.

"Deep down, Aewna wants what's best for the people," I said. "Deep down, Mal-Yin wants what's best for Mal-Yin."

Kirwyn waved his hand back and forth in a *so-so* motion. "I don't completely agree with that statement, but I don't completely disagree. Even if it's true, maybe they'll temper each other."

"Since when did you become his best buddy anyway?" I asked rhetorically.

When Kirwyn fell still and silent, I sat up in bed, skin prickling. "What is it?"

Running a hand through his wet hair, he said, "Mal's ambitious. He might have been born to privilege but he's had ideas and aspirations beyond what he was given. I can relate to that. I'm not behind all his plans and motivations, but some, I am. And not always the altruistic ones."

Kirwyn paused while I searched his face, puzzled. *What was he getting at?*

"Zaria, I can't compete with a king and a keylord. But, fuck it, I can. I just..." he scrubbed his hand down his face, "haven't been given a chance. I wasn't born to these things, but I know what I can do if I have the opportunity."

Oh. *Oh.*

"Kirwyn, you know those things don't matter to me, right? I had a king. I don't want him. I don't care about royal bloodlines."

"It's not *just* a title. It's all the accomplishments someone can achieve with that benefit. You've always had that kind of power, so you don't see. Try to understand what it's like for me. Just as being born in this body, I've always had a power you've been denied all your life, and I try to understand what that's like for you."

"You think Mal will give you the opportunity to prove yourself," I said softly. "You don't have to prove yourself to me."

"To you, to *me*," Kirwyn insisted. "He and I have been discussing plans and we have many ideas in common. We both have an interest in the past, in the way things were done. But this time, being able to start again and pick the best methods from everywhere." Kirwyn locked eyes with me and announced, "I think we can lay the beginnings of a better way forward. I think we should accept his terms. But-"

"But you don't want to change the world just for the world's sake," I said, understanding. "You want power for power's sake. You have that in common with Mal."

Kirwyn shrugged. "I want you more. If you don't want to do this, we won't."

I sighed. *What other choice did I have?* The truth was, I didn't hate the idea, in theory. I just didn't like Mal's manipulation or having to hurt Juls... more than I'd already intended.

"The Man Who Stole a Queen," I whispered pensively,

tracing Kirwyn's lips as I recalled Mal-Yin's words. "Did you steal me?"

"You swam to me," Kirwyn pointed out. "I just took you the rest of the way, and you were more than willing if I recall."

"Eager," I concurred, planting a kiss on his lips. "*Desperate.*"

Sighing, I agreed softly, "Okay. But I'm doing this because of you, not him. I believe in you, I trust you."

Kirwyn's eyes lit. "I believe in you. I've always believed you."

I picked at the bedsheets. "How are you always so confident about everything, including me?"

You are the only one, I thought. *Except, oddly enough, Lazlian believed me capable. He supported my plan for the Oxholde warships and always kept a watchful eye on me. Yet his belief in my abilities didn't mean he didn't want to control them. Control me.*

"I don't even know who I am anymore. When I was young I was so certain. Now..." I spread my hands, helplessly, "I do not wish to be my mother's daughter or my father's. I know I can't change it, but I repent the fact. I do not wish to be Juls's wife." I shook my head, frowning, "I cannot go back to Elowa. I don't want to be Queen of Rythas. And I won't run away to be a freeborn with you. Who am I, Kirwyn?"

"Who do you want to be?"

"I don't know."

He took my chin in his fingers. "But haven't you always wanted the freedom to find out?"

I closed my eyes, admitting, "Yes, but I'm scared."

"Of what?"

"Of never knowing. Of choosing wrong. Of other people disapproving."

Kirwyn made a face between a grimace and a smirk. "I can guarantee the last two will happen."

"Gee, thanks," I muttered, playing with the sheets again.

"And can I promise the first won't. It might take longer than you want or expect, but you'll figure it out."

I huffed and licked my lips. "Can I ask you something and you won't think me weak?"

Kirwyn nodded.

"I'm sure of you. For now, that's all I want. Later, I will do whatever I have to for us to win High Spire and to start all over again and figure out my life... but for now," I met Kirwyn's sharp gaze, nervous as I whispered, "I just want to belong to you. I don't want to be anything else but yours."

"You *are* mine," he declared, kissing me. "And you don't have to be anything else right now." As he coaxed me back onto the bed, my legs fell open and I arched in a silent plea for more. Kirwyn gladly obliged, tossing his towel and positioning himself between my thighs to give me that heavenly fullness I desired.

"I've got you, Zaria," he promised in my ear, punctuating it with a hard stab below, making me gasp. "I won't let anyone take you away again."

Wrapping my legs around his waist, I breathed ineloquently, "Fucking you is treason. But *fuck*, it feels amazing."

Kirwyn chuckled against my cheek. He slid nearly all the way out and drove deep inside me, two times, three... each one eliciting a cry of pain-pleasure from my lips. When he returned to moving close and deep again, grinding in that way that rubbed against my clit, I lost myself to babbling all those embarrassing things I couldn't stop.

Oh god, Kirwyn, oh my god. Please.

As he skillfully brought me to climax, I thought perhaps it wasn't Mal; perhaps Kirwyn was responsible for where we were now. Maybe it all started long ago, in my cave.

Maybe Kirwyn's kiss was the one that cracked kingdoms.

THE IMPROMPTU MEETING with Mal that afternoon was surprisingly informal, considering the weight of what we planned. Kirwyn, Aewna and I found him, expectant, atop one of his roof postings, enjoying the lush forest views spanning for miles. Sun shone brightly and I hoped it was a good omen.

We sat in a circle of chairs while Mal called for one of his clansmen to refresh us with pitchers of iced loquat lemonade.

Once we were alone, I announced, "We've agreed to your terms. *But.* I have my own stipulations. Three."

I caught the corners of Mal's mouth turn down. *Not expecting that, were you?*

"My first stipulation is that the capture of High Spire is done my way, without heavy firepower. I don't want the siege exploding into uncontrolled violence. If you can't agree, we won't proceed."

Mal eyed me for a few seconds, then nodded.

"Secondly, when it's over – *when we succeed* – there will be a discussion of some kind to come to terms. You will not be present at those negotiations. They are between the Dorestes and I." *And Kirwyn,* I thought, but I didn't want to add that now.

Mal's eyes narrowed with displeasure and his jaw clenched in one of his few, genuine reactions. Finally, he gave a tight smile.

"Agreed," he said. But I knew he wasn't happy about it.

"The final stipulation?" he asked.

This was the trickiest one since there were many variables and no way to know what the future held.

"Seeing as how you're interested in pursuing my sister," I declared, without looking to see her reaction to my bluntness, "I have no objections in your following her to Elowa. I know you think it's too small, but there, you'll be able to enact whatever new system of governing you imagine, and I will speak in favor of it in Rythas. Whatever changes you implement, I'll support their spread."

I licked my lips before continuing. "I'll speak favorably of you as well... but I do not have the power to install you as the first leader of its kind in Rythas, even if I wanted to. Maybe it can happen, maybe not. You don't bear their mark and, as an outsider, it would take years to rise to power. Maybe one day we can unite Elowa and Rythas, I don't know. This is uncharted territory. But we can do this the way Kirwyn suggested. I can help see to it that the new ways gain popularity in Rythas and that you are discussed and written about in the history books as the creator. You can be the Father of New Democracy or whatever you want to be called. That's your immortality. But it's up to Aewna as well, seeing as how you'll begin in Elowa."

Mal's gaze shifted to Aewna. She nodded, as we'd earlier agreed. Eyes back on me, Mal said, "Obviously, I'm aware I haven't a history in Rythas, but many who rise to power there have only more recently immigrated – you're proof of that. Will you stand by a division of power between the crown and an elected official, and will you speak up for me as the best candidate, if it comes to pass? Most importantly, will you support the moves I make beforehand to bring it to fruition?"

My stomach fluttered, unsure what this would look like when we were speculating on something many years into the future. But the onus was on Mal to prove himself; I could only do so much. While I didn't believe Mal-Yin was the type of leader who would bring harm to the people he was in charge of protecting, his motivations weren't altruistic either. It was strange... if inherited power could produce anything—either a king like Grahar or a king like Juls—I wondered what qualities clustered in men and women who *actively* sought to rule?

"The deal is that you can begin in Elowa and I will advocate on your behalf in Rythas. But it's up to the people whether or not they want to implement any changes."

Mal cocked a diabolical smile. He and I shook hands and I blinked, startled. *It's done.* There, atop Mal's inland compound, we'd agreed to invade High Spire and change the future for Elowa and Rythas.

I gulped, guilt warring with elation.

Juls will never forgive the betrayal. Lazlian will...

Make me beg for death.

"Her father," Kirwyn quickly reminded, tilting his head in Aewna's direction, face knit with sympathy. "We need you to send your men to take over, and fast. He's plotting with," a nod in my direction, "her mother. If we're all in agreement to proceed, we need him detained so that he cannot send letters. But quietly, so that Queen Pama isn't alerted."

Mal glanced at Aewna who gave one small, sad nod. My heart sank, but I didn't disagree.

"What do you plan to do with your parents after the battle?" Mal asked.

Aewna and I shared a look. "I don't know," I confessed. "I can't think about that now. First, we need them contained and we need to win."

Mal turned to Kirwyn. "Done. We'll meet later to discuss the logistics?"

Kirwyn looked at Aewna and I for approval but we both shook our heads, grateful *not* to be a part of this particular planning.

Lightening the mood, Mal announced to us all, "I'm thrilled at our newfound alliance and I'm arranging a feast for us tonight, to celebrate."

I'm sure you've been arranging it since before we even came up here to solidify the agreement, I thought wryly.

I frowned but Mal didn't notice. A smile, entirely for Aewna, lit his eyes.

CHAPTER 31

A clanswoman knocked on our door early that evening, carrying a gown unlike any I'd seen before. I recognized it as historical, though I couldn't name the era. Constructed from blue silks and satins, the material shone as it moved. The voluminous skirts were too large to fit in any kind of delivery box. I could already tell the neckline fell shockingly low on a woman's chest and the straps slanted outwards, over the tops of a woman's arms and not her shoulders.

Was it a lucky guess or did Mal know blue is my favorite color?

Kirwyn had been instructed to prepare in another room beforehand, and the delivery woman briefly left me alone to don the undergarments. I slid two curious stockings up my legs, reaching only to my thighs and held in place by a discreet elastic band. The accompanying skimpy underwear made me hope that a female clan member, and not Mal himself, had selected the attire.

But with Mal, I could never be sure.

The clanswoman returned to help me dress, lacing me

into a corset that not only dipped as low on my breasts as I'd imagined; it pushed them up and out on display. Layers of white slips beneath the gown bolstered the skirts in a circle around my legs. I was given a wide, collar-like necklace studded with sapphires and two matching ear cuffs.

Rose-colored lip and cheek stain gave me a flushed, pretty hue. I missed Jesi a hundred times a day for a hundred reasons, but this was the first time I wished she were with me to tell me how to line my eyes with that alluring black smudge. Unsure, I didn't bother with the tools. Kirwyn knocked on the door as I finished painting my face to the best of my abilities.

When he entered our room, my heart stuttered and my breath caught. I'd never seen him look like that before.

To say the strange clothing suited him was an understatement. Black leather boots hugged his shins to the knee. Slim pants, practically clinging to his thighs, accentuated his long, toned legs. The high, stiff-backed collar of his jacket added drama and the long cut of the material gave him an even more dashing appearance. From beneath his dark sleeves peeked just the slight edge of pure white from his shirt.

Meeting his eyes, I blushed. I wanted to run my fingers along the fine coat and his even finer frame beneath it. I wanted him to slide his trousers down to those tall boots and take me without taking anything else off.

"Jesus, Zaria."

I blinked. Could he read the lust in my gaze? Was he admonishing me? But no, Kirwyn's eyes roved my attire and I realized he looked as stunned as I felt.

"For a dress I've never loved more, it's strange that all I want to do is tear it off."

I bit my lip, smiling. "A gift from Mal-Yin."

"For you or me?" he asked, still looking me up and down.

I playfully slapped his chest and we left to collect Aewna. She was dressed in an ivory gown not too dissimilar from mine. Her hair, longer than my own, was set in loose curls. Her cheeks already flushed with excitement.

True to his word, Mal's kitchen prepared an unrivaled feast, and it didn't include just the four of us. Soldiers, advisors, and any clanspeople who could fit into his dining hall, crammed every corner. The hall itself had been set up with makeshift tables and at the front, live music played, like the Fae Fête.

My stomach twisted at the memory. I'd enjoyed the holiday. Not all of it, but... parts. *Dancing and laughing with Jesi and Lida. Riding off to watch the sunrise on the beach.*

Everyone in the hall had dressed in a similar historical fashion from an era I did not know. I began to understand that Mal didn't just like to read about the past, he liked to play at it. It was probably why Rythas held such appeal.

Throughout it all, I couldn't take my eyes off Kirwyn. He looked demonically sexy as he sipped his wine, and it gave me the butterflies of a cuspate girl. Somehow, with more layers of complicated clothing than I'd ever seen him wear, he exuded an even greater raw, masculine energy. The more the night wore on, the more I clenched my thighs under the table. A current seemed to pulse between us as his dark green eyes met mine over the rim his wineglass.

I wanted him. *Now.* Slowly, intentionally, I rose from the table.

I could feel Kirwyn's hungry stare follow me as I walked out of the dining hall. It was as if an invisible cord stretched between us. I moved and it drew him to follow. He moved and it pulled me to trail. Without looking back, I knew he'd shadow me, but I was surprised by the speed at which he caught up. Ten paces into the dim corridor and I felt his hands – one grabbed my elbow, the other hugged my waist – quickly escorting me deeper in the darkness. Giddy, I let Kirwyn direct me into little more than an alcove. I was already panting when his hands slid down my back and gently pushed, guiding me to bend toward the wall.

"Don't move, don't you dare move," he whispered against my ear, thrilling me.

I felt him stand back to unbuckle his trousers and the cool air caressed my bare skin as he lifted my voluminous skirts.

I didn't realize my thighs were pressed together again as I'd been unconsciously trying to relieve the ache in my core... not until Kirwyn wedged his legs between mine and forcefully kneed them apart to slide down the skimpy underwear. Just the trail of his fingertips near my intimate regions raised gullbumps all over my skin.

Kirwyn grabbed my hips, and, without warning, drove into me.

"Kirwyn," I gasped.

God, I loved the way he filled me. I felt terribly naughty coupling right outside the dining hall where anyone might catch us, and my whimpers grew to moans as he thrust.

"How do I like you, Zaria?" he asked. I didn't know what he meant, but Kirwyn quickly added, "Spread wider. Bend lower. Arch your back."

I remembered he'd given those commands when he took me from behind in the woods. I followed the instructions again now, moving to suit his pleasure – and mine.

Kirwyn's hands slid up to the neckline of my dress and he gave it a firm yank, exposing and cupping my breasts.

"Shh..." he said, continuing those deliciously hard stabs, stretching me. "You can come but you have to be quiet."

To prove his point, he clapped one hand over my mouth, which only made me moan harder. After a few moments, I wiggled my hips, terribly frustrated, because I desperately wanted release but I couldn't achieve it in the half-bent position. I had no friction against where I most needed it. Struggling under the exquisite torture of being on the edge yet unable to fall over was driving me mad.

Did he know? Because Kirwyn continued talking, saying things he'd never said before.

"You don't want anyone to hear you, do you, Zaria?" He punctuated the question with a powerful thrust. "If someone heard your moans, they'd come running."

His deep voice always turned me on, but for some reason the pointed threat excited me even more. I squeezed my core in response.

"And what would they see? The untouchable princess with her dress around her waist."

Yes, yes they would.

"Getting fucked against the wall like a naughty, filthy girl."

Heat surged through my entire body. *Holy fuck. What was he saying? Why was it making me so hot?*

"They'd see you bent over," Kirwyn whispered. "Willing and wailing. They'd see your legs spread for me, Zaria. They'd see me taking you and you loving it."

Mortification warred with desire. Fear warred with excitement. All of it battled for dominance inside me, spiking my adrenaline. I clenched harder around Kirwyn's shaft as I felt the familiar rise of pleasure. On my next moan, Kirwyn's fingers pushed into my mouth and I eagerly sucked them.

Against my ear, he rasped, "Do you want someone to see that? See me taking you? See my cock glisten as it slides in and out of your wet little pussy?"

Holy fuck.

With a cry, I came undone at his filthy words, his dirty imagery. The ocean roared in my ears, dimming out the sound of Kirwyn climaxing behind me. He slid his fingers out of my mouth with a strange hiss.

My breathing slowed but my cheeks burned as if actual flames danced upon them.

"I can't believe you... said those things," I panted.

I could practically hear Kirwyn's smirk as he whispered, "You enjoyed it. I felt it. I can't believe you bit me."

"What?"

"You bit my fingers when you came." Shaking out his hands, he teased, "Savage."

"You enjoyed it," I teased right back. "I felt it."

"Mm..." Kirwyn mused, kissing my throat. "I'd rather do the biting."

I squeezed my eyes shut and asked, "Where did you learn all this? How do you know how to *do* everything?"

His nose ran the length of my neck, inhaling. "I grew up in a library, remember?"

"But you can't just say those things. It's not... I don't know."

He laughed. "Why not? It's just you and me. They're just words. There's nothing wrong with it."

"I don't know, I just..." I couldn't think of a valid reason. "Do other people talk like this?" I asked, frowning. "What's normal?"

"I don't care what other people do."

So flippant, so sure.

I turned to Kirwyn, searching his gorgeous face. I

wished I had his confidence. I'd *had* it, once, in some matters... then everything happened and my world shattered and it was all different here. His scandalous words echoed in my mind, making me want to cover my eyes. What *was* the big deal? They were just words. But they felt so illicit.

"It's so easy for you," I marveled. "You grew up without rules. Without judgement. It's not – I can't... I don't know how to be like that."

Kirwyn studied my face for several very long seconds, making me look down as heat rose in my cheeks again.

"Then let me lead," he said, threading his fingers through mine, nudging me with his nose to meet his eyes.

"You have been! What do you think you've been doing up until now?" I asked.

"Let me lead us deeper," he said, causing me to shiver.

"Me." I whispered, anxiously. "You mean lead me deeper."

Kirwyn lifted one shoulder, so landdamn casual. "Both. I won't do anything you don't like." He thought for a moment, then added, "Or if I do, I'll stop."

Licking my lips, I took a deep breath and nodded. It was easier if it wasn't me, not my doing. Not yet.

"Tell me what you want, Zaria," Kirwyn ordered. "I know you like words, but what else? Some of the things you're always too afraid to say."

"No," I chewed my lip. "You'll just use it against me."

"Of course I will. And you'll enjoy it."

"You're insufferable."

"You enjoy that too."

Still blushing, I confessed, "I like when we... play. Sexy sort of... games. I don't know how to explain it, but they make me feel safe. You make me feel safe."

Kirwyn cocked a wolfish grin on one side of his face. He slid my undergarments up but stopped mid-thigh. When he reached between my legs I jumped back, too sensitive for more stimulation.

"Shhh..." he soothed. "We're not going again... yet."

"What are you doing?" I asked, as Kirwyn gently spread the sticky fluids dripping out of me onto my stomach and legs.

"Marking you as mine. Keeping you safe. Don't wash it off. I want to know you're wearing my seed underneath your dress when we go back out there."

I let out a soft whimper at his easy, dirty talk, unwittingly encouraging Kirwyn to push further.

"Maybe I want you covered in it each morning," he said, boldly holding my eyes, "so that if another man ever tried to touch you, he's going to see you've already been claimed."

My core clenched and my knees felt weak. At a loss for words, I stuttered a shaky, "O...kay."

Kirwyn licked his teeth, grinning with self-satisfaction. He slid my undergarments back into place and gave me a few gentle pats right between my legs. I couldn't say why the simple act shocked me, but it did, making something warm unfurl low in my belly.

"Let's go," he said casually. He led me back to the celebration pretending like he didn't know I was suddenly terribly aroused and ready to have sex again.

As the night wore on, the feast ended and the musicians retired. Another sound emanated from thin air. I jumped backwards, knocking over the chair and twisting my head to find the source.

"It's safe!" Kirwyn said, pointing to a small, hovering device in the center of the room. "It's from this. It plays songs-"

"A music sphere!" I exclaimed, delighted. "I know it! The Spade emissary gave one to us, but I never heard it play... didn't stay that long..."

A scuffle near one corner of the dining hall caught my attention, cutting me off. I turned to see Aewna amongst a circle of male and female clansmen, her scowl focused on Mal.

In one hand she held a bejeweled dagger.

"What's going on?" I whispered, not expecting an answer.

"It's a game they play," Kirwyn replied. "Spin the dagger. It's placed on the floor and twirled around. When the dagger stops, whoever it lands upon has to accept a cut or a dare by the spinner. The only rule is that the cut must draw blood and the dare cannot."

I blinked. *Madness.* Apparently, Aewna thought so too. I couldn't make out her words but I could hear her scolding the players. She tried to take the dagger away and Mal gently caught her hand at the same time another person intervened, inadvertently hitting Mal's arm. In the struggle it dropped, spinning on the gleaming, polished wood of Mal's floor. Everyone fell silent, watching the rotation.

The point stopped right on her.

I expected Aewna to stomp off, but when everyone began chanting, "Cut or dare! Cut or dare!" she stood, seemingly mesmerized.

Was she playing?

There were so many things Mal could dare Aewna.

I dare you to kiss me.

I dare you to sit in my lap.

I dare you to-

"Cut," he announced, before she could speak. With a gleam in his eyes he said, "Reversed."

What did that mean?

A cheer erupted from the crowd, drinks spilling onto the shining floor. Mal swooped down and retrieved the dagger, holding Aewna's gaze. He ran the blade under an eerie, purple light from a device someone held out for his use.

"Sterilization," Kirwyn whispered, beside me.

Mal threw off his jacket and rolled up the sleeves of his crisp, white shirt, revealing slim, but toned, forearms. I began to understand that "reversed" meant he'd offered to be cut in her place. I guessed this was a secondary rule Kirwyn didn't know and the players excitedly accepted the twist.

Mal turned the blade around, presenting the ornate handle to Aewna. She took it, still under the spell of Mal's gaze. He offered her his forearm and mumbled something I couldn't hear above the crowd's shouts of glee and encouragement.

Don't hit a vein, I imaged he said.

Is she really going to do it? Aewna, of all people, had to find this more barbaric than me.

Staring up at Mal, she took his arm in her delicate hands. The players frenzied, eager to see their leader bleed as one of them, but Mal and Aewna barely noticed. They stared at one another as if in challenge. Even from a distance, I could see Aewna's heavy breathing.

This is about trust, I realized. Mal could have dared

Aewna to do absolutely anything he wanted. But he offered himself up for her to injure instead.

Slowly, she drew the dagger to his skin. Aewna broke eye contact only to gaze down and pierce Mal's flesh with the blade. I couldn't hear it, but I saw Mal hiss through clenched teeth as Aewna drew blood with a small cut.

The circle of players cheered and laughed, slamming back drinks and celebrating. A strange elation shot through me too. Mal brought his forearm to his mouth, sucking the blood and still holding Aewna's gaze before someone rushed forward to tend the minor wound.

Perhaps surprised by her actions, Aewna dropped the dagger to the floor, gathered her skirts, and fled the room.

I watched her with my eyes. As did Mal.

"You're not going to chase her? Check on her?" Kirwyn asked curiously.

"I don't need to," I said, giving him a wry grin. "He's going to give her space, for a moment. And then he'll follow. And then he'll kiss her." I cocked my head. "Maybe more."

I clucked my tongue. "I know because it's exactly what you'd do."

Kirwyn threw back his head and laughed. The music grew louder and the game ended as the players dispersed to dance and drink and celebrate some more.

"Dance with me," Kirwyn said, holding out his hand. "Like we danced in Elowa, but this time... I can touch you."

My heart thumped, taking in his dashing appearance at that moment. Maybe I'd been optimally designed, but Kirwyn was magnetic. Not just outwardly handsome but with something inside him I couldn't resist. He compelled me and it was all the more mystifying *because* I couldn't put my finger on it.

I gave him my hand and he pulled me tight against his strong chest.

How could it simply be lust, as my mother had once said, when it felt so fated? What were the odds that Kirwyn would shipwreck onto my beach, just as I'd run alone one morning, just as he was carried out of the ocean like a gift from Keroe himself...

Kirwyn wrapped one arm low around my back.

For a long time, I'd secretly worried that I'd upset Sea God and been cursed in punishment. But maybe it was the other way around. Maybe Keroe—or whatever gods existed —put Kirwyn and I together because we'd been blessed. Fated to find one another.

Now that I understood how big the world was, how long humans had been walking the Earth, I could barely comprehend how miraculous it was that we found each other that morning.

Kirwyn skillfully spun me around the dining hall, dancing to magical music coming from a tiny metal sphere. No one on Elowa would believe it.

I almost didn't *want* to think about the odds of Kirwyn and I coming together... because a dark, nagging voice in my head worried over how easily we could have missed one another or how easily we could be torn apart. Again.

I was sure Mal didn't disclose our plans to anyone who didn't need to know, but the discussions he had with his closest commanders sent a pulse of nervous anticipation through the room. As we drank and danced, everyone fed off the energy and when the night wore down, I still hadn't.

Kirwyn spun me a final time and suddenly pulled me tight against his chest again.

"I want you to go to our room, take off your dress, and wait for me," he said near my ear.

My heart thumped. "Why?"

"We're going to play a little game," Kirwyn said darkly, then added, "one where I make all the moves."

Just the promise... threat... sent heat coursing through my body.

"It doesn't sound like much of a game if I don't get to move one of the pieces in turn," I pointed out, blinking up at him.

"For this game," Kirwyn arched a sinister brow, "you *are* the piece."

CHAPTER 32

Clad in only my corset, underwear, and white stockings, erotic anticipation coursed through my veins. Kirwyn didn't even need to do anything yet -- my mind did the work for me, making me blush and squirm as I imagined all the things he *might* do. I knew he'd find me wet as soon as he touched me.

I wondered if he'd tease me about it.

I wondered if I liked him smug and teasing.

I wondered if he knew it.

After several minutes, Kirwyn entered the room, seemingly taller and more intimidating than ever before. Not only did he still have on his formal clothing --

-- he wore a *mask.*

It covered the from the tip of his nose upward, and the strangely erotic combination of scary and sexy made my heart thump. The mask was plain, all-black, and had two eyeholes from which dark eyes pinned me to the bed.

"Remember when I told you I'd wear a mask someday?" Kirwyn asked, stalking forward. "At your wedding feast in Elowa?"

Oh, I remembered. But I hadn't truly been able to understand how it would *feel*. I hadn't been able to imagine all the naughty things that could be done along with it.

I had trouble meeting Kirwyn's eyes under that sinister mask. It covered half his cheekbones, but the sharp cut of his jaw and beautiful mouth were still exposed. *Dear god, he was ridiculously handsome.* One glance had my face heating.

When Kirwyn raised a hand holding Old World handcuffs, I didn't even try to hide my wide eyes and rapid breathing.

"Turn around," he instructed.

"Do you want to see my mark?" I teased, recalling the first time we met in Elowa when Kirwyn attacked me and demanded to see my clan tattoo. "I told you," I mimicked my old words, "I don't have one."

"I want to see everything. Starting with your breasts," Kirwyn said, voice husky. "And once you're restrained I'll give you a mark with my mouth."

More heat raced through my veins. *Would he? Would it hurt?*

"We need to get you out of that corset before I handcuff you," Kirwyn explained. "Now turn around."

Lower your dress and show me your mark, he'd threatened that day in my cave. *Or I'll come over there and bare your back myself.*

Echoing those words, I teased again, "Remove my corset and show you my breasts, or you'll come over here and do it for me?"

Kirwyn licked his teeth. "Oh, I'm doing it this time," he said.

Biting my lip, I turned and swept my hair over my shoulders so that Kirwyn could unlace me.

He'd seen my breasts many times before, but having

them exposed within this power-charged dynamic felt more intentional. Electric. I turned around and resisted the urge to cover myself because I knew Kirwyn would only put my hands back at my sides.

"Lie down," he said.

I did as he commanded. He raised my arms above my head, laced the handcuffs through one of the sleek bars on the headboard, and clicked them into place. The metallic locking sound sent a jolt straight to my heart... and another place on my body, too. I trusted Kirwyn but my adrenaline spiked anyway, as I was unable to move.

"Are you going to blindfold me?" I whispered.

Kirwyn cocked a half-smirk. "No. I want you to see everything I'm going to do to you. No hiding. I just don't want you using your arms to interfere." He withdrew a small cloth, like a handkerchief, and a long strip of material from somewhere beside the bed. "Or your mouth."

My breath hitched as Kirwyn lifted what I now understood to be a gag.

"But how will you know if you've gone too far?" I asked, reminding him of his promise to stop if that happened.

Kirwyn paused. "Because I'll watch you. I know you." He brought the cloth to my mouth. "I'm always watching you."

Holding his green eyes through the mask, I nodded, and he slid the handkerchief into my mouth and tied the gag around my head.

"Besides, you can still shout if something's wrong," he admitted.

Once he tied it into place, I realized I could easily cry a muffled *stop,* I just couldn't carry out a conversation. But there was more to it than not only being unable to speak or move... I also didn't have to *worry* about what to say or do.

The inability to use certain parts of my body hyper focused me on others. I was more aware of the air on my chest as Kirwyn stared at my exposed breasts. He rolled my erect nipples between his fingers giving each a pinch just a bit too hard. My body arched in response anyway, so he knew I didn't dislike it. Holding my eyes, he licked my nipples, and his burning gaze aroused me as much as his tongue. He bit one peak a tad too hard and I yelped. Searching my face and grinning like the devil, he slowly moved to the other side. Knowing what he intended intensified my excitement… and fear. He gave another too-hard nip, making me hiss as he sucked away the pain.

When he stopped, I whimpered, but he'd only backed up to slide my stockings and underwear off my body. Reflexively, I squeezed my legs together, but he easily pulled them apart. Even the feel of his strong fingers on my thighs aroused me. I was embarrassed by my canting hips yet I couldn't stop. My body rocked whether I liked it or not, imagining what he'd do next and imagining what I looked like with my hands above my head and all of me on display. He was still fully clothed and I was entirely bare.

"You're so fucking sexy, you have no idea how you drive me insane," Kirwyn rasped. I could see his lust-filled eyes glistening under the mask. "Your legs, your hair, your scent. I look at you and no matter where we are, I want to pick you up and carry you away to devour." He grazed one finger through my center with the lightest, teasing touch. "You don't know how often I picture this when we're together, or even when we're not."

His finger, ghosting my slit without entering, was torture. "I think it would scare you if you knew how often I think about fucking you."

My insides liquefied; I nearly melted into the bed.

Kirwyn purposefully spread my legs wider and I groaned as he stared, knowing what I wanted and prolonging the agony by not giving it to me. He watched me squirm as I tried to find any kind of stimulation. His fingers traced circles on my lower stomach and inner thighs, never going where I most wanted them.

"Or maybe you think about it just as much," Kirwyn teased. "Because you're always wet for me, Zaria, always ready for me to take you."

I screwed my eyes shut, cheeks heating. Was I?

Slowly, Kirwyn moved downward and ran along my outer lips, letting his knuckles nearly brush my sensitive inner folds and clit before backing away without any real stimulation. I pulled at the handcuffs, desperate to grab his hands and *make* him touch me. With my head thrown back, I was out of my mind with desire when his hands left me again. I gave shameless pulses into the air, seeking Kirwyn's fingers and finding nothing.

To my shock, when I finally received full contact it wasn't his hands, but his tongue on my clit. I cried and jerked, but Kirwyn had already gripped my thighs, holding me down, keeping me spread wide. While his mouth worked my swollen clit, his fingers drove inside me, curling, finding that spot I liked deep within. The double-assault was like a powerful drug to my system, taking over my brain, making my eyes roll back in my head.

In less than two minutes of Kirwyn's tongue sweeping my intimate regions, I was screaming my orgasm against the gag and bucking it into his skillful mouth. I pulled on the restraints so hard I was sure I'd bear marks the next day. I didn't care.

I was still coming down from the waves of pleasure when Kirwyn quickly unlocked my handcuffs.

What's he doing? I wondered as he rolled me over, bent my arms behind my back, and refastened the cuffs. Grabbing my waist, Kirwyn pulled my limp body to the side of the bed and planted my feet on the floor so that I was bent over it. He manhandled me with such ease, just his maneuvering made me want another orgasm and I ground into the mattress.

Kirwyn noticed, of course, and I could hear his grin as he asked, "Do you want more, Zaria?"

More, yes, please, now, I longed to beg, but with my mouth gagged and my cheek pressed against the bedding, I only nodded furiously. Kirwyn lined his erection up against my core, sliding it up and down but not entering. I couldn't do anything but whimper and wiggle.

"You want my cock, Zaria? Do you want me to fuck you while you're helpless?"

Delicious heat burned low in my gut. I groaned my desire.

"You're insatiable," Kirwyn teased in my ear. "I love it."

He continued the agonizing torture of running the tip of his erection against me until I thought I'd go mad for another climax. *Finally,* Kirwyn impaled me, giving me the divine fullness I so loved. Reaching between the bed and my hips, his fingers found the spot I needed, rubbing while pistoning into me from behind.

There was nowhere for me to go, no way to move my arms or use my mouth. I could do nothing but *take his cock* and I loved it.

As his motions sped, I knew he was close -- and I didn't doubt that he knew my body well enough to know he'd brought me there, too.

Right before we climaxed, Kirwyn leaned down and sucked hard on my neck. He bared his teeth to give me a bite, marking me, as promised. The pain and possessiveness made me spasm like never before, and I came to the sounds of Kirwyn's own groans in my ear.

Spent, it took several minutes to come back to reality and I was still wobbly. Uncuffing me, Kirwyn rubbed my sore wrists.

"Are you okay?"

"More than, Kirwyn," I whispered, mind curiously hazy. "So much more."

"How do you feel? Tell me," he said softly.

"I – I don't know. Desired. Cared for. I was a little scared, but not in a bad way. It excited me." My words weren't slurred, but they sounded sleepy, dreamy. My body almost felt like it was floating.

"And you?" I asked, quietly. "How do you feel when we do things like this?"

Kirwyn searched for words. "Exalted... powerful."

I realized we were both still slightly drunk and too tired to move. Inelegantly, Kirwyn and I twisted together on the bed until our bodies entwined, my limp one sheltered and shielded within his. I loved how protected he always made me feel.

"I've never known for sure where my home is," I whispered in the dark. "In terms of the land underfoot, I still don't. But I don't need to. Because wherever we go, it's this." I nuzzled closer into his embrace. "My home is in your arms."

~

THE NEXT DAY, we laid together on a blanket in Mal's grassy courtyard. We'd brought a small picnic supplemented by sweet loquats we picked straight from the tree. Surprisingly, I liked the contrast of verdant fields against all the gleaming black and silver of Mal's stronghold, and I especially enjoyed how protected we were, safely ensconced inside the compound itself. Like the Biohazards, he'd created a little oasis of safety amongst the chaos.

"You're different from when we first met," I murmured to Kirwyn. "A little quieter... steadier."

"So are you," he said, giving me gullflesh as his hands caressed up and down the sensitive skin on my sides. "Less prone to flares of temper."

I laughed. "Aren't we condescending? You weren't so self-controlled before either."

Kirwyn's stroking could relax me enough to sleep. Clucking my tongue, I admitted, "But you're not wrong."

I shifted my gaze to the grass, not wanting to meet his eyes as I tried to explain what I'd been thinking about all morning. "It's like... remember that day back on Elowa when I said you were air and earth, together? You were like the air because you had this quality where I felt as if I couldn't touch you, that you would just blow away if I tried?" Kirwyn nodded and I continued, "I don't feel the same anymore. Not after all we've been through. I don't see you as mercurial or unreliable at all. You're more solid to me now. More *earth*." Primly, I teased, "And you're far less broody now, you know."

I kept my eyes on the grass. I knew shouldn't feel embarrassed with Kirwyn. He possessed an imaginative, thoughtful side. But he teased me a lot, too.

"Don't laugh at me, okay?" I asked. "I know you speak differently here than we do in Elowa. But I think about that day a lot and the thing is... I feel something similar happened with me. Do you remember how you told me I was like polarizing elements too? Like fire and water to you? And I feel... less hot now." A laugh burst through my lips and I rubbed my forehead, searching for better words. "That sounds bad, but I mean it as a *good* thing. I feel more in control of myself. If my temperamental wildfires threatened to rage in the past, I've since reined them in. I've always been at home in the water and I feel more at home in my skin now too. More sure of myself. Or, if not entirely sure of who I'm supposed to be, at least sure of what I'm *not.*"

Was I babbling? It was so difficult to explain when mainlanders didn't talk the same way as Elowans.

"What I'm trying to say is, I feel like you are earth and I am water. I can crash into you and be pushed back, but I can reshape you too, over time. And you have the ability to press out and change my course, but I am still essentially *me,* just flowing in an altered direction. And in a way, that is how I picture us – like the earth and the sea, meeting on the beach, a place of magic."

I brought Kirwyn's hand to my lips and kissed his palm. I loved his skillful hands, what they did to me. Already fading on my neck, I bore the love mark he gave me the night before. With a breath for courage, I declared, "I want to get a tattoo with you. A permanent one."

Kirwyn's brows rose in skepticism. "Of what? Where?"

"Just a small one. The symbol of water, for me. And earth, for you." I pressed Kirwyn's hand to my chest. "Here. Above our hearts."

"You want us to create our own marks?" he asked, with the hint of a grin.

"Mm-hm. We'll design them in the same style but with different elements. And not on our backs, like it's something chasing us. Right here," I circled the skin above his heart.

"You want to mark yourself... for me?" Kirwyn asked.

I nodded. "And you for me."

Kirwyn's grin spread across his whole face. "I say we do it right now."

THAT AFTERNOON, Aewna sourced modern equipment for us and even drew some ancient symbols for water and earth. She crafted a copy of the design inside a silver, pen-like mechanism to apply to our skin. I'd known Aewna was an excellent rider, but I'd never known how talented she was in artistic matters as well.

"It won't hurt as much as traditional methods, like on Rythas or in smaller clans," she explained. "This is how the Spades do it. But it's still going to smart a bit."

I tossed back an amber-liquor she'd brought from Mal's reserve, nearly gagging. "Ugh, okay. Give this a few minutes and to kick in and then... just do it."

"Don't you want any?" I asked Kirwyn, lifting his glass.

He shook his head. "I'm curious to see how it feels."

I cringed. "I'd call you a masochist but I think that's the scholar talking."

Following Aewna's movements as she set up a workstation made me woozy. I grabbed Kirwyn's unwanted serving of brown liquor and drank that too, though it didn't go down any easier the second time.

"Don't get me wrong, I'm pleased," Kirwyn said, a bit smugly. "But are you sure? You'll bear the mark for the rest of your life."

His choice of words almost made me shudder. It was for that very reason I too wanted it *now*. We didn't know how much longer our lives may be once we attacked Rythas.

I nodded. *No matter if someone tries to tear us apart again,* I thought, *I'll always have this binding.*

"It'll be quick," Aewna promised. "Grit your teeth for two minutes and it will all be over."

"How do you know? Are you marked?"

She shook her head. "No, but I've done it before."

"When?" I asked, trying to distract myself.

"The boy they dispelled from Elowa, oh, seven years ago. The Mystics sent him to my father and we marked him so that he could join a clan out beyond the Cold Mountains."

"Dispelled?" I asked, confused and suddenly alert. "What boy?"

"The one who touched you when you were younger," Aewna explained, a slight crease in her brow. "Oh! You didn't know."

My mouth fell. He had never actually touched me, but the Mystics thought he did.

"They told us he was sentenced to death..." I whispered. "I was only eleven and they made us believe... all this time..."

Aewna shook her head. "The Mystics are many things, but child murderers isn't one of them. He had to be removed though. Far away."

He'd never been killed. My god, the lies were endless. I rubbed my eyes, trying to process this new information. At least this time the truth was preferable – encouraging, even. *Maybe change in Elowa will go smoother than I thought?*

After a few minutes, Aewna readied the marker. Turning my head and clenching my teeth, I wasn't prepared for how much it would hurt the tender skin on my chest. I howled a string of expletives despite the two strong drinks I'd imbibed.

"Breathe, Zaria, you have to breathe," Kirwyn said. The only thing keeping me from fainting was the ice he rubbed on my forehead.

"Maybe I should have had that drink," he joked, trying to distract me.

A minute later, it was done. My chest bore the symbol of the ocean, about the size of a Spade token. It was small enough to cover up with makeup if I chose. Minor compared to the clan marks everyone wore on their backs, which were about the size of my palm. And it would match Kirwyn's by the decorative ring around the symbol.

He clenched his jaw and hissed, but Kirwyn took the pain a lot better than I did. When his mark was completed, Aewna left us with instructions to care for the red, irritated flesh.

Mesmerized, I traced circles outside the symbol's lines. I felt transformed, tied to Kirwyn in a way superseding my marriage to Juls or my blood-sharing with Lazlian. Those things would fade in time, I told myself.

But this bond with Kirwyn was permanent. No one could take it away.

We slept that night, pressed close like we always did, though with my back to his chest, I was careful not to rub his new mark.

In Kirwyn's arms, everything was so right in our tiny world it was easy to forget that everything outside it was wrong.

CHAPTER 33

Mal-Yin's compound contained an indoor pool unlike any I'd seen before – tile and cement and full of chemicals instead of salt. To prepare for my swim through the Black Passage, I swam laps twice a day. Kirwyn was in his element discussing strategy with Mal's favored commander and training with his soldiers, who showed him weapons and fighting techniques he'd never seen before. Whenever they met, Mal and Kirwyn joked with one another like two brothers separated at birth and reunited after years apart. Aewna laughed and called it a *bromance*. Despite reeling at the change, witnessing it pulled at my heartstrings. Both Kirwyn and I lead a lonely and near-friendless existence in our youth, and I was glad he'd found someone like I'd found Jesi... I just never expected it to be Mal.

I thought about Jesi a lot as I swam. I missed her terribly, especially her easy laughter and her bravery. She was one of the reasons I felt a pull to Rythas and open to the idea of staying there. But Jesi was Rythasian to her core. Lida would understand what I was doing, but how would

Jesi feel when I brought an army to the gate she was sworn to defend?

Would I turn my friend into my enemy?

Throughout the preparatory weeks, the entire compound hummed with the same energy that sparked to life at our feast. Nervous excitement raced through my veins too, but the immense pressure of being the one to deactivate the consoles was my burden alone. Once again, everything depended on me, only this time, in reverse. I needed to emerge victorious in attacking High Spire, not defending her.

Traitor, repeated a voice in my head.

It sounded like Juls. Like Laz.

One evening, a few weeks after we'd begun readying our plans, Mal called me into his dining hall, alone. I found him sitting not at the head of the table, but to the side. He pulled out a chair facing his. I sat, confused and wary.

"You received this," Mal said, producing an envelope too fast for me to see from where he'd stored it, like a magic trick. It was a creamy, thick-stocked paper, sealed with dark red wax.

"It arrived earlier today. It's from your husband."

My stomach flipped. "How did he..."

Lazlian. Of course he'd sailed back and told Juls, as expected. *We've definitely lost the element of surprise,* I thought, heart sinking.

Reading my thoughts, Mal-Yin nodded. "They know we're coming."

"Did you read it?"

Mal shook his head. I folded my arms.

"It's sealed," he shrugged.

I didn't move. "And with all your technology, you've

never found a way around opening and re-sealing this letter?"

Mal smiled, "I was hoping my not reading it might gain some of your trust."

At least he's trying, I thought. Nervously, I took the letter and read.

Dear Zaria,

Come home. I don't know what I've done to make you do this, but we cannot work it out if you remain absent from High Spire. You are my queen and my wife. You belong here.

It will please you to know that Jesi has been made First, under Navere. Lida is studying our laws and customs; she's been granted the necessary funds to continue her work. And I'm happiest to tell you that I've arranged for your friend Marcin to be brought here from Elowa. Tomé has been by his side, helping him acclimate.

We never had the chance to talk about it before you left, but I want you to know that I spoke to the hermit many years ago, when my father decreed our union. The hermit told me our marriage had a good chance of success, so you must believe we can work it out. We can be happy.

Come back to me. That's a king's command.

Your husband,
Juls

There was so much to examine in Juls's letter, I could scarcely breathe. Dazed, I handed it to Mal who eagerly perused it while pacing.

Guilt stabbed my heart, right from the opening. I could see that Juls had obviously done favors for my friends to sway me, but I was grateful for them anyway. I didn't know how much I believed in the hermit's prophecies, considering he'd given me one full of nonsense, but I could tell Juls did. And Juls closed with the words he'd once spoken to me before I swam out to bomb the Oxholde ships. We'd stood together upon the beach that night, never having kissed, barely knowing one another... but starting to. I was terrified for what I was about to do. Juls had stroked my face and said, *"Come back to me, that's a king's command."*

But still...

"There's no love in that letter," I murmured, almost to myself. "Not really." *He never even says the word.*

"There's no love on your part either," Mal pointed out, sliding his hands into his pockets and rocking back on his heels. "Would you return to him if there were, on his?"

"No. But it's something that's needed... to start."

"I think that's what he's trying to do. Begin. Again." Mal resumed his pacing around the firelit dining hall. "You've backed King Juls into a corner. If you truly want to change things without violence, the easiest way to do it might be to give him what he wants. Your return to his side."

Sliding one finger across the long table, as if checking for dust he knew wasn't there, Mal said, "And if you publicly stand by him, he'd probably allow you to privately lay with whomever you choose."

Shocked at his suggestion, I stilled.

"You'd be surprised by the clandestine arrangements the Dorestes have enacted in the past, especially when a marriage sours or an heir is needed."

No, I wouldn't be surprised at all, I thought.

"I'm well aware they do shady things to maintain power."

"Everyone does shady things to maintain power," Mal countered with a careless shrug. "I'm just telling you, don't be surprised if he suggests it."

"I want everything with Kirwyn," I protested, "and I couldn't love two men."

"You're young, you might change your mind," Mal said, as if he were decades and not just a few years older. "Besides, who said anything about loving both?"

I barked a laugh. "No, and anyway, he'd never agree to that. You don't know how rigid Juls can be."

"I think you shattered his idyllic illusions," Mal replied.

"He shattered mine!"

I uncurled fists I hadn't realized I'd clenched. Mal's suggestion made me as angry as the loveless letter. *It never even mentioned the word. In all our time, Juls never even said the word to me.*

"I'm beginning to understand now," I spat. "What I did, what I had to do to survive and what it means. What it would have meant if I'd failed." *All the dark things I don't want to think about. Being commanded into someone's bed, forever.* "The Dorestes were the worst thing that could have happened to me."

"You might be the worst thing that could have

happened to them," Mal countered. "Prince Lazlian probably wanted to protect his brother from you."

Not feeling charitable, I sneered, "Because I shattered Juls's precious illusions of the perfect marriage and docile wife? Poor baby."

"You want to do more than that," Mal said. "You want to shatter his rule."

"No," I argued, "you're the one wanting to dismantle power! I just want to change the rules a little. Change the way he believes some things must be done."

"It's going to have a ripple effect regardless and someone has to fill some gaps. It might as well be me," Mal shrugged. "And you realize you've chosen the more difficult path, don't you? Changing kings is easy, changing minds is hard."

I groaned and chewed my lip, hard enough to intentionally hurt. "I can't believe he still wants me back. Why?"

"You're the Kidnapped Queen. He has to get you back."

"That's his fault!" I scoffed. "Juls didn't need to concoct that story to save face. He has no one to blame but himself."

"What else was he to do?" Mal asked, re-taking the seat opposite me. "When Grahar decided to marry you to Juls, the nobles were enraged. No king before was so selfish. He robbed them of two prizes in one swipe. A pretty Elowan bride for one of their sons, and a handsome king for one of their daughters."

I huffed through my nose remembering Jesi said the same thing.

"They don't even know me," I protested. "I could have been anyone."

"What you represent by your birth is a coveted commodity obscuring whatever or whoever else you are inside. Every noble mother and father with a young son eagerly awaited news of the first-born daughter of Elowa, and Grahar snatched their prize right out of their open hands."

The prize. At least Mal-Yin didn't mince words.

"The apparent love between you and the young king worked like a balm," he continued. "How could anyone argue against the match when you and Juls were so clearly in love? When it was so clearly fated? No noblemen could speak out against it."

I slumped in my chair, not realizing my besotted brae-nese routine worked to the Dorestes' advantage that way, any more than I had known my cover reached Kirwyn's ears.

"Think about it," Mal said, pinning me with his dangerous eyes. "Now, there are only two scenarios if Juls reveals you ran away. One, you didn't truly love the young king in the first place – which will justify the resentment of the nobles. It'll send them into an uproar as they'll be quick to argue you would have been a better match with one of their own. Or two... you did love the king and he did some-thing awful to the Queen of our Hearts to make her run and hide. Which will send everyone into an uproar."

Landdammit. I ran a hand through my hair, twisting it. Before we found each other again, Kirwyn had thought the latter as well. He'd worried Juls hurt me.

"Both options severely and irrevocably damage the dynasty," Mal explained. "I'm sure his pride plays into it, as well as his affection for you. But even if those things didn't, you put Juls in a position with no other option but to persuade you to return to him."

"Why are you trying to convince me if it will make your plans more difficult?" I asked, very suspicious. "You claimed my sister as your lover, my lover as your brother, and me as your songbird. Why would you endanger that when you've got everything you want within your grasp?"

"Maybe I'm not as evil as you think," Mal said, purposefully giving me his most malicious grin to contradict his words. I shot him a look of impatience.

Mal straightened, turning serious. "Neither is Juls. He did have some input in his decision to marry you. There was another option." Mal drummed his fingers on the table, pausing for dramatic effect. "For you to marry the Commander Navere."

My eyes widened in shock.

"Navere is from a noble family, and his sister, Merie, was very friendly with Juls when they were younger. Some speculate there was budding affection between the two, so it was logical. Marry you to Navere and Merie to the king. Their family's power would grow tenfold."

I shook my head. "Navere can't be trusted."

"Exactly. If you married Navere, the Dorestes feared what he might do, given your popularity together."

Navere would take the throne and later dispose of me, as Lida once mentioned.

"By some angles, he was first in line for your hand, and substituting another noblemen might result in grave insult. Easily outranking him, however, was the young king himself, as Grahar had always wanted anyway."

The wheels in my head turned until a realization came so surely it was almost as if I heard an accompanying *click* in my mind, opening a door to a truth that had been obscured.

"Oh... fuck," I breathed. "Juls was protecting his family. And me."

"Taking one for the team is the old expression," Mal-Yin agreed. He stood and resumed pacing.

"But what about Prince Lazlian? Why wasn't he considered?"

Mal shook his head. "Lazlian would have been the *worst* possible choice, even more powerful than Navere. The Elowan bride had to produce offspring with the young king, not his brother, because any child of the keylord's wouldn't be first in line for the throne and could potentially cause a revolt later in life, should that son decide to make a claim."

I dropped my face into my hands. Just when I thought I couldn't feel more guilt, fate piled extra upon my shoulders. To me, Juls was a man who forced me into marriage. But to Juls... he saw himself as having protected me. And possibly sacrificing his own happiness to do so.

Oh god... he *knew* what I'd done to his wine that night in his room, didn't he? And he probably drank it anyway, to protect me.

Why was it all so complicated? Why did simply being free to live my own life have to hurt anyone?

Mal-Yin waited patiently while I remained quiet a long time. Finally, he said ominously, "There is one more letter. It's from Prince Lazlian."

I gulped and looked up to see Mal held a note, already opened.

"You read it?" I frowned.

Mal shrugged. "The keylord didn't bother to seal it."

Part of me wanted to snatch the note from his hands and devour it and part of me wanted to throw it in the fire without reading it at all. As usual, curiosity got the better of me. I reached for the letter cautiously, as if it might bite me, and spread it onto my lap.

In direct contrast to Juls's information-filled missive, this page was almost entirely white, with only three sentences floating near the top. I could almost feel the rage coming from the sharp, hastily scribbled letters, slanting forward like they could reach right off the page to bring their declaration into being.

YOUR BOY IS AS GOOD AS DEAD. AND YOU ARE GOING TO WISH YOU WERE. THAT'S A VOW, LITTLE QUEEN.

My heart hammered and I looked over my shoulder as if Laz could be standing right there, raising a dagger to my throat. In my head I heard the unwritten end to that pledge.

That's a vow, little queen... and I always keep my vows.

There were infinite ways Lazlian could hurt me, clever ones that didn't even require my being in High Spire.

"Jona!" I cried abruptly, realization dawning. "I – I think he's going to take my sister. Use her against me. All this time I thought they'd come for her if I failed to return, but I bet Lazlian has taken her already – or he's going to. Mal, we have to save her, she's just a baby."

Mal-Yin shook his head with regret. "Impossible. Either she's still in Elowa, which is too heavily guarded by sea and will require bloodshed to pass their lines -- something you want to avoid. Or she's already in High Spire, which we'll find out when we get there."

I collapsed my head into my hands.

"If they had taken her, the letters likely would have already used her as leverage," Mal advised. "So it's less probable. But if they have, you know King Juls would never hurt her."

I let out a sound between a whimper and a groan.

"We'll find out as soon as we claim the castle," Mal promised, "And we'll keep her safe."

I heard the rustle of his fine clothing as he stood. I quickly pushed my feelings aside to process later because another thought came to me.

I was no longer the fool I once was.

Mal had risen to leave, as if he wanted to slip away before I worked it out.

"There was another letter, wasn't there?" I asked, stopping him. "The king or the keylord wrote to you, didn't they?"

One side of Mal-Yin's mouth curved as he turned back.

I fixed him with a hard stare. "What did they offer you in exchange for delivering me back to High Spire?" Before he could even construct a lie, I pressed, "We're building trust, remember?"

"Does it matter?" Mal asked. "What you really want to know is, was it worth considering and did I?"

I folded my arms and waited.

"It was. I did."

I blew out a puff of air. *Of course he did.*

"But the scales tip in your favor." Mal said it as if it were only a slight tipping. "You've got better odds at succeeding."

I blinked. "Cut the goatshit, Mal. You mean better odds to get you what you want with Rythas. You mean better odds to get into Aewna's pants."

"Presumptuous of you to assume I want her wearing pants at all," he said.

"She doesn't like vulgar jokes, you know," I scoffed, shooting to my feet. "She won't like you speaking to her that way."

Mal replied evenly, "Presumptuous of you to assume I'd dare upset her like that."

"No, you wouldn't, would you?" I agreed, cocking my head and advancing. "You give everyone one version of yourself and her another, don't you? But what about you is real?"

He considered me with those dangerously dark eyes. "Hiding our true selves is something your sister and I have in common. Something you found exhausting if not downright impossible during your time as the chosen braenese and the young queen. Didn't you?"

Yes, I thought. *It was just another kind of prison, to me.*

"So you're both consummate politicians?" I mused. "Is that what this is?"

Mal afforded me a rare look, a genuine softening of his face. "It's that she doesn't have to be. With me."

Mal might have meant, *when we're alone together,* but I thought he also meant, *in the public's eye.* That he'd shield her from the worst of that.

My own face softened, reflecting his. Mal was dangerous enough to defend Aewna from forces like her father and clever enough to protect her from public assaults. I also thought that he respected her abilities enough to know when to step back and would do so without his ego interfering in those cases.

Relenting, I sighed and gave Mal a small nod I knew he understood. He turned to leave but when he reached the door, he paused.

"Oh, I forgot," he said, returning to stand in front of me. Mal slipped a small velvet box from his pocket and laid it on the table. "This arrived from your husband today, as well."

I sucked in a breath. *What could be inside? A ruby ring to replace the one I threw into the sea? Priceless pearl earrings?* I knew it'd be something enormous and stunning to woo me back.

Without waiting for me to open it, Mal started to leave.

"You know," he mused before departing, "For two people not in love, you and Juls work very hard at protecting each other."

I rose my gaze from the ominous box to meet his eyes.

"But after you move to strike against him…" Mal cautioned, shaking his head.

"I know," I whispered. *He's going to hate me.*

Mal left. Alone, I slowly opened the black box.

My heart thumped.

Inside lay the simple gold band that was my wedding ring.

WHY WAS Rythas so obsessed with this hermit? I wondered, tossing in bed. He must have made several accurate prophecies for the people to believe in him. But his prophesizing reminded me too much of Elowa's own Mystics, who were full of lies. When I sought out the hermit with Jesi, he'd given me no answers. Worse, he'd spoken vague phrases even more meaningless than the Arch Priestess's riddles. His generalities were likely contrived to be easy to apply to any circumstance in an attempt to convey he possessed some kind of soothsaying. Eyes closed, he'd spoken to me through a gummy mouth.

We don't always notice the ground beneath our feet, but it's vital and it's always there. We should remember not to take it for granted.

We can't always see the stars above, but they're necessary and always shining. We should remember to be patient and wait for their light.

Those were his words. Total goatshit.

I'd huffed and turned to leave as I heard his even breathing, telling me he'd probably fallen asleep. When I'd reached the mouth of the hermit's cave, he still lay unmoving in his cot, eyes closed. But his voice carried over one last time and he'd said:

With dire need, stars will appear and illuminate the way. Even when it's light.

I'd struggled not to scoff a laugh. *Well I'm sure they fucking will most nights. And some even appear before it's fully dark. Of course it's only a matter of time.*

As if that vague conclusion was any great prediction. I left ready to tear my hair out at the wasted day.

I used the stars to guide me toward the mainland on my swim to Kirwyn, I used the stars to guide me toward the Oxholde warships, I used the stars to guide me all the time. Everyone did. So what?

I heard the door creak as Kirwyn came into the room and, finding me curled up in our bed, he asked, "What's wrong?"

When I didn't immediately speak, he said, "Do you want to know how I know what's going on in your head?"

I sat up, folding my legs beneath me, instantly at attention. *Yes. My tell. What was it?* Did I twitch my mouth or blink my eyes? And how did he anticipate my desires before I even voiced them?

"I'm good at knowing what people want, how to work them," Kirwyn began.

"And not at all cocky." I rolled my eyes.

"I'm telling you to emphasize my point," he said, giving me a scolding look. "I'm good but... that's not why I know what you're feeling or what you need." He reached out to stroke my hair. "I know because I feel the same, in reverse. You want to be touched somewhere and I want to touch you there. I want to take and you want to be taken. With you, it's not always mind-reading, it's just that we fit together. Like two pieces crafted for one another."

His voice ended on an unsure note, as if I'd be dissatisfied with his explanation. The corners of his mouth turned down in displeasure.

"Do you think I'm disappointed?" I asked, confused. "That you're not some mystical mind reader, that we match, is even *more* magical, to me. It's real. Fated."

Kirwyn leaned down and kissed my forehead. "So now you know I'm not clairvoyant and I can't know everything. But I *can* see you're upset. Tell me what happened."

It wasn't an order, but it wasn't quite a request either.

With leaden feet, I crossed to the chest of drawers and pulled out the letters, handing Juls's to Kirwyn first.

I could read the tension in his shoulders. But he didn't address the content other than to say with business-like evenness, "They're preparing for our attack."

I nodded, minnows swimming in my gut. If it were only Juls, I could count on his actions to follow an honorable course. But Lazlian was a wild card with an unnerving ability to guess my moves and motivations.

Piercing me now were dark green eyes from a man who could see inside me even better.

"Where's the one from the keylord?" Kirwyn asked.

I swallowed. "I was getting to that..." Anxiously, I handed him Lazlian's letter.

"See?" I urged. "He's threatening to *torture* me, Kirwyn. What do you call that, if not fury?"

Kirwyn lifted his gaze from the letter, jaw set.

"Foreplay."

CHAPTER 34

From the bathroom doorway the next morning, Kirwyn watched me getting dressed, rubbing his thumb over his forefinger. His half-grin told me he was enjoying the view, but I didn't think anything else crossed his mind until he said with surprising ease, "Once this is over, we can get married. Your old marriage means nothing. It doesn't count if you were forced."

I froze, dropping my shirt and staring at him, clad only in my undergarments.

"I'm sorry, I shouldn't have brought it up like that," Kirwyn said quickly.

"No, it's just that... I want us together in all ways," I said, placing my hand above my tattoo, "except that one."

Kirwyn's face registered shock. "Why? You said wanted to rule together as king and queen. Why not get married?"

"I don't like it," I scowled. "Don't like what I've seen of it. I've had two weddings already and I'm not even twenty. I don't want to do it again. I feel like..." I shrugged. "How many times can I be married before it ceases to mean anything?"

The folding of Kirwyn's arms and the casual crossing of one foot over the other as he leaned against the doorframe said, *challenge accepted.*

Stubbornly, I crossed my own arms. "What does it matter in this world anyway? You're the one always saying things like that. So why do you want to marry me? Give me one good reason."

"I can give you two."

I narrowed my eyes, suspicious. I'd thrown out the challenge knowing I could counter any *one* statement, yet Kirwyn thought he could come up with *two?* What on earth could marriage possibly bring –

"First, I want you to feel safe." He declared it so firmly that my heart skipped a beat. "You *don't* feel safe, even now," he insisted, gentler this time. "I watch you when you think no one's looking. The show you put on for everyone – even me sometimes – isn't real. You stare into space and bite your nails with your shoulders tensed to your ears. As if someone is going to come behind you at any moment to touch you or take you away."

He'd struck too close to home for me to think up reasons to deny it. I could only whisper, "And the second reason?"

With masculine pride, he declared, "I want the world to know you're mine."

That bold statement made my heart flutter as well. If I'd heard the same from Juls, I'd have bristled. But Kirwyn saying it left me breathless.

You and Lazlian might both know what I'm going to do, I thought. *But only you know what I* need.

I stared at Kirwyn, awed. He'd changed from the volatile, unpredictable boy I'd met in Elowa. Just like his tattoo, he'd become more earth now, more solid. The

Kirwyn I'd first met had danced around his emotions. We'd clash together and come apart, pride wounded... then shyly poke our heads back out again, given enough time.

But this Kirwyn leaning against our doorframe wasn't afraid to assert what he wanted. If I retreated, he didn't retreat in return. He advanced. *Stalked.*

Literally.

He came toward me now, forcing me to tilt my head up to look at him and holding my chin in place with his fingers. His smirk told me he knew exactly what he was doing and though it irritated me, it kinda turned me on, too.

He wasn't dancing around his emotions any longer, he was dancing around *me*.

Kirwyn headed off to train with Mal's men and Aewna knocked on our door while I finished getting ready. Mal-Yin's dogs, Bruel and Terisine, followed at her heels.

"I came to see if you wanted a break outside the compound. Mal and I are going riding," she announced. I could see she was excited, though she tried to conceal it. She'd already dressed in riding clothes and for the first time, Aewna felt safe enough to forgo her camouflage wig.

Sighing, I asked, "Juls was never an option once we came here. Was he?"

Aewna averted her eyes. "The truth is... once I saw Mal," she licked her lips, "my fate was sealed. I just didn't know it or couldn't admit it at the time."

I realized I still held onto the hope that despite Mal-Yin following Aewna to Elowa, there was a small chance she could meet Juls and a spark might ignite.

Feeling guilty I'd persisted when she'd already fallen for Mal, I explained, "I just thought it was the solution that made everyone happy and harmed no one."

"I know and I don't blame you. I *agree* with you. Or I did," Aewna said, enigmatically. "It *seems* to be the smart decision, and no one would think otherwise without knowing our history. Those who don't study the past are doomed to repeat it."

"What do you mean?" I asked. I'd started to tie back my hair but immediately stopped and gave her my full attention.

"That's the other thing I came to talk to you about. Mal and I were up late in his private library last night, talking and reading. The alliance between Elowa and Rythas started with good intentions. Most endeavors do."

"How do you know?" I asked, blinking in surprise.

Aewna smiled, scratching Bruel beneath his head, who'd nudged her for attention. "The history of our people? Guess who has it."

I scowled. "How does he have *everything?*"

"He's a collector." Her grin widened.

"And he's collecting you too? The pretty princess from Elowa?"

Aewna hedged, saying, "It's why that golden cube is so enticing. He doesn't have one."

"Do you know what's on it?"

She nodded. "It's information on the Spade's slave quarters. Locations, numbers, various schedules. One of the many reasons it's hard to successfully win a battle against the Spades is because they use innocent people for defense. If the information on that cube isn't too outdated or if it links to current data, anyone launching an attack might be able to avoid mass casualties of the innocent."

"Does Mal actually care about the innocent?" I challenged.

Aewna flushed a little and stammered, "You know I can tell when someone's lying and I- I'm not saying he's a saint. But a lot of it is a front to keep control. Even the entry hall isn't what you think. Well, it is, but it's not as bad as you believe. They were already dead and volunteered for the... service."

I barely heard her because it was clear Aewna had succumbed to Mal's spell... and she was the *last* person on Earth I'd ever expect to fall so quickly for a man. But, I supposed, Mal-Yin was no typical man.

This is how a devil seduces an angel, I thought. *With books and wine-kisses.*

No, I corrected. *With knowledge and protection.*

Maybe it was as Kirwyn hinted. He was giving her what her father never truly did.

"So what happened in Elowa?" I asked, spreading my hands impatiently. "Tell me everything. Why did our people gather there and why is the chosen braenese shipped off like a prized goat?"

Aewna sat down on the bed. The dogs followed, laying on the floor by her feet.

"Milton was the first Elowan, that much is true. But he didn't come from sea — at least not from underneath it." She knit her brows, scowling prettily. "He came from the mainland. Early in the fighting, his wife and two daughters were killed before his eyes. Apparently, it was horrendously gruesome and it changed him. His family was a part of the Optimal Election program. Back then, people weren't fleeing *to* islands, they were fleeing *from* them. Abandoning their homes when shipments of food, medicine, and other critical supplies to daily life were no longer making it over.

Milton had the foresight – and the resources – to set himself up on Elowa."

Aewna's scowl deepened. "In order to populate Elowa, he began to offer others from the OE program passage. Particularly, those who resembled his deceased wife or their children. Young males were brought too, especially for labor, but for several years Elowa was dominated by Milton and his," Aewna cleared her throat and said pointedly, *"specially selected* beautiful women. For his own purposes."

Oh, fuck. My stomach soured. Thoroughly repulsed, I sat onto the bed beside Aewna. The man we'd worshipped for years was nothing more than a scumbag.

"I don't know what happened exactly, but I imagine it didn't take long for the women to reach their limit on putting up with Milton's... advances. One night, they banded together and killed him. Well, the history book describes it more graphically."

My imagination ran wild. *With their bare hands? Daggers? Slowly?* I wasn't sorry but I wasn't sure I wanted to know.

"What happened next is unclear. Over generations of isolation, the myths began. Classes were formed. The Mystics and the Fire Maidens banded together. But for many years it was largely a time of peace," Aewna explained. "Eventually, the world shifted again and others began stumbling upon Elowa. The women who'd been told the truth didn't want a repeat in the form of another Milton, and they realized that having a concentration of OE descendants made for a tantalizing prospect to outsiders."

I felt my heart pick up speed as I listened, rapt, imagining this long-ago Elowa.

"At the same time, Rythas was solidifying. As the next nearest island, explorers came to Elowa and, as expected, they were enchanted by her people. But this time fate was kinder. A powerful nobleman from Rythas fell in love with a braenese and she loved him in return. He set up the treaty between the two islands to keep Rythas and everyone else out of Elowa. He was forced to offer incentives to persuade the others to help protect her borders, but it began with good intentions. He did it for love," Aewna insisted. "Once a generation, a Daughter of Elowa would come to Rythas and choose a husband. Any Elowan would do, royal or not, and it worked out well as some *wanted* to go. But over the years, it changed."

Aewna looked at me seriously, brow furrowed. "Soon enough, only a braenese was acceptable. Then, only the first-born braenese would do. Years passed and the right for the Daughter of Elowa to choose her own husband was stripped away. Over generations the arrangement morphed into where we are today. The bride has no say the selection of her husband and her purity has to be guaranteed by no male touching her." Sadly, Aewna concluded, "I don't doubt the changes will continue."

I exhaled a long breath, tugging my lip in thought. I didn't doubt it either. Hell, I'd probably be a cause for more rules being added. *Too defiant,* they'd say. *Bring her over sooner.* If a Daughter of Elowa was sent to her husband-to-be at a young age, she'd be more malleable.

I wouldn't be surprised if Lazlian was already arguing to Juls such policies for the future.

"So you see, even if it's an alliance with good intentions, if it's based in marriage," Aewna shook her head, "I fear it has the potential to become the same slippery slope as it's always been."

"I understand," I firmly agreed. "And I would never want that to happen."

"We couldn't know," Aewna said, laying a tentative hand on mine. I didn't pull away. "When the past is shrouded, we're doomed to wear its shackles."

So what would happen when all of Elowa learned the truth? I wondered. *What did an unshackled Elowa look like?*

What did an unshackled me *look like?*

With so many options before us, the future was a blank slate and the idea that I could write anything upon it was overwhelming. If my fate wasn't returning to Elowa, what was it? I knew I belonged with Kirwyn, but what did our life look like? What were we doing?

At least Aewna knew what she wanted.

With such a heavy mood, I broke the silence by teasing, "I understand why you don't want Juls, but *Mal?* You know, Kirwyn had an interesting theory." I raised my eyebrows in a Jesi-like manner and said with obvious implication, "He thinks Mal fills a protective need... that Volmar did not."

Aewna pinked at my suggestion. "N- neither of us had exemplary fathers," she stammered. "Isn't one of the things you love about Kirwyn how he adores and protects you?"

It was my turn to blush. I chose to find the rug very interesting at that moment and changed the subject. "What is happening with Volmar?"

"Kirwyn and Mal have been coordinating to seize Pama's throne once the battle is over, and they're ready to neutralize my father in a few days. His estate will be put under guard so he cannot send letters."

I didn't know why I felt guilty when it was the right thing to do, when they'd both done awful things to us. But she was my *mother.* And I hated to admit it, but he might be my *father.*

"What should we do with them if we win? They're a danger that cannot go unchecked."

"I know," Aewna agreed, absent-mindedly petting Terisine's head. "Mal and Kirwyn have plenty of ideas they want to present to us, of course."

I rolled my eyes at their combined cockiness... but sitting beside Aewna, a strange thought occurred to me. To the world, she and I were two Elowan princesses destined to rule or to marry men like Juls... or Lazlian. Mal and Kirwyn, with no monarchical ties, had come out of nowhere and swept away a pair of royal sisters – stolen us from the grasp of kings and princes.

Staring at Aewna, I felt uncomfortably narcissistic to think it, but I had to admit that seducing us had probably bolstered their swagger.

CHAPTER 35

"Do I really need a blindfold?" I asked, grinning. "You will one-hundred percent peek, I know you."

I pouted but allowed Kirwyn to tie the dark blindfold securely around my head. He clasped my hand and led me down the hall. We made one turn, continued down another room or corridor, and finally I heard a door swing on its hinges. We walked a few more feet before Kirwyn stopped.

"I'm going to remove it now," he said. I could hear the twinge of excitement in his voice and my pulse raced, wondering what I'd see when he took it off.

Muted light greeted me and my mouth dropped as Kirwyn untied the blindfold.

We were under the sea!

I spun in circles, disbelieving. The room was a glass bubble, like a pocket of air surrounded by water. Fish and other sea creatures of all kinds swam around us – to my left and right and above me and even below. The floor itself was glass, allowing us to see fish darting beneath our feet. One doorway led into the space, seeming to connect to a narrow tunnel for exiting. Everything else was cultivated like a sampling of the ocean. Bedrock and sand formed the base and climbed upward, with all kinds of caverns and coral clinging to the sides. Fish of every color – even stingrays and sea turtles – swam by.

"It's magical," I breathed.

"It's an aquarium," Kirwyn said. "A very special one."

I put my hand over my heart, realizing it raced. The room contained one low, tufted cushion for sitting. Round and wide and backless, I didn't know what to call it. But it was somewhere I'd want to lay for hours, watching this enchantment all around me.

"This is incredible." I felt tears well in my eyes. "How does a world that unleashes such horror create this too?"

For a few reverent moments I ambled from one side to the next, awed at the landlocked shrine to the sea.

Watching me, Kirwyn said, "I wanted to do this on the beach but... I figured this was the next best thing."

I didn't know what he meant, but when he lifted a ring unlike any I'd seen before, I gasped.

"Will you marry me?" he asked. Four simple words unleashing a tidal wave of emotion.

"Yes!" I cried, almost before he'd finished. Throwing my arms around a grinning Kirwyn, I kissed him repeatedly through his smiles and he slid the ring onto my finger.

Fit for a Sea Queen.

The circular stone was a shade of blue-green I couldn't name. Teal might be the best term, but that didn't do the color justice. Flanking the main beauty were two diamonds, small enough not to detract from the middle gem, but large enough to add just the right sparkle.

"It's like..." I gasped, "like..."

"Like a drop of the ocean," Kirwyn grinned.

"Yes!" I cried. "It's like the sea... the clear, beautiful sea back home."

I'd never thought I'd care much for jewelry, but I'd never seen an item this special before. I gazed at the stone, utterly dazzled.

"It's like looking into a small, magic gazing glass leading straight to the ocean. It's like carrying a drop of the sea on my finger! I love it. It's so beautiful, I wish I had something for you too. Is that never the way here?"

With some guilt, I realized, *I didn't feel inspired to ask when it was Juls giving me a ring of engagement.*

Kirwyn shook his head. "You're everything I could want."

"But how did you get this?"

"That's my business."

Rolling my eyes, I smiled even wider. "What kind of stone is it?" I turned my finger to watch it sparkle like the sun shining on the waves.

"To be honest, I'm not sure," Kirwyn admitted, rubbing the back of his neck. "It might be a Paraiba or blue-green sapphire or something else entirely. Without an expert, there's no way to know, and we'll never find anyone truly qualified outside Spade City."

I kissed him again. "I don't care. It'll stay a mystery, just like the ocean. Kirwyn, I absolutely love it and I love you so much it hurts."

I threw my arms around him again and he picked me up off the ground as he hugged and spun me.

"I know we might have plenty of time..." he trailed off, setting me on my feet. "But we might not. We don't know what will happen when we leave this compound. I'd marry you now if we could but I know that's not what you want."

"It wouldn't be right or real," I said, brow furrowed. "I

don't know how to explain it but it's not what I want for us. If we're going to do this, if I'm going to do it again, I want it to be right this time."

I remembered something and teased in my haughtiest voice, "Wait a minute. Aren't you supposed to get on your knees to propose? That's what they used to do on the mainland." Proudly, I added, "I read about it."

Kirwyn laughed. "Did you now? You're right. They did."

He walked toward me in a suddenly predatory manner, forcing me backwards. My knees hit the round, backless sofa and Kirwyn leaned forward until I was made to sit. I felt a change in the air and a warming of my skin with his heated stare.

"I'll get on my knees for you," he said in a husky voice, dropping to the floor. With alarming speed, Kirwyn gripped my legs and pulled me so that my back fell onto the sofa as he dove between my thighs. I had that thrilling rush from the strong, easy way he manhandled me. It wasn't careless, it was confident, natural.

Without even removing my undergarments Kirwyn kissed me through the thin material, making me shiver as he backed up to let his hot breath caress me.

Still not moving the cloth aside, he nibbled directly in the center, teasing me. I felt my increasing wetness seep onto my underwear and whimpered, "Kirwyn, please."

"Please, what?" he asked between kisses. "Do you want me to lick you, Zaria?"

"Yes!"

"Do you want me to lick your pretty pussy until you come?"

"*Kirwyn,*" I protested, turning bright red and slapping my hand over my mouth. *My god, you can't just say those things.*

"They're just words, Zaria, remember? They're not bad. Say them," he ordered, pulling aside my underwear to let his breath fall directly on my sex. I writhed, trying to meet his lips, but he wouldn't allow it.

"I want you to lick..." I squeezed my eyes shut. "I can't."

Slowly, Kirwyn slid down my underwear. When I was fully exposed, he parted my legs intentionally wide and wedged himself between them again. Using only one finger, he trailed a line from the base of my slit to the top, circling my clit repeatedly then giving it a gentle squeeze. I nearly jumped off the cushion as I cried out.

Was I so wet it coated my thighs? Had it dripped onto the couch?

"Please..."

"Of course. As soon as you say the words."

I thrashed my head side to side, frustrated.

"You're glistening with need, Zaria," Kirwyn announced smugly. "I can already see how desperately you want me to lick you. Just say it."

"You can be such an asshole sometimes," I panted.

"And I can see yours," he declared, to my complete and total mortification. "Call me that again and I'll stick my tongue there," he threatened.

I didn't think it was possible to turn any redder, but I did. Stuttered choking noises came from my throat. That strange humiliation-arousal warred within me.

"Would you rather I lick somewhere else? Say it," he ordered, strong hands tensing on my inner thighs.

Nodding, I quickly agreed, "Yes, somewhere else! Please lick my... pussy."

The first press of his tongue to my clit made me see stars. My core pulsed with desire and my heart hammered with love. I didn't think it was possible to be happier, to ever want more than I had at that moment.

Kirwyn was *so fucking good* with his tongue, it took no time to bring me to climax. I ran my hands through his dark hair, fisting it when the ecstasy crested. In that magical room with fish swimming all around me, I came loudly, crying out my pleasure to the glass-encased sea.

HOLDING one another as we laid on the tufted cushion, an intrusive and unpleasant thought struck me. The fish dancing all around us – and the turtles and stingrays and seahorses – they'd never swim beyond the bounds of their glass encasement. The sight was beautiful to behold... but they were trapped. I knew in the ocean they'd naturally travel for many leagues, basking under the sun's light.

I suddenly felt sorry for the creatures around me. And a little nervous for myself.

"Promise me... promise me you'll let me stay wild," I whispered to Kirwyn. "That you'll stay wild with me." Thinking about the power games we played in private, I amended, "I don't mean you can't do the things we do when we're alone together in bed. I – I like that. And I don't mean that I do not want a house or children and all of that someday..." I frowned, sitting up and trying to explain. I did not want to be dimmed, muted into another version of myself. The fate I so feared in High Spire.

But it was so difficult to explain when mainlanders spoke differently and I couldn't even explain it to myself.

"I mean, here," I placed my hand to my head. "That our thoughts will always flow freely between us and through us." I brought my hand to my breast. "And here. That our love will always run wild."

"I promise," Kirwyn swore, sitting up to kiss my forehead. "You got it. Wild love, together. You're safe with me, Zaria, I won't hurt you."

Lacing our fingers, we leaned back and watched the fish swimming above us in contented silence.

Leave, came a sudden voice in my head. *You have each other, don't risk it. Leave, together, now.*

Fear shot through my heart. Kirwyn and I had everything we needed. Were we being foolish not to simply run far away together?

I can't, I argued back to the voice. *They'll take Jona or another girl in my place.*

Intentionally trying to distract myself from one fear, I summoned my courage and asked Kirwyn something else I'd anxiously been pondering.

"What do I taste like?" I blurted.

"What?" He nearly choked in surprise.

"Back when we were at Volmar's house one day, you said you liked the way I taste when you do what you just did." I swallowed. "What's it... like?"

Kirwyn thought a moment. "Like candied berries." I could hear his grin. "Tart, but sweet."

My face turned berry-red.

"I want to taste you too," I said, shyly. "Tonight. You're not letting me give you anything... but I want to give you this, I want you to give me this too. I need guidance though. Teach me, Kirwyn. Teach me how to please you."

I'd put my mouth on Kirwyn plenty of times, but I'd never completed the act as I always got nervous about what came next. And since he enjoyed finishing with sex anyway, we'd somehow moved on every time. But maybe he wanted to finish in my mouth and simply wasn't pressuring me?

Kirwyn grabbed my hand and pulled me to standing. "Come on."

"*Now?*" I asked.

"Why wait?"

That answered that question.

Teasing, I replied, "It's only fair. You like to play games where you make *me* wait."

He flashed that charming, but oh-so-smug smirk when he replied, "But you know I don't play fair."

IN THE PRIVACY of our own room, my heart raced with nerves. "How do you want me?" I asked.

"On your knees," Kirwyn grinned. "If you really want to show me how thankful you are."

I swallowed, hard. *Okay, then.*

I slid to the floor, maintaining what I hoped was a seductive look. When Kirwyn lowered his pants, I parted my lips to begin, but he clasped my chin with his thumb and forefinger, lifting my gaze. "I'm not going to stop this time, do you understand? I'm going to come in your mouth, Zaria, and you're going to swallow all of it."

I gulped again, clenching down below as I nodded. Kirwyn's voice and his choice of words sent heat racing through my veins. I never could have imagined this when we first met -- that I'd be kneeling before the demon who washed ashore on my beach. That the boy who taunted and titillated would become the man who stood above me now, making good on all those impish promises in the most erotic ways.

The strange boy who talked a bit too much was a little quieter now, but he always seemed to know the right thing to say. Because Kirwyn's command reverberated in my head, giving me exactly what I needed. A flush of arousal to start, the discipline to finish, and an enthralling connection through the dynamic of our power exchange. It wasn't one-sided, it was fluid. He exercised the authority to tell me what to do and I wielded the power to enrapture him with those acts.

I blinked, noticing Kirwyn's lust-filled eyes. *Or to enchant him simply by gazing up like this. As he arouses me simply by looking down.*

"Lick here," he said, releasing my chin to motion. "On the sensitive underside near the tip."

Tentatively, I pressed my tongue where he'd indicated and watched Kirwyn shudder and groan. After repeating the movement a few times and seeing his obvious pleasure, I kissed and licked Kirwyn's shaft with new hunger. I went further down on him than I'd gone before and was rewarded with more groans. I sucked with vigor, my own body rising with pleasure at his. I pushed down on his erection until I gagged, but he didn't seem to mind at all. When Kirwyn neared his climax, his grip on my head tightened as I'd once imagined it would. The firm hold made me panic and tear a little, but I wanted to please him.

"Every... drop..." Kirwyn panted above me, thrusting faster. "Take all of it, Zaria."

So deep I had difficulty not gagging again, Kirwyn burst into my mouth. A warm stream of salty fluid filled my throat and coated my tongue with its strange taste.

But I liked it because it was Kirwyn. Kirwyn's taste on my tongue.

He moaned so breathlessly at the height of it that I had

difficult making out his stunted words. "...atta, girl... just like that... swallow me, my love."

Dutifully, I swallowed, blinking up at him when I finished.

"Perfect," Kirwyn said, as he slowly withdrew from my mouth. The way his passionate gaze held mine and the way he gently swiped his thumb across my lips made me feel warm and swoony. I realized he answered a question in my eyes.

"Perfect, Zaria."

CHAPTER 36

A week before departure, Kirwyn and I followed the labyrinth of Mal's underground tunnels to meet with his scuba expert, a man named Ener. The air outside the compound had turned cooler and I didn't like it. Groggily, I rubbed my eyes, having trouble sleeping at night as I imagined all the things that could go wrong. In the darkness I stared at the ceiling and tried to formulate contingency plans for each possibility. Kirwyn said that was wise, but that what usually went wrong was what couldn't be anticipated, and that we'd have to pivot and move fast at some point. He argued that a good night's sleep was the best preparation for relying on our quick thinking and followed his own advice.

But he'd always been more disciplined than me when it came to reining in our wild imaginations and impulses.

Memories of that wagon full of children struck at inopportune moments, making breathing difficult. Sometimes I tried to distract myself and shut off my emotions entirely because the horrors overwhelmed me. I'd flash from their young faces to Singen's and Milicena's. At times I wondered

-- if Aewna could tell what a person was *thinking,* did I have an enhanced Elowan ability to understand how they were *feeling?* Did I feel too much?

I was sure Kirwyn would just call it empathy, and maybe it was. Maybe it was the kind that naturally flourished without having been hardened by constant exposure to horror, as he had.

When I awoke from nightmares of Lazlian doing to me what he'd done to Singen, I'd hold Kirwyn loosely, sweating and shaking but trying not to disturb his slumber... or to give him reason to hook me up to sleep monitors again.

Juls would never let those atrocities happen, I consoled myself. *But Lazlian could do other things. Clever tortures where no one would see the evidence, like I'd once feared from Grahar.*

Even if Laz didn't permanently scar or maim me, Mal-Yin was right. Kirwyn would never be spared. And anything bad happening to Kirwyn was worse than if it happened to me.

At least the cool chemical pool worked to jolt me awake each morning. I kept my muscles ready for the long swim and half of the time, Kirwyn joined me. I couldn't deny he was a very strong swimmer, but he wasn't as advanced as I was, and I knew we'd continue arguing about whether he'd swim the Black Passage with me.

The other half of the time, Kirwyn trained with Mal's guard. *Just in case,* he said. *In case things turn violent.*

I knew that too, was wise. But I also knew that if it came to a deadly battle, we were doomed regardless. As we walked to meet with Ener that afternoon, I vowed to do whatever it took to keep things as bloodless as possible.

What if... keeping things bloodless required a bigger sacrifice?

"Kirwyn?" I muttered tentatively. "Mal-Yin thinks Juls might try to cut a deal, that he'll want to keep me by his side publicly and allow us to be together... privately." I gently pulled his hand to stop his walking. "Mal is right about a lot of things and the Dorestes are shady. So what if Juls does require me in some capacity? What if he makes it a condition of the negotiations? I know you want to kill him, but please, talk to me honestly. This is serious and it's bigger than us. There's more than just our happiness at stake." I took a deep breath and whispered, "What if it's the *only* way?"

With his teeth clenched, Kirwyn sighed, bringing a hand to his forehead and rubbing. For a few seconds he didn't speak as he scratched the scruff on his cheeks and huffed through his nose. My heart raced as I awaited his answer. Truthfully, I was scared no matter what he said because such an outcome frightened me whether we'd agree willingly or do our best to fight it.

Finally, Kirwyn met my eyes, staring hard for a moment before saying low, "If there's no other way."

We gazed at one another quietly as unspoken thoughts swirled in the air around us – images of what that might look like. *You must truly love me,* I thought.

"Come here," Kirwyn said, pulling me into his chest when he saw the tears welling in my eyes.

It didn't feel right for him to comfort me. Kirwyn would be suffering just as much in that scenario, maybe more. He wanted to *kill* Juls, after all.

"I will never love anyone the way I love you," I swore into his neck.

"I know."

"I would die without you. I couldn't go on, life would cease to mean anything," I whispered. "Don't tell me no."

Softly, Kirwyn replied, "I can't ask of you something I can't do myself."

～

OUR SCUBA INSTRUCTOR was a broad-shouldered swimmer, like me. He had brown hair that he tied at the nape of his neck in a goat's tail, but it was short enough that pieces had slipped out. His warm smile and obvious expertise immediately put me at ease.

"I know you haven't explored the passage when it's flooded, but have you at least traveled the tunnel by boat?"

"No," I cringed. "But I've seen the entrance and exit."

Ener sucked in a breath. "That's... not ideal. Do you know how long it is? An estimate?"

I pictured High Spire in my mind. "It's not more than a quarter mile."

He nodded. "This won't be as dangerous as normal cave diving since the Black Passage is in part, manmade and direct. But the basic rules still apply. Redundancy is key. You'll need two air tanks and two headlamps in case one fails."

"There are quasi-legal, modern lights in the passage as well," I piped up, eager to contribute my knowledge. "Dimmed and muted underwater, I'm sure, but they're there." I frowned. "Although there's no way to know if Navere will cut the power."

"Right," Ener nodded. "Back up lights will be critical. If one goes out, you're as good as dead down there in the dark."

"I'll have a light for backup as well," Kirwyn said, firmly. "Two, so that's four in total."

My chest tightened in fear. "No, Kirwyn," I protested, too anxious to care if we argued in front of Ener. "You can't. I don't think you can complete the swim as fast as I can," I said gently, trying not to bruise his ego with an audience. "And if Lazlian got his hands on you, I couldn't bear what he'd do."

The image of Singen's mutilation rose to mind and my stomach roiled as if serpents twisted within, making me instantly sick. *Lazlian's a monster inside,* I thought. *And he'd happily make a monster of you, outside.*

Staring at the wetsuit, the memory of when I'd last worn one flashed in my mind, the night Lazlian and I had worked together to protect High Spire.

Is the keylord as horrible as you imagine? another voice in my head asked. *Or were his actions with Singen more isolated? Executed in the heat of the moment and to protect his loved ones?*

I gulped. *Including you?*

If that were the case... I had easily forgiven Kirwyn for torturing the man who attacked Vesper. Would I ever find a way to forgive Lazlian?

If he hurt Kirwyn, never.

"You think I'm going to let him touch you?" I asked. "That I'd take that chance? Kirwyn, please. You said you'd let me lead when it came to Rythas if I let you lead us here."

"And you are leading. But I'm following right behind." Arms folded, he said, "You might as well relent, because you know I'm going to win in the end."

I folded my own arms. He was trying to play power games and it wouldn't work this time...

...but I could make him think it did. I was good at making men believe what they wanted.

Huffing through my nose, I sighed, "Fine. Swear that when we get to Rythas, I'm in command?"

Kirwyn scrutinized my face longer than I'd have liked. I tried not to avert my eyes.

"I swear," he vowed.

Ener motioned us over to the table full of equipment.

"You may have seen pictures with a tank on a diver's back, but that's not how you'll do it. You'll mount each on your side. You're going to be wider than you're used to, but it's more balanced and more comfortable. However, we'll also need to strap all your supplies on your back in a water-proof pack. It's going to feel bulky and it'll slow down your speed."

"Carrying gear on my back is something I've done before," I said, recalling my swim to the Oxholde warships.

"We'll practice each day in the pool," Ener said, spreading his hand to indicate we should follow him.

From that day on, Kirwyn and I donned wetsuits and strapped all the necessary gear onto our backs, learning how to operate the compressed air tanks underwater and practicing swimming with so much loaded onto our bodies.

We also met with a petite woman who instructed us on operating the e-bombs. Unlike regular bombs, this kind didn't explode or emit fire. Unlike Lazlian, this woman was easy to talk to and I felt comfortable learning the basics from her. I didn't worry that she'd rigged anything to fail or to kill me.

Besides the necessary equipment, to subdue the sentries at the Black Passage and for any guards we met along the way, I agreed to carry one tranquilizer gun and *one* bullet gun into High Spire. I had to.

If it's just me, *if it's just* one *gun, it's not likely to set off a chain reaction of violence,* I reasoned.

But I needed Kirwyn to stay behind with Mal's ships. Because having *him* carry a loaded gun in the proximity of Juls or Laz was definitely a concern.

CHAPTER 37

It was the night before we departed for the coast and the tension of imminent battle ran through the compound. Everyone, including Mal's army, departed the next day. I was a sea storm of nerves and needed to be close to Kirwyn, now more than ever.

"Outside," I whispered against Kirwyn's ear, rubbing against his hard body. "If anything goes wrong... I don't want my last memory of us to be in here."

"I know a way," he said, clasping my hand and leading us through the maze of corridors into wings of the stronghold I hadn't yet explored. When we'd ducked into what seemed like our tenth hallway, a guard called out, "Hey! You can't go back there!"

Looking at each other and laughing, Kirwyn and I broke into a run. I had imagined we'd find somewhere secluded in one of the inner farms, but he led me through a set of doors where we popped up *outside* of Mal's thick walls.

"They're going to come looking for us soon," Kirwyn said, jamming the door shut. "Run."

We took off again into the trees, laughing in a much-needed release of tension. Kirwyn pulled us to a stop when he reached an area he liked.

"How long do we have?" I asked.

"Minutes."

"Sounds like a challenge," I grinned, tearing off my shirt.

"That's my job," Kirwyn directed, flipping me around. I grasped the tree for balance and yelped as he yanked my pants and undergarments to the ground. Stepping out, I was already breathing heavily before I slowly turned around, fully naked.

Kirwyn stilled. His eyes lingered on my intimate regions as if it were the first time. *Or the last,* I thought, heart aching.

"You're staring," I blushed. Under such scrutiny I instinctively crossed my arms.

"Put your hands down." His voice was thick with lust.

I lowered my arms. Kirwyn's voice—or his stare—did things to me no other man could do even with the use of better equipment at his disposal. His gaze captured and enflamed my skin and the deep timbre of his voice seemed laced with some magic to compel me.

"Let me look at you, too," I whispered, fighting the urge to squirm.

"In a minute," Kirwyn murmured, spellbound. I was the one not wearing any clothing, yet he gazed, enraptured, as if he were powerless. Kirwyn tucked my hair behind my ear and our eyes locked, wrapping us in that strange cocoon of desire the outside world couldn't penetrate. Those green eyes always reminded of the forest back in Elowa. I inhaled his woodsy scent, like the trees, the earth. Home. Safe.

"You're so beautiful," he rasped in awe.

Everyone told me I was, I thought. *But you were the only one I've ever wanted to be beautiful for.*

Slowly, Kirwyn backed up, stripped his own clothing, and it was my turn to watch, mesmerized. Fully naked he was glorious, from his long legs to his toned chest. My breasts felt heavy and full in anticipation of his touch, tingling as they rose for his skilled hands. I knew Kirwyn would observe the change and the fierce hunger reflected on his face confirmed it. Desire pooled in the area between my legs, and though he couldn't see how I'd grown wet and swollen below, I knew he knew that too.

I could never hide from him. He looked at me and my body responded, readied for his will.

It's the same for him, I thought, mouth dry at the sight of what I'd caused to stiffen.

Naked, we crashed together. I ran my hands along the muscles in his arms and shoulders. Lean, not bulky, but the hardness made him feel so safe, so solid. He slid teasing fingers down the curve of my back and over my rear, squeezing both cheeks in his hands.

I heard the boom of thunder and I jumped a little, but it was far enough away not to be troubling. Drops of rain pelted my bare skin as we kissed, soft at first, but quickly beating faster. Though the weather had chilled a bit, we were both hot enough that I didn't mind the cool caress of the storm.

And *my god,* did Kirwyn look beautiful wet.

He sat on the sodden grass, perhaps taking the brunt of what would soon turn muddy.

"I want to watch you shatter in my lap," he said, lowering me to straddle him. Neither of us broke eye contact despite the pooling rain on our lashes. I couldn't tear my gaze from the chiseled angles of his face if I wanted to. Rain streaked his cheeks and glistened on his wet lips, begging me to kiss them. Kirwyn guided my hips downward, impaling me on his delicious hardness. We'd never done it like this before, but my body knew how to move.

I closed my eyes, arching and rocking against him, offering my breasts to his greedy mouth, to the rain and sky.

"I love you." He mouthed the fierce vow against my throat, sucking. "I will never, *ever* stop loving you."

"I love you, too," I panted. Our slick bodies moved frantically against one another, and I felt an energy build around and through us. "I'm yours. Kirwyn, I was made for you, born for you. And you for me."

"For me..." he echoed as he groaned, stretching and filling me. "Born for me... and I was born for you."

As his lips crashed into mine, my heart swelled to nearly bursting. We mated like wild creatures in the dark, rainy night. But the baser our passion became, the more it seemed to burn away everything material around us, paving the way to somewhere transcendent. The ecstasy surged beyond me; our love made me feel like I touched the infinite.

Kirwyn had always been my sin and my salvation.

He snapped his hips quickly, tilting upwards in a manner that wrested control and made me gasp and shudder, bringing us where I wanted to go, where we could only go together.

"*Kirwyn.*" I breathed his name like a prayer. It was everything at once. A plea not to stop. A cry of gratitude. An invocation of the divine. I prayed to him, I prayed *through* him.

When I climaxed in time with his, I didn't just touch the

stars. I expanded until I burst beyond, until I became infinite.

HAND IN HAND, we returned to Mal-Yin's compound. Part of me wondered if we were followed, caught, *watched*. It made me blush a little, but I couldn't bother to care much. Not when I weighed it against everything we faced in the next few days.

I knew it had been our last time making love before the battle.

But to keep Kirwyn safe, I would have to make him believe we'd have one more chance.

CHAPTER 38

The next day, we marched with Mal-Yin's soldiers to the breezy coast, where a variety of boats bobbed in the bay. Rythas would spy the polished fleet from miles away; there was no way to avoid it. Despite the mismatch in size of the dozen or so vessels, nothing was hodgepodge about their construction, like the Oxholde warships. Whatever their original use, Mal had streamlined each vessel to rigid specifications. Modern motorboats of all sizes were sleek, gray, and formidable, just like his compound.

Mal had insisted Aewna stay back in his stronghold, though not without a fight. I heard them arguing when I passed by her door -- surprised to find she'd returned to her room in the first place. Secretly, I agreed with Mal and I was glad he'd won. Aewna didn't belong in this battle and there was no reason to endanger her life.

I also understood that Mal didn't want to risk her getting captured and being used against him, because I felt the same about Kirwyn. The problem was, I'd already failed to win that argument.

I'd have to outwit him. I couldn't afford to be sorry about it.

As Kirwyn and I boarded Mal-Yin's large flagship, along with the bulk of his soldiers, my heart seemed to beat in time to our footsteps.

The night I'd jumped into the sea, I'd escaped the Dorestes' clutches without any possessions and barely any clothing on my back. I returned now with a small but well-provisioned army.

I'd escaped with the affection of Juls and, at least, some tolerance from Laz. Perhaps I returned now to their burning hate.

I wondered if Juls would ever forgive me. If Jesi would understand. If the people would turn against me.

If Lazlian would catch me and make me beg for death.

So much risk. It was for the girls who would come after me and for all of Elowa... but it was for me too. Control of my body, my *life,* had been handed over to the Dorestes— had never even been mine since before I was born—and I hadn't even known it. So many days I'd looked out my bedroom window in High Spire and wanted to shout my fury to the sea. I couldn't risk being heard, let alone releasing my rage and losing my carefully crafted composure.

Now, this was my scream. But I'd do it with the force of an army and the wisdom of patient strategy.

It would take a day to move the fleet to the coast of Rythas. Kirwyn held out his hand to me as our ship slid out of the harbor. I took it, leaning against his strong body. We were standing by the rail when he pointed northward.

"Look," he said. "I told you."

I gave a small gasp.

"It's the forest of colors," I marveled, eyeing the trees of red, orange, and yellow, far up the coast. It was spectacular, a miracle of nature. Much too stunning to shelter all the horrors of man's nature, shielded below. Despite the beauty, an unexpected relief came over me as we sailed away from the godforsaken mainland and all its terror.

Whatever happened, I vowed never to return.

But I need Juls's pardon – not to mention a divorce – if Kirwyn and I are to stay in Rythas, I worried. *I need our capture of the castle to be done without bloodshed if the people are to continue their support...*

I shook my head to stop the rambling thoughts. The only thing I needed to do was focus on my role and let Mal-Yin's soldiers focus on theirs.

As we crossed into open water, I forced myself to eat, though a sea storm raged in my stomach. *Food is fuel,* Kirwyn insisted, giving me a stern look, and I knew it was prudent to load up on calories and protein.

Thankfully, the seas were calm and each boat in Mal's fleet remained in sight as we crossed the God Sea. Most of the soldiers had to share one large room for sleeping, but Kirwyn and I were given a crammed, private cabin. Several times on our journey, we ran over our tasks with Ener and the bomb specialist.

Besides the bullet gun in my pack, I had four e-bombs. Two were to be used as back-ups. I'd also been given a tranquilizer gun loaded with darts that, when fired into their necks, would cause the guards to sleep. I knew a little of how they worked because Nasero had used something similar to re-capture me back in the tunnels under Elowa, when Kirwyn and I tried to flee so long ago.

The sentries at the Black Passage were one of Kirwyn's best arguments against me going into High Spire alone. Being able to take out two guards myself, especially after a long swim, would be difficult. Back-up was standard proce-dure, he'd often repeated, regardless of a person's skills.

But I refused to risk Kirwyn's life to help me succeed.

Instead, I played along, pretending we'd do it together and bracing for his wrath when he realized I'd tricked him into staying.

For the final items in my pack, I had what looked like a short, black tunic with a concealed bulletproof vest and two flexible, slip-on shoes. The plan was to drag the uncon-scious guards into the recess of the cave where they wouldn't be noticed and to quickly change from my scuba gear and seasuit into my body armor.

Once properly attired, I'd run to the console above the Garden Gate like my life and the lives of many others depended on it.

Because they did.

When the stony towers of High Spire came into view the next day, my heart pounded like an Elowan drum. Twilight burned the sky with vibrant, violent colors, the opposite of when I'd arrived with gray pre-dawn about a year prior, for my deliverance to the Dorestes. The same cascade of colorful flowers, trees, and vines dotted the many balconies and walls of the fortress. So beguilingly stunning, it was hard to believe High Spire was my prison. I knew what others would think. *How could a fairytale castle be a cage? How could a beautiful prince be my captor?*

Because my heart said no. Because it said yes to some-thing else. Some*one* else.

In the sky, clouds rolled in behind us as if we brought them. I could sense the air was charged with more than just the pent-up energy of Mal-Yin's army; it would rain some-time in the night.

Was that better or worse? I didn't have enough battle experience to know. I didn't have any experience, truly. Wet weather couldn't be good for laying siege to tall, stone walls. But we weren't planning on scaling them.

Did anyone even know I was here, or was this attack being blamed entirely on Mal?

Was my uncle Saos in the castle? Was Jesi somewhere marching on the ramparts?

Would they fight me or forgive me?

I didn't know. I turned away from High Spire to hurry to our cabin.

I'd have to work hard to earn Kirwyn's forgiveness for what I was about to do.

I GRABBED Kirwyn's waist before we could depart the tiny quarters. We hadn't made love the night before, we'd only held each other to sleep in the miniscule bed.

"One more time," I begged, nuzzling his neck. "I need you."

"Now?" Kirwyn arched a brow. We were expected above deck in mere minutes.

I nodded, snaking my hand down his pants and finding him already hardening. Kirwyn seemed about to protest but changed his mind and tore off his shirt. As he walked toward the bed, I scurried to my bag and retrieved the handcuffs I'd packed. The ones he'd previously used on me.

He shook his head, grinning. "You want to play? Now? We don't have time."

"I'll be fast, I promise," I said, smiling seductively.

349

"Besides, this will help me... speed things up." I gave a heavy bat of my lashes to imply what was necessary.

Kirwyn shrugged and grabbed me before I could protest. He threw me onto the bed and raised my hands above me, pinning them.

Fuck.

"No!" I cried, eyes wide in horror. "I want to use them on you. I – I want us to switch roles."

Kirwyn stilled and stared down at me with unreadable eyes. I gulped.

"Please," I whispered. "It will be... fun."

I watched Kirwyn's shoulders slowly relax, but his jaw clenched. Reluctantly, he released me and placed the cuffs in my hands. He cocked an almost abrupt half-smirk.

"What are you planning to do with me, Zaria?" he asked, flipping himself onto his back. The husky mockery in voice made me feel as if *he* was leading *me*. He searched for something to hold onto and grabbed the same pipe above the bed that I'd been eying. Simply watching the muscles in his chest and shoulders flex as he grasped the metal felt like a wordless seduction. I couldn't imagine being more attracted to a man than I was to Kirwyn.

"Are you going to tease me? Ride me? Am I allowed to come or will you be using me for your own ends?"

I hoped the flush spreading across my face read as blushing and not nerves.

"You'll have to wait and see." Straddling Kirwyn, I locked the cuffs into place, checking multiple times to make sure they were secure around the pipe before I let go.

Leaning down, I kissed my demon-boy, holding his face and pressing myself against his body.

I'm sorry. I have to keep you safe. I can't risk losing you again. Don't hate me. I love you.

I didn't want the kiss to end. As he swept his tongue with mine, I squeezed my eyes shut and prayed to the Sea God while we still floated in his realm.

If you've ever listened to me, please, hear me now. Whatever happens, keep Kirwyn safe.

I knew ill-concealed remorse colored my face as I pulled back from our kiss. Kirwyn knit his brow, searching my eyes. Slowly, I rose.

"Zaria... what are you doing?"

His voice was a knife to my heart.

"I'm sorry," I breathed, barely able to choke out the words. "You can't come with me. You have to stay here."

Kirwyn was already scraping his handcuffs against the metal pipe before I'd finished.

"*Zaria.*" He made my name a warning.

I stood up and backed away.

"Zaria, take off these fucking handcuffs. Now."

"I can't. I'm sorry. You'll be safe here."

"Zaria!" Kirwyn yelled. "I swear to god, you better take these handcuffs off *right now.*"

Shit, He was shouting. I looked over my shoulder to the door, nervous a passerby would hear.

Grimacing, I made a decision that was only going to anger him more. I fetched the gag from my bag, as well. The same one he'd used on me.

Kirwyn used these items to bring me pleasure, I thought, heart sinking. *And I'm using them to bring him pain.*

When he saw what I held, he began shouting my name even louder. I couldn't silence him as effectively as I wanted because he kept thrashing and closing his mouth whenever I tried to put the cloth inside. But I managed to wrap the gag around his head and wedge it his mouth enough to muffle his shouts. I hoped they could only be heard on our side of the closed door.

Tears streamed down my face by the time I'd finished.

"I'm sorry, I'm sorry," I mumbled. "Please forgive me. You're the most important person in the world to me. If something were to happen to you, I'd die. Please understand, Kirwyn. I love you. You kept me safe, now it's my turn to keep you safe."

Wiping my nose, I took a few deep breaths to get myself together. I couldn't emerge above deck with red eyes. Or maybe it would only look natural to Mal, like Kirwyn and I had a fight?

I knew I'd never forget the way Kirwyn held my eyes as I held his face. He'd stopped thrashing for a moment and looked at me with such pleading and such disbelief at my betrayal.

I hated myself more than I ever thought possible.

I didn't know if Kirwyn would ever forgive me. I wondered if I'd ever forgive myself.

I slid my sea-drop engagement ring from my finger. Kirwyn's pained gaze followed me as I put the jewel in my bag where it could be safely retrieved... after.

With one last look at his agonized green eyes, I slipped out the door.

CLAD ONLY IN MY SEASUIT, I was ready.

"Where's Kirwyn?" Mal immediately asked when I found him on deck. Soldiers scurried to launch boats, readying to invade and attack the Garden Gate without stealth.

"He's not coming," I said evenly, head forward, toward

the sea. "He's not happy about it, of course. But he's sulking with some of your men now, trying to be of use with the wave of soldiers coming in after Juls surrenders."

"Is that so?" Mal's voice edged with suspicion.

I turned to face him now, jutting my chin. "Like you, I protect those I love. Even when they don't like it."

Mal studied me for a moment, then gave a curt nod.

Ener and the e-bomb specialist approached, and I lied to them as well. Someone would find Kirwyn before the battle was over and he'd be released, livid but alive. That was all that mattered.

"This is insanity, no. You need back-up for cave diving," Ener insisted, shaking his head. "Not to mention, for taking out the guards-"

"It's Queen Zaria's plan and she wants to do it solo," Mal-Yin cut him off. "Zaria is our best swimmer and she knows the castle better than anyone."

"That doesn't mean she won't meet with trouble! If she fails-"

Mal held up his hand. "Enough. She's going alone."

Frowning, I studied Mal's face. Ener made sound points and Mal agreed too easily. Something was off. *Why is he supporting me?* Because he understood how I felt about Kirwyn or because...

Because if I failed, did Mal plan to capture High Spire with guns and violence anyway?

Fuck. I didn't know. *Please, Keroe, don't let me fail.*

One last time, I glanced at High Spire over my shoulder. I'd enter the water portside, facing away from the castle, to avoid detection. The violent orange sun was setting. Soon, we'd be plunged into darkness.

"It's high tide," Mal announced, taking a signal from one of his guards.

Ener helped me secure my pack and strapped the dual tanks of compressed air to my sides. I secured the weighted belt around my waist and slid the glass mask over my eyes.

"Ready?" he asked.

I nodded and turned to Mal.

"Just like we discussed. My men will wait to release their full force until we see the control light go out, indicating the gates have been disabled. Then we'll batter her down. When we see the same light deactivated on the Bone Gate, we'll flood the castle from the other side and hem them in."

I nodded again.

"Be quick if you don't want a bloody battle," Mal warned. "I can ask my men to defend themselves against High Spire's attacks without the use of deadly force if avoidable, but I can't ask them to helplessly lay down and die."

I gulped. "If it turns into a bloodbath, I'll lose the support of the people and won't be able to advocate on your behalf," I warned. More firmly, I swore, "I won't fail. Wait for the lights to darken."

From the little deck on the stern, I slipped my feet into the fins. I dropped into the sea backwards, much like a trust fall into Keroe's arms.

Treading water, I oriented my body to swim around Mal's flagship, in the direction of High Spire.

With my first finned-kick, I prayed again.

Please, Keroe. For the brides, for Elowa. Let us win.

PART IV
YOUR PRINCESS, HIS WHORE

CHAPTER 39

Paranoid, I didn't turn on my headlamp. The dying sun left just enough light to see without the device's artificial glow as I swam toward the Black Passage.

It was strange, being under the sea for such an extended period of time. Kirwyn and I had only practiced in Mal's chemical pool, and though I was skilled in deep dives, no human could hold their breath for as long as it took me to cross the bay.

Was I brave? I felt like a fool. Like when Jesi and I lured my kidnappers to me. Though we'd outwitted them and won in the end, I wouldn't do it again given the chance, having learned they'd really come to rescue me.

Or would I? The bald man had been ready to molest me before Jesi stopped him. And if I'd gone with them, things would have turned out very differently. I wouldn't have won any support in Rythas.

Why was nothing simple?

It was simple as I swam below the ocean's surface. The water around me was so peaceful, a part of me didn't ever want to emerge into the chaos above. Chaos I was about to reign.

For most of my life I'd innocently believed this was my fate -- to spend forever under the waves. Looking back with all the knowledge I'd gained, it seemed woefully naïve. Impossible. But when I thought about the undeniable reality – the existence of a war-torn world outside Elowa – it seemed equally unlikely to be true.

What would Elowans think when they were confronted with it?

After a while, I noticed rocks in the distance and risked poking my head above the waves to check if I neared the entrance to the Black Passage. Spying it maybe fifty feet in front of me, to my left, I altered direction. Only about a foot of the archway poked above sea level, barely discernable in the dimness.

My pulse picked up speed. I couldn't hear them, but I knew Mal's soldiers would be taking the beach now, making no attempt at stealth. Juls would order everyone to retreat into the safety of the castle. He'd protect as many people as possible with the advantage of strong, high walls, rather than risk any attack outside the fortress he was sure to lose against Mal's advanced weaponry.

Less than minute later, I reached the tunnel's entrance.

Your traitor has returned, I thought, flipping the switch and activating my headlamp.

Your queen is here, King Juls. Sneaking in through the base of your castle. Will you hate me for it forever?

I swam beneath the arch, entering the eerie channel and leaving behind the open sea.

Your wife has come, seeking vengeance. Can you blame me?

I was helpless when they abducted me and brought me

to High Spire. Forced me to marry a man I did not love, forced me to kiss him and play like a happy couple...

And had I not escaped, I'd have been forced to his bed whenever he wished, forced to bear his children.

How dare you, Juls? Can you really blame me? I thought, with an angry kick of my fins.

He's not a bad man, I argued. *But how dare he? How dare they all?*

The tunnel was large enough not to cause me any claustrophobia and I saw the wisdom in having a backup light. Navere had cut power to High Spire's modest, electric lights, and even if they glowed, I didn't think it would have been enough. Without my headlamp illuminating my surroundings, I'd be plunged into darkness, unable to find the exit. Maybe I could feel my way forward, since the tunnel ran straight, but in something as complex as a real cave, I'd be lost. It seemed a horrible way to go, condemned to utter darkness and waiting for your air to expire, waiting to die alone.

A quarter of the way through the tunnel, I jolted backwards as my headlamp fell upon the seabed and revealed a corpse rotted almost entirely to bone.

I blinked at the gory sight in disbelief. It was as if my intrusive thoughts summoned it into being. Except, this corpse wore no scuba gear or seasuit of any kind. A threadbare dress or shirt clung to its skeletal torso. This person had most likely died above ground and had somehow come to rest below.

What had happened to trap it down here? Did anyone know? Laying on the seabed at the tunnel's base, it would never be revealed, not even during low tide. I might be the first and only person to ever spy it.

I didn't have time to examine the remains, but for some reason I felt sure it was female.

My heart raced. *Was it a bad omen? It couldn't be a good one, could it?* Yet her soul must be at peace, forever at rest beneath the sea.

So that was a good omen... right?

As I swam above her, my heart pounded and I doubled my speed. I had the panicky thought that the skeleton could reanimate, could reach up and grab me.

That she could keep me forever with her, down in the dark tunnel.

Even after I'd left the corpse in my wake, I had visions of it coming up behind me and grabbing my leg. The tunnel was too otherworldly, too eerie. My lamp illuminated floating bits of decaying ocean life or other organic matter all around me, darkness surrounded every bit of space my light didn't shine, and the amplified sound of my own breathing through the air tube sounded creepily in my head.

After a minute, the tunnel widened and light from above shone. My heart leapt.

I'd reached the underground entrance to High Spire.

Still beneath the surface, I kicked off my fins and unstrapped my air tanks, but did not yet remove my breathing tube. I wrapped my weighted belt around the tanks to sink them, but let the fins float up, hitting the tunnel's ceiling.

I gave another glance at the exit to ensure I had enough light and time to make it. Then I tore the mask from my eyes, removed the lamp from my forehead, and pulled the tube from my mouth. With only my pack strapped to my back, I kicked quickly but quietly for the surface.

I felt like a monster or like some kind of sea creature as I slipped above the water, panting equally from the long swim and from my racing nerves. Ahead, I spied the two guards I expected. No more. Hopefully, Juls had ordered all his men to defend the Garden Gate. I had no way of knowing or hearing what was happening. I had to trust that Mal-Yin was doing what he was supposed to.

Which I didn't, under normal circumstances. But I trusted that he needed me badly enough to hold up his end of the bargain. And I trusted that he wanted my sister badly enough not to fuck up his chance.

Creeping forward, I didn't immediately recognize either guard. I could see from behind they were males of average height. I wondered if they had wanted to be a part of the main defense happening above us or if they were happy not to be involved in the immediate danger.

Of course, they couldn't know it was coming from their backs anyway.

At least they'd be uninjured when I was done with them.

Stealthily, in the dark recess of the cave, I crouched and fumbled in my pack for my tranquilizer gun. Not only did I need to make a solid shot for each guard, I needed *time*. The drug within the dart took a few seconds to work its way through a person's system.

Within a few seconds, a lot could happen. I could take a severe punch. A bullet.

It was a dilemma because I needed to get close enough to hit my target on the first shot because once they heard me, I wouldn't have time to make multiple attempts. But I also needed enough distance between us to use those precious seconds as a buffer before the guards charged me in retaliation.

This is the part where Kirwyn would have been able to help, I thought guiltily.

I left my pack where it lay and crept toward the guards with my sleep-gun raised, trying not to tremble. They didn't even turn; they were talking distractedly about what was happening somewhere above our heads.

I sucked in a breath.

Please let my aim be true.

Squeezing the trigger, I released the first dart at the man on the left.

He yelped, and before he even had time to turn, I fired again at the other man, but my arms had started to shake and I missed.

The guard I'd hit charged me, quickly crossing the distance between the entrance to the Black Passage and the mouth of the tunnel. He had no gun, but he'd raised a dagger and yelled loud enough to draw attention.

Oh god. My mind momentarily warred with itself in total terror – should I retreat or hold my ground and fire again?

I made my feet stay planted. The tears leaking from my eyes made me shoot even wilder the next time, completely missing the second man who now had turned and charged me as well.

Please, I begged, forcing my shaking legs to stand their ground though my heart screamed to run. They were shouting and mere seconds away. I was sure I only had one shot left before it would be too late.

I fired.

The second man gave a cry.

I hit him!

But I didn't have enough time to escape their assault before the drug took effect.

I leapt back toward the passage and dove under the sea, kicking wildly into the tunnel's underwater safety. I only needed a few seconds. Turning underwater, I blinked through the bubbles to see if either man followed.

When none appeared, I made myself count to five then tentatively swam back to the exit and poked my head above the surface.

Yes!

But no...

Shit.

Both men had succumbed to the drug, but the first one reached the passage before falling asleep and now floated face-down in the water. I swam to his body and dragged it back onto the rocky landing, praying no one heard the commotion and came to find us. I laid the guard on his back and pressed my head to his mouth.

He's still breathing, I thought with relief. *Thank god.*

I spared a few precious seconds to ensure he continued breathing, before rising and roughly dragging his body into the dark recess of the cave. I repeated the process with the second guard, who'd blessedly fallen asleep on the rocks before reaching the water, and didn't seem to have sustained any injuries in the fall. When I'd hidden them as best I could, I sorted through my pack, first withdrawing the shoes and clothing.

Landdammit. It hit me that I lost the tranquilizer gun under water when I dove to safety, leaving me with only the bullet gun for protection. I was about to fish it out of my bag when I heard a familiar female voice.

"Hands up. Turn around."

CHAPTER 40

"**S**tand up," Jesi ordered. "Turn around slowly."

I did as she commanded, meeting the terrible sight of my best friend with a gun pointed at my head. Despite being in the middle of a siege that would determine the fate of two kingdoms, despite the obvious threat she posed, my heart still leapt to see her.

"Jesi," I cried, tears welling. "How are you here?"

"I had a feeling you'd be inside the castle somewhere. I showed you how the gates work to escape, not to attack!"

"Please," I said as steadily as I could. "I need you to let me go."

"You think because I helped you escape once, I'll help you take High Spire? That was different. I won't let you destroy us, Zaria."

I shook my head rapidly. "No! I don't want to destroy Rythas. I'm *not*. I only need leverage. Juls will never abandon High Spire, not after the Oxholde attacks. I need to make surrender the only option. Without hurting anyone. And once I seize power, I'll return it, I promise! I just need him to listen."

I held Jesi's eyes, pleading, counting out the seconds in heartbeats. Water dripped from my soaked hair onto the smooth rocks of the tunnel's entrance.

"Does anyone... have you told anyone else I might be here?" I asked.

She hesitated before answering reluctantly, "No. I asked for patrol duty on a hunch and I came when I heard the guards shout."

Thank god, I thought, but Jesi deliberated for long seconds I didn't have.

"Please, Jesi, I'm not planning on hurting anyone."

Still pointing her gun at me, she demanded, "What are you planning to do?"

"It's better if you don't know. But I promise, we don't want to kill anyone. And if you don't let me do what I need to do, it might actually start a real battle. One with a body count."

Jesi stood her ground, but I could see she was considering my words.

"This just is about me, the Daughter of Elowa, and Elowa herself. We haven't come to throw Juls from the throne," I swore. "No one needs to get hurt. But you have to let me go for that to happen or this *will* explode into violence."

Jesi blew out a puff of air and shook her head.

"If I let you go and you fail whatever it is you're doing, they'll figure out I was involved, I know it. Questions will be asked and Juls may believe you circumvented me once, not twice. I'll be hanged for High Treason. Or worse."

"No! I won't let that happen," I cried. "We'll win and I'll protect you no matter what. That's what we do Jesi! You and I protect each other. Once I make Juls listen, we'll have demands, negotiations. I'll ensure you're safe, even if Navere suspects something. Please!"

It made my stomach sick to talk to her like this, on opposing sides of a negotiation, like when we'd first met. As if Jesi were a stranger, as if we barely knew one another.

Being on the opposite side of Jesi wasn't – could never be – right.

This is all such a tangle.

"I respect Navere as my commander," Jesi said, "but Lida was right about him. I suspect he'd rather you were dead. And that's nothing compared to what Lazlian will do to you. Zaria, Laz never threatened me after you left. But he made sure to torment me with promises of all the creative ways he was going to hurt you."

I'd be a liar if I said her words didn't frighten me. I shivered hard.

"Juls always believes the best in everyone, he's responsible for getting me promoted," Jesi said. "Zaria, let me take you to him now. He'll shield you as he shielded me."

"No, Jesi, I can't!"

"And I can't let you destroy our kingdom," she countered, firming her grip on her gun.

"I don't want to, I swear! I need you to believe me! I just want some things to change, you can understand that? I don't want to weaken Rythas, I need her *strong*. Think about it. If we can free Elowa and change how things are done there," I held her eyes so she understood my meaning, "we're going to *need* Rythas to help guide the way." *Think about it, Jesi. The hateful ways the Mystics preach.*

"I'm *counting* on Rythas to help Elowa. We can open our two kingdoms to one another. I promise you, I have a plan. Everyone comes out better for it."

I cringed.

Except Elowa's Mystics, losing their ability to lie to the masses.

Except Rythas's nobles, losing their stranglehold on Elowa.

Except the Dorestes, losing their exclusive grip on power.

Shit. It was a fucking tangle. I couldn't pull one string without affecting others.

"Mostly everyone. Mostly better," I amended.

When I saw Jesi considering, I held my breath and prayed. Her choice in this moment decided the fate of everything. If she let me go, we could avoid a battle and save lives… but if she helped me, she'd have to betray her own kingdom to do it.

Fuck, I was a walking catalyst.

"Please help me," I begged. "Not for me, but because if you don't let me go, I know this siege will turn bloody and lives will be lost. Help me for all the people trapped in Elowa who are living a lie. Please. I promise I'll win."

"You can't promise that," Jesi said, evenly.

"We've never let each other down before and I don't plan on starting tonight. Think about all we've been through together. I need to go, *now.*" Holding her shining brown eyes, I said, "Jesi, you save me, I save you, remember?"

Jesi's eyelids fluttered shut and she drew a long, frustrated breath through her nose. Slowly, she lowered her gun, groaning, then let out a soft chuckle.

"Damn you, Zaria. I thought I was a ball of trouble but you're a fucking mountain." She flipped her gun around and handed it to me. "Pistol whip me. Make it look real."

My brief elation was replaced by horror.

Holy fucking no.

"I can't."

Jesi shrugged and replied, "I'd have pistol whipped you if I needed to."

I didn't doubt her. But I couldn't. Anyone else, but not Jesi.

She gave me a hard look. "You're gonna make me do it myself?"

I wasn't sure that was even possible, but I cried, "No! Please, just forget you saw me. Can't you pretend this happened just after your rounds?" I said, lifting my hand toward the sleeping guards.

Jesi shook her head. "Maybe, but only if you win. There will be much more to worry about than speculating on whether or not I'd just passed by when you emerged."

I looked her dead in the eye. "Then I'll win."

"Go," Jesi sighed. "Before I change my mind."

I rushed Jesi and threw my arms around her. "Thank you."

"*Go,*" she commanded, gently removing my arms.

I paused only to retrieve my gun from the bag, to toss my bag onto my back, and to give Jesi one last look of gratitude.

I ran.

I didn't stop until I reached the first control room above the Garden Gate. My heart screamed in fear as my feet beat the floor, but the hallways were empty. My guess was that anyone who could fight swarmed the Garden Gate to protect it, as predicted, and everyone who required shelter had holed up somewhere safe. Distracted by Jesi, I'd forgotten to change into my combat attire. I'd even forgotten to don shoes. My entire outfit lay beside the sleeping guards in the recesses of the Black Passage. I ran barefoot, clad only in my seasuit. I didn't even have the bulletproof vest.

But I carried what I needed. The e-bombs and my gun.

I emerged into the windowless console room above the Garden Gate, dripping sweat, feet filthy and sore. From this room, I could hear the muffled shouts below of Rythasian soldiers bracing to protect High Spire.

Once I deactivated the gate, the real defense would begin. Once that play unfolded, I'd need to be *fast* to get Mal's men in through the Bone Gate before serious violence broke out. I didn't trust him not to follow through with fire-power and I couldn't fathom what Juls might unleash. It would turn into a bloodbath.

Elated, I rushed to the blinking console, and, having no holster, I tucked my gun into my seasuit and fished the first e-bomb out of my bag. The electronic controls were embedded into a gray table about six feet long and four feet high. Everything looked the same as when Jesi showed me the inner workings of the defenses almost a year ago.

I closed my eyes and drew a deep breath.

Please, I prayed to any gods who listened. *Please let this work.*

I opened my eyes, slapped the device onto the sloped, blinking console, and pressed the activation button.

A small *click* sounded and the lights on the modern control table flashed several times before darkening. They did not re-light.

I backed away, eyes wide, and a smile of pure joy broke out on my face.

I did it! I did it!

For a moment, I stared, ensuring nothing flashed back to life. I had to have faith that it worked to disable the gate and that Mal's men saw the corresponding light deactivate below. I had no time to listen for a change in sounds to see if they'd doubled their efforts to batter the door.

I slung my bag onto my back and bolted for the control room above the Bone Gate. It lay on the far side of the castle, above the rocky shore. Long ago, Raoul and Singen first snuck me into High Spire though that entrance, when the tide flooded the Black Passage, making it impassable by boat.

I'd hated every step of my abduction through that gate. *Fitting now that I should destroy it,* I thought, with bitterness and delight.

Faster feet, I commanded, ignoring the pain of my bare soles slapping the stony floor.

To access the second control room—situated lower than the King's Gate—I had to descend a set of stairs branching both up to the King's Gate and down to the Bone Gate. The stairs were long, uneven, and I flew down them so quickly I nearly tumbled over the last few.

I emerged into a room similar to the previous console room, with stone floors and pillars. It was empty but for the modern, electric control table, fortifying the gate below.

My heart soared and I ran halfway across the floor to my goal before I caught sight of another figure emerging from the entrance opposite the stairs.

My heart stopped.

"I knew you would betray us!" Lazlian shouted.

CHAPTER 41

He shot across the room, wild rage personified. Lazlian wasn't wearing the clothing of Rythas; he was dressed for battle in a dark, long-sleeved combat shirt, dark, loose pants and black boots.

He's mad enough to kill me.

I was *so close* to my goal all I could think about were the consequences of losing the battle. With my heart in my throat, I sprinted to the console and slammed the bomb down just as Lazlian slammed into me, shoving me away.

No!

One arm outstretched, my desperate fingers fumbled for the button as I used the other arm to brace my fall forward – a pointless effort as Lazlian quickly fell upon me, smashing me down, hard.

No... so close...

My head bounced off the console table and something metal cut my chest. Blood spilled onto the panel and I thanked Keroe that adrenaline surged too deeply in my veins for me to faint at the sight. Lazlian's hands gripped my shoulders and he hauled me far away from the explosive. As I fell onto the floor, he fell on top of me. I fumbled with my gun and he yanked it from my hands with startling ease. Lazlian tossed the weapon and I watched it scatter to the far corner of the room, beyond my reach. My stomach sank with the lost hope of reaching the detonation button at the same time terror swelled in my breast, unable to rise before Lazlian pushed me back down. Caged by his full weight straddling my chest, he pinned me to the floor, dispelling any chance of reaching the e-bomb. My flailing limbs didn't get the defeated message. As I punched and kicked, Lazlian gripped my wrists and slammed my hands against the stone floor above my head.

"Let me go!" I shouted, bucking wildly.

"Traitor!" he yelled. "I knew you would betray us!"

"I didn't!" I cried. "I couldn't betray you... I was never... on your side to begin with! You knew that!"

You of all people knew.

"I'll have you whipped!" he growled, teeth clenched, face contorted. "I'll do it myself!"

Lazlian transferred both my hands to one of his, giving me more of a chance to free my arms but I still couldn't slip through his grasp. I panicked as his other hand grabbed my neck and squeezed.

"I'll have you whipped for High Treason. Beg for me to spare you!" he shouted as he jerked, scraping the backs of my hands against the stone even more than I was scraping them myself in my effort to escape.

Beg? I couldn't breathe with his hand clutching my throat.

Please, Lazlian, stop, I pled with my eyes, *you're going to kill me.*

"Beg for me to spare you," Lazlian demanded once more. This time, his voice bore less rage and he'd relaxed his death-grip on my neck, but he'd tightened his hold on my wrists. Lazlian panted above me, hunched like a wild animal.

"Beg for me to…" he had a strange look in his hazel eyes.

"Beg for me…" Trailing off, Lazlian again slackened the grip on my throat, but dizziness loomed. I needed more air, fast.

"Lazlian, please," I croaked, using my eyes more than my wheezing words. Tears of despair slipped down my cheeks. Immobilized by his weight, I couldn't buck him from my torso. *Please god, no.* We were going to lose without that gate open. Or Mal-Yin's men would turn violent and we'd lose another way.

I'd failed. Let everyone down.

All because of Lazlian. Because he could predict what I'd do.

"Lazlian…" I wheezed, my vision darkening around the edges.

In a sudden blur, someone slammed into Laz and his body was thrown from mine, freeing me. I made out the tangle of two men throwing fists in a fit of rage as they tumbled.

Kirwyn?

How was he here?

I had no time to ponder answers or to help as he and Lazlian grappled on the floor amidst the sounds of grunting and fists crunching.

Dragging myself to standing and sucking great gulps of air, I stumbled to find my balance and sprang across the room. I leapt the last few feet to the console, threw myself onto the control panel, and slammed the detonation button.

The same flash occurred that I'd witnessed at the

Garden Gate. A mechanical *thrum* sounded – and the console went dark. Deactivated.

We did it.

"Kirwyn!" I cried as I spun. He'd just tossed Lazlian across the room—literally—Laz tumbled and rolled toward the wall.

Eyes wide, I quickly scanned Kirwyn's body for injuries at the same time he took stock of mine. He'd been cut above his brow, but it wasn't too bad. His eyes flicked down to my collarbone...

...and once he saw blood, he was out for it.

Instant, mad rage re-lit Kirwyn's eyes. It was just like the day he tortured and killed the man who maimed Vesper. Only worse, because I meant much more to him than his horse. I could actually see the change on Kirwyn's face the millisecond he registered whatever bruises I'd suffered. It was like he switched off any remaining part of him still possessing the ability to be reasoned with.

No.

I had only seconds to act because I knew exactly what he was going to do.

In a flash, Kirwyn grabbed the gun holstered at his side. Just as quickly, I threw myself in front of Lazlian, now struggling to stand.

"Don't!" I shouted, arms spread wide. My voice came out croaky, pained. "You can't. If you kill him, everything we're working for will fall apart. *Please.*"

Kirwyn's furious gaze went right over my shoulder. He angled his body to shoot around me, forcing me to slide to match him.

Oh god, we were about to lose it all. Juls would never listen to reason if Kirwyn killed his brother. Close behind me, I heard Laz shuffle to his feet. Even though I protected him with my body, that same act made me nervous. I tensed, ready to move forward if he tried to grab me.

Dammit. I didn't trust Kirwyn not to kill Lazlian and I didn't trust Lazlian not to kill me... or not to use me as leverage. I rolled onto the balls of my feet, readying for any outcome. I needed to diffuse the situation. The e-bomb had detonated. Mal-Yin's men would flood the castle in minutes.

How many? Fifteen? Twenty?

I swallowed to wet my vocal cords before trying again. "Kirwyn, *please,* look at me."

His eyes didn't move from over my shoulder. I could see him calculating, trying to figure out the safest shot in case I moved again before a bullet hit Lazlian. I might as well have been trying to reason with a madman. My fears were coming true. This was exactly why I hated guns, exactly why I didn't want them a part of this.

"Please, listen to me," I begged, and finally, something in my voice made him look. Desperate, I angled to protect Laz – the man I'd been fighting only moments before. But I couldn't think about that now.

"You swore that if I listened to you on the mainland, you'd listen to me *here.*"

Kirwyn swung his gaze to Laz. Back to me. I wondered what Lazlian was thinking or doing. He seemed very still behind me.

"You have to trust me, as I trusted you. Maybe not always. Maybe not like when we were hiding from that wagon. But I can't come over there and make you faint with the press of my hands to your neck when you're about to do something we'll both regret."

Once more, Kirwyn's dark green eyes slid back and forth

between Laz and me. Sweat dripped down my back and my heart pounded with fear.

"This is just like that time," I pled. "But I can't physically stop you right now. You need to stop yourself. Listen to what I'm telling you and lower the gun, Kirwyn. Please. If you kill him, everything we've done will be undone."

My heart measured out the beats of silence as Kirwyn stared, muscles tensed in his arms and legs positioned for the perfect shot he'd never miss. That was the truth... no matter how I moved, he wouldn't miss, would he?

Please.

"Can you guess how she thanked me for her engagement ring?" Startling me, Kirwyn spoke over my shoulder, directly to Lazlian. "I'll give you a hint. She was on her knees. A position she'll happily return to as often as I like now that she's agreed to be my wife."

My mouth fell. I blinked hard, unsure I'd heard correctly. I was too shocked and angered to bother blushing.

Dear god, he took a shot of another kind. Several.

Was he intentionally provoking Laz to give him a reason to fire? Or did he just want to get in the jab while he held the gun? I couldn't spare a glance behind me to see Lazlian's reaction, but I could guess. I fixed Kirwyn with my stare once more, this time laced with ire.

Enough. You've tormented him, you've won.

In the long, quiet seconds, I thought the keylord wouldn't respond.

"So you've realized you have a little nymphet on your hands and put her mouth to its best use. Before I offer my congratulations, I'll point out the little whore is my brother's *wife*," Lazlian spat, bitterly. "The only reason she's even had the chance to be with you is because she slipped out of here."

Kirwyn's grin was pure mischief. "Well, I can't thank you enough for your incompetence."

"She has a duty here! And she ran off shirking it like a fucking child."

Kirwyn didn't hesitate. "Then I guess she ran right to *fucking* daddy."

Oh my fucking god.

I wanted to scream but I was too busy choking on air. Kirwyn wielded the statement to not only wound with singular intent, but I was sure Lazlian could read the double meaning as well as I.

"She isn't yours!" Laz shouted. "Anything she's done with you does not make her your betrothed, it makes her an adulteress."

I found my voice and before Kirwyn's temper could escalate the situation again, my own flared. "I'm not a whore or a child or an adulteress!" I cried, tilting my head over my shoulder without taking my eyes off Kirwyn. "You know I had no choice."

Infuriatingly, both men continued the argument as if I wasn't there.

"She is such a bad girl, isn't she?" Kirwyn taunted. His lip curled into a snarl. Blood dripped from the cut on his brow. He looked like the devil in that moment. "But she's a good girl for me."

Once again, my eyes bulged. *Had they both lost their minds?* A battle was imminent, lives were on the line, and kingdoms might topple -- but they wanted to take jabs at one another amidst such high stakes?

Using *me.*

More sweat dripped down my back. This was going to escalate to one of them killing the other.

"If you call this insanity good behavior then we have very different ideas on how to handle her." Lazlian calmed his voice to just below shouting, but even without looking I could picture his clenched teeth.

Please, Kirwyn. I love you, I thought, trying to convey the emotion with my whole body. *Both you and Lazlian are clever but only you are wise. Be wise now.*

Finally, Kirwyn's deep green eyes remained on mine and something shone behind them. After a pause, he flashed a bemused smirk.

Very pointedly, he said, "She can handle herself," and slowly lowered the gun.

I breathed the longest exhale of my life.

Thank you.

Keeping my hands still high and wide, I edged cautiously toward him, as if I approached a dangerous animal. I reached out gradually, afraid he'd change his mind any second and shoot Lazlian dead in the head when I had no chance of angling. Still holding Kirwyn's eyes, I took the gun from his reluctant hands. I heard him grit out the faintest *fuck* under his breath, but he let go.

"Thank you."

My heart soared knowing Kirwyn trusted me enough -- that he actually deferred to me, as promised. Especially because I had a bad track record taking recent events into account. If Kirwyn hadn't managed to follow me somehow, I wouldn't have been able to escape Lazlian and we'd have failed to open the Bone Gate. It was only because he'd knocked Lazlian off me that so many lives were spared. I wanted to say so much in that moment, but I had no time. I backed away before Kirwyn could change his mind.

"Okay," I panted, trying to calm both myself as well as Laz and Kirwyn. "Let's just take a moment here --"

-- Standing halfway between the two men, my world fell apart.

I heard a loud *thump* and the main doors to the control room crashed wide open. I whipped my head to see five Rythasian soldiers storm through and I raised the gun instinctively. Bulky and dressed in black, each man was armed with firepower. One quick, skilled look around and within seconds, all five men pointed their guns at Kirwyn.

Gasping and guessing the origin of the command, I kept my gun high while I turned to see Lazlian not only wearing his usual sneer -- he also wielded a weapon.

I blinked. *Had he been armed with a gun the whole time?* I could see why he couldn't draw when Kirwyn had one aimed at him... but why hadn't he done so beforehand, when he and I were fighting?

Terror gripped my heart as the unavoidable truth sank in. We were outgunned.

Standing between Laz and Kirwyn, I could protect Kirwyn with my body against Laz's bullet, but not from the rest of the soldiers'... and if I shot Laz, the guards would only kill Kirwyn in retaliation. Trying to decide where best to aim, I whipped my outstretched arms back to the five palace guards, but there were too many of them. I spun back to Kirwyn.

Less than five seconds had passed but in that short time, everything had fallen apart. It was so hard to hear from the blood rushing in my ears. Sadness tinged the edges of Kirwyn's eyes.

As if he said goodbye.

I love you, he mouthed.

My heart screamed.

I drew one shaky breath and turned around to Lazlian. His eyes lit with predatory vengeance. He aimed his own weapon over my shoulder at Kirwyn's head and licked his lips, readying to speak, *savoring.*

I knew exactly what he intended on commanding his men.

Hold fire. I'll kill him myself.

What should I do? Who should I shoot?

If I tried to kill Lazlian that would only trigger the soldiers to fire on us.

Where to aim?

I didn't have time to kill all the soldiers before Laz shot Kirwyn, and one of the other guards would take me down before I finished.

Oh god, oh god. There was no way to win.

I heard Kirwyn's words from the woods.

He wants you. Alive.

I did the only thing I could do. I shoved the barrel of the gun against my own head, clammy finger poised on the trigger.

"Kill him and you kill me," I swore, looking Lazlian dead in the eye and freezing the entire room. "I won't live without him."

I didn't want to think about what my action implied; I only hoped it worked.

"That's a vow."

Lazlian's eyes blew wide with fear or fury. I couldn't parse the emotions; I needed a new word to seamlessly mesh the two. His left hand crossed his torso, signaling to the soldiers. One finger pointed slightly higher than the rest – halfway between a *stop* and a *one-moment* motion.

"And I always keep my vows."

I pledged the last part as a reminder of Lazlian's own

words. He looked ready to howl with rage. The keylord's eyes darted back and forth between the gun pressed to my temple and to Kirwyn, calculating. Despite my racing heart, I tightened my finger against the trigger in preparation for any trickery. Though I stared at Laz, I kept watch on the soldiers from the corner of my eye. I had no choice, but I mourned my direction. If these were my last moments alive, I wished I were looking at Kirwyn.

I don't want to die, my mind screamed. *But I won't live without him.*

I could see Lazlian's chest rise and fall with heavy breathing. He was bleeding from somewhere on his scalp and his cheekbone looked to be forming a bruise. Head bent downward and waves of dark hair falling menacingly onto his forehead, his wide-eyed stare bore into mine with that strange horrified-rage.

I'll do it, I swore with my eyes. *Kill him and you kill me.*

I hadn't noticed Lazlian's clenched jaw... until I watched it unclench. Until, bewilderingly, his whole face began to relax...

...making the muscles in *my* body tense, one by one.

Lazlian blinked, slowly. When he reopened his eyes, a new emotion burned within.

Triumph.

"Everything is ready for enemies of Rythas," he said to the guards in a measured tone. "Bring him up atop the King's Stair. Don't do anything until I arrive."

What? What did that mean?

My stomach twisted; fresh fear seized my heart. *What was happening?*

I spun in wild circles, first to the soldiers – now advancing to Kirwyn, muscles coiling – and back to Laz, smirking shamelessly on one side of his mouth.

Should I shoot? Who? Lazlian? A guard? Myself? They weren't killing Kirwyn – yet. But they grabbed him.

"What are you doing?" I cried.

I answered my own question.

Everything is ready. Enemies of Rythas. The King's Stair.

Atop the stair was where the gallows awaited. Where they hanged criminals.

"No!" I cried, lunging forward at the same time Lazlian grabbed me from behind. His hands, bigger and stronger than my own, once again wrested the gun from my frantic and sloppy grasp and tossed it far out of reach. It wouldn't have done much good—it probably would have made the situation worse—but in desperation, I would have started shooting had I managed to hold it a moment longer.

I screamed as Lazlian's arms locked around my torso, pulling me back while soldiers dragged a thrashing Kirwyn toward the stairs. He couldn't know exactly what was to happen, but I was sure he guessed the gist of Lazlian's intentions.

"Lazlian, no! Stop!" I yelled.

"I love you! Zaria, I love you!" Kirwyn called, fighting the grip of the guards and twisting to look at me one last time.

"Kirwyn!" I cried.

CHAPTER 42

"Wait. *Nobody move.*"

Lazlian's command stilled everyone in the room, including me.

"Don't. Move."

We looked around in confusion as the keylord released my waist, but his eyes gave me a stern warning not to budge. Helplessly, I froze on the wild hope that he might spare Kirwyn or had changed his mind in some way. I held my breath while he strode the few feet over to where two guards held him.

Lazlian punched Kirwyn in the jaw with sickening force.

I screamed, not surprised Laz used the opportunity for an unfair shot, but taken aback that he knew how to throw such a punch. As I raced toward Kirwyn, my mind flashed back to when he was ripped from me in Elowa. Guards had held him while Nasero punched his stomach and we were torn apart.

Not again. It couldn't be happening all over again.

The possibility that history was repeating itself—or

worse—made cold water fill my gut. Blood dripped from Kirwyn's downturned mouth onto the floor and I prayed he'd turned his head in time to save his teeth.

I was unable to reach him before a grizzly guard picked me off the ground and tossed me down like I weighed nothing. I howled in pain as I hit the stone floor, but I stumbled back to my feet, ignoring it.

"Touch her again and I'll kill you!" Lazlian yelled. He shoved his way past the guard as I attempted to charge once more. "She is your queen!"

I swore I heard the guard mumble *"She's not my queen,"* as I bolted straight for Kirwyn again. Lazlian caught me before I made it.

"Let me go!" I cried.

"Go," Lazlian commanded his guards over my shoulder. "Take him upstairs. String him up. Collect their guns. I'll follow in a minute."

"Kirwyn!" I shouted.

"Zaria!" he cried. "I love you."

"Please, Lazlian, no! Kirwyn! No, please! I love you!"

Wildly and fruitlessly, I smacked Lazlian's arms, digging my nails into his skin and kicking my legs against the air. He yanked me back while I watched Kirwyn disappear up the long staircase. Struggling with Lazlian, our direction shifted. He scanned the room and seemed to find whatever he was looking for. With a grunt, he abruptly released me, tearing off the long-sleeved combat shirt he wore in a move I didn't understand and didn't have time to comprehend.

I sprinted toward the stairs with renewed energy and made it up two steps before Lazlian yanked my waist again, sending me crashing onto my knees. I kicked backwards but he lifted and carried me across the floor.

"Let me go!" I cried, kicking air again. Reaching from behind me Lazlian grabbed my wrists, twisting the sleeves of the shirt between them and tying them in front of me. I didn't understand what was happening but I knew it was bad. Lazlian dragged me to a stone column in the room's center.

"Lazlian, stop!" I yelled. He dodged my kicks while knotting the shirt around the pillar. The tough, malleable material nearly cut off my circulation.

"You stay put," Lazlian ordered, pulling the knots as tight as he could. They weren't strong enough to hold me indefinitely, but I guessed he only needed to keep me contained until he could reach the door atop the stair... and probably jam it shut behind him so I couldn't follow. "This is for your own good."

"Listen to me, please, stop!" I yelled, twisting my wrists, sweating and shaking. I was quickly making headway with the bindings when he turned and stalked off... but he only needed a few seconds lead time to beat me to the door.

"Don't! You owe me a life, Lazlian!" I screamed, tears streaming down my cheeks. "I saved yours!"

He didn't turn around, but he stopped. "We're even."

Did he mean for not killing me just now when we fought over the bomb? The fact that he carried a gun he could have used? Even still...

"I saved you twice," I shouted, tugging at his shirt, desperate to keep him from walking. I blinked away my tears. I needed to concentrate; Kirwyn's life depended on it. "Once when I had Lida tell you about Singen and once just now. You *owe* me a life."

"Yours," he snarled, turning away from the door to face me. "Not his."

"Mine for his! Hang me instead! I'm the one you hate.

I'm the one you always wanted to kill," I sobbed, beating my breast with my tied, fisted hands. "Is that what you want, Lazlian? Tell me! You want to whip me until I'm dead? Do it! Please, you can do it yourself, I'll go willingly. Just don't hurt him, please."

Lazlian balled his hands into angry fists and tossed his head back in fury, telling me it was the wrong bargain to strike.

"Wait, please! Just *tell* me what to do, Lazlian. You want me to beg?" I threw myself onto my knees, but the bindings didn't have enough give and my arms remained high above my head, still secured to the pillar. I struggled to slide my wrists free while I spoke. Pride was nowhere near a concern. If Lazlian wanted me to kiss his feet like he was the king, I'd do it. There was nothing I wouldn't do for Kirwyn, *nothing.*

"I'm begging," I pled.

"For him," Lazlian sneered, pointing angrily toward the stairs. "Why him?"

Was he asking, 'why not my brother... or why not me?'

I gulped, too scared to answer.

Because he never asked me to. Because he'd do the same for me. Because I love him.

None of those responses were what Lazlian wanted to hear and I couldn't guess what would work. "Please, please, don't do this," I babbled, yanking my bindings.

Lazlian turned and stormed off again just as I'd finally freed my wrists. I shot to my feet, ran across the room, and threw myself at him, catching his arm in an attempt to grab the gun --

-- but he pushed me off his body and I stumbled, making it clear I wasn't going to win a battle of brute strength against him.

"Is it Juls?" I cried, desperate.

Lazlian paused, sparking hope in my chest.

"I'll stay as his wife," I quickly promised. "Quietly. I won't ever speak if that's what you want. Except to say the things you want me to say. Please, just let Kirwyn go and I'll stay with Juls forever."

From behind, I watched Lazlian shake his head and continue walking. If words didn't work, I would have to throw myself at him again and he'd easily throw me back again. Sobbing and sweating, I fought to breathe, to not faint. I needed to keep Lazlian with me, hopefully long enough for Mal-Yin's men to arrive.

What was left? What did Lazlian want?

Not me. It couldn't be me.

But I had nothing else to offer.

I flashed back to the way Lazlian looked at me that night in his bedroom. *It was desire, wasn't it?* It was why he wouldn't let me shoot myself. Why he didn't shoot me now with the gun at his waist. Not for his brother... but for himself.

I remembered what I swore when Kirwyn was nearly captured at Fabroni's safehouse. *My honor isn't worth the risk to your life.* It didn't even come close.

Struggling for air, I cried, "You can have me!"

Lazlian halted.

My heart pounded and I spoke rapidly to keep him detained.

"However you want, however long..."

Lazlian didn't move. Hope blossomed in my breast.

I gulped and finished, "I won't... protest."

One low sound, almost like a pained chuckle, tore from the back of Lazlian's throat. He gave another shake of his head.

Unbelievably, he started walking again. My stomach dropped.

I was wrong. If not me then... what?

"Please! There is nothing I won't do, Lazlian. Just tell me what you want," I sobbed. Tears soaked my face and fell onto my neck and chest. I shook my open hands as if they held something I could surrender. "Tell me and I'll give it to you."

"I don't want," he growled, angry enough to stop. I could see the tension in the muscles of his shoulders and back.

"What do you want?" I pressed, frantic.

"I don't want to want."

"Anything, name it!"

"I don't want to want, Zaria!" he roared as he turned to face me.

"Why not?"

"Because it means I'll resent him!"

Kirwyn? I thought.

"Resent my own brother!" Laz cried.

Oh.

"You belong to my brother," he muttered, almost to himself. Then he raised his arms wide and shouted, "Who doesn't even want you!" Quiet but firm, he added, "Not really."

Lazlian half-chuckled, half-snorted, before turning and re-commencing his walk.

But... I'd just offered myself and he rejected me.

The room came crashing down upon my head. If I could sort through the wreckage, I felt I was so close to touching the key. I needed to distract him, keep him here. But I had nothing left to give, nothing left to try. I'd thought...

thought *I* was what he wanted. Laz seemed to confirm it just now...

I didn't understand.

Oh god, he reached the stairs.

I never understood Lazlian.

His hand clasped the railing.

How he could hurt me so easily.

If I rushed him, he'd just push me back again. Abandon me. Like the day he left me to die.

Why had he left me to die that hateful night? It didn't make sense. If he desired me, why had he done it?

Why, why, why?

Hyperventilating, I struggled to find a solution in my mind. Fight, flight, freeze, flock. None of these conflict responses worked with Lazlian. I needed to invent a new response.

Feint, I thought, hope surging. Just like I played the keylord false when I shoved my dagger into his hands and escaped the castle.

"You broke me!" I cried the lie. "You destroyed me the night you left me on the battlefield."

I was so convincing my voice cracked. Strange though, my deception spread, splintering my body so that I felt like I was falling apart.

"You left me alone to die and I - I hate you so much! Why did you do it? You let me run into the crossfire, alone!"

My performance was so good the very blood in my veins believed it. That terrible shattering crept inward through vital arteries, fracturing closer to one beating organ until that cracked too.

"You hurt me," I sobbed. "Broke me, broke my..." I spoke the last word with such a whimper, such a shuddering breath, that it was barely a word at all.

"...heart."

I must have squeezed my eyes shut to make it more believable, because suddenly, when I opened them, Laz wasn't ascending the stairs.

He was striding across the room, charging me.

I had no time to do anything but gasp as Lazlian grabbed and lifted me. To avoid falling onto the floor and to keep him from walking again, my only choice was to wrap my legs around his waist. Half my body clung to him. The other half, the upper half, fought him with all the repressed rage from that night.

"I hate you!" I bawled, clawing at his bare chest and neck. One sharp scrape of my nails caused Lazlian to bare his teeth in a hiss -- but he didn't stop carrying me backwards.

"*I hate you,*" I snarled between clenched teeth, feeling the unyielding metal of the now-defunct gate console beneath me as Lazlian tossed me onto the sloped control table. In one move, he slammed himself between my open legs and with nothing but my seasuit and his combat pants, I could feel part of Lazlian I hadn't felt before.

What is he doing? My mind screamed.

I used my elbows against the console to support my torso from being pressed lower, but Lazlian didn't push me down. He snaked one hand under my hair, gripping and tugging my head *back.* His other hand clamped my waist as his groin pressed harder between my legs with unmistakable sexual intent.

Oh my god. He's going to kiss me. Assault me.

I nearly scooted away, but in a moment of cunning, I did the opposite. I pushed myself up and against Lazlian's chest.

Reaching around his back, I fumbled for the gun at the

waistband of his pants. Lazlian's left hand was so entangled in my hair he didn't have time to pull it free and his right hand moved too late to cross his body and grab mine.

I shoved the gun against Lazlian's temple.

He froze. And smiled.

"Do it," he challenged, scorched-earth eyes blown wide. "Do it and put me out of my misery."

My hand shook. *Think I won't? Think I'll let you hurt me? If it's you or me, Laz, I can do it. I'll kill you.*

"Do it," Lazlian bit out. I caught the scent of metal from the gun or from him, it was indistinguishable. He always smelled like flint or fire, ready to spark and consume. His grip tightened on my hair, yanking my head further back, so I pushed the barrel of the gun hard enough against his head to jar it sideways as I bared my own teeth.

Lazlian let out a low laugh, releasing my hair and reaching upwards for the gun. In the second I should have shot... I didn't. I panted as his hand closed over mine.

Eyes locked, he challenged, "I'll help you. You want to kill me?" The hand on my waist now reached up to thread my hair and yank my head back again. "Let's do it together."

For some reason, I began vehemently shaking my head, even as I thought, *yes, to protect me from you, I will kill you.* My breath came in quick, short bursts.

I hated these games with Lazlian. I didn't understand the rules. They never made sense. I never won.

"Kill me," Lazlian rasped, and for a moment I thought he might wrest control of the gun and point it at my head. But his words lost their bite and his dark gaze dropped to my mouth. My whole body shook. We hadn't moved – my legs were still wrapped around Lazlian's waist, his fingers still twisted in my hair, and both our hands gripped the gun pressed to his temple.

I can. I can pull the trigger. Save myself, protect myself.

My lip quivered under his intense inspection and new tears pricked the corners of my eyes.

"Do it! Kill me or I'll kill you!" Laz growled, firmly this time, squeezing my hand holding the gun. But his heated gaze darted back to my lips.

I licked a stray tear that fell near my mouth. Lazlian's eyes followed the movement of my tongue.

Oh god, if this was feinting, why did it feel like falling?

With a sudden roar, he yanked the gun from both our hands and threw it on the floor beside us where it clattered out of reach. I had just enough time to draw a deep breath – as one does to prepare before going underwater for a long time – and Lazlian's mouth claimed mine.

I was kissing Lazlian.

He wrapped his arm around my back and crushed me to his chest. Everything slowed and muted, as it does under the sea. Time ceased, sound dimmed, the battle around us melted away. We existed in a pocket outside time, in a space outside reality. I felt something soft between my fingers and realized my hands had woven themselves up into Lazlian's dark waves. I think he liked it because he responded by kissing me deeper, pushing himself harder against me. Or maybe he was angry because he squeezed my waist too fiercely and his teeth nipped my lip. But if they drew blood on their bite it was no matter... I was beneath the sea and the saltwater would soothe it. *Yes... there it was...* the caress of his tongue brushing my lower lip, licking the wound before plunging back into my open mouth. It was an attack. He sucked my will to fight right out through my mouth; drew it from my lips as each sweep of his tongue found any residual resistance and cleared it from his path.

My body's natural response may have been to squeeze my legs a little and pull Lazlian tighter against the area between my thighs. I may have moaned deeper when – if – I did it. It may have been misread as a different desire. I didn't know how long I moaned before I heard the rustle of fabric, muffled beneath the ocean's surface. I felt cool air between my legs, the loss of Lazlian. With one hand he held aside the material of my seasuit; with the other he backed up and lowered his pants.

I emerged back into the reality of the gate room as if I'd shot straight up from the seabed and broke the surface with a gasp for air.

I jerked my hips just as Lazlian pushed the first third of his erection inside me. The thrust would have had him buried deep; only my angling prevented him from going any further. For the moment. A quick readjustment and he'd be back on course.

"Stop," I cried, clutching Laz's shoulders. *"Please."*

To my complete shock, he stilled.

Pain ripped through Lazlian's face. He squeezed his eyes shut, but, mid-thrust, he stopped himself. He didn't push forward.

He didn't pull back either.

Yet it was such an unlikely event, I could only stare, bewildered. Telling him to stop was an instinct, but if I thought about it, I never imagined he'd do it. I was so awestruck, I couldn't move. We hovered together on that precipice, panting in unison, neither of us shifting in either direction. My legs still wrapped themselves around Lazlian's waist, his hand had re-tangled itself under my hair. I could see the sordid picture we made for anyone to look upon should they stumble into the room: bloodied, clothes thrown hastily aside and connected lewdly between my open legs.

Lazlian is inside me, I marveled, with a mixture of terror and… another emotion I didn't want to examine.

And then my body did something it shouldn't have.

Base instinct took over and I squeezed, the walls of my core tightening around the tip of Lazlian's erection, even as I whimpered, *"No."*

His eyes blazed in the dimness of the room, lust-filled, hungry to consume. I could see the indecision reflected there, driving him mad. I had no defense. Even if I were strong enough to battle Lazlian for a few moments, he was already a third of the way *there.* All it would take was a snap of his hips to bury himself to the hilt inside me.

To my horror, I instinctively squeezed around Lazlian's hardness *again,* even as I cried, *"Please, Lazlian. No."*

I'd never seen Lazlian shudder before, but a full-body tremor ran through him.

Shaking my head to contradict what my lower half betrayed, what my moans might have miscommunicated, I implored, "Please, Lazlian, don't."

Utter agony crumpled his face. Trying to breathe through clenched teeth, Lazlian stood stiffly; face strained, shoulders tensed. For several long seconds he didn't move.

Then, with a groan, Lazlian tore himself out of me.

Once again, I was shocked.

What had just happened?

I felt… baffled and bereft. I felt…

Lazlian.

A part of Lazlian that I didn't know existed. It was as if a trick coin had been tossed in the air – the kind unfairly weighted to fall to one side. But rarely, external forces intervened… the wind blew *just so*, or the coin hit an obstruction on the way down and *clink*. It landed on the other side. The side I'd never seen.

In utter awe, the protective walls I always had in place to guard myself around the keylord tumbled down.

My desire flipped with the coin. The moment Lazlian made the other choice, so did I.

A third shock washed over me as I realized…

My eyes were heavy and hooded, my lips were pink and parted, my cheeks were warm and flushed… and my heart thumped with a curious ache.

At that moment, a part of me desired Lazlian, beyond my body's physical response.

He must have read it on my face – a face that always failed to hide my emotions. Because I watched *his* disbelief, and something like awe color *his* face -- stripped bare, raw. Wonder and desire lit his scorched-earth eyes.

My walls were down. His walls were down. It had never happened at the same time before.

Lazlian wasn't inside me, but in that moment, I felt like he penetrated me. I felt connected through the shared awe in our eyes. Everything around us was silent. It was one of the most intense moments of my life, yet not a single word was spoken, not the slightest caress exchanged. We didn't even touch as we gazed at one another. I'd tapped a fleeting part of Lazlian and it shook me. He'd tapped a fleeting part of me and it shook him.

Suddenly, from the hall outside the room, I heard the nearby pounding of boots on stone, making me start.

The next second, Mal-Yin's men burst through the door.

I blinked.

Kirwyn!

Oh god, what kind of person was I? I – I had only meant

to keep Lazlian from the stairs. I blinked again, shaking my head of the strange spell, eyes darting behind the keylord and up to the King's Gate where they'd marched Kirwyn.

Oh my god. Was he okay? What a fucking horrible person I was. I slammed my walls back up around me. How much time had passed? Five minutes? Six? How had so much happened in such a short time?

I hadn't moved away, but Lazlian noticed the change. He wasn't even paying attention to the guards behind him. Men barreled into the room, brandishing weapons and shouting, and Laz stared at me as if chaos wasn't raining down upon us. Oblivious, his fingertips grazed my cheek to recapture my attention. While I scanned the room, he searched my face, anguished, frantic.

Lazlian was still gazing at me with something like desperation when Mal-Yin's men dragged him from my body. He didn't fight them.

It felt like everything happened through a filter.

"Are you alright?"

"Are you hurt?"

Soldiers asked questions but they sounded far away and I ignored them. I slapped at hands trying to assist me, leapt from the console, and bolted toward the staircase. Mal's men forced the keylord to his knees and pulled his hands behind his back, needlessly restraining them with hand-cuffs. He wasn't fighting or even speaking.

As I raced up the stairs, my last glimpse was of his tormented eyes following me.

CHAPTER 43

I took the stairs two at a time, beating my bare feet against the wood without care of silencing my approach. What good would it do to maintain the element of surprise? I had no weapon. I didn't even have proper combat attire.

Stupid.

I should have grabbed some of Mal's men to accompany me. There hadn't been any time to explain but I would have thought they'd follow me... Cocking my head to listen, I heard only silence at my back.

No, not silence. Voices... arguing. Had others entered the control room? Palace Guards?

I pushed the question aside as I burst onto the King's Gate and saw him.

"No!" I screamed in horror along with my heart.

They'd tied Kirwyn's hands behind his back, gagged his mouth, and wound his neck tightly in the noose, readying him for the drop at any moment. Seeing me, all five guards turned.

"Grab her!" the tallest of the soldiers shouted.

"Stop!" I cried. "It's over! Prince Lazlian has been captured, the castle has fallen, our army will be here any minute!"

Will they? I wondered.

Before I reached Kirwyn, two of the men seized my arms.

"Stop!" I repeated, kicking my legs to no avail. "I said it's over! Let us go!"

Finally, the palace guards paused, exchanging looks. I sighed in relief, struggling to catch my breath. Something I didn't understand was communicated between the men's eyes.

"She's *queen,*" one of the soldiers restraining me whispered.

"She's a traitor and a prisoner of war," the other countered. His conspiring tone made coquina clams climb up my spine. He nudged his head in the direction of the gallows. "This is how we deal with enemies of Rythas."

A short pause and then the other man said, "Navere will be pleased to be rid of her."

What? No...

An understanding passed between the guards. One of them moved to cut Kirwyn down from the gallows. I anxiously awaited our dual release, but before I could weep with joy, the guards pulled me toward the dais in his place.

At once, Kirwyn was like a rabid animal – he even managed to knock one of the soldiers down, but two more took his place, shoving Kirwyn to his knees.

No! I don't want to die!

I was dragged onto the hangman's deck, punching and flailing. My screams were silenced by a gag tied around my head and my hands were roughly yanked behind my back and tied as well.

No, oh god, not like this...

But... I thought, never breaking eye contact with Kirwyn. *Better me than him.*

They'd forced Kirwyn flat to the floor, boots pressing into his back to hold him down. He had just enough give to look up at me as he thrashed, red-faced, wild and shouting beneath his gag. Bifurcating the steps behind him, the Water Stairs flowed. It was a cascade of wonder, beginning at the King's Gate and rushing to the gardens below; a fountain from sky to earth I'd once looked upon with delight.

It now appeared ominous, ready to carry my soon-departing soul from the gallows to the ground on a river of plummeting water.

The one particularly tall guard wound the rope around my neck while I sobbed.

At least I can see you. My heart beat with so much love for Kirwyn. *I don't want to die, but at least I can see you. You'll be the last thing I ever see,* I swore, making sure I held Kirwyn's eyes. God, he was so beautiful. So talented and tender and more than I ever imagined a man could be.

I tried but I couldn't catch his scent above the smells of High Spire. Wet stone and sweaty men and my fear.

I love you so much. If I could go back in time, I'd do it all over again, I swore, tears running down my face. *I'd run away with you this time. Straight from Elowa to wherever you wanted to go.*

Kirwyn was beyond hysterically raging. More men came to pin him down.

But if this was the only way to have you, I still wouldn't change it.

All I want, all I wish I had, is more time with you.

I tried so hard to be brave when they tightened the rope.

I didn't want Kirwyn to remember me like this. But tears spilled harder and faster than they ever had in my life, soaking my face.

I love you, Kirwyn.

Without warning, the floor dropped beneath me and I fell.

CHAPTER 44

To my horror, my neck didn't break.

Not a clean death, then.

My feet kicked to find anything but air while my lungs struggled to possess it. I couldn't hold Kirwyn's gaze in those last seconds of my life.

I love you, I screamed in my mind, as my vision blackened around the edges. One last blessing, fainting, my old friend, was going to take me before strangulation did.

"Stop!"

The deep, authoritative command cut across the landing.

"Release her. Now. Cut her down."

Was that...

Juls?

My knees slammed into the floor, the pressure on my neck immediately slacking though not disappearing. Someone pressed against me, bracing me from falling forward with his chest. Blinking, I looked up to see...

Kirwyn.

Like me, his arms were still tied behind him. I burst into

new sobs, blubbering and dripping snot. *I'm alive. You're alive. We're alive.* Without the use of our arms, we nuzzled one another, trying to get close until someone finally cut Kirwyn's bonds and he wrapped his arms around me at the same time someone sawed through the rope around my neck. When my hands were freed, I clung to Kirwyn, weeping hysterically.

Never letting go. Never again. Kirwyn tilted my head back, turning my neck and inspecting it. "She needs a doctor!" he cried.

It took several tries, but I found my voice. "N- no doctor, I'll be okay ..." I protested weakly. Between Lazlian's hands and the noose, my neck hurt, but I didn't want anyone examining me, taking me from Kirwyn. *He* was what I needed most, nothing else. But I had to get my shaking under control to convince him.

Never taking life for granted again.

Kirwyn and I struggled to our feet, holding each other. When a guard reached out to help us, Kirwyn smacked him away.

"Don't you fucking touch her. Lay a hand on her and I'll cut off your fucking arm."

The guard snapped his hand back.

Kirwyn tore off a lightweight combat jacket and wrapped it around my shoulders. He squeezed me to his chest, placing a protective kiss on my forehead. Half-delirious, I pictured what I must look like. Never did I imagine that one of the most pivotal nights of my life would happen while I wore nothing but my seasuit. Though if I thought about it, I shouldn't have been surprised.

From the corner of my eye, I watched Juls stride across the landing, flanked by his own guards. My stomach flipped. Unlike Lazlian, he wore no protective combat shirt.

I wondered if he'd dressed for battle and removed it after surrendering or if he had never bothered to put one on. He wore a black tunic and pants in a style as he would for court, and a silver crown rested upon his regal head.

"On your knees, now, every one of you," he commanded the soldiers. The guards, happy to end my life only moments before, cowed, heads bent as they lined up to kneel.

"You dare attack my queen, your queen?" Juls asked, eyes narrowed. Whenever he affected his *king's voice* it rattled my bones. Juls wasn't especially tall or broad, but his father trained him well in how to rule and he always managed to snap attention with that tone. "You *dare?*"

Juls paced to the tall man, central amongst the five guards. The leader, I assumed, and the same soldier who'd knocked me down at the Bone Gate.

"Your life is forfeit." Juls declared it with such calmness, I jumped at his next action.

Without sentencing the soldier to time in the dungeons, without giving him opportunity to plead his case, without even setting up a proper execution, Juls drew his sword from his waist and in one quick move, pierced it right through the guard's heart, slaying him.

Even after all I'd been through, I gasped. I'd never seen Juls put a man to death with his own blade.

"I would be doing a service to Rythas if I marched each of you up to the noose, in turn."

I heard a sniffle from one of the guards who'd pushed Kirwyn to the ground. The air on the landing was thick with tension as the soldiers awaited their fate.

"But seeing as how there might have been confusion about the true enemy," Juls spoke slowly, pointedly, "I will spare your lives."

I heard more than one whimper of relief.

"No one ever speaks a word of what has happened here," Juls ordered the soldiers. "If I ever hear so much as a whisper, each of you face worse than the noose, so it is in your best interest to quash any rumors. Am I clear?"

Torture and The Isle of Walking Corpses, I assumed he implied.

Solemn nods followed. I stayed pressed to Kirwyn, studying Juls while Kirwyn studied my neck. The king had grown since I'd last seen him. There was something solemn in his countenance that gave him a new maturity. *Had I done that? Had we done it to each other?*

"Leave us," Juls commanded to the guards, not meeting my eyes. "Everyone out. You're lucky I don't execute you now. If you ever speak of this, you'll wish I had."

At his order, the men previously bent on killing both Kirwyn and I scurried back inside the castle with heads bent. They were escorted by some of Juls's personal guards, who carried the body of the executed soldier out with them. But the two guards closest to the king hesitated.

"I'll be fine. He's leaving as well," Juls said.

Kirwyn shook his head, angling his body in front of me. "I'm not going anywhere."

"Water, please," I croaked, needing rehydration but also buying time to figure out what was happening and what I should do. Despite Juls having spared my life, Kirwyn still eyed him as if he'd tear him to shreds any second.

For the first time, Juls truly looked at me. Sadness tinged the edges of his warm, brown eyes, tugging at my heart. He requested one of the guards fetch fresh water and insisted the other one leave for good. The king, Kirwyn and I waited for a tense minute, eyeing one another in an anxious standoff that reminded me of my first awkward dinner at High Spire.

God, how I wish things could have been different. You must hate me now, I thought, angry and guilty at the same time.

I could hear wild commotion below as High Spire surrendered, but I didn't know what was happening and didn't trust Mal to lead it. Either Kirwyn or I – or both of us – needed to get down there quickly.

When the guard fetching water returned, I drank greedily, sure nothing ever tasted as good in my life. Finally, Juls dismissed the last soldier and the three of us were alone.

I licked my lips and said tentatively, "Thank you for saving my life."

"You're my wife and my queen. It's my honor to protect you."

"She is nothing to you and never will be," Kirwyn spat through clenched teeth.

Juls refused to acknowledge Kirwyn. "I've agreed to a surrender," he said, and I could tell he tried to keep the bitterness from his tone. Despite seeing the evidence, my heart leapt to hear it truly spoken.

"It's late and we're all tired," Juls continued. "We can convene in the morning to discuss terms. Until then, you will spend the night here in your bedroom, under my protection. Your friend will return to his men."

My stomach sank as I understood what wasn't being said. I was a bargaining chip to keep things civil. *You've taken the castle, we'll take the queen. Until such time as an agreement can be arranged.*

I squeezed Kirwyn's hand in a silent request to let me speak first.

"I will sleep on Mal-Yin's ship," I declared, calmly.

"I will not allow you to leave the castle," Juls said firmly. "It is out of the question."

"Then Kirwyn will return to my room with me."

"I will not allow him to stay," Juls bit out, shaking his head. "Those are our terms for peace."

Kirwyn cut in, "I'll burn this castle to the ground before I let you touch Zaria again."

"You will leave me alone with my *wife,*" Juls said in his king's voice, still not deigning to look at Kirwyn.

I cringed at the pointed choice of words and braced for Kirwyn's wrath.

"So you can hurt her?"

Kirwyn went for the jugular with a question that was really a statement. My eyes darted back and forth between the two men, ready to intervene.

"It was you who endangered her life every day in the backlands!" Juls declared passionately, finally looking at Kirwyn. "Zaria has always been safe at High Spire."

"Safe against everyone but the boy-king who'd force himself on her?"

Oh fuck.

"I have never touched her without her consent!"

"She was never in a position to give or deny it!"

Fuck, fuck.

"Do you have any idea how she came to me after you and your brother?" Kirwyn shouted. "She was a shell of who she used to be. Afraid for anyone to touch her, jumping at every sound, waking up screaming from nightmares. And that's only after she'd finally fallen asleep, which took fitfully long because she kept glancing at the locked door a hundred times as if someone was going to come in and violate her -- only to reverse the pattern in the day and check the door a hundred times to make sure no one was locking her *in!*"

I gaped at Kirwyn. I knew he was observant, but he'd never said these things before. I was only barely aware that I did them.

"So don't tell me you protected her. Her physical existence might not have been in danger every day here, but inside she was screaming and you couldn't hear it," Kirwyn raged. "You *caused* it."

I badly wanted to process everything Kirwyn said but couldn't spare the time. They were about to come to blows and I saw I needed to diffuse quickly, again.

"Since everyone is so respectful of my wishes," I interrupted, trying to think fast, "Why don't you allow me to express my choices and then, *honor them?*"

Juls looked ready to object so I quickly said, "In a show of goodwill, I agree to stay at High Spire until discussions can begin in the morning."

It was one small concession to let him save face, I told myself. Just a night in my old bedroom in exchange for so much progress.

Juls immediately straightened and I saw a satisfied gleam in his eyes... a kind I hadn't previously recalled seeing. It reminded me of Laz. Before Kirwyn could lose his mind, I clarified, "Mal-Yin's soldiers will accompany me at all times. They will stand guard outside my door for the night."

"Not negotiable," I told Juls firmly. He considered momentarily, then nodded.

I turned to Kirwyn, anticipating a more difficult battle.

"It's okay," I whispered, voice still hoarse from the noose. *Remember your promise to trust me here.* "He won't hurt me."

"You mean more than he already has?" Kirwyn retorted.

"That's over now," I said loudly, hoping it to be true. We needed to proceed peacefully because if we didn't come to an agreement, Juls's men would force Kirwyn from the landing, Kirwyn would return with Mal's men, and things would get messy. If I could buy peace with one night in High Spire, it was worth the price.

"He saved us, saved my life. He's not going to hurt me." Whispering, I added, "Please... you swore to *trust me.*"

With his jaw clenched, Kirwyn and I engaged in a battle of wills.

"I owe him this and you need to manage Mal and the surrender," I argued. "Aewna needs to be contacted, soldiers need to be readied to take my mother out of Elowa..."

There was more to be done than I was capable of handling right now and Kirwyn knew it. He drew in a long breath, then huffed it out. Above my head, he stared at Juls coldly. "If one hair on her head is out of place, if you've upset her in the slightest, I will raze your castle to the ground. And I don't care how many people are inside it, as long as she's out."

My heart thumped at Kirwyn's vow, sure he'd do it. And when his rage subsided, the guilt at killing innocent people would haunt him and he'd never love himself again. And if guilt *didn't* haunt him... then he'd have turned into someone *I* could never love, and it would break my heart.

"Let me remind you again, it's under your *protection* that she was placed in harm's way," Juls countered. "Zaria has and always will be safe in High Spire."

"Your men nearly killed her!" Kirwyn shouted, red-faced.

"Stop," I ordered, before Kirwyn could make things

worse by physically attacking Juls. I laid a hand on his chest. *You swore to listen to me here.*

"I will be safe with Mal's guards outside my room. Please, see what's happening. Get things under control down there. You need to lead. I don't trust them. *Please.*"

Kirwyn sighed deeply, jaw clenched again. He took my chin in his hands, searching my face for several tense seconds before leaning down and kissing me.

"Alright. You deal with him. I'll deal with them. But I'd prefer it the other way around," he said.

"Thank you for trusting me. I will be safe. It's over. We won. I'll see you in the morning and we can do what we've always talked about."

Kirwyn gripped my biceps, unwilling to let go. Finally, he huffed and stepped back.

"The only reason you're still breathing," Kirwyn spat at Juls, pointing to me, "is because she wants you to be. And some of us have enough respect for the people we love to not completely disregard their desires."

"Why do you think it is you're still breathing?" Juls countered.

Fuck, here we go again.

"Because your guards aren't here to do the dirty work for you, you piece of-"

"Stop!" I cried, voice hoarse and wavering, hands balled into fists. "We don't have time for this. If you have to fight, please, just do it in the morning. I'm tired, Kirwyn. Please. I badly need rest."

It wasn't entirely untrue, but I played the damsel in distress card first because I knew it was the fastest way to make them both listen. If they were going to fight dirty, so was I.

Kirwyn's eyes rounded with concern as he turned away

from Juls. *I probably look like I'm about to fall over anyway,* I thought.

"Dammit, Zaria, I don't like this," he protested. "I'm only agreeing because I made you a promise and because you'll have Mal's guards. You stay in your room," Kirwyn ordered. "Get sleep. I'll handle everything down there."

I nodded. Kirwyn kissed me again and walked slowly, unwillingly, from the King's Gate.

"Kirwyn, wait!" I called, remembering.

He turned.

"How did you get here? You couldn't have swum that far and couldn't have unlocked those handcuffs."

"I've known what you were planning since before you even conceived of it yourself," he boasted. His grin was far too cocky for the moment, but a part of me loved that even at a time like this, he could be so wonderfully infuriating. "I wasn't sure how you'd do it, but I knew you were up to something. Mal and I planned an alternate route for me."

"But... how?" I breathed.

Kirwyn's eyes flicked to Juls, but I guessed he decided secrecy no longer mattered. Or maybe he wanted to rub the king's face in his weaknesses.

"In the commotion of Mal's soldiers approaching the Garden Gate, no one noticed a small boat docking on the beach nearest the Black Passage. It's not a far swim through the passage itself. The hard part was climbing the rocks with Ener's gear, and suiting up near the opening without falling into the sea before I finished. When I made it through the passage, I ran straight for the Bone Gate."

I didn't know whether to smack him or kiss him. If Kirwyn hadn't figured out my intentions and followed me, I'd never have escaped Lazlian and deactivated the second console. Everything would have fallen apart.

We do make an incredible team.

Kirwyn's green eyes danced. "I always knew you'd try, but I was never going to let you do this alone."

I swallowed back the lump in my throat. *My demon-boy. You've been incorrigible since the day I met you.*

I wanted to run to him and kiss him deeply, but I didn't, knowing Juls watched us carefully.

Instead I said, "Take care of things down there."

Kirwyn gave one last hate-filled look at Juls and one reluctant one at me before leaving.

Alone with my husband for the first time since I'd spent the night in his room, I wouldn't have known how to act under *normal* circumstances, and the events of the evening were anything but usual.

Needing to break the tension, I spoke first, just as I had the first time we met.

"I'm sorry."

Idiot. It felt woefully inefficient to simply apologize for taking his castle.

"Thank you again for sparing my life."

"I would have executed all the soldiers in a heartbeat," Juls said. "The only reason I am letting them breathe is because they're more useful alive. I now know who to watch."

"Watching them will lead you straight to Navere," I relayed. "They said as much."

"Maybe so," Juls agreed sadly.

"Do you have my sister?" I asked, heart pounding. "Did you take Jona?"

Juls studied me for a moment, then admitted, "No."

I exhaled a sigh of relief.

Head high, he announced, "Lazlian wanted to. But I forbade it."

I knew he'd try. Thank god you stopped him.

For a few awkward moments, neither of us spoke. A different Juls than the one I'd known before eyed me, weary and wary.

"I don't understand you," he said finally, struggling to keep the anger from his voice. "We're both smart, attractive, strong leaders." I could tell he'd wanted to say those words for a long time. "I gave you a kingdom. What more could you want?"

"A choice, Juls. You didn't give me a choice."

"I didn't give myself one either."

Fair point.

"I never thought you'd go this far," Juls said, rubbing his forehead.

"You always underestimated me," I replied, annoyance surfacing.

"You underestimated *me*. I protected you. I never pushed you to take our mark, I kept my father at bay."

"I never asked you to! I asked that you not marry me in the first place! That you let me go!"

"No, Zaria," he said, solemn. "You never asked."

I blinked rapidly. "Well, it should have been obvious when you kidnapped me. I shouldn't have needed to say it."

"Okay, I knew you were reluctant at first," Juls admitted, fussing with his hem and straightening his tunic. "But can you blame me for wanting to make it work? What else was I supposed to do?"

"I don't know, Juls. Can you blame me for being angry?"

"Angry enough to invade my kingdom? *Our* kingdom. To bring an army here in vengeance?" Juls growled. He took a calming breath and ran a hand down his face. "What is it you want?"

"I want my freedom!" I beat my fist against my breast.

"And freedom for all the girls who would come after me. And for Elowa."

"I see. And what of ours did you trade to Mal-Yin to obtain it for you?"

Juls was many things, but a fool wasn't one of them. I looked down, offering a half-shrug. I didn't truly know how far Mal's ideas would take him. But Kirwyn trusted Mal and so did Aewna. Either way, I wasn't ready to discuss what I *did* know until we met in the morning.

"You let the devil in our front door," Juls bit out.

"Well," I replied, "even the devil has a role to play."

Juls shook his head. "Laz always warned that you were like a disease infecting our family." Though his words were harsh, Juls's tone was sad. Tired. It made the insult hurt more.

"Who is the disease and who is the cure depends on your perspective," I returned.

Juls gave me a hard look. "And what are you curing us of, Zaria?"

"Nothing! You're the one who brought it up. I just want Rythas to stop taking Daughters of Elowa as captive brides... and for things to change in Elowa. I want the people to learn about the world beyond. I never wanted to upset your rule."

Juls sighed impatiently. "What is *Mal-Yin* coming to upset?"

I chewed my lip. "All I know is he wants to modernize and democratize things somehow and he wants it to spread. It won't be bad. It will be... helpful."

Juls shook his head. "You were always naïve."

"Well maybe you shouldn't have fucking sheltered me my whole life!"

"Maybe I should have listened to Laz and kept you *more* contained so you couldn't do this kind of damage."

I crossed my arms, seething, but I wasn't surprised. Subduing me, silencing me, locking me in my room. The threat always lurked behind the scenes, even when it wasn't spoken outright.

"You are *my queen,*" Juls said, brows knit in frustration, gesturing with his hands. "We could have been happy. We could have been great. They all love us. We are the golden couple, we can make a golden reign."

I noticed he'd changed tense, clinging to hope. *Even now,* I marveled, *after I seized your castle, you still want to try.*

But it wasn't really *me* with whom he wanted to try -- just what I symbolized or what I could do for him. For all the time we had together, Juls never bothered to know the real me. *We are married and we barely even know each other,* I realized.

"I'm sorry," I sighed, fumbling for words and knowing whatever I said would be inadequate. It always was. Something was lost on the journey from their formation in my head to the tip of my tongue. "Mal told me everything you sacrificed to protect me and I want you to know I'm grateful. I'm sorry I couldn't learn to..."

I almost said *love you.* But we'd never said those kinds of words to each other.

"...be happy with you."

I winced, watching a muscle in his cheek feather as he clenched his jaw.

"But I respect you, Juls." Cringing, I added, "I know it doesn't look like it, given what I've done. I believe you make a good king. I support you, support your rule. But that's all I can give."

Which is more than enough for you to make us work. But not for me.

Juls walked toward me and took my hands in his. Though he was gentle and non-threatening, I didn't feel entirely comfortable being touched by him. I forgot my concerns when I noticed he still wore his gold wedding ring and a pang shot through my heart. Juls brought my hands to his mouth and kissed my knuckles softly. With a shaky breath, I remembered when he'd sucked my knuckle as he presented me with an engagement ring. It felt like it happened so many years ago, like we were children, playing at marriage.

But if we'd married as children then, we parted now as adults.

"You are my *wife,*" Juls repeated, but it was a plea, not a statement, matching the appeal in his eyes. *"You are my wife, Zaria."*

I couldn't help it; I wondered what would have happened if I'd kept his ring, stayed his queen. It was a life unlived, a door closed, possibilities unreached. Gone forever with my decision.

I want to be loved, truly *loved,* I yearned to tell him. But he would consider it a childish notion weighed against the duty of his crown.

"I – I'm sorry," I whimpered. The tears I tried to contain fell anyway.

Juls closed his eyes, inhaling deeply. Slowly, he lowered and released my hands. I wiped my tears and he stepped back, giving me time to collect myself. Or maybe it was time to collect himself.

Maybe it was for us both. Because the moment one of us next spoke, the broken silence would confirm it, would end the possibility for us eternally.

Juls turned his back to me, facing the corridor where his men awaited his command. I hung my head.

"Guards," he called, quietly, resigned. Within seconds soldiers appeared. "Escort the queen to her room."

CHAPTER 45

<p>eing sent to my room like a wayward child when I had done something to displease, or they simply didn't know what to do with me, was an idea all the Dorestes seemed to share.

Despite the fact we played no child's game.

Soldiers from Mal-Yin materialized out of the literal darkness to accompany the palace guard as we marched down the corridors. I knew Kirwyn had ensured our men were ready to move. It made me feel protected by him, even when he wasn't physically beside me, and I relaxed a little knowing he'd effectively manage the chaos below.

It also helped assuage my guilt for not participating. I'd been through too much and I needed a rest. A bath. Quiet.

Mal's men carried complicated weaponry. I was both too exhausted and too relieved from everything that had transpired to muster annoyance at the fact that he'd obviously snuck plenty of guns into Rythas, despite our deal.

At least they'd protect me through the night.

At least no one had started shooting during the invasion. As far as I knew, we had no blood on our hands.

Just shame and guilt on my shoulders.

With no ceremony, Juls's men deposited me at my door, and both his guards and mine took position outside it. I did not realize until later that the door itself had changed. Someone replaced it with a thicker version.

I was too busy gasping at the renovated contents of my room.

The first thing I noticed was the addition of a balcony outside my window, but I didn't have time to explore it before my gaze was recaptured by the updates within my quarters.

The bed had been redressed with lush spreads and pillows, cream-colored and silken. Finer than before. Art hung upon the walls -- pictures of various seascapes. Some were sun-drenched and cheerful, others were dark and moody -- rocky coves at nightfall. Glittering from my dressing table jeweled necklaces, tiaras, rings and bracelets hung on displays. *No wonder Juls showed such restraint in sending only my wedding ring,* I thought, *when all this had been placed in my old room.*

Beguiled, I crossed to the table and sucked in an awe-struck breath at an assortment of gems unlike any I'd ever seen at once. Golden bangles laden with rubies, aquama-rine-and-silver necklaces, pink and orange stones I couldn't name on chains and cuffs whose function on the body I didn't even know.

And more than any other, pearls and diamonds. Glistening on ropes, encrusted in collars, and studded on tiaras.

Yes, Juls had no need to send more than a band of gold when this bounty awaited.

Wide-eyed, I tentatively ran my fingers along a strange body harness of some type, sparkling with diamonds.

My god. It was the riches of a small kingdom. Meant for a queen.

Unworthy, I withdrew my hand like the jewels might bite or burn.

I can't climb into that silken bed in my current state, I thought.

Looking toward the bathroom, I noticed my tub had been filled. For the first time, I realized I had taken it for granted in the past that it was often kept ready. How odd that sometime during the battle or its aftermath, a servant must have been dispatched to fill it, as if this night were like any other.

Eagerly, I stripped my soiled seasuit from my body and climbed inside, soaking my aching muscles and using a coconut soap to clean the sweat and grime from my body, careful over my cuts and bruises. Despite the calming water, spending one last night in my old chambers filled me with an eerie sensation. I felt like I'd stepped into my past, and, at the same time, teetered on a precipice. Candlelight flickered heavy shadows along the furniture and tiled floor, shadows that seemed to reach out to grab and hold me. Make me stay.

I wandered around my chambers half-dazed, feeling as if I were saying goodbye forever. My cuspate phase was ending, and it was permanent. Whatever happened the next day, heavy pieces of the puzzle were sliding into their last places, doors were being shut with finality. I desperately wanted to move on, yet the knowledge that a book in my journey was closing and could never be re-opened, pricked my soul like a knife's blade edged in sorrow. The strange sadness seemed to float in the air like dust motes, infecting my lungs with each labored breath. My bedroom had been a prison and yet there was something poignant about this room and the sea below. I had changed here and somehow, I knew in my bones that when I stepped out for the final time the next day, I could never return to what I once was.

Wandering into the closet-alcove was odder still. New clothing had been hung, stuffed from one wall to the next. My eyes skirted over lushly colored, traditional gowns of Rythas and shorter, modern dresses. There were rows of bodices and armored corset-belts, sandals and slippers and boots for riding. To the back I found sleepwear scandalous enough to make me blush if I wasn't so perplexed. Everything looked a size too small, and I couldn't tell if it was to further eroticize the attire or if someone had purchased it and forgotten my measurements. Perhaps, like the engagement ring Juls once gave me, I was believed to be smaller than I was – a delicately boned, slip of a girl not built for the sea with firm muscles and a broad frame.

The thought made me return to the gazing glass above my table. The air was warm and balmy; I had no need of a robe. Naked, I stood before the mirror, examining myself. I bore a cut on my collarbone and my neck suffered minor bruising. Scrapes decorated the backs of my hands. My thigh had one purple bruise. Nothing too bad. On the outside.

Running my hand down between my breasts, I studied my body. It was a good one, strong, meant for swimming. That had always been the most important thing. But had Elowans been designed, foremost, to attract? How far did the bioengineering go? I studied the curve of my breasts, the tips of my pink nipples. Were they *optimal,* I pondered, creasing my brow... made to please the gaze of men? Was that a choice in the past, or was what I stared at just the luck of nature?

I ran my fingers over my full lips, staring. If Elowans had been created to be beautiful… what was the point of such beauty, truly? Did it all come down to sexual enticement?

My eyes fell upon the brilliant torso-chain and this time, I reverently picked it up and slipped it over my head. I didn't know why I did it. Part of me wondered how it fastened, part of me couldn't tear my eyes from its shining beauty. The chain was long and silver, with tear-shaped and princess-cut diamonds dripping at random intervals throughout, and pearls of different shades dotted in between. Cocking my head, I realized the body jewel ran down between a woman's breasts, gently separating and cupping them, before clasping around her back.

After I secured it, I again stared at myself in the candlelit mirror. The jewels sent sparkles dancing with every rise and fall of my chest. What did it mean that my breath fell heavily?

My fingertips stroked the shining, seductive body necklace. *Fit for a queen. It could feed a family for life, I bet. Maybe several. Maybe a village.* Hanging now, a glittering adornment between my breasts.

I exhaled slowly and made myself remove it.

Scurrying back to my closet to dress for bed, I chose a comparatively modest slip – a cream chemise more sheer than the black ones, but at least an inch longer. I slipped it on eagerly and padded out to the balcony, unsure why I'd avoided it when my heart longed to soak in the view.

As soon as I stepped out, sea air caressed my face and the hush of the ocean lulled me, made me sigh.

How glorious to have this for sleep every night, and to wake up to every morning.

A shuffling noise behind me made the hair on my neck rise. *Footsteps?*

Quickly turning, my heart stopped.

Lazlian stood in the middle of my room.

CHAPTER
46

I *mpossible.*

I gaped, eyes darting to the door behind him -- but it remained firmly shut. My heart pounded against my ribcage. He'd changed – not for sleep, but into a clean, black tunic-vest and pants. *How did he get in here? Did I have time to scream for the guards before he tried to push me off the balcony or... tried something worse?*

Dark, dangerous eyes locked on mine as he prowled forward.

"Lazlian, don't," I croaked.

Don't try to kiss me. Kill me. Fight me. Fuck me.

He continued stalking and I pressed myself to the balcony's rail, preparing to scream and knowing it wouldn't do any good before he attacked.

Lazlian stopped abruptly, cocking his head. "I'm not going to hurt you," he said in a low, husky voice. He raised his hands in surrender, as if... did he think I was going to jump?

"How did you get in here?" I demanded, clutching the polished rail, eyes darting to the door behind him.

Suddenly I felt very aware of my attire. The thin, ivory slip clung to my body. I couldn't hide the outline of my nipples poking through indecently, couldn't cover my bare décolletage, arms, or legs, whose exposure always offended Lazlian. I felt more displayed than I had in my seasuit because, unlike my swim clothes, this slip was designed for desire, sewn to seduce with every stitch.

Maybe to Lazlian, so was I.

I could always jump... rather than... I gulped, casting a quick glance behind me. *What was he going to do?*

The keylord inhaled deeply through his nose, then sighed. "There's a secret passage leading into your room now."

I gritted my teeth, anger flaring at the violation. "I see."

Lazlian sneered, "No, no you *don't*." He stormed onto the balcony and I flattened myself against the ledge, even though he left a good five feet between us. Lazlian's eyes raked my skin too possessively, too hungrily. Grabbing the rail behind me made my chest press out lewdly. I held my breath, waiting for him to determine my fate and hating my helplessness.

"Everything, everything's been taken from me," Lazlian declared, fists clenched.

Are you going to take from me, too? I wondered, hands flexing on the rail. *My life or... something else?* I could feel Lazlian's rage, his sense of injustice, rolling off every inch of his body. I had trouble meeting his wild eyes. My mind flashed back to the night we drank together after the Battle of the Bloody Shoals. *He means his claim,* I thought. *Having been the true first-born.*

"You said you didn't want the throne," I reminded him.

"I didn't," he huffed, "before."

Before... I came with it as a package deal?

Lazlian charged forward with single-minded determination, too fast for me to consider what to do. Panicky butterflies flitted about my stomach and I couldn't help but brace for attack. I didn't trust him; he could toss me into the sea any second. He raised his hand and I cringed, turning my face to my shoulder.

I was so *angry* at myself for cowering, but it was instinctive to lessen the blow.

None came.

Tentatively glancing up, I saw Lazlian's eyes widen as he flinched in return, as if my actions startled *him*. Quickly recovering and resuming course, he smacked his hand to my chest, frowning at the tattoo now visible upon my skin.

Oh.

Scowling, Laz rubbed his thumb over the water symbol as if he could wipe it away. I realized the neck of my seasuit had previously hidden the mark. Most likely guessing it had something to do with Kirwyn, disgust turned the corners of his mouth and rage lit his eyes.

"By law, you were to be queen here," he vehemently declared. "It was pre-ordained. Destiny."

Wait. I blinked, confused. *Queen? Weren't we talking about him? Or was this about Juls?*

"No," I protested, angrily slapping away his hand. "It wasn't pre-ordained, that was your father and a recent development. If he hadn't changed things, I would have been married off to one of your nobles. It was never truly my destiny to be queen or to marry your brother." I licked my lips and continued carefully, "Don't you see... it's Kirwyn. The odds that he washed ashore on my beach just in time for me to find him? That's fate, Lazlian. That's destiny."

A switch flipped and his temper flared.

"A fucking nobody!" Lazlian roared, tearing at his hair. He was scary when he was like this, but I refused to be cowed because it pissed me off when he spoke of Kirwyn that way.

"Is that what bothers you? That he's not royal?"

Eyes blazing and fists clenched, Lazlian shouted, "It bothers me that he fucked you in Elowa when he had no right! It bothers me that he continues to put his cock in you!"

For a moment I was stunned silent at his blunt declaration and strong choice of words.

It's as it's always been, I told myself. *He's angry that his brother was robbed of his supposed claim to my virginity.* We were right back to where we started and it made my head nearly explode. No man could touch the chosen braenese because the Rythasian elite couldn't handle it.

I was sure my face turned red, if not purple. The rage made my hands shake. I pushed Lazlian's shoulders.

"Whose right was it?" I spat. Lazlian smacked my hands away and I pushed him harder. "Not fucking *mine?*" I pushed again at Lazlian's shoulders, furious, shoving him back with my onslaught while he smacked my hands away once more. "Not fucking mine to decide?"

"It was my fucking right!" Lazlian howled, grabbing my wrists to keep me from shoving him again. He needn't bother – his fervent words already stilled me. They'd stilled and silenced everything in me and around us.

Was he saying there was more to it than the hate sex that almost happened in the console room? That being king and being... with me... was stolen from him? But then why had he tried to kill me?

Lazlian's fingers dug into my wrists and his impassioned eyes searched my face as he declared, "You are the first-born daughter of a *queen*. I am the first-born son of a *king*. You belong to *me,* you are my birthright. Fuck my father, fuck the hermit. It was supposed to be *us,* it was always supposed to be us."

I had every intention of screaming at his infuriating speech.

I burst out sobbing.

Breaking free of Lazlian's grip to wipe my tears, I stepped back, tight against the balcony again. *Why was I crying?* I was so angry I didn't even know who or what I was angry at anymore.

"Everything's been stolen from me," Lazlian repeated with resentment.

Of course this was about him. His entitlement.

"You want me to feel sorry for you?" I scoffed, redirecting my ache into anger. "Because you're only *second* in line? The *second* most powerful man in the kingdom? You can have anything you want, any girl you want, all the riches you want!"

I threw my head back as if I cried to the sky, "Your fate is so bad?" I brought my gaze back to his and snarled, "If you had your way, I'd have been imprisoned here to be *raped.*"

Why had I never said the word? Why did no one? We skirted around uncomfortable truths as if it made them less unpleasant, given no voice. But the arranged marriage I was being forced into would have been a lifetime of endless rape. Dressing it up with pretty gowns and building a family upon it didn't change that. Juls might have given me time, but it wasn't indefinite.

"To be raped forever," I whispered, licking a tear that touched my lips. "For the rest of my life."

Lazlian stepped close to my body, raising gullflesh on my neck and shoulders. I caught his flinty scent.

"Not with me," he said, voice low, hard. "It wouldn't have been rape with me."

I closed my eyes and shook my head, unable to process his statement. That Lazlian—a cruel man, a man who was probably capable of many assaults under the right conditions—that, with him, furious sex *wouldn't* be rape... Yet with his brother—gentle, kind—that with Juls encounters would always be rape... they just didn't look obvious on the surface. The bizarre suggestion was backwards and too complex to wrap my head around.

Maybe it meant admitting things I didn't want to confess.

"I'd make you want it," Lazlian swore, hotly.

I snapped my head up, glowering. "By manipulation! Coercion! Trickery!"

"By removing obstacles you throw up between us."

"Me?" I beat my breast with my fist. "You tried to kill me. Twice! I'd call that an obstacle. Those I've thrown up in return have been for good reason. Those barriers are an extension of me. To touch them without my permission is to touch me without permission."

"Permission?" Lazlian scoffed. The scorn in his voice made me brace for a strike. "Since when does a king need permission to take a queen? Since when does a man need permission to touch his wife?"

I couldn't answer because in a fit of rage or desire, he grabbed my hips and lifted me clear off the ground. I scrambled to hold onto Lazlian as he perched me perilously on the balcony's ledge, similar to how he'd positioned me when we were fighting mere hours before. However, despite now having a slip, I wore no undergarments. The chemise was short enough that when Lazlian stood between my knees, nothing impeded his gaze of my exposed sex. I couldn't worry too much about it for a moment because my heart leapt into my throat feeling empty air behind me. I'd drop to my death on the rocks if Laz pushed me or let go.

But if Lazlian's mind trailed his line of vision... it wasn't on murdering me or the sea below or anything above my waist. My gaze locked on his face and his gaze locked... lower. His fiery eyes stared at the apex between my thighs, heating it. Heating me all over my skin. Flushing my cheeks and warming me low in my belly. Lazlian wasn't doing anything other than *looking* yet I couldn't help my squirming hips, making his Adam's apple bob as he swallowed. Lazlian drew a quick breath in and out, and the air from his mouth caressed my bare sex, making my eyelids flutter. Mesmerized, seemingly without consciousness, Lazlian licked his lips as if...

...he wanted to lick the places his eyes stroked.

Overtly, I was at his mercy. One push and I'd fall to my death. Maybe no effort would even be required on his part, maybe the only thing holding me aloft was my grip around his neck and if I let go to fight him off, I'd plummet.

It looked that way, on the surface. *But he'd stopped before when I asked him to.*

It was a pebble of thought, buried deep under the sands of my mind, below the thundering waves of desire. I could scarcely see or hear it... didn't want to.

As he gazed at me, possessed, I started to shake. Lazlian had stood too close to me for too long. I had scented him, felt his warmth, and it caused a betraying wetness where he stared.

A small, shaky whimper from my lips startled him. Lazlian blinked and looked up at my face, studying it. Whatever he found there made him scowl. With control, he lowered me back to the safety of the floor. He didn't step away or release me. My fingers still clutched his hard shoulders. His hand, once gripping my hip, slid lower. Slow enough so that I had time to stop him. My heart pounded wildly and I felt his palm turn and his fingers dip between my thighs. I gasped as he cupped me there.

Lazlian is holding me between my legs, my mind screamed the impossible thought. Blood rushed to my mound, swelling it against his warm palm.

"This was supposed to be mine," he said, the ferocity in his eyes seeming to back up the claim.

I could hardly speak, could hardly breathe as he moved his hand slowly upward, baffling me. Low on my abdomen, Lazlian turned his hand sideways. Long fingers pressed gently-but-firmly into my belly as he declared, "This was supposed to be mine."

I drew in a sharp breath at the confounding onslaught of emotions.

He was talking about my *womb.*

I felt angry and swoony at the same time – then even more enraged for the dizziness. *Who said such things?* Stunned, I stared at Laz for him to say or do something to tell me he wasn't serious. He doubled down, holding that intense look and raising an eyebrow as if daring me to challenge him.

Realizing I gaped, I snapped my mouth shut, but that only made me look as if I accepted his assertion. I reopened my mouth to refute it... but then, wouldn't it be lending credence to his claim to even acknowledge it? Rendered speechless and now opening and closing my mouth like a fish, I felt more flustered than ever.

I was furious at his entitlement.

I was frustrated by some of the things it made me feel.

I was annoyed that he could probably read all of that on my face.

As we gazed at one another, unbidden images came. I pictured it... god help me, I pictured it without wanting to -

As we were earlier against the console, Lazlian between my legs, thrusting into me. One hand pulling my hair, the other, bending one of my knees up and out of the way to push so deep I'd groan... then pistoning hard and fast until neither of us could hold back. Another scene flashed in my mind – Lazlian sitting half-upright on the bed, torso resting against the headboard with his long legs stretched beneath me... as I straddled him, as I rode him... arching and rocking against his lower abdomen until I climaxed in his lap. Then, spent, collapsing on his chest. Feeling his arms tighten around me as our heartrates slowed.

Is this what he pictured when he saw me?

Flushed, my breath fell heavy against his neck.

But... that's not all I saw. The flash of a lifetime with Lazlian flickered through my mind. Mistrust and lies for breakfast. Shouts and betrayal for supper. Violence and rage before bed. I would lose myself, a spark in my spirit, just like I would have in a marriage to his brother. Only, with Lazlian it would be harder to recognize because I'd be distracted, *dazzled,* by the fire in other places.

"I'm not for you," I said, thankful a sea breeze cooled my heated cheeks. "I'm certainly no virgin."

"I. Don't. Care."

Laughing with scorn, I hurled back, "Yes, you do. You hate it."

"Well, it's too late to change!" With a half-smirk he added enigmatically, "Besides, I *know* there are places your boy hasn't yet touched."

Unsure what that meant, I whispered, "Find another.

There are hundreds like me. I never knew, didn't realize before... the sick way our bodies and faces look similar compared to the rest of the world. Dozens of Elowan girls could replace me if you want the same hair or eye color. Another will satisfy you."

Lazlian released my waist and threw back his head as he laughed. "You think I haven't tried? You think there aren't girls in the noble families or the villages or the brothels who have Elowan ancestors from those who came before you?"

I blinked. Of course there were, from generations past or even those who'd come here on their own long ago.

"It takes nothing but a look in their direction to bring them to my room," he boasted. "I'd wrap my hands around their bare necks just like I wanted to do to you. But you want to know a secret, little queen?" Lazlian laughed so mirthlessly it was chilling. "No matter how hard I squeezed I couldn't rise to the occasion. And when the last one nearly passed out, Juls intervened in my... hobby."

Was Lazlian saying he'd almost choked a girl to death? I thought, horrified. *Was he also saying he hadn't... couldn't...*

For a moment, I'd nearly been lulled into something like pity. Then he attacked.

"How's that for irony? All while you've been whoring up the coast. I bet you were like animals out there, weren't you?" Lazlian snarled the last words, pressing close again. The air between us crackled with the energy of pent-up rage.

"Maybe we were!" I cried, defiant. I knew better than to taunt the keylord, especially with the death-drop below me, but he got under my skin in a way that burned. "It's none of your business," I added.

Lightning-fast, his hand gripped my chin, tilting my

head back to look at him. His other hand clutched my hips. I bucked to dislodge him, but he squeezed tighter in both places. "Is that so?"

"You're hurting me," I whimpered, resisting the urge to try to peel back his cruel grip because I knew he'd only press harder.

"Good. You're revolting and so is your behavior." The fire in Lazlian's eyes rose higher. His lips were so close to mine his breath caressed my face as he snarled, "Did he fuck you like a dog in the dirt?"

I refused to acknowledge any shame. Panting made my breasts press against Laz's chest and I didn't like how the contact stiffened my nipples. Trying to push him away would only do more harm, so I kept my arms at my sides. Lazlian's eyes kept dropping to my mouth.

"He did." I straightened my spine and fisted my hands. "I liked it."

Lazlian's laugh was more growl. "My brother should have collared you."

I opened my mouth but before I could speak, he wedged his knee between my legs and pressed his thigh up against my core, hard, making me gasp.

"Lazlian-"

He pushed harder between my splayed legs, unbalancing me, forcing me to clutch his shoulders.

"He should have chained you to the bed. If you acted out, he should have bred you before your wedding whether you liked it or not."

"You mean that's what *you* would do!" I cried, utterly enraged.

"That's exactly what I'd do." His lips nearly brushed mine. His eyes burned with lust. "What you need."

I was so angry I thought I might start screaming and

never stop. Frustrated tears pricked my eyes. Trying to wound, I snapped, "Lucky for me your brother is nothing like you."

The sinister grin pulling one side of Lazlian's mouth pulled the hair on my neck to standing along with it. I braced.

"Lucky he's not, indeed," Lazlian bit out, backing up slightly. Gradually, he lowered his leg. "I encouraged Juls to pick up the slack while you were away and he had no trouble doing so."

"What's that supposed to mean?"

"If you weren't being faithful to your husband, why should he be faithful to you?" Laz shrugged, stepping back.

"He wasn't really my husband! You forced me!"

Yet for some reason I didn't understand and despite having no right, the idea of Juls being with others stung. Was he doing it while simultaneously pleading for me to return? Or was it only after he'd lost hope? Were his sentiments in the letter real?

"Did we?" Laz mocked. "Did we hold a gun to your head or drag you to the altar?"

"Fuck you, Lazlian! You know I didn't have a choice."

Eyes bright with anger, he yelled, "Yet you still seem to make all the wrong ones!"

Who were we talking about? Lazlian or Juls? Because his face said, *me. Why aren't you choosing me?*

"That's what you really desire, isn't it?" I shouted, matching his anger. "For me not to be able to refuse."

Dispelling my confusion on who we discussed, Lazlian grabbed me and half-carried me across the balcony toward my bedroom.

"Stop!" I cried. "Put me down!" Cold fear clutched my heart. Part of it was because being in Lazlian's arms... didn't feel unenjoyable... and part of it was because the line between the balcony and the interior of my chambers felt like a line I couldn't cross. If I set foot within the bedroom itself...

One of my punches got the message through and Lazlian deposited me back on my feet, but he didn't allow me to retreat. He seized my chin again and frantic eyes searched my face.

"Deep down, you want it too. You want it to be my fault so you can have what you want and remain blameless." Even after he'd finished speaking, Lazlian's eyes continued seeking, his stare searing my skin.

"Wow," I scoffed with disgust. "You sound like every other guy out there convincing himself that consent is unclear."

"Wow," Lazlian mimicked, eyes still searching my face. "You sound like someone who didn't outright deny it."

Thump-thump.

A heartbeat of a moment passed between us. His dark, watchful eyes didn't miss a movement of mine. His hands tensed upon my chin and hip.

He seeks a yielding of some kind, I realized. The smallest sigh from my lips or fluttering of my lashes, giving him a wordless *yes.* If I relaxed even the tiniest bit into his grasp, his hands were poised to pull me to him and devour my mouth with his own. To carry me to that bed with silken sheets and ravish me.

It's what he burned for. My surrender to him. All I needed to do was expel the softest whimper and he'd take it from there. And I knew that once I acquiesced in the slightest, there'd be no turning back, no matter how much I protested.

No... crazy... madness...

As if he knew I was about to refuse, Lazlian slid his hand beneath my slip.

"Don't—touch me there," I said, grabbing his forearm.

Touch me there.

"Put your hand down or I will," he threatened, the fire in his eyes backing up the claim.

I let go.

"Lazlian, don't, not there."

He skimmed my inner thigh, close to my aching core, making me shudder. His hungry eyes flashed, utterly possessed. "I don't need to. You're soaked. It's dripping down your leg."

Waves of desire and stunning humiliation washed over me; emotions I didn't even know how to deal with. I could feel it now, the wetness his hand spread as he caressed me. If he moved an inch to the left, I was lost. I wouldn't be able to stop myself from riding his long fingers.

"No..."

Riding *him.*

"You don't need to say a word," he whispered, nuzzling close to my ear.

"I..."

Letting him ride *me.*

"Just listen to my voice. Relax into me."

Begging him to ride me.

"Don't..." My body shook with violent desire in Lazlian's hands.

"Let go and let me lead you."

Oh god... no, no, no.

With a gasp, I tore my chin from his grasp and looked away, breaking the spell. Neither of us moved, listening to our hard breathing and the sea below. What were we doing? God, the bed was *right there.* He could easily carry me to it. Muffle my protests with his hand. Why did he hold back?

Perhaps Lazlian's ego was the only thing protecting me, preventing him from forcing me. His wanting me to want him. Or perhaps his maneuvers were more cunning than that. Perhaps he played a long game, calculating that if he crossed a line with me, I'd hate him forever and he'd lose.

When I felt calm enough, I retreated to the safety of the balcony's rail and said, "Lazlian... no. I don't want to be with anyone but Kirwyn."

I tried not to wince as I watched him visibly deflate. Eyes narrowed, he asked, "Are you lying? I can't tell."

"I learned from the best," I quipped.

Lazlian inhaled, nostrils flaring and the fire re-lighting in his eyes as he readied to charge again.

"I'm sorry but I'm not," I said quickly, holding up my hands. "I love Kirwyn."

"Everything's been taken from me," he growled.

"You want to take everything from me too!" I retorted.

"I want to give you everything."

"Everything on *your* terms. Everything except my free will. Tell me, Lazlian, if you could go back and change the past, somehow have me not meet Kirwyn that day—knowing how much I love him—would you?"

Lazlian didn't reply but his eyes flashed, proving me right. He would take away my happiness to suit himself. He'd willingly prune my past if he could, shape the course of my existence to alter my decisions so that the tree of my life grew in his direction.

It was madness.

"I lied when I told you what the hermit said to my father," Lazlian said suddenly. "About your marriage."

CHAPTER 47

Once again, I remembered that night. It was just over a year ago, though it felt like many years had passed. Lazlian and I had been drinking wine together on the veranda after the Battle of the Bloody Shoals.

"You lied then," I challenged, disbelieving, "but you're telling the truth now?"

"Yes. I know you have no reason to believe me, but I have no reason to lie."

At the time, I had thought it was the one honest conversation I'd had with Lazlian. But he'd been lying for half of it. At least about torturing prisoners. I searched his face, inches from my own. *So why wouldn't he have lied about something else?*

"You're a sociopath. You don't need a reason."

Laz shot me a look of impatience.

"I know what you did to Singen! You lied to me about torturing prisoners," I cried. *You're a monster,* I thought. "I can't look at you without hearing people screaming."

Lazlian flinched, surprised I'd learned the truth. For a

438

moment, he looked away, in what I would have called shame were he any other man. Then his face hardened. "If you think I wouldn't do that to anyone who threatened my brother's well-being, then you don't understand the first thing about me."

He wasn't even sorry. For doing it or for lying to me. *Should I be surprised?*

"Yet you want me to believe you now?" I whispered.

Lazlian didn't answer. "Do you remember when you asked me if my father sought out the hermit? If he asked the old man if you should be married to his son, the young king? I told you the hermit said it was yet to be written in the stars."

I held Lazlian's gaze, waiting.

"I skipped over... a fair bit."

I crossed my arms and jut my chin, unsure if I wanted to humor Lazlian by letting him continue. Everything he said or did was smoke and mirrors. Nothing real. Nothing to believe in.

"My father did ask about you. And the hermit emphatically agreed he should marry you to Juls, not one of the nobles. He said with any other noble family it was unlikely to result in fruition. Whatever that means."

I shrugged, knowing it was probably vagueness to cloak the fraudulence, like the supposedly mystical predictions he'd given me.

"But that wasn't enough for Juls, understandably. When he was older, he sought out the hermit on his own and asked if he'd love you and if you'd make a good queen."

I stiffened, paying attention. *Juls had said the same in his letter.*

"And the hermit told him that you'd be very alluring and the odds were good for both."

Lazlian's story aligned with Juls's version. Was he telling the truth? I studied his face, frowning.

"But that wasn't enough for me," Lazlian insisted. "Shortly thereafter, I trekked all the way out to the hermit's filthy cliff hole. The man was so deep in one of his episodes, I didn't know why I bothered. And I asked him if *you'd* love *my brother.*"

Despite trying not to believe, my heart thumped harder. As if any of this mattered. As if the hermit really possessed mystical powers.

"And *that's* when the old seer invoked the firmament. His words were, 'whether she'll love him or the other one is yet to be written in the stars.'"

Neither of us spoke. After a few seconds, I remembered to breathe.

The other one... as in Kirwyn? Or the other one as in... the other... brother? I knew, as my mind worked out the question, Lazlian had long ago formed the same one.

He seemed to realize I came to that conclusion. His eyes glistened and his mouth quirked.

"Too late, I wished I'd asked him other questions. I felt nothing but contempt that day in his dirty hovel. I clung to my scorn and never returned. And now he's dead."

"You don't believe in any of this nonsense," I countered. What was everyone's obsession with this hermit? He'd told me nothing but rubbish.

Lazlian's mouth quirked again, this time in a humorless smirk. "It was enough to plant the seed of doubt." He gazed at the sea, behind me. Briefly, his eyes fluttered shut. "Every time you looked at me as we dined. Every time you brushed past me in the king's hall. Every time you laughed in my direction or when your body—just for a moment—relaxed against mine as we danced... I wondered..." he shrugged and trailed off.

My heart thumped. *You wondered if, underneath it all, I was falling in love with you.*

Did Lazlian ever *hope?* Did he hate himself for hoping? Oh god... when I'd snuck into his room that night...

"I love my brother," Lazlian declared in a low, heated voice. "And you make me resent him. And I hate you for it." Grinding his teeth, he continued, "You love your mainland boy. And I hate you for it. Sometimes I think I've never hated anyone or anything more."

He'd hurled the words with venom and I was hurt by his bitter disgust. "Then where does that leave us?" I asked, scowling. "Angry sex, Lazlian, like the control room? Is that what you want? You can't build a life on that."

Before he could speak, I continued, "And I don't understand what alternative could satisfy you. Even if I hadn't met Kirwyn, I'd still have come here and married Juls. So don't hate Kirwyn and I meeting. Don't lament your inability to control me," I snapped, "as not getting something you want. Because it was always going to be someone else. No matter what had happened, you'd be fucked."

"You weren't in love," Lazlian scoffed. "Not before. It was infatuation, it would have passed." He waved his hand with angry dismissal.

"Do you have *any* idea what we've gone through to be together?" I shouted. "We've risked our *lives.*"

Ignoring me, he continued, "I've gone back to the night you disappeared a thousand times in my mind. I should have locked you in your room after your dagger stunt that night. Every night," he insisted, with another angry slash of his hand. "If you're in love with him, it's only because of the time you spent together after you fled. If you hadn't run off like bandits in the backlands, you'd have outgrown it."

I hated to admit there was some truth to Lazlian's words. I may have been infatuated with Kirwyn when he washed ashore in Elowa, but I truly grew to love him—to admire and respect him—on our journey together. I had the perspective to see that now.

"*Everything* would be different if I'd locked you in your room and never let you leave High Spire. Say it!" he shouted, making me jump.

"Fine!" I yelled back. "Maybe it would. What do you want me to say Lazlian? *If* I hadn't met Kirwyn, *if* I wasn't promised to your brother, *if* you'd been something other than a homicidal fucking asshole, then we would have had a chance?" I dug my nails into my palms and cried, "There's too many *ifs* between us!"

Lazlian's hand reached up, nearly touching me, but he fisted it and brought it back to his side. "There's only one *if* that matters," he said softly. "If you're in love with me."

I closed my eyes against the question. Gritted my teeth. Swallowed the lump in my throat.

"You're toxic," I whimpered. "You know it. Don't deny it." *You tried to kill me, for crying out loud.*

Lazlian gave me a pleading look. "You make me a better person."

"You make me worse!"

There was the crux of it. It wasn't my job to save Lazlian. He dragged me down. I couldn't lift him up if I wanted to, only he could do that.

I listened to the sea, churning below. Lazlian sighed through his nose. I sighed right back.

"I could have taken your sister, you know. You should

be thanking me. I spared her out of consideration for your feelings."

I scoffed so hard I nearly choked. "You spared her because Juls forbade you touch her! You're such a fucking liar!"

"Fine!" Lazlian sneered, not even ashamed. "I would have used her to keep you in line. It's not like I would have hurt her. Is that so bad?"

"Yes!" I cried. "I don't want a life of lies and drama. I want to be happy, Lazlian."

And guys like you don't make girls happy. Outside the bedroom, came the unbidden thought. It was quickly followed by intimate images I shook away.

"Healthy relationships don't involve attempted murder," I declared, to remind myself as much as the keylord.

"You think your marriage to Juls was so healthy?" Lazlian bit out jealously. "Think he didn't know what my father was capable of doing to you, what he did to you?"

I licked my lips, nervous. "Juls protected me more times than I can count. By marrying me in the first place, by keeping his father at bay when I got myself kidnapped, by knowingly sipping drugged wine when I visited his chambers so that we wouldn't have to sleep together!"

"To a point. He'd protect you to a *point.* You think Juls didn't know you were locked in your room for days before Oxholde attacked? Think he didn't know my father struck you? That he wasn't fully aware of what my father would do to you if he found out you defied him by not sleeping with his son?"

I twisted my hands together. Juls stood up to his brother—to anyone else—but when it came to his father, he was curiously silent on certain matters. He seemed to prefer not to discuss or acknowledge them, to pretend they didn't exist.

But I remembered a time when we were united.

"I know what really happened when Milicena died," I countered. "You were trying to manipulate me, but your plan relied on your brother's good intentions. He spoke to his father on my behalf and convinced him not to send her to The Isle of Walking Corpses."

Lazlian searched my face. "Is that what you think happened?"

"You goaded me to send the plea while Juls conversed with Grahar so that, united, he and I would persuade the king."

Lazlian laughed, stepping into my personal space once more. "I goaded you to send the plea while my brother was with our father so that the king could one-up him by granting your wish. Juls made no such plea."

I frowned. *What did that mean?*

"Are you really so naïve to think my father didn't want to fuck you?" Lazlian asked. "He wanted you for his son and he resented Juls all the same. The late king didn't grant your request out of benevolence, he did it out of bitterness. To stick it to Juls, to show him that even though you were to be his wife, he had ultimate power over everyone, including you."

I couldn't wrap my head around it and protested weakly, "Juls was just trying to make everyone happy."

"Exactly. Juls let you walk all over him at the risk of your own safety. If he truly cared about protecting you, he would have seduced you that night in his chambers," Lazlian insisted. "Spared you from my father's rage – a certainty once he soon learned the truth."

Snarling at Lazlian, I gritted out, "Like you would have

done? Convinced yourself that seducing me was saving me!"

Lazlian's bitter laugh made me want to claw him. He stepped closer again, intimidating me with his size, his height.

"I don't need to convince myself of anything. If you'd been my bride *to ruin, to punish, to breed,*" he relished those words with sadistic pleasure, "I'd have made you toe the line from the beginning. I wouldn't allow you to even think of disobeying me. I'd have done what was necessary to protect you."

Lazlian's words made me so angry that I had trouble seeing, breathing. "You mean you'd make me fear you instead of your father!"

"You're already afraid of me," Lazlian declared, low and matter of fact, making my heart beat faster. He paused before narrowing his scorched-earth eyes and murmuring, "And you're scared that you want me anyway." He added in a husky voice, "I can smell it on you."

A jolt ran through my body and I tore my head to the side. Where had all the air suddenly gone? *He meant it as an animal scents fear, right? Not as if...*

I gulped and squeezed my legs tight, too humiliated to continue the line of thinking.

After a steadying breath, I whispered, "I love Kirwyn." Meeting Lazlian's eyes I repeated, "I love him."

Guilt surged through me at the anguish flitting across Lazlian's face at the same time I was angry at myself for feeling that way.

"Please understand. He's like the earth -- solid and sure," I pled the words, trying to explain to Lazlian and hoping he didn't think me too fanciful, hoping he'd understand me as Kirwyn did. "And I am like the water. Rushing, churning, constantly in motion. We meet on the beach, in a place of magic."

I licked my lips and took a shaky breath before concluding, "But you, Lazlian, you are like fire to my water. We cannot mix without one destroying the other."

Lazlian groaned. He looked to the sky with impatience and sighed, "You should have been brought here sooner. Educated."

"Trained," I countered, scowling with revulsion.

"Protected."

"Groomed!" I shoved his chest, but of course he didn't budge and it only made me angrier. "Are you kidding me, Laz? What is it you want to have happened? Me to be here, locked in this room, pure and chaste and waiting? *You* don't know the first thing about *me*. I'd have only rebelled harder and faster. I'd have fucked dozens of men just to spite you!"

Lazlian's hands seized my hips in a brutal grasp, yanking me to him as his face twisted in fury at my defiance. "Then I'd have strapped you between your legs until you couldn't think of letting anyone touch you. I'd have locked you in a fucking chastity belt and kept the fucking key around my neck! Think I wouldn't?"

I shook with terrible rage, sure my head was going to explode. *No, I don't doubt it. I can feel the idea excites you by the firmness pressed against my stomach.* I dug my fingernails into my temples and screamed, "God, I hate you! You're everything I hate!"

Lazlian's eyes flashed and his mouth broke into something between a sneer and a smirk.

"Then hate me."

Strong hands grabbed my wrists, spun me around, and bent me over the balcony's rail. But it wasn't a jerky or erratic motion. I couldn't deny we moved together with a strange, furious fluidity that reminded me of when Lazlian and I danced in mutual hate at the Fae Fête. Like my body met his movements, knew the steps.

Air greeted my skin as he yanked my slip to my waist.

He's going to... Cold terror froze the scream in my wide, silent mouth as I anticipated something unspeakable.

Instead, to my shock, I heard a resounding *smack* as he struck my backside. A moment later, the pain hit my brain and Lazlian quickly laid another smack on my unprotected rear. My mind frenzied, unsure whether to exhale in relief or to scream in rage. My face heated with sudden, burning shame.

"You never fucking do as you're told," Lazlian seethed, punctuating the accusation with a smack. *I* was the one bent over, yet he had the audacity to sound angry, as if I'd somehow attacked *him* by defying him. "But I could break you."

An onslaught of emotions so confusing warred in my brain that I didn't know what to say or do. Lazlian used the time to lay more hard, open-palmed smacks on my bottom.

"You have no idea how long I've wanted to do this."

He struck me again and again. Rage boiled in my breast, rising to my mouth, ready to pour out in a command for him to stop... but his next hit caught me lower, near my thigh, and it stung more than the rest.

As my head flung back and the cry left my mouth, I was angry at myself, feeling like I gave Lazlian something he wanted. I folded my lips between my teeth and refused to let him affect me at all. At least, I refused to give him the satisfaction of knowing he was affecting me. Because I still felt things as he spanked me. Anger grew, but other strange emotions roiled like a sea storm inside me. Humiliation at being punished like a child. Fear that others outside the castle might hear. And something warm and unwelcome in parts of my body *not* my backside.

I clung to my refusal to cry out, but a strange desire to *cry* built nonetheless. Lazlian didn't hold back and the more he channeled pent-up emotions through each smack, the more it created in me a connected need for release I refused to entertain. Gripping the edge of the stone balustrade, I felt as if everything inside me churned like the waves on the rocks far below.

I didn't know how many hard smacks I endured before Lazlian stopped, leaving me breathless and burning in heavy silence. A delirious part of me wanted to stay bent, stay hidden, because I didn't want him to see the tears welling in my eyes... or anything else on my face.

I gasped when Lazlian palmed my ass, stroking it. I didn't say anything to stop him, but I had the curious feeling like I couldn't; like my tongue lost functionally. My limbs didn't seem willing to heed my commands either. His hand felt *good*, soothing, and I might have moaned.

Lazlian gripped my shoulders, stood me upright, and spun me around. I felt very strange, almost woozy. Like I was a thin glass tower swaying in a terrible storm, ready to topple and shatter. The only thing holding me steady was Lazlian's grip in my hair and his body pressed against mine. His sinister lips were inches from my own. What he'd just done seemed to possess him as much as it had me; I saw it reflected in his gaze. But everything was the opposite. While my eyes were hooded and unfocused, his were wide and wild. While I felt limp and dizzy, he looked tense and alert.

He's made us into two fitted opposites, I realized. Having delivered me into a state of pliability, he'd catapulted into one poised to conquer. I was supple, yielding to molding, and he was brutally hard, ready to shape with ruthless determination.

Lazlian had grown rock-solid against my stomach now.

How dare he touch me, how dare he look as if he is going to devour my mouth after what he just did?

How dare that hardness feel so good?

In my lightheaded state, I struggled to form words. I met his dark stare and swore through gritted teeth, "I hate you even more now," and I both never meant it more and never meant it less.

"Let's check."

Lazlian pushed two fingers into my core.

Oh my fucking god. My tower collapsed and I broke, wailing in rapture.

"Lazlian!" I cried, throwing my head back and arching before clamping my lips shut.

"I knew you'd respond," he gloated, using his knee to nudge my leg into a half-bent position against the balcony. His chest puffed with pride and elation, his eyes gleamed. "My soaked little slut. Open your mouth. Now."

Dizzy thoughts spun in my head and it was as if I spun in place trying to catch them. I didn't move in either direction.

"*Open-*" Lazlian demanded, punctuating the word with a firm thrust of his fingers.

"*Your-*" Another thrust.

"*Fucking-*" Again.

"*Mouth.*" On the last thrust he swiped his thumb over my clit and I couldn't say whether I did as he commanded or if it was the unstoppable gasp, but Lazlian quickly plunged his tongue past my lips when they parted.

As he kissed me, maddeningly, Lazlian's tongue did everything his fingers did not. He took my mouth with burning need but buried deep inside me, his fingers stilled, making my body embarrassingly jerk and wiggle, seeking stimulation I could not find. It was as if he forced me to try to pleasure myself on his hand and in my dizzy, dreamy state my body worked without my mind.

Lazlian broke the kiss and I hated how grateful I felt when he resumed the movement of his long fingers. I was so relieved I whimpered.

"See, I can make you obey," he said against my ear, "I can make you want to."

His words should have upset me more than they did; they almost seemed far away. Delirious moans of pleasure sounded in my head.

"How would you like to be chained to my bed each night? Naked and waiting for me to do whatever I want? Moan for me, my wanton little whore."

"Lazlian, Lazlian, Lazlian."

I heard myself and didn't know how long I'd been babbling. A war raged within me, but I hadn't the capacities to fight it. His words were too much, but I was too out of my mind to protest. I despised what he said, yet, mad with desire, I rocked harder on his long fingers.

"Legs spread... for me..." Lazlian's lust-addled voice breathed hot against my ear. He ground his hard cock into my stomach. "Breed you... *Mine.*"

The hand not compelling me toward a climax suddenly seized my throat.

The lightheadedness that began after he spanked me increased with the loss of air as he squeezed. I began to shake and the only thing holding me up was Lazlian. His tight hand on my throat, his fingers deep inside my core, and his knee wedging my leg against the balcony.

I didn't seek my climax, it was forced upon me.

"That's it, little queen." His voice was pure exaltation as he masterfully rubbed my swollen clit. "Come at my command. Now."

Stars burst behind my eyes as a powerful orgasm shot through my whole body. I fell apart with bucking and whimpering. Shame-filled cries. Anyone could have heard them.

Most of all, I hated that he did.

I felt as if I'd momentarily blacked out and, after a few moments, I sensed Lazlian's lips brushing my neck and grazing my ear. He ordered, "Into the bedroom. Now."

I had slumped, boneless, in his arms. Lazlian entirely supported my weight, but the demand was a wake-up call to my system.

"N- no," I panted, struggling to re-possess my foggy brain and to find my feet.

"Then I'll take you here," he growled, thrusting his hips to press his large erection against my exposed and slippery core.

"No!" I cried, panic rising despite how good it felt. Despite involuntarily rolling up to meet that hardness with my bare sex. "I- I don't know what happened, but I wasn't in my own head..." I couldn't find the words to explain it when I didn't understand it myself. The spanking put me in a drunk-like state, but I was quickly sobering up. It put Lazlian in an altered state of mind too, and I understood his even less, but I knew I needed to jolt him out of it.

"We shouldn't have done this. I love Kirwyn. I don't love you, Lazlian. I... I hate you," I whispered. Though to my ears the declaration didn't sound resolute, the change in Lazlian was fierce. In one second, even the air around us changed, hummed with fury.

He squeezed my arms enough to hurt and panted with more venom than ever before, "I fucking hate you too!"

His rage scared me and I didn't doubt *he* meant it.

I broke, sobbing. It was loud and sudden, with no care to embarrassing myself. Wailing and punching Lazlian's chest with my fists, I screamed, "I figured that out when you tried to kill me! When you watched me nearly die!"

With a roar, Lazlian released me. He spun away and stalked off two steps; to escape the assault of my fists, I assumed. With his back to me, he rested his hands on his slim hips, head bent. I could see his heavy breathing from the rise and fall of his shoulders.

Angrily, I wiped my tears with the back of my hand, half-smacking myself in my urgency to remove their evidence. My addled brain couldn't sort through the tidal wave that had swept over me and the stunningly conflicting emotions left in its wake. For a few moments, I tried to catch my own breath, to cool my blood to a temperature less than boiling. The ocean breeze tickled my skin, soothing most of my fevered flesh, but the heat on my bottom and between my legs remained.

Whatever strange, dreamlike state I had occupied moments before wasn't entirely unfamiliar. Kirwyn had led me to its borderlands, but he'd been gradual, gentle. Lazlian had plunged me to its depths in rapid free fall.

Suddenly, the keylord spun back and charged me so quickly, I panicked that he meant to spank me again or to push me into the sea.

CHAPTER 48

Bewilderingly, Lazlian grasped the neck of his shirt and tore it clean from his body, angrily tossing the tunic to the floor. I gaped at his trim, bare chest, suddenly remembering when I'd presented him mine the night I escaped. I wondered if he meant to do something similar – to shove a dagger in my hand and offer a strike to his heart...

...a heart that still bore the scar I'd seen him carry after the Battle of the Glass Gardens. A diagonal line running up the left side of his chest and to the area beneath his neck.

Seeming to confirm my suspicions, Lazlian grabbed my hand. I tried yanking it back, but he was stronger. Instead of placing a dagger in my grasp, he flattened my palm to his bare skin, left of his key necklace. Right above his heart.

I had the wild urge to dig my nails into his flesh there. To reach through his ribcage and grab his heart. To squeeze it, or toss it into the sea, or to eat it and absorb it into my own body.

I swallowed, thickly.

"I did want you to die in battle," Lazlian said, and *god* -- even though I knew, it crushed me to hear it. I clenched my jaw against the onset of sniveling I'd only just ceased.

"I love my brother," he declared again in a low, heated voice. "And I've always known you were going to destroy us, one way or the other. So I let you run into the crossfire alone, thinking it would be easier for everyone if a bullet took you out."

My lip quivered, but I refused to cry because Lazlian wanted me dead. It wasn't anything I didn't know. And why should I care? I didn't. I didn't.

"You made it to Jesi. Just as you were about to rise, more fire erupted overhead and you slammed back into the ground." Lazlian's eyes briefly fluttered shut, lost in the memory. I remembered, too -- pressing myself into the dirt and thinking I was going to die.

"A soldier spotted you, raised his sword, and charged. You were on your stomach, easy prey." Lazlian's face twisted in anguish. "In that moment, seeing your life about to end... something inside me screamed."

Transfixed, I held Lazlian's strange, hazel eyes. I sucked in a breath and held that too.

"I jumped between you and the soldier and tried to hold him back. We fought. I have some skill, we were moderately trained, but... I'm not a warrior. He slashed me, here - " Lazlian said, pressing his hand harder over mine, pushing it firmly against his heart. "Our swords clashed again and again. I've gone over it a thousand times in my mind. I should have lost. He was better. But somehow, I killed him. A clean strike right through his neck." Lazlian blinked and shook his head. "I don't believe in any gods, but I can't explain how I succeeded."

"You're lying." My voice quaked.

Lazlian's hand tightened on mine. A slight breeze rumpled his hair. He looked at me too deeply. "I'm not. Can't you feel it?"

I felt his warm skin. His strong heartbeat.

His ache.

Tears slipped down my cheeks.

"As you rose, I ran back to the shadows," Lazlian said. "For a moment, I wished you'd seen what I'd done. But you brushed past, refusing to look at me as I bled. I bled for you. As you'd never bled for me! And I wanted to kill you all over again for making me risk my own life."

As he finished, it felt as if I bore the slice of that sword straight down the center of *my* heart, because I knew that when Lazlian said it would be easier for everyone if a bullet took me out... deep down, he meant *himself* more than anyone else.

For a moment, at least, he'd rather let me die than not have me...

As much as it had hurt to believe Lazlian despised me enough to want to kill me, a different sort of agony ripped through me to know it *wasn't* sheer hate, but that he valued his desire over my *life,* for a time long enough that a bullet could have chanced to take me down.

I was only alive because of dumb luck. Twice. He wanted me dead before even meeting me.

Yet he did change his mind and risk his life... and that knowledge hurt too, another way.

"Even if what you say is true, it's not right, Lazlian," I choked out the words through my burning throat. "One minute you want me dead, the next you change your mind, then you want me dead again. That's crazy! I can't rely on that. Trust it. Trust *you.*"

My body shook as I tried to get my crying under control.

I had thought we were done. I thought what happened in the control room was the end, the culmination of whatever repressed emotions existed between Lazlian and me. But now I saw it was just the beginning of truth coming to light and I couldn't handle it. I yanked my hand from his heart and Lazlian let it fall. None of this was like Laz. Why only now did he speak genuinely? Because he had no more hope? A last-ditch effort to persuade me when all else failed?

Or was it all just another manipulation to bring me to heel?

"You were always so hard to read," I breathed. "I thought it a credit to your deceit. And maybe it is, but you know what I just realized? I've had trouble reading you from the start because you're not steady. *You* can't even get a read on what you want. One minute you try to take my life, the next you try to save it? You're not consistent, Lazlian."

"Sometimes I am," he murmured. I didn't follow his meaning as Lazlian very slowly slid a single silver bangle from his left wrist.

"You can't *sometimes* be consistent," I cried, exasperated. "That goes against the very definition."

Holding up his bracelet, Lazlian turned it so that I could see the interior. I caught the outline of a small, flat compartment of some kind, crafted to rest flush against the inner wall.

Lazlian stared at the silver bangle for a few long seconds and I stared at him, perplexed. Everything was silent but the *shhh...* of the sea, below. Finally, he said, "I had this made after you disappeared."

He flipped a miniscule metal latch and the compartment opened to reveal...

...hair?

I furrowed my brow. A lock of blonde hair.

"You weren't thorough in cleaning up when you ran away. You do everything hastily. You missed a piece of the hair you cut."

No... it couldn't be...

A lump the size of High Spire grew in my throat. Impossibly, more tears built.

"I found it on the floor by your wash basin," Lazlian rasped. He didn't meet my eyes, he looked only at the hair. He paused again and I wondered if he debated continuing.

"I had this made. I thought it might... be like a talisman." His voice cracked and it took him a second to recover. "To bring you back to us."

A terrible sound between a whimper and a moan escaped my lips.

"I've worn it since you left. I never remove it, except to bathe," Lazlian confessed, as he closed the tiny compartment, securing the hair safely within. He slid the bangle back onto his left wrist.

I had difficulty hearing, like the times blood rushed and the ocean roared in my ears, except this time it didn't sound like the sea, it sounded like my heart screaming. It *burned.* Warm tears streamed down my cheeks and the attempts at stifling my sobs only made the whimpers worse, so I let them come.

Tentatively, Lazlian reached up, cupping my face. I didn't flinch or turn away, though he'd never held it so completely before. After a moment his thumb swiped across my cheekbone, clearing the tears. My eyes fluttered shut and I turned my cheek into his palm... *my enemy's palm.* The hand that tried to strangle me. The hand that once almost struck my face. The hand that caused the heat still stinging my backside.

"You're right. I can have any girl in the kingdom I want. But you. And you're the one I want."

Lazlian spoke the words against my ear. When had we pressed together? When had his arms encircled me? He held me tightly, yet his muscles tensed. As if he restrained from holding me tighter. My tears wet his bare chest and ran down the scar over his heart. The fanciful part of my brain wished I really were a mermaid, just as I'd dressed the night of the Fae Fête, long ago. Mermaids were believed to have magical tears. Tears that would heal Lazlian's scar, his heart.

Heal mine.

No magic tears fell, but a sudden, soft rain did. Neither Lazlian nor I moved, letting it coat our skin.

I felt his chest ripple.

"I hate you because you don't love me," he bit out. I knew how much it cost him to say those words and I wondered if he only did so under the veil of night rain. "And I hate myself because I love you."

Not love. Madness. Obsession.

"You don't love me," I breathed, licking the rain from my lips. "You love who you think I could be if you changed me to suit you."

"I won't argue with you," Lazlian sighed. "There's no point."

"Fire and water," I whispered against his skin.

I felt another shuddering breath against my head. Rain dripped from Lazlian's face and shoulders onto my cheek.

"Just... *stay.*" He rasped the word with so much anguish, I knew in my heart it would be his final plea. Lazlian's fingers tensed against my biceps, as if trying to keep me. "Stay. You'll be safe here. You'll be cared for."

"I'll be controlled," I whimpered.

Lazlian didn't deny it.

"I can protect you," he tried.

I closed my eyes, struggling not to weep.

"You were always the one I needed to be protected from."

Time passed. Seconds or minutes or hours, it was hard to tell. The rain stopped. I had turned so that we both faced the sea that Lazlian feared so much, with his arms locked around me as I leaned into his chest. Balmy air surrounded us like a blanket, cloaked us in sorrow. That warm, wet air, tinged with his flinty scent as it enveloped Lazlian and me, was as close as we'd ever get to a union. If he was fire, my waves extinguished his pyre. If I was water, his flames burned me into nothingness.

I didn't know what brought the realization, but some-how, with his arms caging my waist, it struck me that Juls did not stock my closet or buy the jewels or re-design my chambers.

Oh my god.

Perhaps, at night, Lazlian strangled girls who looked like me. But come morning he purchased baubles and re-shaped my bedroom.

"Why did you build this balcony?" I asked him, quietly.

He didn't immediately reply and I wondered if he'd deny it.

"I thought it would make you feel more... contented," he finally said.

"And the secret passage?"

"I thought it would make me feel more contented."

I let out a soft, sorrowful laugh. Another realization cut it off.

"Were you... watching me?" I asked, holding my breath, remembering how before he showed himself, I'd tried on the strange body-necklace in the mirror, fully naked. Examined myself. *Touched myself.*

Lazlian stiffened. Breathed in. Out. "Yes."

Deep down, I was only surprised he admitted it. Too tired to work through the emotions the confession stirred, I gazed upwards in surrender. Even the sea had no power to soothe me on a night like this. A night that changed the course of history. Mine, and the world's. In ways I couldn't yet foresee.

"There are no stars tonight," I breathed, looking up at low, heavy clouds.

"No," Lazlian rasped by my ear. "They wouldn't shine for us, now would they?"

I swallowed back a lump in my throat.

"Maybe... in another world..." I couldn't finish. Feeling my chest shake to fight the tears, Lazlian's arms wrapped tighter around my torso.

"There's a small saltwater pool in the royal tower," he began, perhaps to distract me. "I don't think you've seen it. Juls wanted to surprise you after... well, your nights together never went as planned. No one uses the pool. Juls is too busy and I - "

"Hate the water," I finished for him. I felt Lazlian's head dip in a nod, behind me.

"The courtyard is small, but exquisite. It's been cultivated with rare, flowering plants and trees I can't name. For all I know they've gone extinct elsewhere. Besides the gardeners who tend it, the court is private, as only Juls and I have windows to face it. It's utterly quiet and empty. Sometimes, looking down out my window, I'd picture you there. I'd imagine you swimming..." Lazlian trailed off, swallowing before continuing. "...that you'd teach your children to swim in that pool."

Sadness ripped through me at the image of the other-worldly, desolate courtyard. *Whose children?* I wondered, remembering his hand on my belly. *Your brother's or... did your mind ever stray? Did you picture... ours?* The unused garden tugged at my heart with a such a melancholic yearning it made breathing difficult.

I whispered, "Maybe Juls's kids will swim there someday."

"Maybe," Laz replied.

Time passed again. Seconds or minutes or hours.

"Can I stay?" Lazlian asked, with unusual trepidation. "I promise I won't touch you. Not in that way. I just want... we'll never have... a night like this again."

I turned around to look up at Lazlian, still in his embrace. I told myself it cost me nothing to give the keylord this. That I'd outmaneuvered him and beaten him, and, compared to all that, it mattered little to concede to this one, small request. But another truth nagged at me, like the surf tumbling against the sand again and again, refusing to depart.

I didn't want to be alone. I wanted him to hold me.

Swallowing hard, I nodded. Lazlian scooped me off my feet and I threw my arms tightly around his neck. I couldn't help it -- once again I worried he'd toss me over the balcony and into the sea.

That he only carried me gently to the bed hurt worse.

Carefully, like I was a fragile doll, Lazlian laid me down on the silken sheets, never breaking eye contact. I wanted so badly to reach up and pull him toward me, but to what end? I ached to do something to take away the misery I saw in his glossy eyes, but I had nothing to offer. Other than... whatever this was.

Lazlian laid his long body on the bed and pulled me to

him. I wore only my short negligée and he wore only his thin black pants. I rested my head on his warm chest and he wrapped his arm around my shoulders. Besides Juls, long ago, I hadn't laid with a man other than Kirwyn, and a flurry of confusing emotions washed over me. This was *not Kirwyn.* It didn't matter who held me, the fact that it was *not Kirwyn* made it strange. I vowed to confess everything to him in the morning and I hoped it didn't set him off in a murderous rage again, leading him to do something that would throw away all the success we might have.

The odd melancholy that first seized me upon entering my room rose anew. *This is my last night in my old bed,* I thought. As if I'd ever asked for this bed. Ever wanted it. So why did I hurt knowing I was leaving it, never to return? Why was I comforted to have Lazlian, my tormentor, hold me, help me through my... goodbye?

I whimpered and felt his lips brush my forehead in a soft kiss.

"I'm so scared, Lazlian," I whispered, feeling small and child-like again. "I'm scared of what comes next."

I wanted him to say the right words, as Kirwyn would... but he didn't speak.

"Aren't you?" I prompted.

"I don't have anything to be afraid of anymore."

I AWOKE BEFORE DAWN, covered in sweat from the worst night terror I had in my entire life. It was so *real.* I might have even shouted in the real world.

Vulnerable, yearning, I reached for Lazlian. I didn't know what I intended. Sometimes... I didn't want to think about it.

But my hands felt only emptiness beside me.

I shot up in bed.

Lazlian was gone.

Drawing my knees to my chest, I tucked my head against them. Of course he was gone.

CHAPTER 49

The next morning, I met Kirwyn in the hall and practically knocked him over as I threw myself at him.

"I have something to tell you. It's not about Juls. And it's not what you think," I blurted, because I didn't want Kirwyn to imagine Lazlian and I had sex. *Although we almost did.* "But I need to explain."

I didn't have to say his name or specify what I implied. Kirwyn's green eyes bore into me, right through to my bones, to the marrow within my bones. I was laid bare for him, as always.

"No, you don't," he said, surprising and scaring me a little. "I'm going to ask you just one question. And you will answer it. And that's the end of this."

I nodded, not at all minding his bossiness. But I wasn't grateful he'd simplified the matter; my stomach knotted as I feared the answer to his question would only make things worse.

Do you love him? he'd ask. And I'd be forced to confess...
No, but.

But there's a desire buried deep that I don't understand. But something more than sexual tugs at me.

Or worse.

Yes, but.

But it's not at all like I love you. Not even close.

Or maybe Kirwyn would simply ask, *do you want to fuck him?*

And though admitting it made it hard to breathe, the truth was...

A dark part of me, deep down, almost wished there was a way they could both-

"Do you want to be with him?" Kirwyn asked, cutting off my thoughts and studying my face.

Shocked, I blinked and cried, "No! It's not even a question. I want to be with you, to build a life with you."

Kirwyn's shoulders subtly relaxed and his jaw unclenched. "Then unless you *need* to talk, to get something off your chest, this discussion is over," he said. "Agreed?"

"I – uh – agreed," I replied, frowning. I didn't know what else to say and now certainly wasn't the time to talk, but it didn't feel over. "Are you planning to attack him?"

"No," Kirwyn said, taking my hand as we walked up to the war tower, "because that's exactly what he wants – for his actions to divide us. I won't let them."

As we entered the war tower, I heard the keylord coming up behind us. Even before he spoke, I felt the change in Lazlian. His eyes glided over our surroundings, bored. His overly relaxed posture radiated insolence. His lips intermittently twitched, holding back their perpetual sneer.

I knew it was all fake, all a show because I'd wounded his ego... but it was so good I doubted myself. Regardless, it hurt. The way Lazlian closed off, the way he refused to meet my eyes with any acknowledgement of what happened the previous night... left me alone with it. I wouldn't selfishly burden Kirwyn with any details he didn't want, and I couldn't explain it to Jesi or even confide in Lida. But unshared, it was as if it happened in my own head. Lazlian's disappearance and his denial left me achingly lonely with... whatever it was.

Kirwyn and Lazlian's eyes met.

The tense, threatening silence felt heavy enough to suffocate all of us. I didn't expect otherwise; they'd only tried to kill each other the night before. But this meeting was about negotiating the future and it was vital for all of us to remain civil.

"No fighting," I warned shakily, eyeing them both as they sized up one another, subtly shifting shoulders back and chests out.

"You won," I said softly to Kirwyn, laying a hand on his torso.

"You surrendered," I reminded Lazlian firmly, shifting only my eyes.

I didn't know what would happen next, but we were interrupted by Juls walking into the war tower... accompanied by Merie. My face must have registered surprise.

"Oh, don't you know?" Laz whispered, as we resumed walking. "She's to be your replacement."

Kirwyn's body radiated defense with Lazlian in close proximity. His grip on my hand tightened. I swallowed, eyeing the petite brunette. "If I'm bringing his, he wanted mine."

"Actually, I think he wanted to keep her out, but she insisted. She has that willful behavior in common with you.

Or should I say, Merie *politely requested*. A deference not so common to you."

I shot Laz a look a look of annoyance. He shrugged. Kirwyn looked ready to beat the keylord bloody.

These negotiations weren't going to go smoothly.

"Still, it's interesting that my brother can't seem to get away from meddlesome women."

I had no right to be upset—it was actually a hopeful sign for being granted a divorce—but it didn't make me feel wonderful that Juls seemingly had Merie waiting in the wings. Lazlian was right. Juls never wanted *me*. Not really. He wanted a queen who'd fit the role he'd carve her.

It's as it should be, I thought, eyeing Merie, who carried herself with quiet confidence into a room that could easily have intimidated someone else. *She's probably always loved him.*

I received another shock as Lida walked in, closing the door behind her. I instinctively looked to Juls, confused, and he gave a curt nod of confirmation.

"I thought negotiations would proceed smoothest under the direction of someone who has lived amongst both our clans, and who has proven herself to be wise and impartial," Juls said. "Lida has been granted my authorization to conduct the proceedings."

Lida offered me the tiniest smile of encouragement and I nodded in eager agreement. I'd assumed I'd be fighting Juls on every point; his arranging a third party to manage the discussion was another hopeful sign.

Approaching the war table, Juls sat at one head and Lida, the other. Merie sat to the left of Juls, and Lazlian to his right. Kirwyn took the seat beside Laz in a move I knew he saw as keeping him from me, and I was left with the chair between Merie and Lida.

Shuffling some papers, Lida stood, commanding attention. "We'll open the discussions by laying out the terms Juls is willing to set-"

"We're willing to return your horse to you," Lazlian cut her off in a smarmy manner that communicated he was determined to play my adversary.

My mouth fell. "Szirena?" I asked, confused. "You have her? When? How?"

"Do you care?" Lazlian taunted, in a tone that told me he knew I did. "You abandoned her at the bridge you destroyed, don't you remember?"

I went back to that day in my mind. We'd left her on the other side, but I assumed the bomb spooked her and she bolted. Lazlian must have caught her somehow. *Szirena.* My heart leapt. We'd be reunited.

"It was troublesome bringing her here, across the sea. She needed a firm hand the entire journey." Lazlian enunciated every word in an unmistakably antagonistic manner. *He's trying to unsettle you before negotiations,* I warned myself. His head was bent, holding my gaze and waiting for my reaction.

"But worth the effort for such fine breeding stock."

My eyes rounded at the implication and I slammed my fist against the table. "She wasn't to be bred. I didn't want that for her and it wasn't your decision to make!"

"It seems she wanted it for herself. The island sun in winter is as good as a mainland summer." Lazlian smirked and I wanted to scream. "And in the presence of my stallion, she went right into estrus."

Against the table, my hands shook.

"Zaria..." Kirwyn warned.

"It would have been cruel to leave her in such a state. Have you ever seen a mare in heat? Lifting her tail and squatting? Whining and winking? Not her beautiful, blue eyes. Do you know what winks on a mare when she's begging to be taken? Do you know how my stallion satiated her?"

"That's enough, Lazlian," Juls interjected.

Eyes bright with glee, Laz said pointedly, "He mounted her for days."

"Fuck you, Lazlian!" I cried, shooting to my feet and leaning half across the table. I was so mad for his little game and for the cocky way he acted. As if nothing happened between us the night before. "She was not to be mated! Not *her*. I never wanted to endanger her health like that and it wasn't your right to decide."

He waved his hand in the dismissive Doreste manner that got under my skin. "Breeding rights have always been ours to decide."

The double meaning was unmistakable to me, if not everyone in the room. My hands fumbled for the nearest object and landed on a glass of water laid upon the table. Hoping I hit his smug face, I threw it directly at Lazlian's head. He ducked and it shattered on the floor behind him.

"I can see we're off to a good start," Lida sighed, drumming her fingers on the table.

Landdammit. I huffed back into my chair, knowing I'd performed exactly as Lazlian intended. Whether it was to rile me before negotiations or to take revenge on the night prior – or both – I'd certainly behaved as he'd wanted.

Kirwyn gave me a scolding look. Seething, I vowed to do better the next time.

Either to soothe tempers or to redirect the discussion, Lida opened our negotiations by dropping a bomb.

"The king has agreed to grant you the title of Princess," she announced, and I froze, suffering whiplash from the change in course. "There have only ever been princes and princesses who are direct descendants of the king and queen. Juls is bestowing you a princessdom with a regional title, the Princess of Mid-Spire or Low Spire, it's your choice."

My mind couldn't catch up. *Did that mean he was granting me a divorce? But... why would he make me a princess? Where was the trick?*

"You'll be a princess..." Lida said, swinging her eyes to Kirwyn, "and he'll be a prince."

I generally thought myself to be somewhat clever, but in that moment, I felt like a complete idiot, entirely unable to grasp what was happening.

My frowned deepened and I looked around the room, disbelieving. Juls stared at us hard, his elbow propped on the table and his hand resting pensively under his chin.

"Whose idea was this? What do you want in return? No, this isn't right," I accused Juls. "Because I know you didn't come up with this yourself and couldn't have possibly agreed to it unless someone blackmailed you."

In the silence that followed, I heard Kirwyn's low chuckle. "Oh, but he did. All on his own. Didn't you?" Kirwyn held the king's gaze and Juls stared back with a new coldness in his dark eyes. Palpable tension crackled in the air above our table.

Kirwyn turned to me and explained, "He's worked out some of Mal's intentions and he's securing your inability to speak out too much against the monarchy by folding you back into it, while at the same time, preventing either of us from heading any new leadership. It's not a concession, it's a chain."

Juls's lips twitched as he stared at Kirwyn.

Still not fully comprehending, I asked Juls, "But… why are you being so generous to Kirwyn?"

"He's not," Kirwyn answered, sneering. "He's being magnanimous, don't you see? Being the bigger man in the situation and ensuring the public's goodwill with his gracious transfer of you, to me."

"You're *posturing?*" I asked Juls, scowling. "Why is everything so fake with your family? It's always a move to protect reputations!"

"I protect my reputation to protect my *family*. My family protects my *dynasty*. My dynasty protects my *country*," Juls replied, tapping the table and looking at me, pointedly. "Not all of us have the freedom to go off and do whatever we want, whenever we want."

I nearly screamed. "You of all people can't seriously think I was given that freedom."

"No, you took it. Without thinking about the consequences to others."

"All I thought about were the consequences – for everyone!"

"Enough," Lida ordered, and I could see how much she'd also grown in a short time. Having the confidence to command kings – to direct everyone in this room – was no mean feat. But her poise and her talents were always there, under the surface in Elowa. As she'd said, she'd just never been given a chance to utilize them.

"Juls has been generous," Lida said to me. "You will henceforth be known as Princess Zaria and he will be Prince Kirwyn upon your marriage. It is a title you can pass on to your children. In return…"

Juls's solemn gaze fell upon me. "In return I require Zaria to swear allegiance to the crown and for her support of my rule."

I blinked, "You must know I will, Juls. I think you make a great king. I won't stand in the way of your reign."

"On the surface, yes. But you've paid lip service before and subverted us the moment you had the chance. You pledged loyalty and then pulled stunts like tossing your ring to gain popularity and sway the people."

I never pledged loyalty, I thought, but I bit back the words. He was right about the second part.

"I don't want you to swear fealty then turn around and hinder our ability to get anything done with small acts of dissent," Juls said. "I want your solidarity and support in public and private."

I took a deep breath. "I can agree to that, but it can't conflict with the vows I've made to Mal-Yin. I..." I shrugged, "have to support you both."

Juls rubbed his head in frustration. "We'll get to that." He waved an annoyed hand at Lida to continue.

"You will be provided with a stipend and required to engage in royal affairs," Lida announced. "And you will be granted an uncontested divorce."

I clutched the table, still reeling. I'd imagined I'd still have to fight Juls for freedom, but he was handing it over. More than simply giving it, he was offering rank and title and funds to live. Buying us off?

"What's the spin?" Kirwyn asked, keen gaze locked on Lida.

Lida shook back her long braid and announced, "The people will continue to know Zaria as the Kidnapped Queen. We will tell them she was abducted beyond the Green Mountains. However," she swung her gaze back to Kirwyn, "A freeborn man heard her cries and tracked her party. He rescued her, slaying her abductors."

Turning to me, Lida explained, "He was dashing,

daring, and saved you from death or defilement. On the long journey back to the coast, you couldn't help but fall in love," her face beamed in an imitation of desire. "Rythas loves a good love story. This is one we can tell with minimal damage to everyone's reputation."

I fought to keep my mouth from falling. *Well, this is bloody ironic. We'll spin a fake story to cover the real story, which is actually pretty damn close to the lie. Kirwyn did save me, in another manner.*

I wondered what Lazlian thought of all this. If Juls had no choice but to make me a princess, then Kirwyn had to be a prince upon marriage. *A fucking nobody,* Lazlian once said.

"Whatever," Kirwyn huffed and leaned back in his chair, arms crossed.

"There's only one catch..." Lida began, and my stomach dropped.

I knew it. Something to hurt.

"You know the law," she said. "Anyone seeking a divorce must serve a prison sentence, time to reflect upon their decision."

"I'm being sent to jail?" I gasped.

Lida held up her hand. "Exceptions can't be made for you. How would it look? However, considering your status, you can't quite be thrown into a normal prison either."

"Which is why we should just put her in the royal dungeons," Lazlian suggested. "After she's tried and whipped."

"Which is *why,*" Lida quickly corrected, "Juls has agreed to a period under house arrest." Before I could panic, she added, "Kirwyn can join you. You'll serve a term of six months of house arrest together. We've already located an appropriate estate to sequester you both."

I tried not to let my head collapse into my hands, but I

couldn't keep from rubbing it. *From Kidnapped Queen to Imprisoned Princess. I guess that's an improvement?*

There were so many other matters to discuss. Why did we begin with me? Was Juls just buttering me up for the slaughter?

"What about the next Daughter of Elowa?" I asked. "I don't want any more brides stolen from my people. And what about Elowa herself? I want her freed."

"We've been up all night outlining steps to make the changes we knew you'd seek. As a part of the surrender, Juls is willing to sign his cooperation in those negotiations effective immediately," Lida declared, withdrawing papers she carried in a bag and distributing them to us. "Everyone is exhausted and not every step can be done today. We'll have time to hammer out the finer points. We've drafted an outline of the process you can peruse at your leisure."

Kirwyn's eyes immediately began roving the documents, but without looking I refused.

"No."

"Why not?" Lazlian asked. "You'll have plenty of time during your house arrest and not much else to do. Unless you didn't get the whoring out of your system in the backlands? Perhaps you'll be too busy mating like adultering little rabbits together. Maybe when you pop out of prison, you'll already be bursting to pop out a little princeling."

This time, I was ready for Lazlian's instigation.

Smirking, I confessed, "Oh, but I took the birth control shot long ago. I'll need a booster, but I haven't been able to get pregnant, well, pretty much my entire time here."

The quiet rage on Lazlian's face could have burst his head into flames and set fire to the room around us. For a moment I gloated, then I spared Juls a glance and immediately regretted it when I saw the hurt in his eyes.

Lazlian twitched as if he was ready to toss the entire table over on its side. "You conniving little-"

"Because I wouldn't let you breed me?" I mocked, batting my lashes. "I'll keep my bodily autonomy thank-you-very-much."

Kirwyn briefly glanced up at us with a clenched jaw, but he quickly returned to his perusal of the outline Lida provided. Wisely refusing to be distracted, I supposed. Conversely, Lazlian seethed, hand fisted on the table. He panted like he couldn't fill his lungs with air and stared at me with wild, unblinking eyes.

"You have one duty as queen," he gritted out with intentional cruelty. "To lie back and wail when you're fucked and wail when you whelp."

I leaned back in my chair, grinning. "Not. Anymore."

"And for this deceit you should wail as you're whipped!"

"Oh, but Lazlian," I bat my lashes, intervening before Kirwyn could, "I'm so enjoying listening to your pitiful wailing right now."

I watched the rage on Lazlian's face with glee, but I cut him off from exploding further by returning to the more important topic, casually, as if entirely relaxed.

"I can't trust that you will follow through on our demands," I told Juls, lifting my chin.

"Do you think I can stop it?" he cried, barely concealing *his* anger. "Mal-Yin's men are crawling all over Rythas. I want them out as soon as possible. They can go to Elowa for all I care and start messing up things there. But I want him the hell out of here!"

"Zaria," Kirwyn caught my attention with a snap of his fingers. "It's legit. You can accept these terms as a starting point and work from here. The Daughter of Elowa will no longer be gifted to Rythas and there's steps in place to dismantle the secrecy of Elowa. There's a lot of unknown variables in that regard, but it's a start."

Kirwyn was calm, authoritative, and it made my heart skip a beat. We'd all been bickering – even Juls – but Kirwyn filtered out the noise and did what was necessary. Maybe it was easier for him, being on the outside. Still...

You would have made a great king, I thought. *Applying the knowledge you spent years acquiring, leveraging your ability to make tough decisions, and utilizing the way you protect those you love.*

Everyone fell silent, looking at me. I looked only at Kirwyn and nodded.

Lida blew out a puff of air. "This was easier than I anticipated. I commend everyone on their maturity through these difficult proceedings and I'd like to thank King Juls in particular for trusting me to arbitrate," she stated. "In the spirit of cooperation, I'd like to invoke a process known as the Last Request."

Kirwyn and I shifted suspiciously, but Juls didn't look surprised, so I assumed he'd arranged it beforehand.

"It is a wish, of sorts, that may or may not pertain to the general agreement," Lida explained. "As long as it is a reasonable request, it must be granted."

"Define reasonable," Kirwyn said, voice hard.

CHAPTER 50

"You can't ask to negate parts of the agreement we've just solidified, for example," Lida instructed.

"I'll assume that requesting any member of this assembly pitch themselves out the window would be deemed impermissible as well?" Kirwyn asked.

Lazlian snarled, but before he could reply, Lida qualified, "Requesting death or significant harm – mental or physical – to anyone within or without the assembly is not permitted."

"Pity," Kirwyn snapped.

Lida nodded to Juls. "The king will go first."

"I didn't think it proper to include in our terms, but there will be a-" he grimaced, "royal wedding for you, as a princess. At the ceremony, I will give you away this time."

Oh, I badly wanted to laugh, though not with mirth.

I didn't need Kirwyn to catch me up, the posturing was clear now. *Give me away.* To publicly, graciously, transfer me to Kirwyn and save face. To show that the king wasn't at all in opposition. Perhaps to make it look like it was *his* choice.

With a glance at Kirwyn for approval, I shrugged to Juls, "Agreed."

But I had my own plan forming in the back of my head when it came to marrying Kirwyn.

Lida scribbled a note on some papers and called, "Merie?"

I realized we were going in a circle, and I'd be next.

"I'm too new to these matters," Merie said cautiously, tucking a strand of smooth brown hair behind her ear. "I'd like to save my request for another time."

"No," Kirwyn immediately interjected. He looked at Lida. "That sounds suspect. It must be declined."

Lida scrunched her lips, "If the assembly agrees, she can temporarily abstain. Whether it's made now or later, the request still must be reasonable. You may abstain too, if you like," she told Kirwyn.

He shook his head. "I know what I want."

He did?

I felt everyone's eyes hot upon my face as my turn came. There were so many things I could request, I didn't know where to begin. A wish for myself and Kirwyn, or for Elowa, or for the people of Rythas... but all that would be covered under future negotiations, wouldn't it?

As soon as I had an idea, a voice answered.

It's not your job to save him. You can't save him. Only he can save himself.

But, I argued with the voice, *I can give him a start.*

I drew a long breath. "I don't know what will happen with prisoners in the future. Someday, I hope you'll work to... restructure... tactics. I understand it's not black-and-white, that there's a lot of gray between prisoner discomfort and unspeakable torture." I eyed everyone around the table slowly before letting my gaze fall on Laz.

"But whatever happens, my request is that Lazlian is no longer a part of it. He cannot have any contact with the prisoners or authority over or even knowledge of the decisions made concerning their imprisonment."

The room was silent for several long seconds.

"Juls?" Lida asked, softly.

He leaned back in his chair. "Granted."

Merie nodded. Kirwyn shrugged. Everyone looked at Laz.

I stared, attempting to discern his real emotions, to decipher the subtext of whatever he would say. The keylord did not meet my eyes. Refused.

With a wave of his hand, Laz casually decreed, "Whatever she wants."

I exhaled. A part of me felt lighter, a weight having been lifted. No matter what happened in the future, Lazlian was spared his own torture.

My heart beat a little faster as we all turned to Kirwyn next. I wondered if he'd request something to hurt Lazlian or to protect me.

"I don't want Zaria and I to be prince and princess in title only. If we're doing this, we'll have an active role, serving as the liaison between the Rythas and Elowa, between the king, Mal-Yin, and her sister Aewna. If Zaria wishes to abstain, I still want knowledge of important decisions regarding both clans and an advisory role in those decisions."

I blinked at him. A power grab? Or was this Kirwyn's way of protecting me? It was a ballsy fucking ask. Kirwyn had no history here, no ties to Rythas. But if Juls was already conceding to give him a title, it wasn't an unreasonable request...

"I won't accept council from the interloper," Juls scoffed. "Denied."

"We were together first, so who's the fucking interloper?" Kirwyn snapped, leaning forward onto the table as if he could reach across and attack Juls.

"You had no right," Juls shouted, fists clenched.

"*You* had no right," Kirwyn replied, raising his voice above the king's.

I looked at Lazlian – not because I expected him to interject *his* supposed rights – but because the only thing to make this moment worse would be Lazlian adding fuel to the fire with some snarky quip. But the keylord only watched, carefully, quietly.

"I'm sorry," Juls said softly, turning to Merie and rubbing a hand over his face. "I didn't mean-"

Merie laid a gentle hand upon Juls's. "I know," she said.

"He's not asking for authority to make decisions or for you to even heed his advice," Lida noted, "just to be kept in the loop and for you to hear him out."

Juls didn't budge and I couldn't blame him. Asking him to include the man who – in his eyes, stole his wife... for the man he most despised to be brought into his inner circle of royal exclusivity...

"I will hear him out," Merie piped up, surprising us. "As Kirwyn acts as a go-between for Rythas and Elowa, I will liaise between the prince and the Dorestes. Would that work for everyone?"

I caught Laz rubbing his lips in thought over the unexpected turn of events and realized I was doing the same. Juls searched Merie's face and I couldn't help but wonder if he searched for duplicity... if he looked for me in her face. Whatever he saw in her eyes satisfied him. Intent upon his next bride, he nodded in acquiescence.

"Agreed," he sighed.

Lazlian's turn was last and the room fell silent in anticipation. I braced for a clever move to seize power or undo some of the good our negotiations had done – literally, my fingertips pressed harder into the tabletop as I mentally prepared for battle.

Laz shifted his gaze to me. I couldn't claim to be surprised.

"She takes our mark."

I was floored.

I shook my head, thinking I misheard.

"Our tattoo?" Juls asked, equally confused. "If she plans to stay, she must eventually do so."

"And yet she avoided it before. For almost a year. My request is that she take it. *Now*. Before leaving this room." Lazlian stared at me, eyebrows raised. "If she's going to take the mark anyway, it's a reasonable request."

I started to sweat, both at the idea of being marked, right here, right now, and the knowledge of how painful it would be.

I hate needles. They know I do.

"We don't have the time right now," Juls pointed out, to my relief. "It will take hours to bring in the artist, set up his work, and complete the tattoo."

"Ah, but we have a new process, like the Spades," Lazlian said. "The minute marker we've been perfecting. Once the artist is here it would take ten minutes, tops."

"Yes, but we haven't been using it because though you've manipulated the instrument to work faster, it causes more pain in exchange," Juls pointed out, speaking slowly.

I had to stop myself from throwing my head back and roaring with mad laughter.

As if Lazlian cares. It's probably more enjoyable for him this way.

He shrugged. "Give her a drink first. It's a reasonable request."

Son of a bitch. Lazlian went last. And Lazlian had the last laugh.

Kirwyn, rubbing his thumb over his fists, looked ready to deck the keylord.

Lida turned to me. "I concede it's reasonable. Do you accept?"

I shot Lazlian my darkest look. I hadn't suspected this request, but I knew damn well what he was doing. That tattoo meant something different to me than it did anyone else. The crown and the key were like Juls and Laz on my back forever. But I couldn't think of an excuse. I *had* secretly meant to escape the marking somehow and he knew it.

I gritted my teeth and sighed through my nose. "I accept."

How fitting. I used my one wish to free Lazlian. And he used his to cage me.

Water and Fire.

"Excellent," Lazlian replied smugly, making me want to deck him as well. "Fetch the artist, will you, Lida? There's some rum in the cabinet she can have before he arrives."

KNEELING ON A CHAIR, I was bent from the waist onto the war table with the top of my dress cut down its center to bare my back. It wasn't dignified and it wasn't really consensual and both were probably Lazlian's point.

"Stop," Kirwyn ordered, as the tattoo artist approached.

Roughly, he stripped his own shirt from his body. "I'm going first."

I sprang from the table, surprised, holding my dress in front to cover myself. "No, Kirwyn."

"Yes." He balled up his shirt and tossed it aside.

The artist—a man who seemed capable enough, judging from span of tattoos covering his own body— looked around the room. The rest of us looked to Lazlian, unsure if this act was covered under the umbrella of his request.

"I don't give a shit what he does," Laz dismissed, acting as if he barely paid attention.

"No," Kirwyn agreed, sauntering beside me with a one-sided grin, "but she does."

He folded himself over the table, right next to where I had just bent.

"Don't," I whispered my protest, ignoring everyone else in the room. "You never wanted to be marked. You're a free-born, like your family."

Kirwyn shook his head, once. "You're my family now."

I reached out and stroked his face. *God, I love him so much.*

"Besides," Kirwyn added, "I don't think one can be a prince of a clan without the clan's mark."

Fair point. He was going to have to take it someday, too.

I leaned down and kissed him before stepping back to allow the tattoo artist to get to work. After he'd prepped Kirwyn's skin, he used a threatening-looking metal tool to create the design. It resembled a torture device to me, and when Kirwyn grunted loudly, I knew it felt like one.

My hands fumbled for the rum and I took a swig directly from the bottle, eyes wide in fear. Kirwyn gritted his teeth but I could tell from the sweat beading his forehead that he was trying to remain calm so as not to worry me.

"*Fuck,*" he hissed when it was nearly over. "*Shit.*"

I almost couldn't believe it as I stared at Kirwyn's back, now bearing the symbol of Rythas. The tattoo artist sprayed something over the design and ordered Kirwyn to lie down for a few minutes, but Kirwyn waved him off and took my face in his hands.

"I won't lie to you," he said, eyes searching mine. "It's going to hurt. But it's fast. You can do it. I'll be with you the whole time."

Wordlessly, I nodded and eased myself back over the table, letting my dress fall open once more. Kirwyn moved aside, holding my hand and blocking me from Lazlian. "Hey. Look at me. It will be over in a few minutes."

"Try not to faint," the artist warned. "If you faint, I have to stop and it will take longer."

The last thing I wanted to do was cry in front of the entire room. But the minute the needle touched me the pain was unbearable. It was *not* like the Spade method Aewna used. Sweat broke out all over my body.

"Stop, please."

"She has to lay still or I'll mess it up," the artist warned.

Kirwyn rotated around the table's edge and reached over, gently-but-firmly pressing my head and shoulder down.

I started crying. It hurt too much.

"Zaria, stay with me," Kirwyn urged. He rubbed my face frantically, trying to keep me conscious. "Don't faint. Just another minute or two."

I'd worried I might not escape the mark someday, but never did I imagine it would happen like this. It was Lazlian's order, but Kirwyn holding me in place. To everyone else, it was the symbol of Rythas, worn proudly. But to me, the crown was Juls and Laz, the key. Forever branded upon my back. I couldn't see it, but I'd always know it was there.

Bent over the war table in the castle that was my prison, I was permanently marked.

It's behind you, I told myself. *Your past. Kirwyn's on your front, he's your future.*

I'd won so much; *we'd* won so much.

But, to get there, we'd made more sacrifices than I could imagine and most of them in ways I was only starting to understand. My beliefs about the world and myself were forever changed -- and I had a feeling this was only the beginning.

In my mind, I tried to hold onto all we'd achieved. A new path would unfold for Elowa. Her daughters would never been surrendered as brides to Rythasian nobles. I'd saved the next chosen braenese from a fate like my own. We'd changed *the world.*

And, for myself, I was no longer condemned to dwell the halls of High Spire on the arm of a man I did not love. I'd be free to live a life with Kirwyn, a royal one, where we'd still be able to do some good, as we'd always discussed. On top of it all, I'd get to live a happy life amongst the friends and family I'd deeply missed.

One book in my life has closed, I thought. *But I'm about to crack the spine on a new one, a better one.*

Part V

Queen of *Their* Hearts

CHAPTER 51

Our house arrest was more like a voluntary isolation in a fairy-tale manor by the sea. The home wasn't very large, but it was well-appointed, and Kirwyn and I didn't need much. What the property lacked in square footage for the dwelling itself, it made up for in the expanse of land. Set back safely from the beach, we had our own sprawling path to the shoreline and a few acres on either side.

"What will we do with all this time alone together?" Kirwyn teased, coming up behind me as we surveyed our temporary home on the outskirts of Mid-Spire. I could hear the grin in his voice. He wrapped his arms around my waist and I relaxed into the safety of his embrace.

"Just be," I sighed. "We've earned it. We can explore each other on our own time, slowly. Inside and out. Find out who we are without the pressures of the world telling us to be something. Without having to run or to hide from anything or anyone."

I turned and wrapped my arms around Kirwyn's neck.

"I want to just exist for a while, quietly, with you."

Kirwyn lifted me, wrapping my legs around either side of his waist. "Can you be quiet, Zaria?" He grinned, walking me over to the nearest sofa. "I highly doubt it. But I'll help you try," he said, laying me down on the pillows and running his hands up my dress.

"Let's see if I can make you scream yourself hoarse."

WE'D BEEN under house arrest less than a month when I heard about the first strange occurrence. We received weekly packages of food and other vital supplies, often delivered by Jesi, who also brought news and gossip.

I didn't think much of it when the first of Lazlian's guards – the ones who attempted to hang me – died under unusual circumstances. But the skin on my neck prickled when the second perished in an accident a few weeks later. Two deaths were too coincidental.

Juls wasn't behind it, I was sure. He wanted the men alive in order to play them.

That left two men whose rage burned so bright that it might drive them to murder, fuck the consequences. But which?

Under house arrest, Kirwyn couldn't access the information to set up any vengeance killings. How would he learn where the men lived, their habits, and so on, in order to plan their deaths? And Lazlian might be able to gain that knowledge, but how could he escape his brother's notice to assassinate the men? Who would he trust enough to execute a murder that flew in the face of the king's pardon?

While Kirwyn was unpacking the latest supplies from Jesi one day, I mused with false innocence, "It's odd that the guards who tried to hang me are mysteriously dying."

I thought we'd have to play cat-and-mouse games before he confessed anything, but Kirwyn shocked the sea out of me by replying coldly, "It's not odd at all. It's fantastic. The only odd thing, the only *frustrating* thing, is that I can't get it done alone from here."

Wide-eyed, I collapsed into the chair behind me. I'd noticed Kirwyn was especially tired some mornings and had taken to napping for long afternoons. Could he have slipped out of the house at night, without my waking? Could Lazlian have come by, or sent a trusted messenger, to work *with* Kirwyn?

"Are you saying that... no. I don't believe you."

"Believe it, princess," Kirwyn replied, still unboxing supplies as if this were a casual conversation. "The only thing the keylord and I agree on is that those men need to die. And they will. If they don't flee Rythas first."

It wasn't the image of Kirwyn assassinating the guards or even Lazlian deciding they needed to be executed that surprised me. It was that the two men who'd tried to kill each other could actually stomach working together for my benefit. They must have had no other choice. They must hate it.

I clutched the arms of the chair to steady myself. "But... how?"

"You sleep a lot more soundly now that you feel safe," Kirwyn answered, finally pausing in his work. "And I'll sleep a lot more soundly once they're all dead."

Shrugging one dismissive shoulder, Kirwyn said, "I guess he will too."

∿

OVER THE NEXT few months under house arrest, our fake story spread. Juls knew what his people wanted. The nobles weren't thrilled, but after a period of adjustment, Rythas accepted Merie as the new queen. Juls solidified his reputation as the gracious king by bestowing Kirwyn the title of *prince* upon his marriage to me, and by nobly stepping back and handing me over to Kirwyn in the first place.

He did it to be a thorn in Mal's side, and it worked. After a period of utter shock I understood first-hand, Elowa began rapidly enacting new ways to govern under Mal and Aewna's guidance. While those changes might be enticing in Rythas, there was nothing to rebel against when we possessed such a beloved king.

I might be untouchable, but so was Juls. Everyone came out untarnished. For a time.

Rythas embraced Kirwyn and I as a newly-titled royal couple. They compared us to Guinevere and Lancelot and asked, *how could any girl not lose her heart to such a dashing rescuer?*

Helping popularize the lie, a game was set up in the brothels and I couldn't help but wonder if Lazlian was behind it. Clients actually *paid* to play at being Kirwyn. They'd fight off a group of men and "rescue" a girl who looked like me before she was assaulted by her "evil kidnappers." Of course, this allowed a patron to benefit from the girl's gratitude and eager participation as he ravished her himself.

That was the *less* insulting version.

The alternative was to watch a play unfold where the hero did not make it in time.

In such a case, a man short on coin could split the cost with a few others. The clients did not participate but were instead treated to a show. In the discounted version, a brothel worker in an Elowan tunic failed to meet her Kirwyn-rescuer and was "forced" to service her kidnappers for the viewer's pleasure.

Jesi had relayed the news over guava cakes one afternoon and I was reminded of her previous words of wisdom.

There's a price to fame. And for women, it usually looks like this.

The more I thought about it, the more I was sure Lazlian had conceived of such a brutal show-- and likely watched it unfold more than once. If I were to ask him about it, he'd probably deflect, telling me it was for my own good to popularize our fake story.

But I couldn't confront him because he was gone.

After the last of his guards died suspiciously, Lazlian sailed away from Rythas. I had no way of knowing what the keylord was making of his life other than from odd bits of information I collected after I completed my jail term and was formally granted a divorce.

Free to move, Kirwyn and I chose a property not unlike where we'd served in isolation, having grown to enjoy beach accessibility and room for riding. The land didn't cost much of our royal funds as the run-down property required a lot of work. We repaired as much as possible with our own labor, while at the same time we geared up for our required, royal wedding.

Yet I had one more trick up my sleeve.

Juls would give me away at the affair for all the nobles to see, as I'd agreed... but first, Kirwyn and I had a secret ceremony on the beach in front of our home.

It was just the two of us. It was everything I'd always dreamed and always been denied.

I wore a simple white dress, short, not unlike an Elowan tunic. I had no crown but for the flowers Kirwyn picked himself and wove into a circlet for my hair. He wore a white shirt with buttons, similar to the one he'd worn when I found him ashore on Queen's Beach. His trousers were similar too, although they were cream-colored this time.

Lida had found an obscure Rythasian law that said a priest wasn't needed, as long as two witnesses signed proof that the ceremony occurred. Later that evening, she and Jesi stopped by to sign such a document, but had respectfully left Kirwyn and I alone to conduct our own ceremony in the surf that day.

He and I first met at sunrise, in the blue-gray predawn, but we married with the sun at its apex, shining down in full strength -- an Elowan sign of good fortune.

At sunset, we consummated our union again and again, right in the waves.

WITH OUR NEWFOUND TIME, space, and money, we set up a free camp on one part of our land. I'd had the idea when I was thinking about the young girl's face, the one who'd been carted off on the mainland. We'd failed to save her but with our royal money, we could help other children.

Kirwyn divided our funds, using half to set up dizzying businesses for trade and speculative investments I barely understood. He was astoundingly good at money—making it, managing it—and he worked easily with Mal and Aewna. Motivated by not wanting to depend on Juls, Kirwyn produced enough revenue streams that we didn't need to take coin from the crown after the first year, and we paid it all back by the second. With interest.

Immediately after we captured High Spire, Queen Pama was disposed and Aewna took over as regent for Jona. We sequestered my mother, along with Volmar and Enith, back on the mainland. Jona, Gereth, and Naseroson stayed with Pama, but as they grew they were required regular lengthy stays in Elowa, to be raised in part under Aewna's care.

Two years passed during which I was free to learn, to rest, and to help manage the back end of the camp a bit. For a while, that's all I wanted. We hired staff to handle most of our organization, but once a week, Kirwyn led a class on horseback riding and once a week, I taught the younger kids how to swim.

One day, on my way out the door to meet with Jesi for my birth control shot, Kirwyn grabbed my wrist.

"Don't," he said, pinning me with those deep green eyes. "Don't take it."

We weren't too young to conceive by Elowan or Rythasian standards, but I felt a little unprepared and vulnerable with his suddenness.

I swallowed, also feeling the deep *thump-thump* of my heart. Just looking at Kirwyn's sexy body in repose made my cheeks blush and my body tingle. Even after all this time, the idea that this gorgeous man wanted a family with me didn't cease to astound me.

"Are you sure?"

"Don't even question it," he said, staring at me as if the world around us had suddenly disappeared. Though the drug still worked through my system, Kirwyn's eyes already lit with a new kind of hunger as he rose from the sofa, stalked forward, and slid the straps of my seasuit from my shoulders.

When I bled the next month, indicating the medicine no longer ran through my veins, it was as if my body cast a spell on Kirwyn. His ceaseless, single-minded desire to make a baby worked my own into a frenzy. We made love each night, sometimes multiple times a day, and Kirwyn's dirty talk expanded into regions I hadn't known possible... but excited me, nonetheless.

"I'm going to fill you up, Zaria," he'd whisper in my ear, weaving our fingers together on one hand. "There's nothing stopping me now. No other people in our way, no distance, not even any protection. When I come, it's going here," he'd say, pressing his other hand low on my belly, "and we're going to make our baby inside you."

I no longer cared if other people talked this way.

He did. We did.

That was all that mattered.

It only took one moon cycle.

Though it happily turned out I was very fertile, my body didn't handle the pregnancy well. Kirwyn and I were strolling to the beach one day when I fainted, and we knew.

For the duration of the pregnancy, I was barely able to walk or even keep food or water down. Juls ordered royal doctors to our house, who injected me with those hated IVs again. Tomé and Marcin often came to visit, keeping me company. Like Kirwyn and me, they'd married in a private ceremony and split their time between a business crafting and selling Elowan carvings, and an organization helping other Elowans acclimate to life beyond such cruelty as they'd suffered.

When the time came, I expected my labor to be as difficult as the pregnancy, but in an odd twist of fate, our baby was born in less than an hour. In the privacy of our own home and with only an Elowan healer to assist, Teddy came into this world.

Little Theo had dark hair like Kirwyn, but bright blue eyes, like me. Even as a baby those eyes were sharp and clever, often finding their way to mischievousness. From the beginning, Kirwyn rode horseback with Teddy strapped to his chest, scaring the sea out of me each time. But I took young Teddy into the waves, acclimating him to the ocean from the moment he was born. It never failed to make Kirwyn hover anxiously, as if it wasn't natural for babies to swim.

A DEVASTATING BLACK Squall hit Rythas four years after I returned. Those nearest were able to shelter in High Spire, but so many others were killed, injured, or missing. Houses were completely destroyed and families lost generations of possessions in one day.

Mal-Yin heroically swooped in, using his men and his money to help rebuild the areas hardest hit. If there had been any way to facilitate the disaster, I'd have suspected Mal of controlling the weather to do so, lives be damned. He rode in at the head of a fleet like an emissary from Keroe himself, boats laden with supplies from the mainland.

More frequently, people began speaking highly of him for his introduction of *democratic ways* in Elowa -- ways I supported, like a good little songbird. If I was step one in Mal's plan to foster the adoration of Rythas, my sister made a happy step two in securing Elowa as the showgrounds. On one hand, Mal had an uphill battle against Juls's popularity. On the other, the changes we made from our negotiations caused increasing unrest amongst the elite. Mal was right -- messing with the TORR had a ripple effect I feared reached as far as Spade City.

Kirwyn's good looks and charm made our love story easy to sell to Rythas. But it didn't help in his endeavor to persuade Juls to incorporate any new ideas he'd learned about in his childhood library, or those currently meeting with success in Elowa. Merie heard him out, as promised, but she couldn't make Juls act. I could see it was frustrating for Kirwyn to be a royal puppet with no real power in court... to be required to attend events and fall in line when ordered, but not to be able to have any input.

I was used to it.

And I never failed to feel immense gratitude that our lives came with so many more blessings than we'd imagined.

Yet... in those years, I thought often of Lazlian. I wondered where he was and if he'd ever return.

It was hard to predict what the keylord would do.

CHAPTER 52

"No man can serve two masters," Kirwyn warned.

"I am not a man," I retorted, slinging my bag over my shoulders, "and they are not my masters."

The last five years, I'd worked a delicate and difficult balance of both backing Juls as king *and* supporting the democratization Mal encouraged. I was on my way to a meeting that afternoon when a knock on our door sounded, just as I'd raised my hand to open it.

The only thing that could have shocked me more than seeing King Juls and Queen Merie standing on my doorstep was that Lazlian stood behind them, towering over them.

A full-body jolt ran through me.

I hadn't seen him in five years. We were cuspate boys and girls back then.

No longer.

Lazlian looked... different. He'd grown his hair out a bit and styled it somewhat slicked back, smoothing out the waves. Similar to Kirwyn, he didn't bother shaving his stubble, giving him a rugged, masculine look. Most noticeably, Lazlian filled out. Whatever he'd been doing on the mainland, it hadn't been sitting idly on a throne somewhere. He wasn't overly bulky, but he bore muscle where none before existed. Beneath his tight tunic, I glimpsed his firm chest and toned arms. Involuntarily, I swallowed.

What are they doing here?

I felt Kirwyn instantly beside me.

"Come in," he tentatively invited. Having spent more time with Juls and Merie than I did, he may have felt more comfortable to lead.

Not that Kirwyn was making any progress in their meetings.

My questions raged like a sea storm as we walked to the glass-encased patio at the back of our house. I'd assumed we'd sit the table, but everyone stood, awkwardly.

Why are they here and why does the air feel so charged?

Where had Lazlian been all this time? Why had he returned?

I looked from Laz to Juls to Merie. Something very strange was happening and I couldn't tell what to expect from their faces. My heart pounded.

"We've known one another for a long time," Juls said. "So I'm going to get right to the point."

I straightened my spine, readying for anything.

"I'm considering giving the throne to Lazlian or naming any child of his - regardless of gender - my heir."

I blinked, stunned.

"But... why?" I breathed, noticing Merie gave Juls an encouraging squeeze between their clasped hands.

"I can't produce an heir," Juls said, stiffly. "Without a solid line of succession, there will be a fight and worse, Navere will try to seize power. Your disruptions upset the TORR and Spade clients are no longer visiting the brothels as they used to. The nobles have lost money and they blame the crown. Several will support Navere if I can't name an heir and stabilize our dynasty."

I let out a long breath, trying to quell that storm inside me, but it raged harder every time I looked at Laz. *Lazlian who would be... king?*

"I'm sorry," I whispered. "I'm so sorry."

Kirwyn, arms folded beside me, frowned and asked, "Has there been a solid history of brothers handing the crown to brothers? Yours is not well-liked, you know," he pointed out. I knew the wheels in Kirwyn's head spun as he spoke.

Juls drew another long breath. "We are going to ask those who were present at the time of our birth to come forward and speak the truth – that Lazlian was really the first born. If that's not enough, we'll fabricate the evidence," he said with a dismissive wave of his hand.

Kirwyn wasn't convinced. "The keylord has a reputation for arrogance, for caring more about the nobles than everyone else. What makes you think the people will accept him or his offspring as their new king when you're so beloved?"

A heavy silence fell upon the room. Juls and Merie shifted. She drew a long breath; Juls's gaze flicked to me.

Kirwyn snarled. "How dare you come into my house and even think to suggest-"

"You're only here by *my* grace!" Juls threw back at Kirwyn.

"Stop," I demanded, hating when my mind worked a step behind Kirwyn's. "Will someone tell me what's going on?"

Kirwyn gave a mirthless chuckle in Juls's direction. "You

don't even have the fucking nerve to say it." Kirwyn looked at me and declared, "He wants you carry the heir."

I was sure I'd heard incorrectly. I literally shook my head, almost comically, as if I could shake out whatever lodged itself in my ears, clogging and confusing them.

"It's the only way to ensure the people accept it," Kirwyn explained. "A child of his brother's is still a Doreste, still of the royal line, and a child from *The Queen of our Hearts* would be embraced by the people."

Everyone looked to me for a reaction but I wasn't capable of giving one. I'd frozen in disbelief, staring stupidly. I must have misheard. A conversation like this couldn't happen anywhere, anytime, but certainly not in my sunroom on a beautiful afternoon.

"Zaria?" Merie asked. "Are you okay? I know this is a lot to process..."

Why was she speaking as if any of this were real?

Of course. *It's a joke.*

"You're terribly funny," I said. "Good one, coming in here-"

"Do you think I have time to make jokes?" Juls asked, incredulous. "Zaria, I have never been more serious in my life." He affected his *king's voice* and it cracked across the room like a whip.

But I didn't look at Juls. In my confusion, I looked to Kirwyn for confirmation. *Is this a dream? A nightmare?*

"Rythas loves you," Kirwyn huffed. "They'll support your child on the throne as the next best after Merie's. Juls wants to use you to make everyone accept Lazlian as king or regent or at least to seamlessly crown his next of kin by making it *your* offspring."

What... the... fuck?

Lazlian had been eerily quiet as we spoke. My mind began to accept what was happening and I blamed him, suspected he was behind it somehow. Therefore, in the tense, heavy pause that followed, I directed my rage to Laz when I exploded.

"Fuck you, Lazlian, fuck you!"

He relaxed against the table. "Well, yes. That would be the general idea."

I looked wide-eyed at Kirwyn, worried he'd jump at the bait, but he was too clever. Instead, he'd turned cold eyes to Juls. I supposed it made sense -- all the power to decide anything lay with Juls. If Kirwyn was going to hate anyone, the king was the practical target.

Laz pushed, making things worse, as usual.

"It's not like it'd be the first time," he taunted. "Remember our night together when you attacked High Spire?"

Oh no.

Smugly, Lazlian looked at Kirwyn and declared, "While you were in the noose, I was in her."

I spun wildly on my heel to face the keylord. "Are you crazy? That's not – Kirwyn," I spun around again. "That's not-"

Fuck. It wasn't entirely untrue, but Lazlian twisted it. Pleadingly, I looked at my husband. "That's not exactly... it's not what you think."

Kirwyn never failed to amaze me. I was ready to punch Lazlian, but he was utterly unruffled as he cocked a lazy grin. Pointedly, he said, "I'm sure what's between Zaria and I is *big* enough to erase whatever *small* memory that might be."

Ouch. I spun back to Laz.

He shrugged in return. "Perhaps. But the memory of

what happened later that evening is a much *longer* one. I was in her bed all night, after all."

Fucking Laz! I knew that'd come back to haunt me! All these years...

Whirling back to Kirwyn, I protested, "It's not how it sounds. *Nothing happened in bed.* I swear to you."

I spun yet again back to Laz. I was doing nothing but spinning in circles like a fool, trying to diffuse tension when I wanted to scream. It was just like when Laz and Kirwyn nearly shot each other and I had stood between them, trying to prevent *that* catastrophe. Fate forced me into the middle once more.

"You're twisting everything around, Lazlian. Stop it. And you weren't there all night. You were gone before morning, remember?"

"Did you miss me?" he mocked.

Unwillingly, I thought back to that horrible nightmare I'd had. How scared and alone I was. My stupid face must have answered Laz's question with a *yes* or reflected the fear I'd felt upon waking with no one to comfort me. Because Lazlian saw something in my expression. His brow furrowed and he blinked. He turned his head, disengaging.

Juls and Merie had taken a seat, watching us carefully, hands clasped for support.

"This is insane. I'm not entertaining this discussion. You want an heir?" I asked, angrily. "Then let Lazlian try with Merie. That's even better. He's good at keeping secrets and it would still be in your family."

I'd only half-meant it, but in the tense silence that followed, I realized I'd struck on something.

Oh my god... Had they already tried?

Mouth agape, I looked to Lazlian, wondering if he'd gloat somehow, but he only averted his eyes, confirming it.

Oh my god. Oh, Keroe. How could this happen? My head was going to explode trying to comprehend it.

Lazlian had slept with his brother's wife.

They *were* truly desperate.

I didn't want to picture it, but I couldn't stop myself. What was I thinking? Of course Laz wasn't happy about it. He respected his brother and his brother's marriage too much for that.

But he'd done it for the very same reason.

Realizing I'd covered my mouth with inconsiderate shock, I lowered my hand.

"I'm not asking you to do anything I haven't done myself," Merie whispered, breaking the silence to dispel any lingering doubt.

I realized...*she's infertile. Juls and Merie both are.*

I needed a chair. A drink.

They must have tried many times. Lazlian and Merie must have had sex repeatedly to be sure. Oh my god, he must have been... well, honestly, I had no idea what Lazlian felt, how he... psyched himself up to perform. But I knew it had to be profoundly awful and awkward for them both.

But how did they know Lazlian wasn't infertile too?

"I don't understand..." I had difficulty meeting anyone's eyes. "Who's to say Lazlian can even have children?"

The room stilled with more ominous tension. Subtly, Laz nodded to Juls.

"Lazlian had a son," Juls said softly, sadly. "I had a nephew. Both the boy and the mother perished in a mainland attack."

My hand fell to my heart and I looked at Laz with newfound sympathy, scarcely breathing. I couldn't read his eyes, yet I had so many questions I wished he'd answer.

Five years... it made sense he'd had sex with someone in

all that time. My mind raced with scenarios. Maybe it had been a one-off? Maybe she'd gotten him drunk and had seduced him, determined to bear royal offspring? Maybe he'd seduced her? Maybe he loved her?

Maybe I'd never know the truth.

So much pain he'd endured in his life.

"I'm so sorry," I whispered. Lazlian's face was a mask; he only nodded his acceptance.

"Only my brother or my brother's child will wear the crown," Juls declared, bringing the conversation back to business. "This is my decree. We're here with a royal request for you to help provide that heir."

"But this can't be your plan," I protested. "I did everything I could to help you keep the throne! Everything!"

"Then do this one thing more to help us stabilize it," Juls replied.

"You're not just asking me to visit his bed," I cried. "You're asking me to tear apart my family!"

"As you asked me to tear apart my kingdom!" Juls shouted, slamming his hand so hard on the tabletop I was surprised he didn't break the wood. Or his hand.

I froze. The room fell silent.

Fuck. I did worse than that. I didn't ask.

"Is this your way of punishing me?" I asked, teeth clenched. "Conscripting me as a womb for your brother?"

"Is it really such a punishment?" Juls retorted. "Do you think I was oblivious back then? You were never that accomplished in courtly guile."

An involuntary blush heated my face as I fumbled for words. Obviously, Juls had been hurt by whatever he sensed between Lazlian and I. With a raised brow, it was as if Juls challenged, *maybe you should just sleep together and get it over with.*

But that's just it, I thought. *It would never be over.* It's not like I could sleep with Lazlian once and *poof* – I'd conceive, first try. And I wasn't so naïve to think Lazlian wouldn't suggest additional children, back-ups, as soon as I birthed the first. And for their education and safety, any child would need to be raised at High Spire. And to be with them and for my own safety, I would be held there too...

I could see exactly how it would go. Or worse, I couldn't see all the possibilities and *that* frightened me.

"You can't command me," I warned Juls. "You're not my husband any longer."

"No, but I am your king."

Who was this new Juls? Pointing angrily, I declared, "If you're going to be a king like that, then I welcome Mal-Yin hurrying to shrink your power. Better for the people."

"Perhaps," Juls said evenly. "But I could treat you to a night in the dungeons as it's still treason to speak that way."

"Technically, it's sedition," Kirwyn murmured.

Juls shot him a look.

I gaped, open-mouthed.

"Since when did you rule with such an iron fist?"

"Since *you,*" he snarled.

I flinched as if I'd been slapped. After a breath to calm myself, I said, "What you're suggesting is adultery. What you've *already* encouraged your brother and your wife to do is treason."

Oh my god. I audibly gasped at the realization that *Mal-Yin was right.*

All those years ago, he'd warned me that Juls would suggest something dubious to maintain power.

Mal just guessed the wrong brother.

"Zaria, Mal wants to move too fast and you know it,"

Merie spoke up. "We are not the blank slate Elowa was. We need to keep him and my brother at bay."

"I'm giving you options," Juls said. "You can divorce your husband, marry Lazlian, and bear the next heir. Or you can have an indiscretion in which you are caught. It's not my preferred course, it's riskier. But it will still be a child of *yours.* If there were another they'd accept, legitimate or illegitimate, I wouldn't be here."

"No," I scoffed. "Everyone would hate me for the infidelity and it wouldn't work. Think about it. I'd have gone from you to Kirwyn to Laz?" I shook my head. "Not even my reputation can withstand that."

"It can. Only yours. The people love you." Juls waved a hand to indicate the camp we'd built.

Sensing some resentment in his voice, I countered, "I didn't do this as a publicity stunt! I did it because I wanted to help!"

"That's precisely why they love you."

I groaned. *How bloody ironic.* Everything I did to step away from rule only embroiled me further with the crown.

"You're wrong," I repeated. "My reputation couldn't weather this. It's crazy."

Juls stared hard, giving me chills. "There is a basis."

"What do you mean?"

"Before we married, when you lived in High Spire... do you remember when you tried to steal the key to the Forbidden Texts? You were noticed and rumors spread... whispers of the two of you together."

Those drawings in the drinking halls.

The people thought Lazlian and I had a secret affair in the past?

How could that one night from years ago come back to bite me?

"I don't even understand what you're saying," I cried. "Is Lazlian king or not in this scenario?"

"We can work out the best way to roll it out. Who sits the throne and for how long, if there's a regency role, when to name the heir... the key is having the heir in the first place. We're flexible on how it's done."

"Oh, you're *flexible*," I scoffed. "How generous."

"Now that you point it out, I have been," Juls retorted angrily. "You and your husband live here by my benevolence. You were given a start on royal coin by my charity. Your very lives were spared by my mercy."

I crossed my arms. "Kirwyn's work for Rythas has far out-earned any monies you've provided. We give away more than we initially took."

Merie cut in, "My brother has support of the army and many nobles now. We lost their allegiance after the changes you started supporting which has been lessening their power. Navere will use the lack of a suitable heir to steal the throne and undo all the good we've been trying to do. It will all have been for nothing. Everything Lazlian and I... it will have been for nothing."

Merie looked it at me, eyes glistening with tears as she shot to her feet. "If you care about us, about Rythas, I'm asking you to do this. I'm using my Last Request. I – I need a moment," she said, fleeing out the glass doors to our rear gardens.

"Excuse me," Juls said, quickly following on her heels.

Kirwyn gave Lazlian a hard look. "I'm going out there to talk some sense into the king." He pointed at me. "If you touch her, I'll tear your hands off. If you upset her, I'll rip your tongue out."

Lazlian blinked. "I suppose neither hands nor tongues are required to make an heir, but they do help the process."

I groaned loudly. "Just go," I said, before Kirwyn attacked Lazlian. "I'll be fine."

Truthfully, I wanted a moment with Laz to see if I could figure out what was going on without anyone interfering.

With a last, stern look at the keylord, Kirwyn left, storming after the king and queen now sitting on one of our benches in the gardens.

Alone, awkward silence descended upon Lazlian and me. It was strange seeing him after those long years apart, after all we'd been through. Surreal.

"You know, I think my brother grows weary of the crown," Laz said finally. "I feel like we're all heading toward a game of musical chairs. Except, when the music stops, we're all trying *not* to be the one on the throne."

"Except to keep it from Navere," I said softly. Lazlian dipped his head in assent.

"Funny enough, your boy is probably the only one who would want the responsibility." Lazlian grinned maliciously. "But he doesn't have the pedigree."

"He's a prince," I reminded. "And he's done plenty for Rythas."

"He's a foreigner."

"So am I."

"You're a woman," Lazlian dismissed. "You are what your husband is."

If smoke could have blown from my ears, it would have. I fisted my hands to restrain myself from throttling Lazlian. Instead, I countered, "Are you trying to incite me? *He* is my *husband.*"

"We can fix that," Lazlian waved a hand. "I'll tell you what. I can be generous. I'll make him keylord and allow him to continue his counsel. He'll all but rule, behind the scenes. In fact, with the business of producing an heir, I'll be far too busy," he suggested lasciviously.

"If you do not shut up, I swear I will thrash you."

"I'll name Teddy next in line for the throne, after our own children. Wouldn't your mainland boy like to see his son in line for the crown?"

"Children?" I scoffed. "As in plural? That's not the deal. It's for *one.*"

"You accept then?" he smirked. "Okay, I agree. One child between us."

"That's not what I said! Oh my god, Lazlian, I really am going to murder you and then this won't be a discussion at all. And besides, I don't believe you would heed Kirwyn's advice on anything."

"I want you in my bed," Laz declared, with a boldness perhaps borne from years of thinking about it... from five years of maturing into someone more direct. My face heated. "I don't care about the kingdom."

"That's a lie and we both know it," I huffed. "You care about Rythas, you care about your family, and you certainly care about your legacy. If you're trying to prove you've changed, you're not off to a good start."

Lazlian threw his head back and sighed through his nose. "Fine. I admit that your boy isn't stupid. His advisement wouldn't be foolish."

I crossed my arms and raised my eyebrows.

"He's... clever. Given more power, it's not as if he'd run the kingdom into the ground," Lazlian hedged.

I continued staring.

"You're so stubborn," Lazlian decreed, exasperated. "Fine. It's as I've always said. You and I aren't suited to it. It wouldn't be the worst thing in the world if your boy made *some* decisions, if someone listened to his suggestions more than my brother does. He came from *fucking* nowhere and he's somehow married a princess, become the right hand to Mal-*fucking*-Yin, and the people praise every *fucking* thing he does like he's their goddamn hero. The nobles respect me, the people love you, and Kirwyn has Mal in his pocket. We'd be unmatched... working together," he grumbled the last two words under his breath, with obvious resentment. "Happy?"

"More so. But if you think Kirwyn would trade me for power," I scoffed, "you don't know the first thing about him."

"I don't think he would. But I think he's inclined to want to make you happy *and* select the best solution to problems... and if those two things are one in the same?"

Lazlian thought this plan made me *happy? What fucking arrogance.*

I snorted. "You're insane. Juls is insane. This whole thing is insane. I'm not divorcing Kirwyn. Ever. Get it out of your head. I love him and he is my husband."

"Then don't," Laz said, voice hard. "Just give me an heir. It can be done. There's a precedent for it."

Curious, I asked the question against my better judgement, "What would that even make me? Queen... consort?" I tried, furrowing my brow and searching my mind for anything historically close.

Lazlian's lip quirked. "Not married to someone else, no."

Seeing his mouth fight a smirk, I narrowed my eyes and pressed, "Then *what?*"

"The title is H.R.M.," Lazlian said, scratching his stubble and not meeting my gaze. He had the wisdom to look a *tad* sheepish as he tried – and failed – to suppress his chuckle while elaborating, "His Royal Mistress."

Oh, you would just love that, wouldn't you? I thought. But I didn't say it, because I *knew* Lazlian would only counter with some lewd comment about what I'd love too. Lacking a handy weapon, I did my best to shoot daggers at Lazlian with my eyes.

"Juls fights Kirwyn—and Mal—every step of the way," Lazlian argued. "Think about it. I love my brother, but he's never been one inclined toward change. You want to divvy up some of the crown's judiciary power? As king, I'd grant it. Fuck if I want to sit and hear peasants petition all day."

I sucked in a breath. *Oh, did Lazlian make a tantalizing offer. And he knew it.*

"This way... you win," he said. "Your boy wins. I win. Mal wins. My brother wins. Merie wins. Everyone wins."

"Everyone wins *something* by compromising something else," I pointed out.

"That's life, little queen."

"I'm not a queen. Not anymore. And by your designs, I'm good enough to breed, not to lead."

"Do you want to lead?" Lazlian asked.

"No," I admitted. "Do you?"

He shrugged. "There are worse fates."

"That's not an answer."

"The important thing is to keep our family in power. Whatever it takes."

Yes, I thought, still stunned. *You've already proven that by joining your brother's wife in bed.*

"All Merie ever wanted was Juls," Lazlian said, daring to step closer to me. "She believes if he renounces the throne and retires to a quiet life in Low Spire without stress, they might conceive naturally."

I pondered that and Lazlian added, "I think a part of Juls always wanted Merie. Or he would have, but he never let himself feel those feelings because he knew she was never to be his. The Doreste men are good at that."

"You want irony?" Lazlian asked, voice low, edging closer to where I stood. "I've suffered the fate you always feared. He is my brother. You cannot imagine..."

"I cannot imagine your hell, Lazlian, but I can come close," I replied, breathing harder. "You were willing, at least. I never was."

"I'm not asking you to come to me unwilling either," he declared boldly, holding my gaze with those scorched-earth eyes.

Dear god, how had this happened?

I blinked and Lazlian was the master manipulator. Maneuvering people to get his way, placing me beside him, the queen to his king. Placing me *under* him, the captive lover to his depraved desires. Cocky, smug, triumphant to have bent everyone to his will. I could see it shining in his eyes.

I blinked again and he was just as helplessly caught as I was. Without power, without better choices, forced to stud himself, to breed under the directive of the crown in order to save the land and family he loved. Bent, sorrowful, and sorry it had come to this. I could see it shining in his eyes.

Which was real?

"You know, it's interesting. I couldn't do this even if I tried." Lazlian chuckled. He began pacing a bit. "Hate me all you want but you did this all by yourself."

Grinding my teeth, I waited for him to continue.

"If you had come here as originally intended, married Juls and hated me... your marriage would have proved unfruitful, but my brother would never have tried to persuade you into bed with me. He'd love and respect you too much to hurt you like that, if it were truly against your wishes. He'd find another way, another stud for his heir."

I refused to let Lazlian's blunt talk color my cheeks. I was an adult now, *dammit.*

"And if you hadn't lost him the support our family needs amongst the nobles, Juls could have slid me in as king, and, in such a stable scenario, any other bride would have been accepted. Now you've made waves... and while the nobles don't like you and your changes, the people do, and the elite can't fight your popularity amongst the people." Lazlian spread his hands, indicating our camp. "From the Queen of Our Hearts to charity's princess."

My shoulders slumped. *When he put it that way...*

"Popularity you worked so hard to achieve," Lazlian smirked. "And the icing on the clandestine cake, when you snuck into my room that night, *you* spurred the rumors of us bedding in secret long ago, setting the stage for it to make sense now."

My mind spun. Had I sealed my own fate?

"If you hadn't made such waves," Lazlian continued with an arrogant shrug, "it wouldn't have worked out this way. Everything *you've* done has led you here. It's almost like you set it all up to be the only candidate qualified to take the role. It's almost like you fought for this."

The wheels in my head were turning so swiftly I felt dizzy. I knew I stood dumbstruck, but I couldn't wipe the look from my face. Laz was using my good intentions against me, *as usual.*

"I need to think... think my way out. Forward," I insisted. "There's *always* a solution."

"Don't think too hard, little queen. It seems your scheming leads you right in the direction you claim you don't want to go."

"They'll never accept you as king. Generally, people don't like you, Lazlian."

"Common people," he remarked off-handedly. "Ah, but the nobles. While you were busy emptying their coffers by taking back first rights to Elowan wares, I was busy filling their pockets with new goods from mainland clans."

Is that what Lazlian was doing on the mainland? Building ties?

A flash of insight struck.

"You're neutralizing me, aren't you?" I whispered, working out the possibility as I spoke. "Further bringing me back into the fold? Are some nobles actually supporting this to nullify me?"

I'd never seen such a shit-eating grin in my life.

"They believe I can bring you to heel."

I smirked right back at him. "And how's that worked out for you so far?"

"I'll have more tools at my disposal once you're on your back," Lazlian quipped. Stroking his chin with mock-consideration, he added, "Or front. Or all fours…"

I coughed on air despite not wanting to give him the reaction he desired.

Keying into my struggle, the bastard taunted, "You know, you didn't have to wage war and topple kingdoms just to writhe beneath me. I would have let you if you asked." He licked his lips, as if considering. "Though I am partial to begging, as you know."

My face flamed and the blood in my veins burned. I dug my fingernails into my palms.

"What is it you once told me?" Lazlian began, smugly overacting as if trying to recall. "I think you're right." He lowered his head, glared up at me heatedly, and repeated my long-ago words from the balcony. *"No matter what had happened, I'd be fucked."*

I ground my teeth so hard I wondered if I'd break them.

Lazlian raised his eyebrows, adding, "Although I think you'll find that in my bed, I prefer to do the fucking."

I exploded.

"You haven't changed a bit!" I cried. "You think you're different? You come back here after five years with a new hairstyle and looking buff or something-"

"Buff?" Lazlian mused with a pleased grin.

"-and you think you're different, but you're still the same guy inside!"

"I look buff?"

"Shut up! Oh my god, for once in your life, shut up!" I grabbed my hair, tugging.

Lazlian, of course, didn't listen. He stepped into my personal space, backing me against the table. My heart raced and my muscles coiled. Leaning forward, he said, "You look the same..." he paused for dramatic effect.

"Breedable."

My hand flew before I had the thought that he'd said it just to rile me.

Iron fingers clamped my wrist, a mirror of when I'd attempted to slap him years ago and he'd stopped me. Only this time, it wasn't hatred simmering in Lazlian's gaze. I jerked my head back, more fearful of what I saw there now. He remained calm while I panted, and I didn't like that change either. No, not calm... his face was far from indifferent. He was alert, *aroused*.

Gulping and flustered, I tore my gaze from his, eyes settling where his hand held my wrist --

-- only to gasp in surprise again.

Lazlian still wore the silver bangle? The one with my hair coiled within?

Blinking up at Laz, my eyes asked the silent question.

The slightest dip of his head answered it.

I exhaled slowly, searching his face. *He couldn't still... so many years...*

"Let me go, Lazlian," I whispered the plea with double meaning.

He released my wrist. But shook his head.

Against my will, it made my heart flutter.

I can't keep fighting you, I thought. *I don't even know that I want to.*

One of the things I loved most about Kirwyn was that he genuinely respected me, valued my wishes. Enough that if I told him I *truly* did not want to be with him... he would fight hard for me and might always love me... but he would eventually honor my decision.

So how was it that, deep down, a part of me warmed at the *exact opposite* behavior in Lazlian?

I don't know what to do. I practically cried the plea aloud.

I'd thought my life was settled, but I was wrong. My fate had lain dormant, like a volcano. Now the earth shook and fire erupted, forcing me to again make choices that would determine the destinies of entire kingdoms.

Lazlian drew in a deep breath, his chest rising upwards with the motion and causing his tunic-vest to spread. He must have been wearing an old one because it was too tight on his newly widened torso, and he hadn't buttoned the top few buttons as he'd done since getting his scar.

I caught sight of something sharp, black, and pointed on his chest. Had he gotten a tattoo?

Curious, I slowly moved my hands to further unbutton Lazlian's shirt. I glanced up, giving him time to stop me if he chose -- but he only watched the movement of my fingers, standing still to allow my inspection.

I pushed aside the material to reveal a new tattoo, as suspected. Somewhere along the way, Lazlian had marked himself with a small constellation of stars, intertwining the scar he bore over his heart. It wasn't in the same shape, but it reminded me a little of my own tattoo, of Kirwyn's. Kirwyn had earth and I had water... but this wasn't fire.

Watching my face carefully, it was as if Lazlian read my thoughts. He said, "Stars burn too. But they don't consume the sea."

No, they guide people on their journeys, I thought.

Old words sounded in my mind so loudly, I gasped. I traced my fingers delicately over the bare skin on Lazlian's mark, awed. His eyes fluttered at my touch and he sucked in a breath.

With dire need, stars will appear and illuminate the way. Even when it's light.

The hermit's prophecy all those years ago. Could it mean... this?

Perhaps Kirwyn was my sun and Lazlian, my moon. Or was Lazlian the stars, and I, the moon? But Kirwyn had taught me the sun was also a star...

It was all so tangled. We were all so landdamn tangled. Even Juls and Merie. The lives of all five of us had entwined so deeply that it was impossible to pull the string of one and not unravel the others.

"This isn't... normal," I protested, weakly.

"Neither are we." Laz gave an arrogant shrug. "We're royal."

"The people wouldn't like it."

"We can show them whatever they like to see and behind closed doors do whatever we want."

Was I actually considering this? What would Kirwyn say? He and Lazlian worked together once before... could they do so again?

What did this make me?

Kirwyn's princess? Lazlian's whore?

A thought sparked. *There is* one *alternative.*

I heard the door creak and Kirwyn entered the sunroom with Juls and Merie behind him. Merie's eyes were dry, at least. I watched Kirwyn anxiously, wondering what they'd discussed.

"Are you okay?" Kirwyn asked, wrapping his arms around me and whispering the question against my ear.

"As long as you're with me, always." I inhaled his piney, comforting scent.

Kirwyn took my chin between his thumb and his forefinger, bringing my gaze to meet his. He paused and said heavily, "Forever."

We all sat the table in our sunroom and I spoke first.

"There is another way," I began, lifting my chin. "Especially if Lazlian has been building relationships with mainland clans. The Spades have fertility treatments," I reminded. "If relations have soured anyway and they're increasingly turning an eye to Elowa... we can band together and fight them. With Mal-Yin and the alliance of other clans, it might be enough."

Astonished, Juls asked, "You'd bring half the world to war just to avoid having sex with my brother?"

I opened my mouth to refute -- *it's not just sex you're asking* -- but no words came out. Everything I could counter seemed infinitesimal against the prospect of war. And if an acceptable heir could not be named, the dynasty would fall and perhaps Rythas with it.

Jesi once asked me long ago -- in the choice between love and duty, which would I choose?

I'd said I wanted not to have to choose.

It seemed Fate answered... in the most twisted way possible.

Love and duty had flipped around and meshed so that I couldn't distinguish the two, couldn't sort out between the choices before me which was which.

I stared at my husband sitting beside me – steadfast, confident, gorgeous. After all these years, my breath still caught when I really looked at him. Kirwyn wasn't boiling with rage, as he would have when we were younger. The pensive furrowing of his brow told me he was deep in thought. Not having been born to privilege like the rest of us, Kirwyn's life depended on his wits, and he'd perhaps honed them to be sharper than we had. I hoped so because I needed his wisdom... and maybe his understanding, too.

A bead of sweat dripping down Merie's neck caught my attention. The room had grown hot, but no one dared move. I crossed to our windows and threw them wide to allow a breeze.

Better, I thought, inhaling the salt air. Slowly, I turned around to meet the weight of everyone watching me expectantly.

In that moment, so much power was mine. Not because anyone gave it to me, but because I'd *fought* for it, earned it. Whether I'd schemed a risky solution or by kicking and clawing my way forward, dirt beneath my jagged nails. I'd battled and had the scars to prove it, inside and out.

I had what I always wanted -- the freedom to make my own choices.

But... though the choice I made might affect me first, it didn't affect *just* me -- not by a longshot. That feeling of change hung in the air again. Doors were opening once more, new pathways illuminating.

Swallowing, I strode back to the table.

Any incalculable number of outcomes stood before us, altering people's lives forever. It wasn't just a personal decision.

I took a seat.

"No one leaves this room," I said, locking eyes with Juls, Merie, Lazlian and Kirwyn.

I had the power. And with my next words, I shared it with everyone around me.

"We talk this out," I said slowly. "The five of us, here and now. Until together, we come to an agreed-upon solution."

Despite declaring one another enemies at one point, despite our attempts at killing each other, despite even going to war... I trusted everyone beside me to make thoughtful decisions. I trusted that no one wanted to see me hurt, not even Laz. We weren't the same people that we used to be.

Lazlian sat on my left, and Kirwyn, my right.

"And I agree to proceed with whatever solution we, together, decide is best," I swore.

Beneath the table, I took Kirwyn's strong hand and gave it a squeeze.

I love you more than anything in this world, I thought. Meeting his green eyes was enough to make my heart thump. *Nothing will ever change how deeply I love you.*

For the first time ever, my other hand took Lazlian's... and gave that a squeeze, as well. His surprised eyes found mine. For a moment he looked vulnerable, as he had that night at the gate console, just before Mal's men tore him off me.

In the fleeting moments his walls were down, that look made my heart beat faster too.

Why should I deny it now, especially when faced with a situation like this?

Five years ago, I'd had a thought I was terrified to finish.

A dark part of me, deep down, almost wished there was a way they could both--

--be mine. And I, theirs.

I didn't know exactly what that looked like. But the thought didn't feel dark any longer. It felt so light a smile touched my lips.

Had destiny called to me from so far away I couldn't heed its direction, as I'd once lamented... Or had I always known what I wanted and stubbornly covered my ears?

No man can serve two masters, Kirwyn had said minutes before, when speaking of Juls and Mal.

I am not a man, I'd argued. *And they are not my masters.*

I looked at Kirwyn and Lazlian.

Without needing the discussions to begin, in my heart I already knew my fate.

I tightened my grip on their hands, where, out of plain sight, I'd united the three of us.

The End

**Borne to Salt and Sin will continue in Book IV,
to be released in 2024**

ALSO BY ELORA MORGAN

<u>Beyond the God Sea Series</u>

Beyond the God Sea (Betrothed)

Bound by Dark Waters (Wed)

Borne to Salt and Sin (Fated)

Book 4: Coming 2024